THE CRY OF THE HALIDON

Jonathan Ryder is the pseudonym of an American author making a bid for best-sellerdom in his new fiction 'The Cry of the Halidon' – a bid which deserves to succeed. This is one of those stories which impresses the reader by the large lines on which the plot has been conceived.

It possesses also a compulsive start which sets up a quickening vibration of uneasiness and suspense that is maintained throughout the book.

A top American geo-physicist (geological surveyor, in common parlance) is invited to London and offered a million dollars to lead a survey into the Jamaican interior. No sooner is he back in his room at the Savoy than a British Intelligence agent tells him some rather nasty facts. Dunstone Ltd – the mysterious firm who approached him – are a world-wide organization bent on controlling world-wide trade. The agent tells the American that if he were to back out now, Dunstone would undoubtedly have him killed, and that the mission he is to conduct will be the second one (no one at all having returned from the first). Fast-travelling and sophisticated, there are odd peeps of Greenland (that territory on the map of modern fiction) in 'The Cry of the Halidon'. Characterization is minimal, but in such a well-planned chess-problem of a novel its absence is not felt.
– *The Scotsman*

Also by Jonathan Ryder

TREVAYNE

Jonathan Ryder

The Cry of the Halidon

Futura Publications Limited
A Futura Book

A Futura Book

First published in Great Britain in 1974
by Weidenfeld & Nicolson Ltd

First Futura Publications edition 1976

ISBN 0 8600 7389 0
Printed in Great Britain by
Hazell Watson & Viney Ltd
Aylesbury, Bucks

Futura Publications Limited
110 Warner Road
Camberwell, London SE5

For Marge and Don Wilde
Wonder Bread and hibiscus
and quiet flights to the islands,
and for God's sake, stay out
of the sun! Watch your language;
they cut off telephones!
Best always . . .

ONE

Port Antonio/
London

1

Port Antonio, Jamaica

THE WHITE SHEET of ocean spray burst up from the coral rock and appeared suspended, the pitch-blue waters of the Caribbean serving as a backdrop. The spray cascaded forward and downward and asserted itself over thousands of tiny, sharp, ragged crevices that were the coral overlay. It became ocean again, at one with its source.

Timothy Durell walked out on the far edge of the huge free-form pool deck, imposed over the surrounding coral, and watched the increasing combat between water and rock. This isolated section of the Jamaican north coast was a compromise between man and natural phenomenon. Trident Villas were built on top of a coral sheet, surrounded by it on three sides, with a single drive that led to the roads in front. The villas were miniature replicas of their names: guest houses that fronted the sea and the fields of coral. Each an entity in itself; each isolated from the others, as the entire complex was isolated from the adjoining territory of Port Antonio.

Durell was the young English manager of Trident Villas, a graduate of London's College of Hotel Management, with a series of letters after his name indicating more knowledge and experience than his mid-twenties appearance would seem to support. But Durell was good; he knew it, the Trident's owners knew it. He never stopped looking for the unexpected—that, along with routine smoothness, was the essence of superior management.

He had found the unexpected now. And it troubled him.

It was a mathematical impossibility. Or, if not impossible, certainly improbable in the extreme.

It simply did not make sense.

"Mr. Durell?"

He turned. His brown Jamaican secretary, her skin and features bespeaking the age-old coalition of Africa and Empire, had walked out on the deck with a message.

"Yes?"

"Lufthansa flight 16 from Munich will be late getting into Montego."

"That's the Keppler reservation, isn't it?"

"Yes. They'll miss the in-island connection."

"They should have come into Kingston . . ."

"They didn't," said the girl, her voice carrying the same disapproval as Durell's statement, but not so sternly. "They obviously don't wish to spend the night in Montego; they had Lufthansa radio ahead. You're to get them a charter . . ."

"On three hours' notice? Let the Germans do it! It's their equipment that's late . . ."

"They tried. None available in Mo'Bay."

"Of course, there isn't . . . I'll ask Hanley. He'll be back from Kingston with the Warfields by five o'clock."

"He may not wish to . . ."

"He will. We're in a spot. I trust it's not indicative of the week."

"Why do you say that? What bothers you?"

Durell turned back to the railing overlooking the fields and cliffs of coral. He lighted a cigarette, cupping the flame against the bursts of warm breeze. "Several things. I'm not sure I can put my finger on them all. One I *do* know." He looked at the girl, but his eyes were remembering. "A little over twelve months ago, the reservations for this particular week began coming in. Eleven months ago they were complete. All the villas were booked . . . for this particular week."

"Trident's popular. What is so unusual?"

"You don't understand. Since eleven months ago, every one of those reservations has stood firm. Not a single cancellation, or even a minor change of dates. Not even a day."

"Less bother for you. I'd think you'd be pleased."

"Don't you see? It's a mathematical imp—well, inconsistency, to say the least. Twenty villas. Assuming couples, that's forty families, really—mothers, fathers, aunts, uncles, cousins . . . For eleven months nothing has happened to change anyone's plans. None of the principals died—and at our rates we don't cater exclusively to the young. No misfortunes of consequence, no simple business interferences, or measles or mumps or weddings or funerals or lingering illness. Yet we're not the Queen's coronation; we're just a week-in-Jamaica."

The girl laughed. "You're playing with numbers, Mr.

Durell. You're put out because your well-organized waiting list hasn't been used."

"And the way they're all arriving," continued the young manager, his words coming faster. "This Keppler, he's the only one with a problem, and how does he solve it? Having an aircraft radio ahead from somewhere over the Atlantic. Now, you'll grant *that's* a bit much . . . The others? No one asks for a car to meet them, no in-island confirmations required, no concerns about luggage or distances. Or anything. They'll just be here."

"Not the Warfields. Captain Hanley flew to Kingston for the Warfields."

"But *we* didn't know that. Hanley assumed that we did, but we didn't. The arrangements were made privately from London. He thought we'd given them his name; we hadn't. *I* hadn't."

"No one else would . . ." The girl stopped. "But everyone's . . . from all over."

"Yes. Almost evenly divided. The States, England, France, West Germany, and . . . Haiti."

"What's your point?" asked the girl, seeing the concern on Durell's face.

"I have a strange feeling that all our guests for the week are acquainted. But they don't want us to know it."

London, England

The tall, light-haired American in the unbuttoned Burberry trench coat walked out the Strand entrance of the Savoy Hotel. He stopped for an instant and looked up at the English sky between the buildings in the court. It was a perfectly normal thing to do—to observe the sky, to check the elements after emerging from shelter—but this man did not give the normally cursory glance and form a judgment based primarily on the chill factor.

He looked.

Any geologist who made his living developing geophysical surveys for governments, companies and foundations knew that the weather was income; it connoted progress or delay.

Habit.

His clear gray eyes were deeply set beneath wide eyebrows, darker than the light brown hair that fell with irritating regularity over his forehead. His face was the color of a man's exposed to the weather, the tone permanently stained by the sun, but not burned. The lines at the sides and below his eyes seemed stamped more from his work than from age; again a face in constant conflict with the elements. The cheekbones were high, the mouth full, the jaw casually slack; for there was a softness also about the man . . . in abstract contrast to the hard, professional look.

This softness, too, was in his eyes. Not weak, but inquisitive; the eyes of a man who probed . . . perhaps because he had not probed sufficiently in the past.

Things . . . things . . . had happened to this man.

The instant of observation over, he greeted the uniformed doorman with a smile and a brief shake of his head, indicating a negative.

"No taxi, Mr. McAuliff?"

"Thanks, no, Jack. I'll walk."

"A bit nippy, sir."

"It's refreshing—only going a few blocks."

The doorman tipped his cap and turned his attention to an incoming Jaguar sedan. Alexander McAuliff continued down the Savoy Court, past the theater and the American Express office to the Strand. He crossed the pavement and entered the flow of human traffic heading north toward Waterloo Bridge. He buttoned his raincoat, pulling the lapels up to ward off London's February chill.

It was nearly one o'clock; he was to be at the Waterloo intersection by one. He would make it with only minutes to spare.

He had agreed to meet the Dunstone company man this way, but he hoped his tone of voice had conveyed his annoyance. He had been perfectly willing to take a taxi, or rent a car, or hire a chauffeur . . . if any or all were necessary; but if Dunstone was sending an automobile for him, why not send it to the Savoy? It wasn't that he minded the walk; he just hated to meet people in automobiles in the middle of congested streets. It was a goddamn nuisance.

The Dunstone man had had a short, succinct explanation that was, for the Dunstone man, the only reason necessary—for all things:

"Mr. Julian Warfield prefers it this way."

He spotted the automobile immediately. It had to be Dunstone's—and/or Warfield's. A St. James Rolls-Royce, its glistening black, hand-tooled body breaking space majestically, anachronistically, among the petrol-conscious Austins, MGs, and European imports. He waited on the curb, ten feet from the crosswalk into the bridge. He would not gesture or acknowledge the slowly approaching Rolls. He waited until the car stopped directly in front of him, a chauffeur driving, the rear window open.

"Mr. McAuliff?" said the eager, young-old face in the frame.

"Mr. Warfield?" asked McAuliff, knowing that this fiftyish, precise-looking executive was not.

"Good heavens, no. The name's Preston. Do hop in; I think we're holding up the line."

"Yes, you are." Alex got into the back seat as Preston moved over. The Englishman extended his hand.

"It's a pleasure. I'm the one you've been talking to on the telephone."

"Yes . . . Mr. Preston."

"I'm really very sorry for the inconvenience, meeting like this. Old Julian has his quirks, I'll grant you."

McAuliff decided he might have misjudged the Dunstone man. "It was a little confusing, that's all. If the object was precautionary—for what reason I can't imagine—he picked a hell of a car to send."

Preston laughed. "True. But then, I've learned over the years that Warfield, like God, moves in mysterious ways that basically are quite logical. He's really all right. You're having lunch with him, you know."

"Fine. Where?"

"Belgravia."

"Aren't we going the wrong way?"

"Julian and God—basically logical, chap."

The St. James Rolls crossed Waterloo, proceeded south to The Cut, turned left until Blackfriars Road, then left again, over Blackfriars Bridge and north into Holborn. It was a confusing route.

Ten minutes later the car pulled up to the entrance canopy of a white stone building with a brass plate to the right of the glass double doors that read "SHAFTSBURY ARMS." The doorman pulled at the handle and spoke jovially.

"Good afternoon, Mr. Preston."

"Good afternoon, Ralph."

McAuliff followed Preston into the building, to a bank of three elevators in the well-appointed hallway. "Is this Warfield's place?" he asked, more to pass the moment than for inquiry.

"No, actually. It's mine. Although I won't be joining you for lunch. However, I trust cook implicitly; you'll be well taken care of."

"I won't try to follow that . . . 'Julian and God.' "

Preston smiled noncommittally as the elevator door opened.

Julian Warfield was talking on the telephone when Preston ushered McAuliff into the tastefully—elegantly—decorated living room. The old man was standing by an antique table in front of a tall window overlooking Belgravia Square. The size of the window, flanked by long white drapes, emphasized Warfield's shortness. He is really quite a small man, thought Alex as he acknowledged Warfield's wave with a nod and a smile.

"You'll send the accrual statistics on to Macintosh, then," said Warfield deliberately into the telephone; he was not asking a question. "I'm sure he'll disagree, and you can both hammer it out. Good-bye." The diminutive old man replaced the receiver and looked over at Alex. "Mr. McAuliff, is it?" Then he chuckled. "That was a prime lesson in business. Employ experts who disagree on just about everything and take the best arguments from both for a compromise."

"Good advice generally, I'd say," replied McAuliff. "As long as the experts disagree on the subject matter and not just chemically."

"You're quick. I like that . . . Good to see you." Warfield crossed to Preston. His walk was like his speech: deliberate, paced slowly. Mentally confident, physically unsure. "Thank you for the use of your flat, Clive. And Virginia, of course. From experience, I know the lunch will be splendid."

"Not at all, Julian. I'll be off."

McAuliff turned his head sharply, without subtlety, and looked at Preston. The man's first-name familiarity with old Warfield was the last thing he expected. Clive Preston smiled and walked rapidly out of the room as Alex watched him, bewildered.

"To answer your unspoken questions," said Warfield, "although you have been speaking with Preston on the telephone, he is not with Dunstone, Limited, Mr. McAuliff."

Alexander turned back to the diminutive businessman. "Whenever I phoned the Dunstone offices for you, I had to give a number for someone to return the call—"

"Always within a few minutes," interrupted Warfield. "We never kept you waiting; that would have been rude. Whenever you telephoned—four times, I believe—my secretary informed Mr. Preston. At his offices."

"And the Rolls at Waterloo was Preston's," said Alex.

"Yes."

"So if anyone was following me, my business is with Preston. Has been since I've been in London."

"That was the object."

"Why?"

"Self-evident, I should think. We'd rather not have anyone know we're discussing a contract with you. Our initial call to you in New York stressed that point, I believe."

"You said it was confidential. Everyone says that. If you meant it to this degree, why did you even use the name of Dunstone?"

"Would you have flown over otherwise?"

McAuliff thought for a moment. A week of skiing in Aspen notwithstanding, there *had* been several other projects. But Dunstone *was* Dunstone, one of the largest corporations in the international market. "No, I probably wouldn't have."

"We were convinced of that. We knew you were about to negotiate with I.T.T. about a little matter in southern Germany."

Alex stared at the old man. He couldn't help but smile. "That, Mr. Warfield, was supposed to be as confidential as anything you might be considering."

Warfield returned the good humor. "Then we know who deals best in confidence, don't we? I.T.T. is patently obvious . . . Come, we'll have a drink, then lunch. I know your preference: Scotch with ice. Somewhat more ice than I think is good for the system."

The old man laughed softly and led McAuliff to a mahogany bar across the room. He made drinks rapidly, his ancient hands moving deftly, in counterpoint to his walk. He offered Alex a glass and indicated that they should sit down. "I've learned quite a bit about you, Mr. McAuliff. Rather fascinating."

"I heard someone was asking around."

They were across from one another, in armchairs. At McAuliff's statement, Warfield took his eyes off his glass and looked sharply, almost angrily, at Alex. "I find that hard to believe."

"Names weren't used, but the information reached me. Eight sources. Five American, two Canadian, one French."

"*Not* traceable to Dunstone." Warfield's short body seemed to stiffen; McAuliff understood that he had touched an exposed nerve.

"I said names weren't mentioned."

"Did *you* use the Dunstone name in any ensuing conversations? Tell me the truth, Mr. McAuliff."

"There'd be no reason not to tell the truth," answered Alex, a touch disagreeably. "No, I did not."

"I believe you."

"You should."

"If I didn't, I'd pay you handsomely for your time and suggest you return to America and take up with I.T.T."

"I may do that anyway, mightn't I? I *do* have that option."

"You like money."

"Very much."

Julian Warfield placed his glass down and brought his thin, small hands together. "Alexander T. McAuliff. The 'T' is for Tarquin, rarely, if ever, used. It's not even on your stationery; rumor is you don't care for it . . ."

"True. I'm not violent about it."

"Alexander Tarquin McAuliff, thirty-eight years old. B.S., M.S., Ph.D., but the title of Doctor is used as rarely as his middle name. The geology departments of several leading American universities, including California Tech and Columbia, lost an excellent research fellow when Dr. McAuliff decided to put his expertise to more commercial pursuits." The man smiled, his expression one of how-am-I-doing; but, again, not a question.

"Faculty and laboratory pressures are no less aggravating than those outside. Why not get paid for them?"

"Yes. We agreed you like money?"

"Don't you?"

Warfield laughed, and his laugh was genuine and loud. His thin, short body fairly shook with pleasure as he brought Alex his glass. "Excellent reply. Really quite fine."

"It wasn't that good . . ."

"But you're interrupting me," said Warfield as he returned to his chair. "It's my intention to impress you."

"Not about myself, I hope."

"No. Our thoroughness . . . You are from a close-knit family, secure academic surroundings—"

"Is this necessary?" asked McAuliff, fingering his glass, interrupting the old man.

"Yes, it is," replied Warfield simply, continuing as though his line of thought was unbroken. "Your father was—and is, in retirement—a highly regarded agro-scientist; your mother, unfortunately deceased, a delightfully romantic soul adored by all. It was she who gave you the 'Tarquin,' and until she died you never denied the initial or the name. You had an older brother, a pilot, shot down in the last days of the World War; you yourself made a splendid record in Korea . . . Upon receipt of your doctorate, it was assumed that you would continue the family's academic tradition. Until personal tragedy propelled you out of the laboratory. A young woman—your fiancée—was killed on the streets of New York. At night. You blamed yourself . . . and others. You were to have met her. Instead, a hastily called, quite unnecessary research meeting prohibited it . . . Alexander Tarquin McAuliff fled the university. Am I drawing an accurate picture?"

"You're invading my privacy. You're repeating information that may be personal but hardly . . . classified. Easy to piece together. You're also extremely obnoxious. I don't think I want to have lunch with you."

"A few more minutes. Then it is your decision."

"It's my decision right now."

"Of course. Just a bit more . . . Dr. McAuliff embarked on a new career with extraordinary precision. He hired out to several established geological-survey firms, where his work was outstanding; then left the companies and underbid them on upcoming contracts. Industrial construction knows no national boundaries: Fiat builds in Moscow; Moscow in Cairo; General Motors in Berlin; British Petroleum in Buenos Aires; Volkswagen in New

Jersey, U.S.A.; Renault in Madrid—I could go on for hours. And everything begins with a single file folder profuse with complicated technical paragraphs describing what is and what is not possible in terms of construction upon the land. Such a simple, taken-for-granted exercise. But without that file, nothing else is possible."

"Your few minutes are about up, Warfield. And, speaking for the community of surveyors, we thank you for acknowledging our necessity. As you say, we're so often taken for granted." McAuliff put his glass down on the table next to his armchair and started to get up.

Warfield spoke quietly, precisely. "You have twenty-three bank accounts, including four in Switzerland; I can supply the code numbers if you like. Others in Prague, Tel Aviv, Montreal, Brisbane, São Paulo, Kingston, Los Angeles, and, of course, New York, among others."

Alexander remained immobile at the edge of his chair and stared at the little old man. "You've been busy."

"Thorough . . . Nothing patently illegal; none of the accounts is enormous. Altogether they total three hundred and eighteen thousand four hundred-odd U.S. dollars, as of several days ago when you flew from New York. Unfortunately, the figure is meaningless. Due to international tax agreements regarding financial transfers, the money cannot be centralized."

"Now I know I don't want to have lunch with you."

"Perhaps not. But how would you like one million dollars? Free and clear, all American taxes paid. Deposited in the bank of your choice."

McAuliff continued to stare at Warfield. It was several moments before he spoke.

"You're serious, aren't you?"

"Utterly."

"For a *survey?*"

"Yes."

"There are five good houses right here in London. For that kind of money, why call on me? Why not use them?"

"We don't want a firm. We want an individual. A man we have investigated thoroughly; a man we believe will honor the most important aspect of the contract. Secrecy."

"That sounds ominous."

"Not at all. A financial necessity. If word got out, the speculators would move in. Land prices would skyrocket, the project would become untenable. It would be abandoned."

"What is it? Before I give you my answer, I have to know that."

"We're planning to build a city. In Jamaica."

2

MCAULIFF politely rejected Warfield's offer to have Preston's car brought back to Belgravia for him. Alex wanted to walk, to think in the cold winter air. It helped him to sort out his thoughts while in motion; the brisk, chilling winds somehow forced his concentration inward.

Not that there was so much to think about as to absorb. In a sense, the hunt was over. The end of the intricate maze was in sight, after eleven years of complicated wandering. Not for the money per se. But for money as the conveyor belt to independence.

Complete. Total. Never having to do what he did not wish to do.

Ann's death—murder—had been the springboard. Certainly the rationalization, he understood that. But the rationalization had solid roots, beyond the emotional explosion. The research meeting—accurately described by Warfield as "quite unnecessary"—was symptomatic of the academic system.

All laboratory activities were geared to justify whatever grants were in the offing. God! How much useless activity! How many pointless meetings! How often useful work went unfinished because a research grant did not materialize or a department administrator shifted priorities to achieve more obvious *progress* for *progress*-oriented foundations.

He could not fight the academic system; he was too angry to join its politics. So he left it.

He could not stand the companies, either. *Jesus!* A different set of priorities, leading to only one objective: profit. Only profit. Projects that didn't produce the most favorable "profit picture" were abandoned without a backward glance.

Stick to business. Don't waste time.

So he left the companies and went out on his own. Where a man could decide for himself the price of immediate values. And whether they were worth it.

All things considered, everything . . . everything Warfield proposed was not only correct and acceptable, it was glorious. An unencumbered, legitimate million dollars for a survey Alex knew he could handle.

He knew vaguely the area in Jamaica to be surveyed: east and south of Falmouth, on the coast as far as Duncan's Bay; in the interior into the Cock Pit. It was actually the Cock Pit territory that Dunstone seemed most interested in: vast sections of uninhabited—in some cases, unmapped—mountains and jungles. Undeveloped miles ten minutes by air to the sophistication of Montego Bay, fifteen to the expanding, exploding New Kingston.

Dunstone would deliver him the specific degree marks within the next three weeks, during which time he was to assemble his team.

He was back on the Strand now, the Savoy Court several blocks away. He hadn't resolved anything, really; there was nothing to resolve, except perhaps the decision to start looking for people at the university. He was sure there would be no lack of interested applicants; he only hoped he could find the level of qualification he needed.

Everything was fine. Really *fine*.

He walked down the alley into the court, smiled at the doorman, and passed the thick glass doors of the Savoy. He crossed to the reservations desk on the right and asked for any messages.

There were none.

But there was something else. The tuxedoed clerk behind the counter asked him a question.

"Will you be going upstairs, Mr. McAuliff?"

"Yes . . . yes, I'll be going upstairs," answered Alex, bewildered at the inquiry. "Why?"

"I beg your pardon?"

"Why do you ask?" McAuliff smiled.

"Floor service, sir," replied the man, with intelligence in his eyes, assurance in his soft British voice. "In the event of any cleaning or pressing. These are frightfully busy hours."

"Of course. Thank you." Alex smiled again, nodded his appreciation, and started for the small brass-grilled elevator. He had tried to pry something else from the Savoy man's eyes, but he could not. Yet he knew something else was there. In the six years he had been staying at the hotel, no one had ever asked him if he was "going upstairs." Considering English . . . Savoy propriety, it was an unlikely question.

Or were his cautions, his Dunstone cautions, asserting

themselves too quickly, too strongly?

Inside his room, McAuliff stripped to shorts, put on a bathrobe, and ordered ice from the floor steward. He still had most of a bottle of Scotch on the bureau. He sat in an armchair next to the window and opened a newspaper, considerately left by room service.

With the swiftness for which the Savoy stewards were known, there was a knock on his corridor door. McAuliff got out of the chair and then stopped.

The Savoy stewards did not knock on hallway doors—they let themselves into the foyers. Room privacy was obtained by locking the bedroom doors, which opened onto the foyers.

Alex walked rapidly to the door and opened it. There was no steward. Instead, there was a tall, pleasant-looking middle-aged man in a tweed overcoat.

"Mr. McAuliff?"

"Yes?"

"My name is Holcroft. May I speak with you, sir?"

"Oh? Sure . . . certainly." Alex looked down the hallway as he gestured the man to pass him. "I rang for ice; I thought you were the steward."

"Then may I step into your . . . excuse me, your lavatory, sir? I'd rather not be seen."

"What? Are you from Warfield?"

"No, Mr. McAuliff. British Intelligence."

"THAT was a sorry introduction, Mr. McAuliff. Do you mind if I begin again?" Holcroft walked into the bedroom-sitting room. Alex dropped ice cubes into a glass.

"No need to. I've never had anyone knock on my hotel door, say he's with British Intelligence, and ask to use the bathroom. Has kind of a quaint ring to it . . . Drink?"

"Thank you. Short, if you please; a touch of soda will be fine."

McAuliff poured as requested and handed Holcroft his glass. "Take off your coat. Sit down."

"You're most hospitable. Thank you." The Britisher removed his tweed overcoat and placed it carefully on the back of a chair.

"I'm most curious, that's what I am, Mr. Holcroft." McAuliff sat by the window, the Englishman across from him. "The clerk at the desk; he asked if I was going upstairs. That was for you, wasn't it?"

"Yes, it was. He knows nothing, however. He thinks the managers wished to see you unobtrusively. It's often done that way. Over financial matters, usually."

"Thanks very much."

"We'll set it right, if it disturbs you."

"It doesn't."

"I was in the cellars. When word reached me, I came up the service elevator."

"Rather elaborate—"

"Rather necessary," interrupted the Englishman. "For the past few days, you've been under continuous surveillance. I don't mean to alarm you."

McAuliff paused, his glass halfway to his lips. "You just have. I gather the surveillance wasn't yours."

"Well, you could say we observed—from a distance—both the followers and their subject." Holcroft sipped his whisky and smiled.

"I'm not sure I like this game," said McAuliff quietly.

"Neither do we. May I introduce myself more completely?"

"Please do."

Holcroft removed a black leather identification case from his jacket pocket, rose from the chair, and crossed to McAuliff. He held out the flat case and flipped it open. "There is a telephone number below the seal. I'd appreciate it if you would place a call for verification, Mr. McAuliff."

"It's not necessary, Mr. Holcroft. You haven't asked me for anything."

"I may."

"If you do, I'll call."

"Yes, I see . . . Very well." Holcroft returned to his chair. "As my credentials state, I'm with Military Intelligence. What they do not say is that I have been assigned to the Foreign Office and Inland Revenue. I'm a financial analyst."

"In the Intelligence service?" Alex got out of his chair and went to the ice bucket and the whisky. He gestured at them; Holcroft shook his head. "That's unusual, isn't it? I can understand a bank or a brokerage office, not the cloak-and-dagger business."

"The vast majority of . . . Intelligence gathering is allied with finance, Mr. McAuliff. In greater or lesser degrees of subtlety, of course."

"I stand corrected." Alex replenished his drink and realized that the ensuing silence was Holcroft's waiting for him to return to his chair. "When I think about it, I see what you mean," he said, sitting down.

"A few minutes ago, you asked if I were with Dunstone, Limited."

"I don't think I said that."

"Very well. Julian Warfield—same thing."

"It was a mistake on my part. I'm afraid I don't remember asking you anything."

"Yes, of course. That's an essential part of your agreement. There can be no reference whatsoever to Mr. Warfield or Dunstone or any *one* or *thing* related. We understand. Quite frankly, at this juncture we approve wholeheartedly. Among other reasons, should you violate the demands of secrecy, we think you'd be killed instantly."

McAuliff lowered his glass and stared at the Englishman, who spoke so calmly, precisely. "That's preposterous," he said simply.

"That's Dunstone, Limited," replied Holcroft softly.

"Then I think you'd better explain."

"I shall do my best . . . To begin with, the geophysical survey that you've contracted for is the second such team to be sent out—"

"I wasn't told that," interrupted Alex.

"With good reason. They're dead. I should say, 'disappeared and dead.' No one's been able to trace the Jamaican members; the whites are dead, of that we are sure."

"How so? I mean, how can you be sure?"

"The best of all reasons, Mr. McAuliff. One of the men was a British agent."

McAuliff found himself mesmerized by the soft-spoken Intelligence man's narrative. Holcroft might have been an Oxford don going over the blurred complexities of a dark Elizabethan drama, patiently clarifying each twist of an essentially inexplicable plot. He supplied conjectures where knowledge failed, making sure that McAuliff understood that they were conjectures.

Dunstone, Limited, was not simply an industrial-development company; that was to say, its objectives went far beyond those of a conglomerate. And it was not solely British, as its listed board of directors implied. In actuality, Dunstone, Limited, London, was the "corporate" headquarters of an organization of international financiers dedicated to building global cartels beyond the interferences and controls of the European Common Market and its trade alliances. *That* was to say—by conjecture—eliminating the economic intervention of governments: Washington, London, Berlin, Paris, The Hague, and all other points of the financial compass. Ultimately, these were to be reduced to the status of clients, not origins of resource or negotiation.

"You're saying, in essence, that Dunstone is in the process of setting up its own government."

"Precisely. A government based solely on economic trade factors. A concentration of financial resources unheard of since the pharaohs. Along with this economic catastrophe, and no less important, is the absorption of the government of Jamaica by Dunstone, Limited. Jamaica is Dunstone's projected base of operations. They can succeed, Mr. McAuliff."

Alex put his glass on the wide windowsill. He began slowly, trying to find words, looking out at the slate rooftops converging into the Savoy Court. "Let me try to understand . . . from what you've told me and from what I know. Dunstone anticipates investing heavily in Jamaican development. All right, we agree on that, and the figures *are* astronomical. Now, in exchange for this investment, they expect to be awarded a lot of clout from a grateful Kingston government. At least, that's what I'd expect if I were Dunstone. The normal tax credits, importing concessions, employment breaks, real estate . . . general incentives. Nothing new." McAuliff turned his head and looked at Holcroft. "I'm not sure I see any financial catastrophe . . . except, maybe, an English financial catastrophe."

"You stood corrected; I stand rebuked," said Holcroft. "But only in a minor way. You're quite perceptive; it's true that our concerns were—at *first*—U.K.-oriented. English perversity, if you will. Dunstone is an important factor in Britain's balance of trade. We'd hate to lose it."

"So you build a conspiracy—"

"Now, just a minute, Mr. McAuliff," the agent broke in, without raising his voice. "The highest echelons of the British government do not *invent* conspiracies. If Dunstone were what it is purported to be, those responsible in Downing Street would fight openly for our interests. I'm afraid that is not the case. Dunstone reaches into extremely sensitive areas in London, Berlin, Paris, Rome . . . and, most assuredly, in Washington. But I shall return to that . . . I'd like to concentrate on Jamaica for the moment. You used the terms 'concessions,' 'tax breaks' . . . 'clout' and 'incentives.' I say 'absorption.' "

"Words."

"*Laws*, Mr. McAuliff. Sovereign; sanctioned by prime ministers and cabinets and parliament. Think for a minute, Mr. McAuliff. An existing, viable government in a strategically located independent nation controlled by a huge industrial monopoly with world markets. It's not outlandish. It's around the corner."

Alex did think about it. For more than a minute. Prodded by Holcroft's gently spoken, authoritatively phrased "clarifications."

Without disclosing M.I.5's methods of discovery, the Britisher explained Dunstone's *modus operandi*. Enormous sums of capital had been transferred from Swiss banks to Kingston's King Street, that short stretch of the block that housed major international banking institutions. But the massive cash flow was not deposited in British, American, or Canadian banks. Those went begging, while the less secure Jamaican banks were stunned by an influx of hard money unheard of in their histories.

Few knew that the vast new Jamaican riches were solely Dunstone's. But for these few, proof was supplied by the revolving transfers of a thousand accounts within an eight-hour business day.

Heads spun in astonishment. A few heads. Selected men in extraordinarily high places were shown incontrovertibly that a new force had invaded Kingston, a force so powerful that Wall Street and Whitehall would tremble at its presence.

"If you know this much, why don't you move in? Stop them."

"Not possible," answered Holcroft. "All transactions are covered; there's no one to accuse. It's too complex a web of financing. Dunstone is masterminded by Warfield. He operates on the premise that a closed society is efficient only when its various arms have little or no knowledge of each other."

"In other words, you can't prove your case and—"

"We cannot expose what we cannot prove," interrupted Holcroft. "That is correct."

"You could threaten. I mean, on the basis of what you know damn well is true, you could raise one hell of a cry . . . But you can't chance it. It goes back to those 'sensitive' areas in Berlin, Washington, Paris, et cetera. Am I correct about that, too?"

"You are."

"They must be goddamn sensitive."

"We believe they comprise an international cross section of extraordinarily powerful men."

"In governments?"

"Allied with major industries."

"For instance?"

Holcroft held Alex's eyes with his own. His message was clear. "You understand that what I say is merely . . . conjecture."

"All right. And my memory is short."

"Very well." The Britisher got out of the chair and walked around it. His voice remained quiet, but there was no lack of precision. "Your own country: conceivably the Vice-President of the United States or someone in his office and, certainly, unknown members of the Senate and the President's cabinet. England: prominent figures in the House of Commons and undoubtedly various department directors at Inland Revenue. Germany: ranking *vorsitzen* in the Bundestag. France: elitist holdovers from the pre-Algerian Gaullists . . . Such men as I have described *must* exist relative to Warfield. The progress made by Dunstone would have been impossible without influence in such places. Of that we are certain."

"But you don't know who, specifically."

"No."

"And you think, somehow, I can help you?"

"We do, Mr. McAuliff."

"With all the resources you have, you come to me? I've been contracted for a Dunstone field survey, nothing else."

"The *second* Dunstone survey, Mr. McAuliff."

Alexander stared at the Englishman.

"And you say that team is dead."

Holcroft returned to his chair and sat down once more. "Yes, Mr. McAuliff. Which means Dunstone has an adversary. One that's either quite powerful or very knowledgeable or both. And we haven't the slightest idea what it is . . . who they are. Only that it exists, *they* exist. We wish to make contact with those who want the same thing we do. We can guarantee the safety of your expedition. You are the key. Without you, we're stymied. Without us, you and your people might well be in extreme jeopardy."

McAuliff shot out of the chair and stood above the British agent. He took several short, deep breaths and walked purposefully away from Holcroft; then he aimlessly paced the Savoy room. The Englishman seemed to understand Alex's action. He let the moment subside; he said nothing.

"*Jesus!* You're something, Holcroft!" McAuliff returned to his chair, but he did not sit down. He reached for his drink on the windowsill, not so much for the whisky as to hold the glass. "You come in here, build a case against Warfield by way of an economics lecture, and then calmly tell me that I've signed what amounts to my last contract if I don't cooperate with you."

"That's rather black and white, chap . . ."

"That's rather exactly what you just said! Suppose you're mistaken?"

"We're not."

"You know goddamn well I can't prove *that* either. If I go back to Warfield and tell him about this little informal chat, I'll lose the contract the second I open my mouth. And the largest fee any surveyor was ever offered."

"May I ask the amount? Just academic interest."

McAuliff looked at Holcroft. "What would you say to a million dollars?"

"I'd say I'm surprised he didn't offer two. Or three . . . Why not? You wouldn't live to spend it."

Alex held the Englishman's eyes. "Translated, that means if Dunstone's enemies don't kill me, Dunstone will?"

"It's what we believe. There's no other logical conclusion. Once your work is finished."

"I see . . ." McAuliff walked slowly to the whisky and poured deliberately, as if measuring. He did not offer anything to Holcroft. "If I confront Warfield with what you've told me, you're really saying that he'd . . ."

"Kill you? Are those the words that stick, Mr. McAuliff?"

"I don't have much cause to employ those kind of words, Mr. Holcroft."

"Naturally. No one ever gets used to them . . . Yes, we think he would kill you. Have you killed, of course. After picking your brains."

McAuliff leaned against the wall, staring at the whisky in his glass, but not drinking. "You're not giving me an alternative, are you?"

"Of course we are. I can leave these rooms; we never met."

"Suppose someone sees you? That surveillance you spoke of."

"They won't see me; you will have to take my word for that." Holcroft leaned back in the chair. He brought his fingers together pensively. "Of course, under the circumstances, we'd be in no position to offer protection. From either faction—"

"Protection from the unprovable," interjected Alex softly.

"Yes."

"No alternative . . ." McAuliff pushed himself away from the wall and took several swallows of whisky. "Except one, Holcroft. Suppose I cooperate, on the basis that there *may* be substance to your charges . . . or theories, or whatever you call them. But I'm not accountable to you."

"I'm not sure I understand."

"I don't accept orders blindly. No puppet strings. I want that condition—on the record. If that's the phrase."

"It must be. I've used it frequently."

McAuliff crossed in front of the Englishman to the arm of his chair. He sat on the edge. "Now, put it in simple words. What am I supposed to do?"

Holcroft's voice was calm and precise. "There are two objectives. The first is Dunstone's opposition; those who destroyed—killed the first survey team. It is conceivable that they will lead you to the second and, obviously, primary objective: the names of Dunstone's unknown hierarchy. The faceless men in London, Paris, Berlin, Washington . . . even one or two. We'd be grateful for anything specific."

"How do I begin?"

"With very little, I'm afraid. But we do have something. It's only a word, a name, perhaps. We don't know. But we have every reason to think it's terribly important."

"A word?"

"Yes . . . 'Halidon.' "

IT WAS LIKE working in two distinct spheres of reality, neither completely real. During the days, McAuliff conferred with the men and women in the University of London's geophysics laboratories, gathering personnel data for his survey team. The university was Dunstone's cover—along with the Royal Historical Society—and neither was aware that Dunstone's finances were behind the expedition.

During the nights, into the early morning hours, he met with R. C. Holcroft, British Intelligence, in small, guarded houses on dimly lit streets in Kensington and Chelsea. These locations were reached by two changes of vehicles—taxis driven by M.I.5. And for each meeting Alex was provided with a cover story regarding his whereabouts: a dinner party, a girl, a crowded restaurant he was familiar with; nothing out of the ordinary, everything easily explained and verifiable.

The sessions with Holcroft were divided into areas of instruction: the political and financial climate of Jamaica, M.I.5 contacts throughout the island, and basic skills—with instruments—in communication and counter-surveillance.

At several sessions, Holcroft brought in West Indian "specialists"—black agents who were capable of answering just about any question McAuliff might raise. McAuliff had few questions; he had surveyed for the Kaiser bauxite interests near Oracabessa a little over a year ago, a fact he suspected had led Julian Warfield to him.

When they were alone, R. C. Holcroft droned on about the attitudes and reactions Alex should foster.

Always build on part of the truth . . . keeping it simple . . . the basics easily confirmed . . .

You'll find it quite acceptable to operate on different levels . . . naturally, instinctively. Your concentration will separate independently . . .

Very rapidly your personal antennae will be activated . . . second nature. You'll fall into a rhythm . . . the connecting link between your divided objectives . . .

The British agent was never emphatic, simply redundant. Over and over again, he repeated the phrases, with minor variations in the words.

Alex understood. Holcroft was providing him with fundamentals: tools and confidence.

"Your contact in Kingston will be given you in a few days; we're still refining. Kingston's a mess; trust isn't easily come by there."

"Whose trust?" asked McAuliff.

"Good point," replied the agent. "Don't dwell on it. That's our job. Memorize everyone else."

Alex looked at the typewritten names on the paper that was not to be removed from the house in Kensington. "You've got a lot of people on your payroll."

"A few too many. Those that are crossed out were on double rosters. Ours and the C.I.A.'s. Your Central Intelligence Agency has become too political in recent years."

"Are you concerned about leaks?"

"Yes. Dunstone, Limited, is alive in Washington. Elusive, but very much alive."

The mornings found him entering the other sphere of reality, the University of London. He discovered that it was easier than he'd thought to shut out the previous night's concerns. Holcroft's theory of divided objectives was borne out; he did fall into a rhythm. His concentration was now limited to professional concerns—the building of his survey team.

It was agreed that the number should not exceed eight, preferably fewer. The areas of expertise would be the normal ones: shale, limestone, and bedrock stratification; water and gas-pocket analyses; vegetation—soil and botanical research; and finally, because the survey extended into the interior regions of the Cock Pit country, someone familiar with the various dialects and outback customs. Warfield had thought this last was superfluous; Alex knew better. Resentments ran high in Jamaica.

McAuliff had made up his mind about one member of the team, a soil analyst from California named Sam Tucker. Sam was an immense, burly man in his fifties, given to whatever excesses could be found in any immediate vicinity, but a top professional in his field. He was also the most reliable man Alex had ever known, a strong friend who had worked surveys with him from Alaska to last year's Kaiser job in Oracabessa. McAuliff implied that if Julian Warfield withheld approval from Sam, he might have to find himself another surveyor.

It was a hollow threat, all things considered, but it was worth the embarrassment of having to back down. Alex wanted Sam with him in Jamaica. The others would be new, unproven; Tucker had worn well over the years. He could be trusted.

Warfield ran a Dunstone check on Sam Tucker and agreed there was nothing prejudicial beyond certain minor idiosyncrasies. But Sam was to be no different from any other member; none was to be informed of Dunstone's interest. Obviously.

None would be. Alex meant it. More than Warfield realized. If there was *any* truth to R. C. Holcroft's astonishing pronouncements.

Everyone on the survey would be told the same story. Given a set of facts engineered by Dunstone, Limited. Even the organizations involved accepted the facts as truth; there was no reason not to. Financial grants were not questioned; they were academic holy writ. Coveted, revered, never debated.

The geological survey had been made possible through a grant from the Royal Historical Society, encouraged by the Commonwealth Activities Committee, House of Lords. The expedition was to be a joint endeavor of the University of London and the Jamaican Ministry of Education.

All salaries, expenses, disbursements of any kind were to be made through the bursar's office at the university. The Royal Society would establish lines of bank credit, and the university was to draw on these funds.

The reason for the survey was compatible with the endeavors of the Commonwealth Committee at Lords, whose members peopled and paid for most royal societies. It was a patrimonial gift to the new, independent nation—another not-to-be-forgotten link with Britannia. A study which would be acknowledged in textbooks for years to come. For, according to the Jamaican Ministry, there were no records of this particular territory having been subjected to a geophysical survey of any dimensions.

Obviously.

And if there were, certainly no one was going to bring them up.

Academic holy writ.

The university rip-off. One did not question.

The selection of Alexander McAuliff for the post of survey director was acknowledged to be an embarrassment to both the society and the university. But the American was the Jamaican Ministry's choice. One suffered such insults from the colonies.

One took the money; one did not debate.

Holy writ.

Everything was just complicated enough to be academically viable, thought McAuliff. Julian Warfield understood the environs through which he maneuvered.

As did R. C. Holcroft of British Intelligence.

And Alex began to realize that he would have to catch up. Both Dunstone, Limited, and M.I.5 were committed to specific objectives. He could get lost in those commitments.

In some ways, he had lost already.

He intended doing something about that in the not-too-distant future. Certain . . . things would have to be made clear.

But choosing the team was his immediate concern.

McAuliff's personnel approach was one he had used often enough to know it worked. He would not interview anyone whose work he had not read thoroughly; anyone he did interview had already proven himself on paper. Beyond the specific areas of expertise, he cared about adaptability to the physical and climatic requirements, and to the give-and-take of close-quarters association.

He had done his work. He was ready.

"My secretary said you wanted to see me, Dr. McAuliff." The speaker at the door was the chairman of the geophysics department, a bespectacled, gaunt academician who tried not to betray his resentment of Alex. It was obvious that the man felt cheated by both the Royal Society and Kingston for not having been chosen for McAuliff's job. He had recently completed an excellent survey in Anguilla; there were too many similarities between that assignment and the Jamaican grant for comfort.

"Good Lord," said Alex. "I expected to come to your

office." He crossed to his desk and smiled awkwardly. He had been standing by the single window, looking out over a miniature quadrangle, watching students carrying books, thankful that he was no longer part of that world. "I think I'll be ready to start the interviews this afternoon."

"So soon?"

"Thanks mainly to you, Professor Ralston. Your recommendations were excellent." McAuliff wasn't being polite; the academician's candidates were good—on paper. Of the ten final prospects, exactly half were from Ralston; the remaining five were free-lancers highly thought of by two London survey firms. "I'm inclined just to take your people without seeing any others," continued Alex, now being polite. "But the Kingston Ministry is adamant that I interview these." McAuliff handed Ralston a sheet of paper with the five non-university names.

"Oh, yes. I recognize several," said Ralston, his voice now pleasantly acknowledging Alex's compliment. "A couple here are . . . a couple, you know."

"What?"

"Man-and-wife team. The Jensens."

"There's one Jensen. Who's the woman?"

"R. L. Wells. That's Ruth Wells, Jensen's wife."

"I didn't realize . . . I can't say that fact is in their favor."

"Why not?"

"I'm not sure," answered Alex sincerely. "I've never had a married couple on a survey. Silly reaction, isn't it? Do you know anybody else there?"

"One fellow. I'd rather not comment."

"Then I wish you would."

"Ferguson. James Ferguson. He was a student of mine. Very outspoken chap. Quite opinionated, if you know what I mean."

"But he's a botanist, a plant specialist, not a geology man."

"Survey training; geophysics was his curriculum secondary. Of course, it was a number of years ago."

McAuliff sorted out some papers on the desk. "It couldn't have been too many. He's only been on three tours, all in the past four years."

"It wasn't, actually. And you should see him. He's considered quite good, I'm told."

"Here are your people," said Alex, offering a second page to Ralston. "I chose five out of the eight you submitted. Any more surprises there? Incidentally, I hope you approve."

Ralston read the list, adjusting his spectacles and pursing his lips as he did so. "Yes, I thought you'd select these. You realize, of course, that this Whitehall chap is not one of us. He was recommended by the West Indies Studies. Brilliant fellow, according to the chairs. Never met him myself. Makes quite a lot of money on the lecture circuits."

"He's black, isn't he?"

"Oh, certainly. He knows every tongue, every dialect, every cultural normality and aberration in the Antilles. His doctoral thesis traced no fewer than twenty-seven African tribes to the islands. From the Bushwadie to the Coromantees. His research of Indian-African integration is the standard reference. He's quite a dandy, too, I believe."

"Anyone else you want to talk about?"

"No, not actually. You'll have a difficult time deciding between your shale-bedrock experts. You've two very decent ones here. Unless your . . . immediate reactions take precedence. One way or the other."

"I don't understand."

Ralston smiled. "It would be presumptuous of me to comment further." And then the professor added quickly, "Shall I have one of our girls set up the appointments?"

"Thanks, I'd appreciate it. If schedules can be organized with all ten, I'd like an hour apiece over the next few days; whatever order is convenient for everyone."

"An hour . . ."

"I'll call back those I want to talk with further—no sense in wasting everyone's time."

"Yes, of course."

One applicant disqualified himself the moment he walked into McAuliff's cubicle. The fact that he was more drunk than sober at one o'clock in the afternoon might have been explained, but, instead, it was used as the excuse to eliminate him for a larger problem: He was crippled in his right leg. Three men were crossed off for identical conditions: Each was obviously hostile to West

Indians—a spreading English virus, Britain's parallel to *Americus Redneckus.*

The Jensens—Peter Jensen and Ruth Wells—were delightful surprises, singly and together. They were in their early fifties, bright, confident, and good-natured. A childless couple, they were financially secure and genuinely interested both in each other and in their work. His expertise was ore minerals; hers, the sister science of paleontology—fossils. His had direct application, hers was removed but academically justifiable.

"Might I ask you some questions, Dr. McAuliff?" Peter Jensen packed his pipe, his voice pleasant.

"By all means."

"Can't say that I know much about Jamaica, but this seems like a damned curious trip. I'm not sure I understand—what's the point?"

Alex was grateful for the opportunity to recite the explanation created by Dunstone, Limited. He watched the ore man closely as he spoke, relieved to see the light of recognition in the geologist's eyes. When he finished, he paused and added, "I don't know if that clears up anything."

"Oh, my word, it certainly does, chap. *Burke's Peerage* strikes again!" Peter Jensen chuckled, glancing at his wife. "The royal *H* has been hard pressed to find something to do. Its members at Lords simply provided it. Good show . . . I trust the university will make a pound or two."

"I'm afraid the budget's not that loose."

"Really?" Peter Jensen held his pipe as he looked at McAuliff. "Then perhaps I *don't* understand. You'll forgive me, but you're not known in the field as a particularly inexpensive director . . . quite rightfully, let me add; your reputation precedes you."

"From the Balkans to Australia," added Ruth Wells Jensen, her expression showing minor irritation with her husband. "And if you have a separate arrangement, it's none of Peter's bloody business."

Alex laughed softly. "You're kind, both of you. But there's nothing special. I got caught, it's as simple as that. I've worked for companies on the island; I hope to again. Often. All geophysical certificates are issued by Kingston, and Kingston asked for me. Let's call it an investment."

Again McAuliff watched Peter Jensen closely; he had

rehearsed the answer. The Britisher looked once more at his wife. Briefly. Then he chuckled, as he had done seconds before.

"I'd do the same, chap. But God help the survey I was director on."

"It's one I'd avoid like a May Day in Trafalgar," said Ruth, matching her husband's quiet laugh. "Who have you set, if it's proper to ask. Anyone we might know?"

"Nobody yet. I've really just started—"

"Well," interrupted Peter Jensen, his eyes alive with humor, "since you suffer from inadequate freight charges, I should tell you we'd rather not be separated. Somewhat used to each other by now. If you're interested in one of us, the other would take half-till to straggle along."

Whatever doubts that remained for Alex were dispelled by Ruth Wells Jensen's words. She mimicked her husband's professional tones with good natured accuracy. "Half-till, old chap, can be negotiated. Our flat's damned cold this time of year."

The Jensens would be hired.

The third non-university name, James Ferguson, had been accurately described by Ralston as outspoken and opinionated. These traits, however, were the results of energy and impatience, it seemed to McAuliff. Ferguson was young—twenty-six—and was not the sort to survive, much less thrive, in an academic environment. Alex recognized in Ferguson much of his younger self: consummate interest in his subject, intolerance of the research world in which it was studied. A contradiction, if not a conflict of objectives. Ferguson free-lanced for agro-industry companies, and his best recommendation was that he rarely was out of work, in a market not famous for excessive employment. James Ferguson was one of the best vegetation specialists around.

"I'd love to get back to Jamaica," said the young man within seconds after the preliminary interview began. "I was in Port Maria for the Craft Foundation two years ago. It's my judgment the whole bloody island is in the middle of a gold mine if the fruit and synthetic industries would allow development."

"What's the gold?" asked McAuliff.

"The baracoa fibers. In the second growth stages. A banana strain could be developed that would send the nylon and the tricot boys into panic, to say nothing of the fruit shippers."

"Can you prove it?"

"Damn near did, *I* think. That's why I was thrown out by the foundation."

"You were thrown out?"

"Quite unceremoniously. No sense hiding the fact; don't care to, really. They told me to stick to business. Can you imagine? You'll probably run across a few negatives about me, if you're interested."

"I'm interested, Mr. Ferguson."

The interview with Charles Whitehall disturbed McAuliff. That was to say, the man disturbed him, not the quality of information received. Whitehall was a black cynic, a now-Londoner whose roots and expertise were in the West Indies but whose outlook was aggressively self-perpetuating. His appearance startled McAuliff. For a man who had written three volumes of Caribbean history, whose work was, in Ralston's words, "the standard reference," Charles Whitehall looked barely as old as James Ferguson.

"Don't let my appearance fool you, Mr. McAuliff," said Whitehall, upon entering the cubicle and extending his hand to Alex. "My tropic hue covers the years better than paler skin. I'm forty-two years old."

"You read my thoughts."

"Not necessarily. I'm used to the reaction," replied the black, sitting down, smoothing his expensive blazer, and crossing his legs, which were encased in flared pin-striped trousers.

"Since you don't waste words, Dr. Whitehall, neither will I. Why are you interested in this survey? As I gather, you can make a great deal more money on the lecture circuit. A geophysical survey isn't the most lucrative employment."

"Let's say the financial aspects are secondary; one of the few times in my life that they will be, perhaps." Whitehall spoke while removing a silver cigarette case from his pocket. "To tell you the truth, Mr. McAuliff, there's a certain ego fulfillment in returning to one's country as an expert under the aegis of the Royal Historical Society. It's really as simple as that."

Alex believed the man. For, as he read him, Whitehall

was a scholar far more honored abroad than at home. It seemed that Charles Whitehall wanted to achieve an acceptance commensurate with his scholarship that had been denied him in the intellectual—or was it social?—houses of Kingston.

"Are you familiar with the Cock Pit country?"

"As much as anyone who isn't a runner. Historically and culturally, much more so, of course."

"What's a runner?"

"Runners are hill people. From the mountain communities. They hire out as guides . . . when you can find one. They're primitives, really. Who have you hired for the survey?"

"What?" Alex's thoughts were on runners.

"I asked who was going with you. On the survey team. I'd be interested."

"Well . . . not all the posts have been filled. There's a couple named Jensen—ores and paleo; a young botanist, Ferguson. An American friend of mine, a soil analyst, name of Sam Tucker."

"I've heard of Jensen, I believe. I'm not sure, but I think so. I don't know the others."

"Did you expect to?"

"Frankly, yes. Royal Society projects generally attract very high-caliber people." Whitehall delicately tapped his cigarette on the rim of an ashtray.

"Such as yourself?" asked McAuliff, smiling.

"I'm not modest," replied the black scholar, returning Alex's smile with an open grin. "And I'm very much interested. I think I could be of service to you."

So did McAuliff.

The second shale-bedrock analyst was listed as A. Gerrard Booth. Booth was a university applicant personally recommended by Ralston in the following manner:

"I promised Booth I'd bring these papers and articles to your attention. I do believe Booth would be a fine asset to the survey."

Ralston had given McAuliff a folder filled with A. Gerrard Booth's studies of sheet strata in such diverse locations as Iran, Corsica, and southern Spain. Alex recalled having read several of the articles in the *National Geologist*, and remembered them as lucid and professional. Booth was good; Booth was better than good.

Booth was also a woman. A. Gerrard Booth was known to her colleagues as Alison Booth; no one bothered with the middle name.

She had one of the most genuine smiles McAuliff had ever seen. It was more a half laugh—one might even say masculine, but the word was loudly denied by her complete femininity. Her eyes were blue and alive and level—the eyes of a professional. Her handshake was firm, again professional. Her light brown hair was long and soft and slightly waved—brushed repeatedly, thought Alex, for the interview. Her age was anywhere from late twenties to middle thirties; there was no way to tell by observation, except that there were laugh lines at the corners of her eyes.

Alison Booth was not only good and a woman; she was also, at least on first meeting, a very attractive, outgoing person. The term "professional" kept recurring to McAuliff as they spoke.

"I made Rolly promise to omit the fact that I was a woman. Don't hold him responsible."

"Were you so convinced I was anti-liberation?"

The girl raised her hand and brushed her long, soft hair away from the side of her lovely face. "No preformed hostility, Dr. McAuliff. I just understand the practical obstacles. It's part of my job to convince you I'm qualified."

And then, as if she were aware of the possible double-entendre, Alison Booth stopped smiling and smoothed her skirt . . . professionally.

"In field work and the laboratory, I'm sure you *are* qualified . . ."

"Any other considerations would be extraneous, I should think," said the girl, with a slight trace of English aloofness.

"Not necessarily. There are environmental problems, degrees of physical discomfort, if not hardship."

"I can't conceive of Jamaica being in that league with Iran or Corsica. I've surveyed in those places."

"I know—"

"Rolly told me," interrupted Alison Booth, "that you would not accept tour references until you had interviewed us."

"Group isolation tends to create fallible judgments. Insupportable relationships. I've lost good men in the past because other good men reacted negatively to them for the wrong reasons."

"What about women?"

"I used the term inclusively, not exclusively."

"I have very good references, Dr. McAuliff. For the right reasons."

"I'll request them."

"I have them with me." Alison unbuckled the large leather purse on her lap, extracted two business envelopes, and placed them on the edge of McAuliff's desk. "My references, Dr. McAuliff."

Alex laughed as he reached for the envelopes. He looked over at the girl; her eyes locked with his. There was both a good-humored challenge and a degree of supplication in her expression. "Why is this survey so important to you, Miss Booth?"

"Because I'm good and I can do the job," she answered simply.

"You're employed by the university, aren't you?"

"On a part-time basis, lecture and laboratory. I'm not permanent . . . by choice, incidentally."

"Then it's not money." McAuliff made a statement.

"I could use it; I'm not desperate, however."

"I can't imagine your being desperate anywhere," he said, with a partial smile. And then Alex saw—or thought he saw—a trace of a cloud across the girl's eyes, an instant of concern that left as rapidly as it had come. He instinctively pressed further. "But why *this* tour? With your qualifications, I'm sure there are others. Probably more interesting, certainly more money."

"The timing is propitious," she replied softly, with precise hesitation. "For personal reasons that have absolutely nothing to do with my qualifications."

"Are there reasons why you want to spend a prolonged period in Jamaica?"

"Jamaica has nothing to do with it. You could be surveying Outer Mongolia for all that it matters."

"I see." Alex replaced the two envelopes on the desk. He intentionally conveyed a trace of indifference. The girl reacted.

"Very well, Dr. McAuliff. It's no secret among my friends." The girl held her purse on her lap. She did not grip it; there was no intensity about her whatsoever.

When she spoke, her voice was steady, as were her eyes. She was the total professional again. "You called me 'Miss Booth'; that's incorrect. 'Booth' is my married name. I regret to say the marriage was not successful; it was terminated recently. The solicitousness of well-meaning people during such times can be boring. I'd prefer to be out of touch."

McAuliff returned her steady gaze, trying to evoke something beyond her words. There *was* something, but she would not allow his prying further; her expression told him that . . . professionally.

"It's not relevant. I apologize. But I appreciate your telling me."

"Is your . . . responsibility satisfied?"

"Well, my curiosity, at any rate." Alex leaned forward, elbows on the desk, his hands folded under his chin. "Beyond that, and I hope it's not improper, you've made it possible for me to ask you to have dinner with me."

"I think that would depend on the degree of relevance you ascribed to my acceptance." Alison's voice was polite but not cold. And there was that lovely humor in her eyes.

"In all honesty, I *do* make it a point to have dinner or a long lunch . . . even a fair amount of drinks with those I'm thinking about hiring. But right now, I'm reluctant to admit it."

"That's a very disarming reply, Dr. McAuliff," said the girl, her lips parted, laughing her half laugh. "I'd be delighted to have dinner with you."

"I'll do my damnedest not to be solicitous. I don't think it's necessary at all."

"And I'm sure you're never boring."

"Not relevantly."

5

MCAULIFF stood on the corner of High Holborn and Chancery and looked at his watch. The radium hands glowed in the mist-laden London darkness; it was 11:40. Preston's Rolls-Royce was ten minutes late. Or perhaps it would not appear at all. His instructions were that if the car did not arrive by midnight, he was to return to the Savoy. Another meeting would be scheduled.

There were times when he had to remind himself whose furtive commands he was following, wondering whether he in turn was being followed. It was a degrading way to live, he reflected: the constant awareness that locked a man into a pocket of fear. All the fictions about the shadow world of conspiracy omitted the fundamental indignity intrinsic to that world. There was no essential independence; it was strangling.

This particular evening's rendezvous with Warfield had necessitated a near-panic call to Holcroft, for the British agent had scheduled a meeting himself, for one in the morning. That is, McAuliff had requested it, and Holcroft had set the time and the place. And at 10:20 that night the call had come from Dunstone: Be at High Holborn and Chancery at 11:30, an hour and ten minutes from then.

Holcroft could not, at first, be found. His highly secret, private telephone at the Foreign Office simply did not answer. Alex had been given no other number, and Holcroft had told him repeatedly never to call the F.O. and leave his name. Nor was he ever to place a call to the agent from his rooms at the Savoy. Holcroft did not trust the switchboards at either establishment.

So Alex had to go out onto the Strand, into succeeding pubs and chemists' shops to public telephones until Holcroft's line answered. He was sure he was being observed—by someone—and thus he had to pretend annoyance each time he hung up after an unanswered call. He found that he had built the fabric of a lie, should Warfield question him. His lie was that he was trying to reach Alison Booth and cancel a lunch date they had for the following day. They did have a lunch date which he had no intention of canceling, but the story possessed sufficient truth to be valid.

Build on part of the truth . . . Attitude and reaction. M.I.5.

Finally, Holcroft's telephone was answered, by a man who stated casually that he had gone out for a late supper.

A late supper! Good God! . . . Global cartels, international collusion in the highest places, financial conspiracies, and a late supper.

In reasoned tones, as opposed to McAuliff's anxiety, the man told him that Holcroft would be alerted. Alex was not satisfied; he insisted that Holcroft be at his telephone—if he had to wait all night—until he, Alex, made contact after the Warfield appointment.

It was 11:45. Still no St. James Rolls-Royce. He looked around at the few pedestrians on High Holborn, walking through the heavy mist. He wondered which, if any, was concerned with him.

The pocket of fear.

He wondered, too, about Alison. They had had dinner for the third night in succession; she had claimed she had a lecture to prepare, and so the evening was cut short. Considering the complications that followed, it was a good thing.

Alison was a strange girl. The professional who covered her vulnerability well; who never strayed far from that circle of quiet humor that protected her. The half laugh, the warm blue eyes, the slow, graceful movement of her hands . . . these were her shields, somehow.

There was no problem in selecting her as his first choice . . . professionally. She was far and away the best applicant for the team. Alex considered himself one of the finest rock-strata specialists on both continents, yet he wasn't sure he wanted to pit his expertise against hers. Alison Gerrard Booth was good.

And lovely.

And he wanted her in Jamaica.

He had prepared an argument for Warfield, should Dunstone's goddamn security computers reject her. The final clearance of his selections was the object of the night's conference.

Where *was* that goddamned black ship of an automobile? It was ten minutes to midnight.

"Excuse me, sir," said a deep, almost guttural voice behind McAuliff. He turned, and saw a man about his own age, in a brown mackinaw; he looked like a longshoreman or a construction worker.

"Yes?"

"It's m' first time in London, sir, and I thinks I'm lost."

The man then pointed up at the street sign, barely visible in the spill of the lamp through the mist. "This says Chancery Lane, which is *supposed* to be near a place called Hatton, which is where I'm supposed to meet m' friends. I can't *find* it, sir."

Alex gestured to his left. "It's up there two or three blocks."

The man pointed again, as a simpleton might point, in the direction of McAuliff's gesture. "Up there, sir?"

"That's right."

The man shook his arm several times, as if emphasizing. "You're sure, sir?" And then the man lowered his voice and spoke rapidly. "Please don't react, Mr. McAuliff. Continue as though you are explaining. Mr. Holcroft will meet you in Soho; there's an all-night club called The Owl of Saint George. He'll be waiting. Stay at the bar, he'll reach you. Don't worry about the time . . . He doesn't want you to make any more telephone calls. You're being watched."

McAuliff swallowed, blanched, and waved his hand—a little too obviously, he felt—in the direction of Hatton Garden. He, too, spoke quietly, rapidly. *"Jesus!* If *I'm* being watched, so are *you!"*

"We calculate these things—"

"I don't like your addition! What am I supposed to tell Warfield? To let me off in *Soho!"*

"Why not? Say you feel like a night out. You've nothing scheduled in the morning. Americans like Soho; it's perfectly natural. You're not a heavy gambler, but you place a bet now and then."

"Christ! Would you care to describe my sex life?"

"I could, but I won't." The guttural, loud North Country voice returned. "Thank you, sir. You're very kind, sir. I'm sure I'll find m' friends."

The man walked swiftly away, into the night mist

toward Hatton Garden. McAuliff felt his whole body shiver; his hands trembled. To still them, he reached into his pocket for cigarettes. He was grateful for the opportunity to grip the metal of his lighter.

It was five minutes to twelve. He would wait several minutes past midnight and then leave. His instructions were to "return to the Savoy"; another meeting would be set. Did that mean it was to be scheduled later that night? In the morning hours? Or did "return to the Savoy" simply mean that he was no longer required to remain at the corner of High Holborn and Chancery Lane? He was free for the evening?

The words were clear, but the alternate interpretation was entirely feasible. If he chose, he could—with a number of stops—make his way into Soho, to Holcroft. The network of surveillance would establish the fact that Warfield had not appeared for the appointment. The option was open.

My God! thought Alex. *What's happening to me? Words and meanings . . . options and alternates. Interpretations of . . . orders!*

Who the hell *gave him orders!*

He was *not* a man to be commanded!

But when his hand shook as he raised his cigarette to his lips, he knew that he was . . . for an indeterminate period of time. Time in a hell he could not stand; he was not free.

The radium hands on his wristwatch converged. It was midnight. To goddamn hell with all of them! He *would* leave! He would call Alison and tell her he wanted to come over for a drink . . . ask her if she would let him. Holcroft could wait all night in Soho. Where was it? The Owl of Saint George. Silly fucking name!

To hell with him!

The Rolls-Royce sped out of the fog from the direction of Newgate, its deep-throated engine racing, a powerful intrusion on the otherwise still street. It swung alongside the curb in front of McAuliff and stopped abruptly. The chauffeur got out of his seat, raced around the long hood of the car, and opened the rear door for Alex.

It all happened so quickly that McAuliff threw away his cigarette and climbed in, bewildered; he had not adjusted to the swift change of plans. Julian Warfield sat in the far right corner of the huge rear seat, his tiny frame dwarfed by the vehicle's expansive interior.

"I'm sorry to have kept you waiting until the last minute, Mr. McAuliff. I was detained."

"Do you always do business with one eye on secrecy, the other on shock effect?" asked Alex, settling back in the seat, relieved to feel he could speak with confidence.

Warfield replied by laughing his hard, old-man's laugh. "Compared to Howard Hughes, I'm a used-car salesman."

"You're still damned unsettling."

"Would you care for a drink? Preston has a bar built in right there." Warfield pointed to the felt back of the front seat. "Just pull on that strap."

"No, thank you. I may do a little drinking later, not now." *Easy. Easy, McAuliff,* he thought to himself. *For Christ's sake, don't be obvious. Holcroft can wait all night. Two minutes ago, you were going to let him do just that!*

The old man took an envelope from his jacket pocket. "I'll give you the good news straight off. There's no one we objected to strenuously, subject to minor questions. On the contrary, we think you finalized your selections rather ingeniously . . ."

According to Warfield, the initial reaction at Dunstone to his list of first choices was negative. Not from security—subject to those minor questions; nor in quality— McAuliff had done his homework. But from a conceptual viewpoint. The idea of female members on a geological survey expedition was rejected out-of-hand, the central issue being that of less strength, not necessarily weakness. Any project entailing travel had, by tradition, a masculine identification; the intrusion of the female was a disquieting component. It could only lead to complications—any number of them.

"So we crossed off two of your first choices, realizing that by eliminating the Wells woman, you would also lose her husband, Jensen . . . Three out of the first five rejected; knew you'd be unhappy, but then, you *did* understand . . . Later, it came to me. By George, you'd out-thought the lot of us!"

"I wasn't concerned with any strategies, Warfield. I was putting together the best team I could." McAuliff felt he had to interject the statement.

"Perhaps not consciously, and qualitatively you have a splendid group. But the inclusion of the two ladies, one a wife and both superior in their fields, was a profound improvement."

"Why?"

"It provides—they provide—a unique ingredient of innocence. A patina of scholarship, actually; an aspect we had overlooked. A dedicated team of men and women—on a grant from the Royal Society . . . so different somehow from an all-male survey expedition. Really, most remarkable."

"That wasn't my intention. I hate to disabuse you."

"No disabusement whatsoever. The result is the same. Needlessly said, I pointed out this consideration to the others, and they agreed instantly."

"I have an idea that whatever you might 'point out' would be instantly agreed to. What are the minor questions?"

" 'Incidental information you might wish to consider' is a better description." The old man reached up and snapped on a reading lamp. He then removed several pages from his overcoat, unfolded them, and placed them in front of the envelope. He adjusted his glasses and scanned the top paper. "The husband and wife, this Jensen and Wells. They're quite active in leftish political circles. Peace marches, ban-the-bombing, that sort of thing."

"That doesn't have any bearing on their work. I doubt they'll be organizing the natives." McAuliff spoke wearily—on purpose. If Warfield intended to raise such "questions," he wanted the financier to know he thought them irrelevant.

"There is a great deal of political instability in Jamaica; unrest, to be precise. It would not be in our interests for any of your people to be outspoken on such matters."

McAuliff shifted in his seat and looked at the little old man—tiny lips pursed, the papers held in his thin, bony fingers under the pin spot of yellow light, giving his ancient flesh a sallow color. "Should the occasion arise—and I can't conceive of it—when the Jensens make political noises, I'll quiet them . . . On the other hand, the inclusion of such people might be an asset to you. They'd hardly, knowingly, work for Dunstone."

"Yes," said Warfield quietly. "That, too, occurred to us . . . This chap, Ferguson. He ran into trouble with the Craft Foundation."

"He ran into a potentially vital discovery concerning baracoa fibers, that's what he ran into. It scared the hell out of Craft and Craft's funding resources."

"*We* have no fight with Craft. We don't want one. The fact that he's with you could raise eyebrows. Craft's well thought of in Jamaica."

"There's no one as good as Ferguson, certainly not the alternate, and *he* was the best of those remaining. I'll keep Ferguson away from Craft."

"That is essential. We cannot permit him otherwise."

Charles Whitehall, the black scholar-dandy, was a psychological mess, according to Dunstone's data banks. Politically he was a conservative, a black conservative who might have led the Kingston reactionaries had he remained on the island. But his future was not in Jamaica, and he had recognized it early. He was bitter over the fact. Warfield hastened to add, however, that this negative information was balanced—and more so—by Whitehall's academic standing. His interest in the survey was ultimately a positive factor; his inclusion tended to remove any commercial stain from the project. To compound the complications of this very complex man, Whitehall was a Class Triple A Black Belt practitioner of Jukato, a more intricate and deadly development of Judo.

"Our contacts in Kingston are quite impressed with his being with you. I suspect they'll offer him a chair at the West Indies University. I think he'll probably accept, if they pay him enough . . . Now, we come to the last submission." Warfield removed his glasses, placed them on his lap with the papers, and rubbed the bridge of his thin, bony nose. "Mrs. Booth . . . Mrs. Alison Gerrard Booth."

Alex felt the stirrings of resentment. Warfield had already told him that Alison was acceptable; he did not want to hear intimate, private information dredged up by Dunstone's faceless men or whirring machines.

"What about her?" asked McAuliff, his voice careful. "Her record speaks for itself."

"Unquestionably. She's extremely qualified . . . And extremely anxious to leave England."

"She's explained that. I buy it. She's just been divorced, and the circumstances, I gather, are not too pleasant . . . socially."

"Is that what she told you?"

"Yes. I believe her."

Warfield replaced his glasses and flipped the page in front of him. "I'm afraid there's a bit more to it than that, Mr. McAuliff. Did she tell you who her husband was? What he did for a living?"

"No. And I didn't ask her."

"Yes . . . Well, I think you should know. David Booth is from a socially prominent family—viscount status, actually—that hasn't had the cash flow of a pound sterling for a generation. He is a partner in an export-import firm whose books indicate a barely passable subsistence . . . Yet Mr. Booth lives extremely well. Several homes—here and on the Continent—drives expensive cars, belongs to the better clubs. Contradictory, isn't it?"

"I'd say so. How does he do it?"

"Narcotics," said Julian Warfield, as if he had just given the time of day. "David Booth is a courier for Franco-American interests operating out of Corsica, Beirut, and Marseilles."

For the next few moments both men were silent. McAuliff understood the implication, and finally spoke. "Mrs. Booth was on surveys in Corsica, Iran . . . and southern Spain. You're suggesting that she's involved."

"Possibly; not likely. If so, unwittingly. After all, she did divorce the chap. What we are saying is that she undoubtedly learned of her husband's involvement; she's afraid to remain in England. We don't think she plans to return."

Again, there was silence, until McAuliff broke it.

"When you said 'afraid,' I presume you mean she's been threatened."

"Quite possibly. Whatever she knows could be damaging. Booth didn't take the divorce action very well. Not from the point of view of affection—he's quite a womanizer—but, we suspect, for reasons related to his travels." Warfield refolded the pages and put them back into his overcoat pocket.

"Well," said Alex, "that's quite a . . . minor explosion. I'm not sure I'm ready for it."

"I gave you this information on Mrs. Booth because we thought you'd find out for yourself. We wanted to prepare you . . . not to dissuade you."

McAuliff turned sharply and looked at Warfield. "You want her along because she might . . . might possibly be valuable to you. And not for geological reasons." *Easy, McAuliff. Easy!*

"Anything is conceivable in these complicated times."

"I don't like it!"

"You haven't thought about it. It is our opinion that she's infinitely safer in Jamaica than in London . . . You are concerned, aren't you? You've seen her frequently during the past week."

"I don't like being followed, either." It was all Alex could think to say.

"Whatever was done was minimal and for your protection," replied Warfield quickly.

"Against what? For Christ's sake, protection from whom?" McAuliff stared at the little old man, realizing how much he disliked him. He wondered if Warfield would be any more explicit than Holcroft on the subject of protection. Or would he admit the existence of a prior Jamaican survey? "I think I have a right to be told," he added angrily.

"You shall be. First, however, I should like to show you these papers. I trust everything will be to your satisfaction." Warfield lifted the flap of the unsealed envelope and withdrew several thin pages stapled together on top of a single page of stationery. They were onionskin carbons of his lengthy Letter of Agreement signed in Belgravia Square over a week ago. He reached above, snapped on his own reading lamp, took the papers from Warfield and flipped over the carbons to the thicker page of stationery. Only it wasn't stationery; it was a Xerox copy of a Letter Deposit Transfer from the Chase Bank in New York. The figures were clear: On the left was the amount paid into his account by a Swiss concern; on the right, the maximum taxes on that amount, designated as income, to the Swiss authorities and the United States Internal Revenue Service.

The net figure was $333,000.

He looked over at Warfield. "My first payment was to have been twenty-five percent of the total contract upon principal work of the survey. We agreed that would be the team's arrival in Kingston. Prior to that date, you're responsible only for my expenses and, if we terminate, two hundred a day for my time. Why the change?"

"We've very pleased with your preliminary labors. We wanted to indicate our good faith."

"I don't believe you—"

"Besides," continued Warfield, raising his voice over Alex's objection, "there's been no contractual change."

"I know what I signed."

"Not too well, apparently . . . Go on, read the agreement. It states clearly that you will be paid a *minimum* of twenty-five percent, *no later* than the end of the business day we determined to be the start of the survey. It says nothing about an excess of twenty-five percent; no prohibitions as to an earlier date . . . We thought you'd be pleased." The old man folded his small hands like some kind of Ghandi of peace in Saville Row clothes.

McAuliff reread the transfer letter from Chase. "This bank transfer describes the money as payment for services rendered as of today's date. That's past tense, free and clear. You'd have a hard time recouping if I didn't go to Jamaica. And considering your paranoia over secrecy, I doubt you'd try too hard . . . No, Mr. Warfield, this is out of character."

"Faith, Mr. McAuliff. Your generation overlooks it." The financier smiled benignly.

"I don't wish to be rude, but I don't think you ever had it. Not that way. You're a manipulator, not an ideologue . . . I repeat: out of character."

"Very well." Warfield unfolded his delicate hands, still retaining the Ghandi pose under the yellow light. "It leads to the protection of which I spoke and which, rightly, you question . . . You are one of us, Alexander Tarquin McAuliff. A very important and essential part of Dunstone's plans. In recognition of your contributions, we have recommended to our Directors that you be elevated—in confidence—to their status. Ergo, the payments made to you—in gross terms, amounting to close to a million—are the initial monies due one of our own. As you say, it would be out of character for such excessive payments to be made otherwise."

"What the hell are you driving at?"

"In rather abrupt words, don't ever try to deny us. You are a consenting participant in our work. Should you at any time, for whatever motive, decide you do not approve of Dunstone, don't try to separate yourself. You'd never be believed."

McAuliff stared at the now smiling old man. "Why would I do that?" he asked softly.

"Because we have reason to believe there are . . . elements most anxious to stop our progress. They may try to reach you; perhaps they have already. Your future is with us. No one else. Financially, perhaps ideologically . . . certainly, legally."

Alex looked away from Warfield. The Rolls had proceeded west into New Oxford, south on Charing Cross, and west again on Shaftesbury. They were approaching the outer lights of Piccadilly Circus, the gaudy colors diffused by the heavy mist.

"Who were you trying to call so frantically this evening?" The old man was not smiling now.

McAuliff turned from the window. "Not that it's any of your damned business but I was calling—not frantically—Mrs. Booth. We're having lunch tomorrow. Any irritation was due to your hastily scheduled meeting and the fact that I didn't want to disturb her after midnight. Who do you think?"

"You shouldn't be hostile—"

"I forgot," interrupted Alex. "You're only trying to protect me. From . . . elements."

"I can be somewhat more precise." Julian Warfield's eyes bore into Alex's, with an intensity he had not seen before. "There would be no point in your lying to me, so I expect the truth. What does the word 'Halidon' mean to you, Mr. McAuliff?"

6

THE SCREAMING, hysterical cacophony of the acid-rock music caused a sensation of actual pain in the ears. The eyes were attacked next, by tear-provoking layers of heavy smoke, thick and translucent—the nostrils reacting immediately to the pungent sweetness of tobacco laced with grass and hashish.

McAuliff made his way through the tangled network of soft flesh, separating thrusting arms and protruding shoulders gently but firmly, finally reaching the rear of the bar area.

The Owl of Saint George was at its undulating peak. The psychedelic lights exploded against the walls and ceiling in rhythmic crescendos; bodies were concave and convex, none seemingly upright, all swaying, writhing violently.

Holcroft was seated in a circular booth with five others: two men and three women. Alex paused, concealed by drinkers and dancers, and looked at Holcroft's gathering. It was funny; not sardonically funny, humorously funny. Holcroft and his middle-aged counterpart across the table were dressed in the "straight" fashion, as were two of the three women, straight and past forty. The remaining couple was young, hip, and profuse with beads and suede and flowing hair held back with headbands. The picture was instantly recognizable: parents indulging the generation gap, uncomfortable but game.

McAuliff remembered the man's words on High Holborn. *Stay at the bar, he'll reach you.* He maneuvered his way to within arm's length of the mahogany and managed to shout his order to the black Soho bartender with an Afro haircut. He wondered when Holcroft would make his move; he did not want to wait long. He had a great deal to say to the British agent.

"Pardon, but you *are* a chap named McAuliff, aren't you?" The shouted question caused Alex to spill part of his drink. The shouter was the young mod from Holcroft's table. Holcroft was not wasting time.

"Yes. Why?"

"My girl's parents recognized you. Asked me to invite you over."

The following moments, McAuliff felt, were like a play within a play. A brief, staged exercise with acutely familiar dialogue, acted out in front of a bored audience of other, more energetic actors. But with a surprise that made Alex consider Holcroft's skill in a very favorable light.

He *did* know the middle-aged man across from Holcroft. And his wife. Not well, of course, but they were acquaintances. He'd met them two or three times before, on previous London trips. They weren't the sort of memorable people one recognized on the street—or in The Owl of Saint George—unless the circumstances were recalled.

Holcroft was introduced by his correct name, and McAuliff was seated next to him.

"How the hell did you arrange this?" asked Alex after five excruciating minutes remembering the unmemorable with the acquaintances. "Do they know who you are?"

"Laugh occasionally," answered Holcroft with a calm, precise smile. "They believe I'm somewhere in that great government pyramid, juggling figures in poorly lit rooms . . . The arrangements were necessary. Warfield has doubled his teams on you. We're not happy about it; he may have spotted us, but, of course, it's unlikely."

"He's spotted something, I guarantee it." Alex bared his teeth, but the smile was false. "I've got a lot to talk to you about. Where can we meet?"

"Here. Now," was the Britisher's reply. "Speak occasionally to the others, but it's perfectly acceptable that we strike up a conversation. We might use it as a basis for lunch or drinks in a day or two."

"No way. I leave for Kingston the morning after next."

Holcroft paused, his glass halfway to his lips. "So soon? We didn't expect that."

"It's insignificant compared to something else . . . Warfield knows about Halidon. That is, he asked me what *I* knew about it."

"What?"

"Mr. McAuliff?" came the shouted inquiry from across the table. "Surely you know the Bensons, from Kent . . ."

The timing was right, thought Alex. Holcroft's reaction to his news was one of astonishment. Shock that changed swiftly to angered acceptance. The ensuing conversation about the unremembered Bensons would give Holcroft time to think. And Alex wanted him to think.

"What *exactly* did he say?" asked Holcroft. The revolving psychedelic lights now projected their sharp patterns on the table, giving the agent a grotesque appearance. "The exact words."

" 'What does the word "Halidon" mean to you?' That's what he said."

"Your answer?"

"What answer? I didn't have one. I told him it was a town in New Jersey."

"I beg your pardon?"

"Halidon, New Jersey. It's a town."

"Different spelling, I believe. And pronunciation . . . Did he accept your ignorance?"

"Why wouldn't he? I'm ignorant."

"Did you conceal the fact that you'd heard the word? It's terribly important!"

"Yes . . . yes, I think I did. As a matter of fact, I was thinking about something else. Several other things—"

"Did he bring it up later?" broke in the agent.

"No, he didn't. He stared hard, but he didn't mention it again . . . What do you think it means?"

Suddenly a gyrating, spaced-out dancer careened against the table, his eyes half focused, his lips parted without control. "Well, if it ain't old Mums and Dadsies!" he said, slurring his words with rough Yorkshire. "Enjoying the kiddie's show-and-tell, Mums?"

"Damn!" Holcroft had spilled part of his drink.

"Ring for the butler, Pops! Charge it to old Edinburgh. He's a personal friend! Good old Edinburgh."

The solo, freaked-out dancer bolted away as quickly as he had intruded. The other middle-aged straights were appropriately solicitous of Holcroft, simultaneously scathing of The Owl's patrons; the youngsters did their best to mollify.

"It's all right, nothing to be concerned with," said the agent good-naturedly. "Just a bit damp, nothing to it." Holcroft removed his handkerchief and began blotting his front. The table returned to its prior and individual conversations. The Britisher turned to McAuliff, his resigned smiling belying his words. "I have less than a minute;

you'll be contacted tomorrow if necessary."

"You mean that . . . collision was a signal?"

"Yes. Now, listen and commit. I haven't time to repeat myself. When you reach Kingston, you'll be on your own for a while. Quite frankly, we weren't prepared for you so soon—"

"Just a minute!" interrupted McAuliff, his voice low, angry. "Goddamn you! *You* listen . . . and commit! You guaranteed complete safety, contacts twenty-four hours a day. It was on that basis I agreed—"

"Nothing has changed." Holcroft cut in swiftly, smiling paternalistically—in contradiction to the quiet hostility between them. "You *have* contacts; you've memorized eighteen, twenty names—"

"In the north country, not Kingston! You're supposed to deliver the Kingston names!"

"We'll do our best for tomorrow."

"That's not good enough!"

"It will have to be, Mr. McAuliff," said Holcroft coldly. "In Kingston, east of Victoria Park on Duke Street, there is a fish store called Tallon's. In the last extremity—and only then—should you wish to transmit information, see the owner. He's quite arthritic in his right hand. But, mind you, all he can do is transmit. He's of no other use to you . . . Now, I really must go."

"I've got a few other things to say." Alex put his hand on Holcroft's arm.

"They'll have to wait—"

"One thing . . . Alison Booth. You knew, didn't you?"

"About her husband?"

"Yes."

"We did. Frankly, at first, we thought she was a Dunstone plant. We haven't ruled it out . . . Oh, you asked about Warfield's mention of Halidon; what he meant. In my judgment, he knows no more than we do. And he's trying just as hard to find out."

With the swiftness associated with a much younger man, Holcroft lifted himself up from the booth, sidled past McAuliff, and excused himself from the group. McAuliff found himself seated next to the middle-aged woman he presumed had come with Holcroft. He had not listened to her name during the introductions, but as he looked at her now, he did not have to be told. The concern—the fear—was in her eyes; she tried to conceal it, but she could not. Her smile was hesitant, taut.

"So you're the young man . . ." Mrs. Holcroft stopped and brought the glass to her lips.

"Young and not so young," said McAuliff, noting that the woman's hand shook, as his had shaken an hour ago with Warfield. "It's difficult to talk in here with all the blaring. And those godawful lights."

Mrs. Holcroft seemed not to hear or be concerned with his words. The psychedelic oranges and yellows and sickening greens played a visual tattoo on her frightened features. It was strange, thought Alex, but he had not considered Holcroft as a private man with personal possessions or a wife or even a private, personal life.

And as he thought about these unconsidered realities, the woman suddenly gripped his forearm and leaned against him. Under the maddening sounds and through the wild, blinding lights, she whispered in McAuliff's ear: "For God's sake, go after him!"

The undulating bodies formed a violently writhing wall. He lunged through, pushing, pulling, shoving, finally shouldering a path for himself amid the shouted obscenities. He tried looking around for the spaced-out intruder who had signaled Holcroft by crashing into the table. He was nowhere to be found.

Then, at the rear of the crowded, flashing dance floor, he could see the interrupted movements of several men pushing a single figure back into a narrow corridor. It was Holcroft!

He crashed through the writhing wall again, toward the back of the room. A tall black man objected to Alex's assault.

"Hey, mon! Stop it! You own The Owl, I think not!"

"Get out of my way! Goddamn it, take your hands off me!"

"With pleasure, mon!" The black removed his hands from McAuliff's coat, pulled back a tight fist, and hammered it into Alex's stomach. The force of the blow, along with the shock of its utter surprise, caused McAuliff to double up.

He rose as fast as he could, the pain sharp, and lurched for the man. As he did so, the black twisted his wrist somehow, and McAuliff fell into the surrounding, nearly oblivious dancers. When he got to his feet, the black was gone.

It was a curious and very painful moment.

The smoke and its accompanying odors made him dizzy; then he understood. He was breathing deep breaths; he was out of breath. With less strength but no less intensity, he continued through the dancers to the narrow corridor.

It was a passageway to the restrooms, *"Chicks"* to the right, *"Roosters"* to the left. At the end of the narrow hallway was a door with a very large lock, an outsized padlock, that was meant, apparently, to remind patrons that the door was no egress; The Owl of Saint George expected tabs to be paid before departure.

The lock had been pried open. Pried open and then reset in the round hasps, its curving steel arm a half inch from insertion.

McAuliff ripped it off and opened the door.

He walked out into a dark, very dark, alleyway filled with garbage cans and refuse. There was literally no light but the night sky, dulled by fog, and a minimum spill from the windows in the surrounding ghettolike apartment buildings. In front of him was a high brick wall; to the right the alley continued past other rear doorways, ending in a cul-de-sac formed by the sharply angled wall. To his left, there was a break between The Owl's building and the brick; it was a passageway to the street. It was also lined with garbage cans, and the stench that had to accompany their presence.

McAuliff started down the cement corridor, the light from the street lamps illuminating the narrow confines. He was within twenty feet of the pavement when he saw it. Them: small pools of deep red fluid.

He raced out into the street. The crowds were thinning out; Soho was approaching its own witching hour. Its business was inside now: the private clubs, the all-night gambling houses, the profitable beds where sex was found in varying ways and prices. He looked up and down the sidewalk, trying to find a break in the patterns of human traffic: a resistance, an eruption.

There was none.

He stared down at the pavement; the rivulets of blood

had been streaked and blotted by passing feet, the red drops stopping abruptly at the curb. Holcroft had been taken away in an automobile.

Without warning, McAuliff felt the impact of lunging hands against his back. He had turned sideways at the last instant, his eyes drawn by the flickering of a neon light, and that small motion kept him from being hurled into the street. Instead, his attacker—a huge black—plunged over the curb, into the path of an onrushing Bentley, traveling at extraordinary speed. McAuliff felt a stinging pain on his face: Then man and vehicle collided; the anguished scream was the scream at the moment of death; the screeching wheels signified the incredible to McAuliff. The Bentley raced forward, crushing its victim, and sped off. It reached the corner and whipped violently to the left, its tires spinning above the curb, whirring as they touched stone again, propelling the car out of sight. Pedestrians screamed, men ran, whores disappeared into doorways, pimps gripped their pockets, and McAuliff stood above the bloody, mangled corpse in the street and knew it was meant to be him.

He ran down the Soho street; he did not know where, just away. Away from the gathering crowds on the pavement behind. There would be questions, witnesses . . . people placing him at the scene—*involved*, not placed, he reflected. He had no answers, and instinctively he knew he could not allow himself to be identified—not until he had some answers.

The dead black was the man in The Owl of Saint George, of that he was certain: the man who had stunned him with a savage blow to the stomach on the dance floor and twisted his wrist, throwing him onto the surrounding gyrating bodies. The man who had stopped him from reaching Holcroft in the narrow corridor that led past the *"Chicks"* and the *"Roosters"* into the dark alleyway beyond.

Why had the black stopped him? Why for Christ Almighty's sake had he tried to kill him?

Where was Holcroft?

He had to get to a telephone. He had to call Holcroft's number and speak to someone, anyone who could give him some answers.

Suddenly, Alex was aware that people in the street were staring at him. Why? . . . Of course. He was running—well, walking too rapidly. A man walking rapidly at this hour on a misty Soho street was conspicuous. He could not be conspicuous; he slowed his walk, his aimless walk, and aimlessly crossed unfamiliar streets.

Still they stared. He tried not to panic. What *was* it?

And then he knew. He could feel the warm blood trickling down his cheek. He remembered now: the sting on his face as the huge black hands went crashing past him over the curb. A ring, perhaps. A fingernail . . . what difference? He had been cut, and he was bleeding. He reached into his coat pocket for a handkerchief. The whole side of his jacket had been ripped.

He had been too stunned to notice or feel the jacket ripping, or the blood.

Christ! What a sight! A man in a torn jacket with blood on his face running away from a dead black in Soho.

Dead? Deceased? Life spent?

No. Murdered.

By the method meant for him: a violent thrust into the street, timed to meet the heavy steel on an onrushing, racing Bentley.

In the middle of the next block—what block?—there was a telephone booth. An English telephone booth, wider and darker than its American cousin. He quickened his pace as he withdrew coins from his pocket. He went inside; it was dark, too dark. Why was it so dark? He took out his metal cigarette lighter, gripping it as though it were a handle that, if released, would send him plunging into an abyss. He pressed the lever, breathed deeply, and dialed by the light of the flame.

"We know what's happened, Mr. McAuliff," said the clipped, cool British voice. "Where precisely are you calling from?"

"I don't know. I ran . . . I crossed a number of streets."

"It's urgent we know where you are . . . When you left The Owl, which way did you walk?"

"I ran, goddamn it! I *ran*. Someone tried to *kill* me!"

"Which *way* did you run, Mr. McAuliff?"

"To the right . . . four or five blocks. Then right again; then left, I think, two blocks later."

"All right. Relax, now . . . You're phoning from a call booth?"

"Yes. No, damn it, I'm *calling* from a *phone* booth! . . . Yes. For Christ's sake, tell me what's happening! There aren't any street signs; I'm in the middle of the block."

"Calm down, please." The Englishman was maddening: imperviously condescending. "What are the structures outside the booth? Describe anything you like, anything that catches your eye."

McAuliff complained about the fog and described as best he could the darkened shops and buildings. "Christ, that's the best I can do . . . I'm going to get out of here. I'll grab a taxi somehow; and then I want to see one of you! Where do I go?"

"You will *not* go *anywhere*, Mr. McAuliff!" The cold British tones were suddenly loud and harsh. "Stay right where you are. If there is a light in the booth, smash it. We know your position. We'll pick you up in minutes."

Alex hung up the receiver. There was no light bulb in the booth, of course. The tribes of Soho had removed it . . . He tried to think. He hadn't gotten any answers. Only orders. More commands.

It was insane. The last half hour was madness. What was he *doing?* Why was he in a darkened telephone booth with a bloody face and a torn jacket, trembling and afraid to light a cigarette?

Madness!

There was a man outside the booth, jingling coins in his hand and pointedly shifting his weight from foot to foot in irritation. The command over the telephone had instructed Alex to wait inside, but to do so under the circumstances might cause the man on the pavement to object vocally, drawing attention. He could call someone else, he thought. But who? . . . Alison? No . . . He had to think about Alison now, not talk with her.

He was behaving like a terrified child! With terrifying justification, perhaps. He was actually afraid to move, to walk outside a telephone booth and let an impatient man jingling coins go in. No, he could not behave like that. He could not freeze. He had learned that lesson years ago— centuries ago—in the hills of Panmunjung. To freeze was to become a target. One had to be flexible within the perimeters of common sense. One had to, above all, use his natural antennae and stay intensely alert. Staying alert, retaining the ability and capacity to move swiftly, these were the important things.

Jesus! He was correlating the murderous fury of Korea with a back street in Soho. He was actually drawing a parallel and forcing himself to adjust to it. Too goddamn much!

He opened the door, blotted his cheek, and mumbled apologies to the man jingling coins. He walked to a recessed doorway opposite the booth and waited.

The man on Holcroft's telephone was true to his word. The wait wasn't long, and the automobile recognizable as one of those Alex and the agent had used several times. It came down the street at a steady pace and stopped by the booth, its motor running.

McAuliff left the darkness of the recessed doorway and walked rapidly to the car. The rear door was flung open for him, and he climbed in.

And he froze again.

The man in the back seat was black. The man in the back seat was supposed to be dead, a mangled corpse in the street in front of The Owl of Saint George!

"Yes, Mr. McAuliff. It is I," said the black who was supposed to be dead. "I apologize for having struck you, but then, you were intruding. Are you all right?"

"Oh, my God!" Alex was rigid on the edge of the seat as the automobile lurched forward and sped off down the street. "I thought . . . I mean, I *saw* . . ."

"We're on our way to Holcroft. You'll understand better then. Sit back. You've had a very strenuous past hour . . . Quite unexpectedly, incidentally."

"*I saw you killed!*" McAuliff blurted out the words involuntarily.

"You saw a black man killed; a large black man like myself. We *do* weary of the bromide that we all look alike. It's both unflattering and untrue. By the way, my name is Tallon."

McAuliff stared at the man. "No, it's not. Tallon is the name of a fish store near Victoria Park. In Kingston."

The black laughed softly. "Very good, Mr. McAuliff. I was testing you. Smoke?"

Alex took the offered cigarette gratefully. "Tallon" held

a match for him, and McAuliff inhaled deeply, trying to
find a brief moment of sanity.

He looked at his hands. He was both astonished and
disturbed.

He was cupping the glow of the cigarette as he had
done . . . centuries ago as an infantry officer in the hills
of Panmunjung.

They drove for nearly twenty minutes, traveling swiftly
through the London streets to the outskirts. McAuliff did
not try to follow their route out the window; he did not
really care. He was consumed with the decision he had to
make. In a profound way it was related to the sight of his
hands—no longer trembling—cupping the cigarette. From
the nonexistent wind? From betraying his position? From
enemy snipers?

No. He was not a soldier, had never been one really.
He had performed because it was the only way to survive.
He had no motive other than survival; no war was his or
ever would be his. Certainly not Holcroft's.

"Here we are, Mr. McAuliff," said the black who called
himself "Tallon." "Rather deserted place, isn't it?"

The car had entered a road by a field—a field, but not
grass-covered. It was a leveled expanse of ground, perhaps
five acres, that looked as though it was being primed for
construction. Beyond the field was a river bank; Alex presumed it was the Thames, it had to be. In the distance
were large square structures that looked like warehouses.
Warehouses along a river bank. He had no idea where
they were.

The driver made a sharp left turn, and the automobile
bounced as it rolled over a primitive car path on the
rough ground. Through the windshield, McAuliff saw in
the glare of the headlamps two vehicles about a hundred
yards away, both sedans. The one on the right had its inside lights on. Within seconds, the driver had pulled up
parallel with the second car.

McAuliff got out and followed "Tallon" to the lighted
automobile. What he saw bewildered him, angered him,
perhaps, and unquestionably reaffirmed his decision to remove himself from Holcroft's war.

The British agent was sitting stiffly in the rear seat, his
shirt and overcoat draped over his shoulders, an open ex-

panse of flesh at his midsection revealing wide, white bandages. His eyes were squinting slightly, betraying the fact that the pain was not negligible. Alex knew the reason; he had seen the sight before—centuries ago—usually after a bayonet encounter.

Holcroft had been stabbed.

"I had you brought here for two reasons, McAuliff. And I warrant you, it was a gamble," said the agent as Alex stood by the open door. "Leave us alone, please," he added to the black.

"Shouldn't you be in a hospital?"

"No, it's not a severe laceration—"

"You got cut, Holcroft," interrupted McAuliff. "That's no laceration."

"You're melodramatic; it's unimportant. You'll notice, I trust, that I am very much alive."

"You're lucky."

"Luck, sir, had nothing whatsoever to do with it! That's part of what I want you to understand."

"All right. You're Captain Marvel, indestructible nemesis of the evil people."

"I am a fifty year old veteran of Her Majesty's Service who was never very good at football . . . soccer, to you." Holcroft winced and leaned forward. "And it's quite possible I would not be in these extremely tight bandages had you followed my instructions and not made a scene on the dance floor."

"What?"

"But you provoke me into straying. First things first. The instant it was apparent that I was in danger, that danger was removed. At no time, no moment, was my life in jeopardy."

"Because you say so? With a ten-inch bandage straddling your stomach? Don't try to sell water in the Sahara."

"This wound was delivered in panic caused by you! I was in the process of making the most vital contact on our schedule, the contact we sought *you* out to make."

"Halidon?"

"It's what we believed. Unfortunately, there's no way to verify. Come with me." Holcroft gripped the side strap, and with his right hand supported himself on the front seat as he climbed painfully out of the car. Alex made a minor gesture of assistance, knowing that it would be re-fused. The agent led McAuliff to the forward automobile, awkwardly removing a flashlight from his draped overcoat as they approached. There were several other men in shadows; they stepped away, obviously under orders.

Inside the car were two lifeless figures: one sprawled over the wheel, the other slumped across the rear seat. Holcroft shot the beam of light successively on both corpses. Each was male, black, in his mid-thirties, per-haps, and dressed in conservative, though not expensive, business suits. McAuliff was confused: There were no signs of violence, no shattered glass, no blood. The inte-rior of the car was neat, clean, even peaceful. The two dead men might have been a pair of young executives tak-ing a brief rest off the highway in the middle of a long business trip. Alex's bewilderment was ended with Hol-croft's next word.

"Cyanide."

"Why?"

"Fanatics, obviously. It was preferable to revealing in-formation . . . unwillingly, of course. They misread us. It began when you made such an obvious attempt to follow me out of The Owl of Saint George. That was their first panic; when they inflicted . . . this." Holcroft waved his hand just once at his midsection.

McAuliff did not bother to conceal his anger. "I've about had it with your goddamn caustic deductions!"

"I told you it was a gamble bringing you here—"

"Stop *telling* me things!"

"Please bear in mind that without us you had a life ex-pectancy of four months—at the outside."

"Your version, Holcroft." But the agent's version had more substance than McAuliff cared to think about at the moment.

"Do men take their lives because versions are false? Even fanatics?"

Alex turned away from the unpleasant sight. For no particular reason, he ripped the torn lining from the base of his jacket and leaned against the hood of the car. "Since you hold me responsible for so much tonight, what happened?"

The Britisher told him. Several days ago, M.I.5's sur-veillance had picked up a second "force" involved with

Dunstone's movements. Three, possibly four, unidentifi-
able subjects who kept reappearing. The subjects were
black. Photographs were taken, fingerprints obtained by
way of restaurants, discarded objects—cigarette packs,
newspapers, and the like—and all the data fed into the
computers at New Scotland Yard and Emigration. There
were no records; the subjects were in the country illegally.
Holcroft had been elated; the connection was so possible.
It was obvious that the subjects were "negative" insofar as
Dunstone was concerned. Obvious . . . then proven without doubt earlier in the evening, when one of the subjects
killed a Dunstone man who spotted him.

"We knew then," said Holcroft, "that we had centered
in; the target was accurate. It remained to make positive
contact, *sympathetic* contact. I even toyed with the idea of
bringing these men and you together in short order, perhaps this morning. So much resolved so damned
quickly . . ."

A cautious preliminary contact was made with the subjects: "so harmless and promising, we damn near offered
what was left of the Empire. They were concerned, of
course, with a trap."

A rendezvous was arranged at The Owl of Saint
George, a racially integrated club that offered a comfortable environment. It was scheduled for 2:30 in the morning, after Holcroft's meeting with McAuliff.

When Alex made his panicked—and threatening—call
to Holcroft's number, insisting that they meet regardless
of time, the agent left his options open. And then made
his decision. Why not The Owl of Saint George? Bring
the American into Soho, to the club, and if it proved the
wrong decision, McAuliff could be stopped once inside. If
the decision was the right one, the circumstances would be
optimal—all parties present.

"What about Warfield's men?" asked Alex. "You said
he doubled his teams on me."

"I lied. I wanted you to remain where you were. Warfield had a single man on you. We diverted him. The
Dunstone people had their own anxieties: One of their
men had been killed. You couldn't be held responsible for
that."

The night progressed as Holcroft had anticipated: without incident. The agent made arrangements for the ta-

ble—"we know just about everyone you've met in London, chap"—and awaited the compatible merging of elements.

And then, in rapid succession, each component fell apart. First was Alex's statement that the survey team was leaving in two days—M.I.5 was not ready for it in Kingston. Then the information that Warfield had spoken the name of "Halidon"; it was to be expected, of course. Dunstone would be working furiously to find the killers of the first survey team. But, again, M.I.5 had not expected Dunstone to have made such progress. The next breakdown was the spaced-out agent who crashed into the table and used the word "Edinburgh"—used it twice.

"Each twenty-four-hour period we circulate an unusual word that has but one connotation: 'abort, extreme prejudice.' If it's repeated, that simply compounds the meaning: Our cover is blown. Or misread. Weapons should be ready."

At that moment, Holcroft saw clearly the massive error that had been made. His agents had diverted Warfield's men away from Alex, but not one of the blacks. McAuliff had been observed in Warfield's company at midnight for a considerable length of time. Within minutes after he had walked into The Owl, his black surveillance had followed, panicked that his colleagues had been led into a trap.

The confrontation had begun within the gyrating, psychedelic madness that was The Owl of Saint George.

Holcroft tried to stop the final collapse.

He broke the rules. It was not yet 2:30, but since Alexander McAuliff had been seen with him, he dared not wait. He tried to establish a bridge, to explain, to calm the raging outburst.

He had nearly succeeded when one of the blacks—now dead behind the wheel—saw McAuliff leap from his seat in the booth and plunge into the crowds, whipping people out of his way, looking frantically—obviously—for Holcroft.

This sight triggered the panic. Holcroft was cut, used as a shield, and propelled out the rear door into the alley by two of the subjects while the third fled through the crowds in front to alert the car for escape.

"What happened during the next few minutes was as distressing as it was comforting," said Holcroft. "My people would not allow my physical danger, so the instant my captors and I emerged on the pavement, they were taken. We put them in this car and drove off, still hoping to reestablish good will. But we purposely allowed the third man to disappear—an article of faith on our part."

The M.I.5 had driven out to the deserted field. A doctor was summoned to patch up Holcroft. And the two subjects—relieved of weapons, car key removed unobtrusively—were left alone to talk by themselves, hopefully to resolve their doubts, while Holcroft was being bandaged.

"They made a last attempt to get away but, of course, there were no keys in the vehicle. So they took their deadly little vials or tablets and, with them, their lives. Ultimately, they could not trust us."

McAuliff said nothing for several moments. Holcroft did not interrupt the silence.

"And your 'article of faith' tried to kill me."

"Apparently. Leaving one man in England we must try to find: the driver . . . You understand that we cannot be held accountable; you completely disregarded our instructions—"

"We'll get to that," broke in McAuliff. "You said you brought me out here for two reasons. I get the first: Your people are quick, safety guaranteed . . . if instructions aren't 'disregarded.' " Alex mimicked Holcroft's reading of the word. "What's the second reason?"

The agent walked directly in front of McAuliff and, through the night light, Alex could see the intensity in his eyes. "To tell you you have no choice but to continue now. Too much has happened. You're too involved."

"That's what Warfield said."

"He's right."

"Suppose I refuse? Suppose I just pack up and leave?"

"You'd be suspect, and expendable. You'd be hunted down. Take my word for that, I've been here before."

"That's quite a statement from a . . . what was it, a financial analyst?"

"Labels, Mr. McAuliff. Titles. Quite meaningless."

"Not to your wife."

"I beg your—" Holcroft inhaled deeply, audibly. When he continued, he did not ask a question. He made a quiet, painful statement. "She sent you after me."

"Yes."

It was Holcroft's turn to remain silent. And Alex's option not to break that silence. Instead, McAuliff watched the fifty year old agent struggle to regain his composure.

"The fact remains, you disregarded my instructions."

"You must be a lovely man to live with."

"Get used to it," replied Holcroft with cold precision. "For the next several months, our association will be very close. And you'll do exactly as I say. Or you'll be dead."

TWO

Kingston

7

THE RED-ORANGE sun burned a hole in the streaked blue tapestry that was the evening sky. Arcs of yellow rimmed the lower clouds; a purplish-black void was above. The soft Caribbean night would soon envelop this section of the world. It would be dark when the plane landed at Port Royal.

McAuliff stared out at the horizon through the tinted glass of the aircraft's window. Alison Booth was in the seat beside him, asleep.

The Jensens were across the 747's aisle, and for a couple whose political persuasions were left of center, they adapted to B.O.A.C.'s first-class accommodations with a remarkable lack of guilt, thought Alex. They ordered the best wine, the foie gras, duck à l'orange, and Charlotte Malakof as if they had been used to them for years. And Alex wondered if Warfield was wrong. All the left-oriented he knew, outside the Soviet block, were humorless; the Jensens were not.

Young James Ferguson was alone in a forward seat. Initially, Charles Whitehall had sat with him, but Whitehall had gone up to the lounge early in the flight, found an acquaintance from Savanna-La-Mar, and stayed. Ferguson used the unoccupied seat for a leather bag containing photographic equipment. He was currently changing lens filters, snapping shots of the sky outside.

McAuliff and Alison had joined Charles Whitehall and his friend for several drinks in the lounge. The friend was white, rich, and a heavy drinker. He was also a vacuous inheritor of old southwest Jamaican money, and Alex found it contradictory that Whitehall would care to spend much time with him, and it was a little disturbing to watch Whitehall respond with such alacrity to his friend's alcoholic, unbright, unfunny observations.

Alison had touched McAuliff's arm after the second drink. It had been a signal to return to their seats; she had had enough. So had he.

Alison?

During the last two days in London there had been so

much to do that he had not spent the time with her he had wanted to, intended to. He was involved with all-day problems of logistics: equipment purchases and rentals, clearing passports, ascertaining whether inoculations were required (none was), establishing bank accounts in Montego, Kingston, and Ocho Rios, and scores of additional items necessary for a long geological survey. Dunstone stayed out of the picture but was of enormous help behind the scenes. The Dunstone people told him precisely who to see where; the tangled webs of bureaucracy—governmental and commercial—were untangled.

He had spent one evening bringing everyone together—everyone but Sam Tucker, who would join them in Kingston. Dinner at Simpsons. It was sufficiently agreeable; all were professionals. Each sized up the others and made flattering comments where work was known. Whitehall received the most recognition—as was appropriate. He was an authentic celebrity of sorts. Ruth Jensen and Alison seemed genuinely to like each other, which McAuliff had thought would happen. Ruth's husband, Peter, assumed a paternalistic attitude toward Ferguson, laughing gently, continuously at the young man's incessant banter. And Charles Whitehall had the best manners, slightly aloof and very proper, with just the right traces of scholarly wit and unfelt humility.

But Alison.

He had kept their luncheon date after the madness at The Owl of Saint George and the insanity that followed in the deserted field on London's outskirts. He had approached her with ambiguous feelings. He was annoyed that she had not brought up the questionable activities of her recent husband. But he did not accept Holcroft's vague concern that Alison was a Warfield plant. It was senseless. She was nothing if not independent—as he was. To be a silent emissary from Warfield meant losing independence—as he knew. Alison could not do that, not without showing it.

Still, he tried to provoke her into talking about her husband. She responded with humorously "civilized" clichés such as leaving sleeping dogs lie, which he had. Often. She would not, at this point, discuss David Booth with him.

It was not relevant.

"Ladies and gentlemen," said the very masculine, in-charge tones over the aircraft's speaker. "This is Captain Thomas. We are nearing the northeast coast of Jamaica; in several minutes we shall be over Port Antonio, descending for our approach to Palisados Airport, Port Royal. May we suggest that all passengers return to their seats. There may be minor turbulence over the Blue Mountain range. Time of arrival is now anticipated at 8:20, Jamaican. The temperature in Kingston is seventy-eight degrees, weather and visibility clear . . ."

As the calm, strong voice finished the announcement, McAuliff thought of Holcroft. If the British agent spoke over a loudspeaker, he would sound very much like Captain Thomas, Alex considered.

Holcroft.

McAuliff had not ended their temporary disassociation—as Holcroft phrased it—too pleasantly. He had countered the agent's caustic pronouncement that Alex do as Holcroft instructed with a volatile provision of his own: He had six hundred sixty-odd thousand dollars coming to him from Dunstone, Limited, and he expected to collect it. From Dunstone or some other source.

Holcroft had exploded. What good was a million dollars to a dead geologist? Alex should be paying for the warnings and the protection afforded him. But, in the final analysis, Holcroft recognized the necessity for something to motivate Alexander's cooperation. Survival was too abstract; lack of survival could not be experienced.

In the early morning hours, a Letter of Agreement was brought to McAuliff by a temporary Savoy floor steward; Alex recognized him as the man in the brown mackinaw on High Holborn. The letter covered the conditions of reimbursement in the event of "loss of fees" with a *very* clear ceiling of six hundred and sixty thousand dollars.

If he remained in one piece—and he had every expectation of so doing—the loss was six thousand dollars.

He would live with it. He mailed the agreement to New York.

Holcroft.

He wondered what the explanation was; what could explain a wife whose whispered voice could hold such fear? He wondered about the private, personal Holcroft, yet knew instinctively that whatever private questions he had would never be answered.

Holcroft was like that. Perhaps all the people who did what Holcroft did were like that. Men in shadows; their women in unending tunnels of fear. Pockets of fear.

And then there was . . .

Halidon.

What did it mean? What was it?

Was it black?

Possibly. Probably not, however, Holcroft had said. At least, not exclusively. It had too many informational resources, too much apparent influence in powerful sectors. Too much money.

The word had surfaced under strange and horrible circumstances. The British agent attached to the previous Dunstone survey had been one of two men killed in a bush fire that began inside a bamboo camp on the banks of the Martha Brae River, deep within the Cock Pit country. Evidence indicated that the two dead members of the survey had tried to salvage equipment within the fire, collapsed from the smoke, and burned in the bamboo inferno.

But there was something more; something so appalling that even Holcroft found it difficult to recite it.

The two men had been bound by bamboo shoots to separate trees, each next to valuable survey equipment. They had been consumed in the conflagration, for the simple reason that neither could run from it. But the agent had left a message, a single word scratched on the metal casing of a geoscope.

Halidon.

Inspection under a microscope gave the remainder of the horror story: particles of human tooth enamel. The agent had scratched the letters with broken teeth.

Halidon . . . holly-dawn.

No known definition. A word? A name? A man? A three-beat sound?

What did it mean?

"It's beautiful, isn't it," said Alison, looking beyond him through the window.

"You're awake."

"Someone turned on a radio and a man spoke . . . endlessly." She smiled and stretched long legs. She then inhaled in a deep yawn, which caused her breasts to swell against the soft white silk of her blouse. McAuliff watched. And she saw him watching, and smiled again—in humor, not provocation. "Relevancy, Dr. McAuliff. Remember?"

"That word's going to get you into trouble, Ms. Booth."

"I'll stop saying it instantly. Come to think, I don't believe I used it much until I met you."

"I like the connection; don't stop."

She laughed, and reached for her pocketbook, on the deck between them.

There was a sudden series of rise-and-fall motions as the plane entered air turbulence. It was over quickly, but during it Alison's open purse landed on its side—on Alex's lap. Lipstick, compact, matches, and a short thick tube fell out, wedging themselves between McAuliff's legs. It was one of those brief, indecisive moments. Pocketbooks were unfair vantage points, somehow unguarded extensions of the private self. And Alison was not the type to reach swiftly between a man's legs to retrieve property.

"Nothing fell on the floor," said Alex awkwardly, handing Alison the purse. "Here."

He picked out the lipstick and the compact with his left hand, his right on the thick tube, which, at first, seemed to have a very personal connotation. As his eyes were drawn to the casing, however, the connotation became something else. The tube was a weapon, a compressor. On the cylinder's side were printed words:

312 GAS CONTENTS
FOR MILITARY AND/OR POLICE USE ONLY
AUTHORISATION NUMBER 4316
RECORDED: 1-6

The authorization number and the date had been handwritten in indelible ink. The gas compressor had been issued by British authorities a month ago.

Alison took the tube from his hand. "Thank you" was all she said.

"You planning to hijack the plane? That's quite a lethal-looking object."

"London has its problems for girls . . . women these days. There were incidents in my building. May I have a cigarette? I seem to be out."

"Sure." McAuliff reached into his shirt pocket and

withdrew his cigarettes, shaking one up for her. He lighted it, then spoke softly, very gently. "Why are you lying to me, Alison?"

"I'm not. I think it's presumptuous of you to think so."

"Oh, come on." He smiled, reducing the earnestness of his inquiry. "The police, especially the London police, do not issue compressors of gas because of 'incidents.' And you don't look like a colonel in the Women's Auxillary Army." As he said the words, Alex suddenly had the feeling that perhaps he was wrong. Was Alison Booth an emissary from Holcroft? Not Warfield, but British Intelligence?

"Exceptions are made. They really are, Alex." She locked her eyes with his; she was not lying.

"May I venture a suggestion? A reason?"

"If you like."

"David Booth?"

She looked away, inhaling deeply on her cigarette. "You know about him. That's why you kept asking questions the other night."

"Yes. Did you think I wouldn't find out?"

"I didn't care . . . no, that's not right; I think I wanted you to find out if it helped me get the job. But I couldn't tell you."

"Why not?"

"Oh, Lord, Alex! Your own words; you wanted the best professionals, not personal problems! For all I knew, you'd have scratched me instantly." Her smile was gone now. There was only anxiety.

"This Booth must be quite a fellow."

"He's a very sick, very vicious man . . . But I can handle David. I was always able to handle him. He's an extraordinary coward."

"Most vicious people are."

"I'm not sure I subscribe to that. But it wasn't David. It was someone else. The man he worked for."

"Who?"

"A Frenchman. A marquis. Chatellerault is his name."

The team took separate taxis into Kingston. Alison remained behind with McAuliff while he commandeered the equipment with the help of the Jamaican government people attached to the Ministry of Education. Alex could feel the same vague resentment from the Jamaicans that he had felt with the academicians in London; only added now was the aspect of pigmentation. Were there no black geologists? they seemed to be thinking.

The point was emphasized by the Customs men, their khaki uniforms creased into steel. They insisted on examining each box, each carton, as though each contained the most dangerous contraband imaginable. They decided to be officially thorough as McAuliff stood helplessly by long after the aircraft had taxied into a Palisados berth. Alison remained ten yards away, sitting on a luggage dolly.

An hour and a half later, the equipment had been processed and marked for in-island transport to Boscobel Airfield, in Ocho Rios. McAuliff's temper was stretched to the point of gritted teeth and a great deal of swallowing. He grabbed Alison's arm and marched them both toward the terminal.

"For heaven's sake, Alex, you're bruising my elbow!" said Alison under her breath, trying to hold back her laughter.

"Sorry . . . I'm *sorry*. Those goddamned messiahs think they inherited the earth! The *bastards!*"

"They recently inherited their own island—"

"I'm in no mood for anti-colonial lectures," he interrupted. "I'm in the mood for a drink. Let's stop at the lounge."

"What about our bags?"

"Oh, Christ! I forgot . . . it's this way, if I remember," said Alex, pointing to a gate entrance on the right.

"Yes," replied Alison. " 'Incoming Flights' usually means that."

"Be quiet. My first order to you as a subordinate is not to say another word until we get our bags and I have a drink in my hand."

But McAuliff's command, by necessity, was rescinded. Their luggage was nowhere in sight. And apparently no one knew where it might be; all passenger baggage stored on Flight 640 from London had been picked up. An hour ago.

"*We* were on that flight. We did *not* pick up our bags. So, you see, you're mistaken," said Alex curtly to the luggage manager.

"Then you look-see, mon," answered the Jamaican, irritated by the American's implication that he was less than efficient. "Every suitcase taken—nothing left. Flight 640 all *here,* mon! No place other."

"Let me talk to the B.O.A.C. representative. Where is he?"

"Who?"

"Your boss, goddamn it!"

"I top mon!" replied the black angrily.

Alex held himself in check. "Look, there's been a mix-up. The airline's responsible, that's all I'm trying to say."

"I think not, mon," interjected the luggage manager defensively as he turned to a telephone on the counter. "I will call Bo-Ack."

"B.O.A.C." McAuliff spoke softly to Alison. "Our bags are probably on the way to Buenos Aires." They waited while the man spoke briefly on the phone.

"Here, mon." The manager held the phone out for Alex. "You talk, please."

"Hello?"

"Dr. McAuliff?" said the British voice.

"Yes. McAuliff."

"We merely followed the instructions in your note, sir."

"What note?"

"To First Class Accommodations. The driver brought it to us. The taxi. Mrs. Booth's and your luggage was taken to Courtleigh Manor. That *is* what you wished, is it not, sir?" The voice was laced with a trace of over-clarification, as if the speaker were addressing someone who had had an extra drink he could not handle.

"I see . . . Yes, that's fine," said Alex quietly. He hung up the telephone and turned to Alison. "Our bags were taken to the hotel."

"Really? Wasn't that nice." A statement.

"No, I don't think it was," answered McAuliff. "Come on, let's find that bar."

They sat at a corner table in the Palisados observation lounge. The red-jacketed waiter brought their drinks while humming a Jamaican folk tune softly. Alex wondered if the island's tourist bureau instructed all those who served visitors to hum tunes and move rhythmically. He reached for his glass and drank a large portion of his double Scotch. He noticed that Alison, who was not much of a drinker, seemed as anxious as he was to put some alcohol into her system.

All things considered—all things—it was conceivable that his luggage might be stolen. Not hers. But the note had specified his and Mrs. Booth's.

"You didn't have any more artillery, did you?" asked Alex quickly. "Like that compressor?"

"No. It would have set off bells in the airline X-ray. I declared this prior to boarding." Alison pointed to her purse.

"Yes, of course," he mumbled.

"I must say, you're remarkably calm. I should think you'd be telephoning the hotel, see if the bags got there . . . oh, not for me. I don't travel with the Crown jewels."

"Oh, Lord, I'm sorry, Alison." He pushed his chair back. "I'll call right away."

"No, please." She reached out and put her hand over his. "I think you're doing what you're doing for a reason. You don't want to appear upset. I think you're right. If they're gone, there's nothing I can't replace in the morning."

"You're very understanding. Thanks."

She withdrew her hand and drank again. He pulled his chair back and shifted his position slightly, toward the interior of the lounge. Unobtrusively, he began scanning the other tables.

The observation lounge was half filled, no more than that. From his position—their position—in the far west corner of the room, Alex could see nearly every table. And he slowly riveted his attention on every table, wondering, as he had wondered two nights ago on High Holborn, who might be concerned with *him*.

There was movement in the dimly lighted entrance. McAuliff's eyes were drawn to it: the figure of a stocky man in a white shirt and no jacket standing in the wide frame. He spoke to the lounge's hostess, shaking his head slowly, negatively, as he looked inside. Suddenly, Alex blinked and focused on the man.

He knew him.

A man he had last seen in Australia, in the fields of Kimberly Plateau. He had been told the man had retired to Jamaica.

Robert Hanley, a pilot.

Hanley was standing in the entranceway of the lounge, looking for someone inside. And Alex knew instinctively that Hanley was looking for him.

"Excuse me," he said to Alison. "There's a fellow I know. Unless I'm mistaken, he's trying to find me."

McAuliff thought, as he threaded his way around the tables and through the subdued shadows of the room, that it was somehow right that Robert Hanley, of all the men in the Caribbean, would be involved. Hanley, the open man who dealt with a covert world because he was, above all, a man to be trusted. A laughing man, a tough man, a professional with expertise far beyond that required by those employing him. Someone who had miraculously survived six decades when all the odds indicated nearer to four. But then, Robert Hanley did not look much over forty-five. Even his close-cropped, reddish-blond hair was devoid of gray.

"Robert!"

"Alexander!"

The two men clasped hands and held each other's shoulders.

"I said to the lady sitting with me that I thought you were looking for me. I'll be honest, I hope I'm wrong."

"I wish you were, lad."

"That's what I was afraid of. What is it? Come on in."

"In a minute. Let me tell you the news first. I wouldn't want the lady to see you uncork your temper." Hanley led Alex away from the door; they stood alone by the wall. "It's Sam Tucker."

"*Sam?* Where is he?"

"That's the point, lad. I don't know. Sam flew into Mo'Bay three days ago and called me at Port Antone'; the boys in Los Angeles told him I was here. I hopped over, naturally, and it was a grand reunion. I won't go into the details. The next morning, Sam went down to the lobby to get a paper, I think. He never came back."

8

ROBERT HANLEY was flying back to Port Antonio in an hour. He and McAuliff agreed not to mention Sam Tucker to Alison. Hanley also agreed to keep looking for Sam; he and Alex would stay in touch.

The three of them took a taxi from Port Royal into Kingston, to the Courtleigh. Hanley remained in the cab and took it on to the small Tinson Pen Airfield, where he kept his plane.

At the hotel desk, Alex inquired nonchalantly, feeling no casualness whatsoever, "I assume our luggage arrived?"

"Indeed, yes, Mr. McAuliff," replied the clerk, stamping both registration forms and signaling a bellhop. "Only minutes ago. We had them brought to your rooms. They're adjoining."

"How thoughtful," said Alex softly, wondering if Alison had heard the man behind the desk. The clerk did not speak loudly, and Alison was at the end of the counter, looking at tourist brochures. She glanced over at McAuliff; she had heard. The expression on her face was noncommittal. He wondered.

Five minutes later, she opened the door between their two rooms, and Alex knew there was no point speculating further.

"I did as you ordered, Mister Bossman," said Alison, walking in. "I didn't touch the—"

McAuliff held up his hand quickly, signaling her to be quiet. "The *bed*, bless your heart! You're all heart, luv!"

The expression now on Alison's face was definitely committal. Not pleasantly. It was an awkward moment, which he was not prepared for; he had not expected her to walk deliberately into his room. Still, there was no point standing immobile, looking foolish.

He reached into his jacket pocket and withdrew a small, square-shaped metal instrument the size of a cigarette pack. It was one of several items given him by Holcroft. (Holcroft had cleared his boarding pass with B.O.A.C. in London, eliminating the necessity of his declaring whatever metallic objects were on his person.)

The small metal box was an electronic scanner with a miniaturized high-voltage battery. Its function was simple, its mechanism complex, and Holcroft claimed it was in very common use these days. It detected the presence of electronic listening devices within a nine-by-nine-foot area. Alex had intended to use it the minute he entered the room. Instead, he absentmindedly had opened the doors to his small balcony and gazed for a brief time at the dark, majestic rise of the Blue Mountains beyond in the clear Kingston night.

Alison Booth stared at the scanner and then at McAuliff. Both anger and fear were in her eyes, but she had the presence of mind to say nothing.

As he had been taught, Alex switched on the instrument and made half circles laterally and vertically, starting from the far corner of the room. This pattern was to be followed in the other three corners. He felt embarrassed, almost ludicrous, as he waved his arm slowly, as though administering some occult benediction. He did not care to look at Alison as he went through the motions.

Then, suddenly, he was not embarrassed at all. Instead, he felt a pain in the center of his upper stomach, a sharp sting as his breath stopped and his eyes riveted on the inch-long, narrow bar in the dial of the scanner. He had seen that bar move often during the practice sessions with Holcroft; he had been curious, even fascinated at its wavering, stuttering, movements. He was not fascinated now. He was afraid.

This was not a training session in an out-of-the-way, safe practice room with Holcroft patiently, thoroughly explaining the importance of overlapping areas. It was actually happening; he had not really thought that it *would* happen. It all had been . . . well, basically *insincere*, somehow so improbable.

Yet now, in front of him, the thin, inch-long bar was vibrating, oscillating with a miniature violence of its own. The tiny sensors were responding to an intruder.

Somewhere within the immediate area of his position was a foreign object whose function was to transmit everything being said in this room.

He motioned to Alison; she approached him warily. He gestured and realized that his gestures were those of an unimaginative charade contestant. He pointed to the scanner and then to his lips. When she spoke he felt like a goddamned idiot.

"You promised me a drink in that lovely garden downstairs. Other considerations will have to wait . . . *luv*." She said the words quietly, simply. She was very believable!

"You're right," he answered, deciding instantly that he was no actor. "Just let me wash up."

He walked swiftly into the bathroom and turned the faucets on in the basin. He pulled the door to within several inches of closing; the sound of the rushing water was discernible, not obvious. He returned to where he had been standing and continued to operate the scanner, reducing the semicircles as the narrow bar reacted, centering in on the location of the object as he had been taught to do by Holcroft.

The only non-stunning surprise was the fact that the scanner's tiny red light went on directly above his suitcase, against the wall on a baggage rack.

The red light indicated that the object was within twelve inches of the instrument.

He handed Alison the scanner and opened the case cautiously. He separated his clothes, removing shirts, socks, and underwear, and placing them—throwing them—on the bed. When the suitcase was more empty than full, he stretched the elasticized liner and ran his fingers against the leather wall.

McAuliff knew what to feel for; Holcroft had showed him dozens of bugs of varying sizes and shapes.

He found it.

It was attached to the outer lining: a small bulge the size of a leather-covered button. He let it stay and, as Holcroft had instructed, continued to examine the remainder of the suitcase for a second, back-up device.

It was there, too. On the opposite side.

He took the scanner from Alison, walked away from the area, and rapidly "half circled" the rest of the room. As Holcroft had told him to expect, there was no further movement on the scanner's dial. For, if a transmitter was planted on a movable host, it usually indicated that it was the only source available.

The rest of the room was clean. "Sterile" was the word Holcroft had used.

McAuliff went into the bathroom; it, too, was safe. He turned off the faucets and called out to Alison.

"Are you unpacked?" *Now why the hell did he say that? Of all the stupid . . .*

"I'm an old hand at geo trips," came the relaxed reply. "All my garments are double-knit; they can wait. I really want to see that *lovely* garden. Do hurry."

He pulled the door open and saw that the girl was closing the balcony door, drawing the curtains across the floor-to-ceiling glass. Alison Booth was doing the right thing, he reflected. Holcroft had often repeated the command: *When you find a transmitter, check outside sightlines; assume visual surveillance.*

He came out of the bathroom; she looked across at him . . . No, he thought, she did not look at him, she stared at him.

"Good," she said. "You're ready. I think you missed most of your beard, but you're presentable. Let's go . . . *luv.*"

Outside the room, in the hotel corridor, Alison took his arm, and they walked to the elevator. Several times he began to speak, but each time he did so, she interrupted him.

"Wait till we're downstairs," she kept repeating softly.

In the patio garden, it was Alison who, after they had been seated, requested another table. One on the opposite side of the open area; a table, Alex realized, that had no palms or plants in its vicinity. There were no more than a dozen other couples, no single men or unescorted women. McAuliff had the feeling that Alison had observed each couple closely.

Their drinks arrived; the waiter departed, and Alison Booth spoke.

"I think it's time we talked to each other . . . about things we haven't talked about."

Alex offered her a cigarette. She declined, and so he lighted one for himself. He was buying a few seconds of time before answering her, and both of them knew it.

"I'm sorry you saw what you did upstairs. I don't want you to give it undue importance."

"That would be funny, darling, except that *you* were halfway to hysterics."

"That's nice."

"What?"

"You said 'darling.' "

"Please. May we stay professional?"

"Good Lord! Are you? Professional, I mean?"

"I'm a geologist. What are you?"

McAuliff ignored her. "You said I was . . . excited upstairs. You were right. But it struck me that you weren't. You did all the correct things while I was fumbling."

"I agree. You were fumbling. Alex . . . were you told to hire me?"

"No. I was told to think twice or three times before accepting you."

"That could have been a ploy. I wanted the job badly; I would have gone to bed with you to get it . . . Thank you for not demanding that."

"There was no pressure one way or the other about you. Only a warning. And that was because of your recent husband's sideline occupation, which, incidentally, apparently accounts for most of his money. I say money because it's not considered income, I gather."

"It accounts for *all* of his money, and is not reported as income. And I don't for a minute believe the Geophysics Department of London University would have access to such information. Much less the Royal Society."

"Then you'd be wrong. A lot of the money for this survey is a grant from the government funneled through the society and the university. When governments spend money, they're concerned about personnel *and* payrolls." McAuliff was pleasantly surprised at himself. He was responding as Holcroft said he would: creating instant, logical replies. *Build on part of the truth, keep it simple . . .* Those had been Holcroft's words.

"We'll let that dubious, American-oriented assessment pass," said Alison, now reaching for his cigarettes. "Surely you'll explain what happened upstairs."

The moment had come, thought Alex, wondering if he could carry it off the way Holcroft said: *Reduce any explanation to very few words, rooted in common sense and simplicity, and do not vary.* He lighted her cigarette and spoke as casually as possible.

"There's a lot of political jockeying in Kingston. Most of it's petty, but some of it gets rough. This survey has controversial overtones. Resentment of origin, jealousies, that sort of thing. You saw it at Customs . . . There are people who would like to discredit us. I was given that goddamned scanner to use in case I thought something very unusual happened. I thought it had, and I was right." Alex drank the remainder of his drink and watched the girl's reaction. He did his best to convey only sincerity.

"Our bags, you mean," said Alison.

"Yes. That note didn't make sense, and the clerk at the desk said they got here just before we did. But they were picked up at Palisados over two hours ago."

"I see. And a geological survey would drive people to those extremes? That's hard to swallow, Alex."

"Not if you think about it. Why are surveys made? What's generally the purpose? Isn't it usually because someone—some people—expect to build something?"

"Not one like ours, no. It's too spread out over too great an area. I'd say it's patently, *obviously* academic. Anything else would—" Alison stopped as her eyes met McAuliff's. "Good Lord! If it *was* anything else, it's unbelievable!"

"Perhaps there are those who *do* believe it. If they did, what do you think they'd do?" Alex signaled the waiter by holding up two fingers for refills. Alison Booth's lips were parted in astonishment.

"Millions and millions *and millions,*" said the girl quietly. "My God, they'd buy up everything in sight!"

"Only if they were convinced they were right."

Alison forced him to look at her. When, at first, he refused, and glanced over at the waiter, who was dawdling, she put her hand on top of his and made him pay attention. "They *are* right, aren't they, Alex?"

"I wouldn't have any proof of it. My contract's with London University, with countersigned approvals from the Society and the Jamaican Ministry. What they do with the results is their business." It was pointless to issue a flat denial. He was a professional surveyor, not a clairvoyant.

"I don't believe you. You've been primed."

"Not primed. Told to be on guard, that's all."

"Those . . . deadly little instruments aren't given to people who've only been told to be on guard."

"That's what I thought. But you know something? You and I are wrong, Alison. Scanners are in . . . common use these days. Nothing out of the ordinary. Especially if you're working outside home territory. Not a very nice comment on the state of trust, is it?"

The waiter brought their drinks. He was humming and moving rhythmically to the beat of his own tune. Alison continued to stare at McAuliff. He wasn't sure, but he began to think she believed him. When the waiter left, she leaned forward, anxious to speak.

"And what are you supposed to do now? You found those awful . . . things. What are you going to do about them?"

"Nothing. Report them to the Ministry in the morning, that's all."

"You mean you're not going to take them out and step on them or something? You're just going to leave them there?"

It was not a pleasant prospect, thought Alex, but Holcroft had been clear: If a bug was found, let it remain intact and *use* it. It could be invaluable. Before eliminating any such device, he was to report it and await instructions. A fish store named Tallon's, near Victoria Park.

"They're paying me . . . paying us. I suppose they'll want to quietly investigate. What difference does it make? I don't have any secrets."

"And you *won't* have," said the girl softly but pointedly, removing her hand from his.

McAuliff suddenly realized the preposterousness of his position. It was at once ridiculous and sublime, funny and not funny at all.

"May I change my mind and call someone now?" he asked.

Alison slowly—very slowly—began to smile her lovely smile. "No. I was being unfair . . . And I *do* believe you. You're the most maddeningly unconcerned man I've ever known. You are either supremely innocent or superbly ulterior. I can't accept the latter; you were far too nervous upstairs." She put her hand back on top of his free one. With his other, he finished the second drink.

"May I ask why you weren't? Nervous."

"Yes. It's time I told you. I owe you that . . . I shan't be returning to England, Alex. Not for many years, if ever. I can't. I spent several months . . . cooperating with Interpol. I've had experience with those horrid little buggers. That's what we called them. Buggers."

McAuliff felt the stinging pain in his stomach again. It was fear, and more than fear. Holcroft had said British Intelligence doubted she would return to England. Julian Warfield suggested that she might be of value for abstract reasons having nothing to do with her contributions to the survey.

He was not sure how—or why—but Alison was being used.

Just as he was being used.

"How did *that* happen?" he asked with appropriate astonishment.

Alison touched on the highlights of her involvement. The marriage was sour before the first anniversary. Succinctly put, Alison Booth came to the conclusion very early that her husband had pursued and married her for reasons having more to do with her professional travels than for anything else.

". . . it was as though he had been ordered to take me, use me, absorb me . . ."

The strain came soon after they were married: Booth was inordinately interested in her prospects. And, from seemingly nowhere, survey offers came out of the blue, from little-known but good-paying firms, for operations remarkably exotic.

". . . among them, of course, Beirut, Corsica, southern Spain. He joined me each time. For days, weeks at a time . . ."

The first confrontation with David Booth came about in Corsica. The survey was a coastal-offshore expedition in the Capo Senetosa area. David arrived during the middle stages for his usual two- to three-week stay, and during this period a series of strange telephone calls and unexplained conferences took place, which seemed to disturb him beyond his limited abilities to cope. Men flew into Ajaccia in small, fast planes; others came by sea in trawlers and small ocean-going craft. David would disappear for hours, then for days at a time. Alison's field work was such that she returned nightly to the team's seacoast hotel; her husband could not conceal his behavior, nor the fact that his presence in Corsica was not an act of devotion to her.

She forced the issue, enumerating the undeniable, and brutally labeling David's explanations for what they were:

amateurish lies. He had broken down, wept, pleaded, and told his wife the truth.

In order to maintain a life style David Booth was incapable of earning in the marketplace, he had moved into international narcotics. He was primarily a courier. His partnership in a small importing-exporting business was ideal for the work. The firm had no real identity; indeed, it was rather nondescript, catering—as befitted the owners—to a social rather than a commercial clientele, dealing in art objects on the decorating level. He was able to travel extensively without raising official eyebrows. His introduction to the world of the *contrabandists* was banal: gambling debts compounded by an excess of alcohol and embarrassing female alliances. On the one hand, he had no choice; on the other, he was well paid and had no moral compunctions.

But Alison did. The geological surveys were legitimate, testimonials to David's employers' abilities to ferret out unsuspecting collaborators. David was given the names of survey teams in selected Mediterranean sites and told to contact them, offering the services of his very respected wife, adding further that he would confidentially contribute to her salary if she was hired. A rich, devoted husband only interested in keeping an active wife happy. The offers were invariably accepted. And, by finding her "situations," his travels were given a twofold legitimacy. His courier activities had grown beyond the dilettante horizons of his business.

Alison threatened to leave the Corsican job.

David was hysterical. He insisted he would be killed, and Alison as well. He painted a picture of such widespread, powerful corruption-without-conscience that Alison, fearing for both their lives, relented. She agreed to finish the work in Corsica, but made it clear their marriage was finished. Nothing would alter *that* decision.

So she believed at the time.

But one late afternoon in the field—on the water, actually—Alison was taking bore samples from the ocean floor several hundred yards offshore. In the small cabin cruiser were two men. They were agents of Interpol. They had been following her husband for a number of months. Interpol was gathering massive documentation of criminal evidence. It was closing in.

"Needless to say, they were prepared for his arrival.

My room was as private as yours was intended to be this evening . . ."

The case they presented was strong and clear. Where her husband had described a powerful network of corruption, the Interpol men told of another world of pain and suffering and needless, horrible death.

"Oh, they were experts," said Alison, her eyes remembering, her smile compassionately sad. "They brought photographs, dozens of them. Children in agony; young men, girls destroyed. I shall never forget those pictures. As they intended I would not . . ."

Their appeal was the classic recruiting approach: Mrs. David Booth was in a unique position; there was no one like her. She could do *so* much, provide *so* much. And if she walked away in the manner she had described to her husband—abruptly, without explanation—there was the very real question of whether she would be allowed to do so.

My God, thought McAuliff as he listened, *the more things change . . . The Interpol men might have been Holcroft speaking in a room at the Savoy Hotel.*

The arrangements were made, schedules created, a reasonable period of time specified for the "deterioration" of the marriage. She told a relieved Booth that she would try to save their relationship, on the condition that he never again speak to her of his outside activities.

For half a year Alison Gerrard Booth reported the activities of her husband, identified photographs, planted dozens of tiny listening devices in hotel rooms, automobiles, their own apartment. She did so with the understanding that David Booth—whatever the eventual charges against him—would be protected from physical harm. To the best of Interpol's ability.

Nothing was guaranteed.

"When did it all come to an end?" asked Alex.

Alison looked away, briefly, at the dark, ominous panorama of the Blue Mountains, rising in blackness several miles to the north. "When I listened to a very painful recording. Painful to hear; more painful because I had made the recording possible."

One morning after a lecture at the university, an Interpol man arrived at her office in the geology department. In his briefcase he had a cassette machine and a cartridge that was a duplicate of a conversation recorded between her husband and a liaison from the Marquis de Chatellerault, the man identified as the overlord of the narcotics operation. Alison sat and listened to the voice of a broken man drunkenly describing the collapse of his marriage to a woman he loved very much. She heard him rage and weep, blaming himself for the inadequate man that he was. He spoke of his refused entreaties for the bed, her total rejection of him. And at the last, he made it clear beyond doubt that he loathed using her; that if she ever found out, he would kill himself. What he had done, almost too perfectly, was to exonerate her from any knowledge whatsoever of Chatellerault's operation. He had done it superbly.

"Interpol reached a conclusion that was as painful as the recording. David had somehow learned what I was doing. He was sending a message. It was time to get out."

A forty-eight-hour divorce in Haiti was arranged. Alison Booth was free.

And, of course, not free at all.

". . . within a year, it will all close in on Chatellerault, on David . . . on all of them. And somewhere, someone will put it together: Booth's wife . . ."

Alison reached for her drink and drank and tried to smile.

"That's it?" said Alex, not sure it was at all.

"That's it, Mr. McAuliff . . . Now, tell me honestly, would you have hired me had you known?"

"No, I would not . . . I wonder why I didn't know."

"It's not the sort of information the university, or Emigration, or just about anyone else would have."

"Alison?" McAuliff tried to conceal the sudden fear he felt. "You *did* hear about this job from the university people, didn't you?"

The girl laughed and raised her lovely eyebrows in mock protest. "Oh, Lord, it's tell-all time! . . . No, I admit to having a jump; it gave me time to compile that *very* impressive portfolio for you."

"How did you learn of it?"

"Interpol. They'd been looking for months. They called me about ten or twelve days before the interview."

McAuliff did not have to indulge in any rapid calculations. Ten or twelve days before the interview would place the date within reasonable approximation of the afternoon he had met with Julian Warfield at Belgravia Square.

And later with a man named Holcroft from British Intelligence.

The stinging pain returned to McAuliff's stomach. Only it was sharper now, more defined. But he could not dwell on it. Across the dark-shadowed patio, a man was approaching. He was walking to their table unsteadily. He was drunk, thought Alex.

"Well, for God's sake, *there* you are! We wondered where the hell you were! We're all in the bar inside. Whitehall's an absolute riot on the piano! A bloody black Noel Coward! . . . Oh, by the way, I trust your luggage got here. I saw you were having problems, so I scribbled a note for the bastards to send it along. If they could read my whiskey slant."

Young James Ferguson dropped into an empty chair and smiled alcoholically at Alison. He then turned and looked at McAuliff, his smile fading as he was met by Alex's stare.

"That was very kind of you," said McAuliff quietly.

And then Alexander saw it in Ferguson's eyes. The focused consciousness behind the supposedly glazed eyes.

James Ferguson was nowhere near as drunk as he pretended to be.

9

THEY EXPECTED to stay up most of the night. It was their silent, hostile answer to the "horrid little buggers." They joined the others in the bar and, as a good captain should, McAuliff was seen talking to the maître d'; all knew the evening was being paid for by their director.

Charles Whitehall lived up to Ferguson's judgment. His talent was professional; his island patter songs—filled with Caribbean idiom and Jamaican black wit—were funny, brittle, cold, and episodically hot. His voice had the clear, high-pitched thrust of a Kingston balladeer; only his eyes remained remote. He was entertaining and amusing, but he was neither entertained nor amused himself, thought Alex.

He was performing.

And finally, after nearly two hours, he wearied of the chore, accepted the cheers of the half-drunken room, and wandered to the table. After receiving individual shakes, claps, and hugs from Ferguson, the Jensens, Alison Booth, and Alex, he opted for a chair next to McAuliff. Ferguson had been sitting there—encouraged by Alex—but the young botanist was only too happy to move. Unsteadily.

"That was remarkable!" said Alison, leaning across McAuliff, reaching for Whitehall's hand. Alex watched as the Jamaican responded; the dark Caribbean hand—fingernails manicured, gold ring glistening—curled delicately over Alison's as another woman's might. And then, in contradiction, Whitehall raised the girl's wrist and kissed her fingers.

A waiter brought over a bottle of white wine for Whitehall's inspection. He read the label in the nightclub light, looked up at the smiling attendant, and nodded. He turned back to McAuliff; Alison was now chatting with Ruth Jensen across the table. "I should like to speak with you privately," said the Jamaican casually. "Meet me in my room, say, twenty minutes after I leave."

"Alone?"

"Alone."

"Can't it wait until morning?"

Whitehall leveled his black eyes at McAuliff and spoke softly but sharply. "No, it cannot."

James Ferguson suddenly lurched up from his chair at the end of the table and raised his glass to Whitehall. He weaved and gripped the edge with his free hand; he was the picture of a very drunk young man. "Here's to Charles the First of Kingston! The bloody black Sir Noel! You're simply fan*testic*, Charles!"

There was an embarrassing instant of silence as the word "black" was absorbed. The waiter hurriedly poured Whitehall's wine; it was no moment for sampling.

"Thank you," said Whitehall politely. "I take that as a high compliment, indeed . . . Jimbo-mon."

"*Jimbo-mon!*" shouted Ferguson with delight. "I love it! You shall call me *Jimbo-mon!* And now, I should like—" Ferguson's words were cut short, replaced by an agonizing grimace on his pale young face. It was suddenly abundantly clear that his alcoholic capacity had been reached. He set his glass down with wavering precision, staggered backward and, in a slow motion of his own, collapsed to the floor.

The table rose en masse; surrounding couples turned. The waiter put the bottle down quickly and started toward Ferguson; he was joined by Peter Jensen, who was nearest.

"Oh, Lord," said Jensen, kneeling down. "I think the poor fellow's going to be sick. Ruth, come help . . . You there, waiter. Give me a hand, chap!"

The Jensens, aided by two waiters now, gently lifted the young botanist into a sitting position, unloosened his tie, and generally tried to reinstate some form of consciousness. And Charles Whitehall, standing beside McAuliff, smiled, picked up two napkins, and lobbed them across the table onto the floor near those administering aid. Alex watched the Jamaican's action; it was not pleasant. Ferguson's head was nodding back and forth; moans of impending illness came from his lips.

"I think this is as good a time as any for me to leave," said Whitehall. "Twenty minutes?"

McAuliff nodded. "Or thereabouts."

The Jamaican turned to Alison, delicately took her hand, kissed it, and smiled. "Good night, my dear."

With minor annoyance, Alex sidestepped the two of

them and walked over to the Jensens, who, with the waiters' help, were getting Ferguson to his feet.

"We'll bring him to his room," said Ruth. "I warned him about the rum; it doesn't go with whiskey. I don't think he listened." She smiled and shook her head.

McAuliff kept his eyes on Ferguson's face. He wondered if he would see what he saw before. What he had been watching for for over an hour.

And then he did. Or thought he did.

As Ferguson's arms went limp around the shoulders of a waiter and Peter Jensen, he opened his eyes. Eyes that seemingly swum in their sockets. But for the briefest of moments, they were steady, focused, devoid of glaze. Ferguson was doing a perfectly natural thing any person would do in a dimly lit room. He was checking his path to avoid obstacles.

And he was—for that instant—quite sober.

Why was James Ferguson putting on such a splendidly embarrassing performance? McAuliff would have a talk with the young man in the morning. About several things, including a "whiskey-slanted" note that resulted in a suitcase that triggered the dial of an electronic scanner.

"Poor lamb. He'll feel miserable in the morning." Alison had come alongside Alex. Together they watched the Jensens take Ferguson out the door.

"I hope he's just a poor lamb who went astray for the night and doesn't make a habit of it."

"Oh, come on, Alex, don't be old-auntie. He's a perfectly nice young man who's had a pint too many." Alison turned and looked at the deserted table. "Well, it seems the party's over, doesn't it?"

"I thought we agreed to keep it going."

"I'm fading fast, darling; my resolve is weakening. We also agreed to check my luggage with your little magic box. Shall we?"

"Sure." McAuliff signaled the waiter.

They walked down the hotel corridor; McAuliff took Alison's key as they approached her door. "I have to see Whitehall in a few minutes."

"Oh? How come? It's awfully late."

"He said he wanted to speak to me. Privately. I have no idea why. I'll make it quick." He inserted the key, opened the door, and found himself instinctively barring Alison in the frame until he had switched on the lights and looked inside.

The single room was empty, the connecting door to his still open, as it had been when they left hours ago.

"I'm impressed," whispered Alison, resting her chin playfully on the outstretched, forbidding arm that formed a bar across the entrance.

"What?" He removed his arm and walked toward the connecting door. The lights in his room were on—as he had left them. He closed the door quietly, withdrew the scanner from his jacket, and crossed to the bed, where Alison's two suitcases lay alongside each other. He held the instrument above them; there was no movement on the dial. He walked rapidly about the room, laterally and vertically blessing it from all corners. The room was clean. "What did you say?" he asked softly.

"You're protective. That's nice."

"Why were the lights off in this room and not in mine?" He had not heard her words.

"Because I turned them off. I came in here, got my purse, used some lipstick, and went back into your room. There's a switch by the door. I used it."

"I don't remember."

"You were upset at the time. I gather my room isn't the center of attention yours is." Alison walked in and closed the corridor door.

"No, it's not, but keep your voice low . . . Can those goddamn things listen through doors and walls?"

"No, I don't think so." She watched him take her suitcases from the bed and carry them across the room. He stood by the closet, looking for a luggage rack. There was none. "Aren't you being a little obvious?"

"What?"

"What are you doing with my bags? I haven't unpacked."

"Oh." McAuliff could feel the flush on his face. He felt like a goddamn idiot. "I'm sorry. I suppose I could say I'm compulsively neat."

"Or just compulsive."

He carried the bags back to the bed and turned to look at her, the suitcases still in his hands. He was so terribly tired. "It's been a rotten day . . . a very confusing day," he said. "The fact that it's not over yet is discouraging as hell; there's still Whitehall to go . . . And in the next room, if I snore or talk in my sleep or go to the bathroom with the door open, everything is recorded somewhere on a tape. I can say it doesn't bother me, but it doesn't make me feel any better, either . . . I'll tell you something else, too, while I'm rambling. You are a lovely, lovely girl . . . and you're right, I'm compulsive . . . for example, at this moment I have the strongest compulsion to hold you and kiss you and feel your arms around me, and . . . you are so goddamn desirable . . . and you have such a beautiful smile and laugh . . . when you laugh I just want to watch you and touch your face . . . and all I want to do is hold you and forget everything else . . . Now I'm finished rambling, and you can tell me to go to hell because I'm not relevant."

Alison Booth stood silently, looking at McAuliff for what seemed to him far too long. Then she walked slowly, deliberately, to him.

"Do you know how silly you look holding those suitcases?" she whispered as she leaned forward and kissed him on the lips.

He dropped the bags; the noise of their contact with the floor made them both smile. He pulled her to him and the comfort was splendid, the warm, growing excitement a special thing. And as he kissed her, their mouths moistly exploring, pressing, widening, he realized Alison was trembling, gripping him with a strength that was more than a desire to be taken. Yet it was not fear; there was no hesitancy, no holding back, only anxiety.

He lowered her gently to the bed; as he did so, she unbuttoned the silk blouse and guided his hand to her breasts. She closed her eyes as he caressed her and whispered.

"It's been a terribly long time, Alex. Do you think Whitehall could wait a while longer? You see, I don't think I can."

They lay beside each other, naked, under the soft covers. She rose on her elbow, her hair falling over her face, and looked at him. She traced his lips with her fingers and bent down, kissing him, outlining his lips now with her tongue.

"I'm absolutely shameless," she said, laughing softly. "I

want to make love to you all night long. And most of the
day . . . I'm parched and I've been to the well and I want
to stay here."

He reached up and let her hair fall through his fingers.
He followed the strands downward to the swell of her
body and cupped her left breast. "We'll take the minimum
time out for food and sleep."

There was the faint ring of a telephone. It came from
the direction of the connecting door. From his room.

"You're late for Charles Whitehall," said Alison. You'd
better go answer it."

"Our goddamn Sir Noel." He climbed out of the bed,
walked rapidly to the door, opened it, and went into the
room. As he picked up the telephone, he looked at the
drawn curtains of his balcony doors; he was grateful for
Alison's experience. Except for his socks—why his
socks?—he was naked.

"I said twenty minutes, Mr. McAuliff. It's nearly an
hour." Whitehall's voice was quietly furious.

"I'm sorry. I told you 'thereabouts.' For me, an hour is
'thereabouts.' Especially when someone gives me orders at
this time of night and he's not bleeding."

"Let's not argue. Will you be here soon?"

"Yes."

"When?"

"Twenty minutes." Alex hung up the telephone a bit
harder than was necessary and looked over at his suitcase.
Whoever was on the other end of *that* line knew he was
going out of the room to meet someone who had tried to
issue him orders at three o'clock in the morning. He
would think about it later.

"Do you know how positively handsome you are? All
over," said Alison as he came back into the room.

"You're right, you're shameless."

"Why do you have your knee socks on? It looks peculiar." She sat up, pulling the sheet over her breasts, and
reached for the cigarettes on the night table.

"Light me one, will you please? I've got to get dressed."
McAuliff looked around the bed for the clothing he had
removed in such haste a half hour ago.

"Was he upset?" She handed him a cigarette as he
pulled on his trousers and picked up his shirt from the
floor.

"He was upset. He's also an arrogant son of a bitch."

"I think Charles Whitehall wants to strike back at someone, or something," said Alison, watching him absently. "He's angry."

"Maybe it's recognition. Not granted to the extent he thinks it should be." McAuliff buttoned his shirt.

"Perhaps. That would account for his dismissing the compliments."

"The what?" he asked.

"His little entertainment downstairs tonight was frighteningly thought out. It wasn't prepared for a nightclub. It was created for Covent Garden. Or the grand hall of the United Nations."

He tapped gently on Whitehall's door, and when it opened, McAuliff found the Jamaican dressed in an embroidered Japanese *hopi* coat. Beneath the flowery garment, Whitehall wore his flared pin-stripe trousers and velvet slippers.

"Come in, please. This time you're early. It's not yet fifteen minutes."

"You're obsessed with time. It's after three in the morning; I'd rather not look at my watch." Alex closed the door behind him. "I hope you have something important to tell me. Because if you don't, I'm going to be damned angry."

The black had crossed to the bureau; he picked up a folded piece of paper from the top and indicated a chair for McAuliff. "Sit down, please. I, too, am quite exhausted, but we must talk."

Alex walked to the armchair and sat down. "Go ahead."

"I think it's time we had an understanding. It will in no way affect my contributions to the survey."

"I'm relieved to hear that. I didn't hire you to entertain the troops downstairs."

"A dividend," said Whitehall coldly. "Don't knock it; I'm very good."

"I know you are. What else is new?"

The scholar tapped the paper in his hands. "There'll be periods when it will be necessary for me to be absent. Never more than a day or two at a time. Naturally, I'll give you advance notice, and if there are problems—

where *possible*—I shall rearrange my schedule."

"You'll *what?*" McAuliff sat forward in the chair. "Where . . . *possible* . . . you'll fit your time to *mine?* That's goddamn nice of you. I hope the survey won't be a burden."

Whitehall laughed, impersonally. "Not at all. It was just what I was looking for. And you'll see, you'll be quite pleased . . . although I'm not sure why I should be terribly concerned. You see, I cannot accept the stated reasons for this survey. And I suspect there are one or two others, if they spoke their thoughts, who share my doubts."

"Are you suggesting that I hired you under false pretenses?"

"Oh, come now," replied the black scholar, his eyes narrowing in irritation. "Alexander McAuliff, a highly confidential, one-man survey company whose work takes him throughout the world . . . for very large fees, abruptly decides to become academically *charitable?* To take from four to six months away from a lucrative practice to head up a *university survey?*" Whitehall laughed like a nervous jackal, walked rapidly to the curtains of the room's balcony doors, and flipped one side partially open. He twisted the latch and pulled the glass panel several inches inward; the curtain billowed in the night breeze.

"You don't know the specifics of my contract," said Alex noncommittally.

"I know what universities and royal societies *and* ministries of education pay. It's not your league, McAuliff." The Jamaican returned to the bed and sat down on the edge. He brought the folded paper to his chin and stared at Alex.

McAuliff hesitated, then spoke slowly. "In a way, aren't you describing your own situation? There were several people in London who didn't think you'd take the job. It was quite a drop in income for you."

"Precisely. Our positions are similar; I'm sure for very different reasons . . . Part of *my* reasoning takes me to Savanna-la-Mar in the morning."

"Your friend on the plane?"

"A bore. Merely a messenger." Whitehall held up the folded piece of paper. "He brought me an invitation. Would you care to read it?"

"You wouldn't offer unless it was pertinent."

"I have no idea whether it is or not. Perhaps *you* can tell *me*."

Alex took the paper extended to him and unfolded it. It was hotel stationery. The George V, Paris. The handwriting was slanted, the strokes rapid, words joined in speed.

> My dear Whitehall—
>
> Forgive this hastily written note but I have just learned that we are both en route to Jamaica. I for a welcome rest and you, I understand, for more worthwhile pursuits.
>
> I should deem it an honor and a pleasure to meet with you. Our mutual friend will give you the details. I shall be staying in Savanna-la-Mar, albeit incognito. He will explain.
>
> I do believe our coming together at the earliest would be mutually beneficial. I have long admired your past (?) island activities. I ask only that our meeting and my presence in Jamaica remain confidential. Since I so admire your endeavors, I know you will understand.
>
> *Chatellerault*

Chatellerault . . . ?
The Marquis de Chatellerault.
David Booth's "employer." The man behind a narcotics network that spread throughout most of Europe and the Mediterranean. The man Alison feared so terribly that she carried a lethal-looking cylinder of gas with her at all times!

McAuliff knew that Whitehall was observing him. He forced himself to remain immobile, betraying only numbness on his face and in his eyes.

"Who is he?" asked McAuliff blandly. "Who's this Chatel . . . Chatellerault?"

"You don't know?"

"Oh, for Christ's *sake*, Whitehall," said Alex in weary exasperation. "Stop playing games. I've never heard of him."

"I thought you might have." The scholar was once again staring at McAuliff. "I thought the connection was rather evident."

"What connection?"

"To whatever *your* reasons are for being in Jamaica. Chatellerault is . . . among other things . . . a financier with considerable resources. The coincidence is startling, wouldn't you agree?"

"I don't know what you're talking about." McAuliff glanced down at Chatellerault's note. "What does he mean by your past question mark island activities?"

Whitehall paused before replying. When he did, he spoke quietly, thus lending emphasis to his words. "Ten years ago I left my homeland because the political faction for which I worked . . . devotedly, and in secret . . . was forced underground. Further underground, I should say. For a decade we have remained dormant—on the surface. But only on the surface . . . I have returned now. Kingston knows nothing. It never associated me with the movement. But Chatellerault knows, and therefore demands confidentiality. I have, with considerable risk, broken this confidence as an article of faith. For you . . . please. Why are you here, McAuliff? Perhaps it will tell me why such a man as Chatellerault wishes a conference."

Alex got out of the chair and walked aimlessly toward the balcony doors. He moved because it helped him concentrate. His mind was racing; some abstract thoughts signaling a warning that Alison was in danger . . . others balking, not convinced.

He crossed to the back of the chair facing Whitehall's bed and gripped the cloth firmly. "All right, I'll make a deal with you. I'll tell you why I'm here, if you'll spell out this . . . activity of yours."

"I will tell you what I can," replied Charles, his eyes devoid of deceit. "It will be sufficient, you will see. I cannot tell you everything. It would not be good for you."

"That's a condition I'm not sure I like."

"Please. Trust me."

The man was not lying, that much was clear to Alex. "Okay . . . I know the north coast; I worked for Kaiser's bauxite. I'm considered very pro—that is, I've put together some good teams and I've got a decent reputation—"

"Yes, yes. To the point, please."

"By heading up this job, the Jamaican government has guaranteed me first refusal on fifty percent of any industrial development for the next six years. That could mean hundreds of thousands of dollars . . . It's as simple as that."

Whitehall sat motionless, his hands still folded beneath his chin, an elegant little boy in a concerned man's body. "Yes, that is plausible," he said finally. "In much of Kingston, everything's for sale. It could be a motive for Chatellerault."

Alex remained behind the chair. "All right. Now, that's why *I'm* here. Why are you?"

"It is good you told me of your arrangement . . . I shall do my best to see that it is lived up to. You deserve that."

"What the hell does that mean?"

"It means I am here in a political capacity. A solely Jamaican concern. You must respect that condition . . . and my confidence. I'd deny it anyway, and you would soil your foreigner's hands in things Jamaican. Ultimately, however, we will control Kingston."

"Oh, Christ! Comes the goddamn revolution!"

"Of a different sort, Mr. McAuliff. Put plainly, I'm a fascist. Fascism is the only hope for my island."

10

MCAULIFF opened his eyes, raised his wrist from beneath the covers, and saw that it was 10:25. He had intended to get up by 8:30—9:00 at the latest.

He had a man to see. A man with arthritis at a fish store called Tallon's.

He looked over at Alison. She was curled up away from him, her hair sprayed over the sheets, her face buried in the pillow. She had been magnificent, he thought. No, he thought again, *they* had been magnificent together. She had been . . . what was the word she used? Parched. She had said: "I've been parched and I've been to the well . . ." And she had been.

Magnificent.

Yet still the thoughts came back.

A name that meant nothing to him twenty-four hours ago was suddenly an unknown force to be reckoned with, separately put forward by two people who were strangers a week ago.

Chatellerault. The Marquis de Chatellerault.

Currently in Savanna-la-Mar, on the southwest coast of Jamaica.

Charles Whitehall would be seeing him shortly, if they had not met by now. The black fascist and the French financier. It sounded like a vaudeville act.

But Alison Booth carried a deadly cylinder in her handbag, in the event she ever had occasion to meet him. Or meet with those who worked for him.

What was the connection? Certainly there had to be one.

He stretched, taking care not to wake her. Although he wanted to wake her and hold her and run his hands over her body and make warm love to her in the morning.

He couldn't. There was too much to do. Too much to think about . . .

He wondered what his instructions would be. And how long it would take to receive them. And what the man with arthritis at a fish store named Tallon's would be like.

And, no less important, where in God's name was Sam

Tucker? He was to be in Kingston by tomorrow. It wasn't like Sam to just take his leave without a word; he was too kind a man. And yet, there had been times . . .

When would they get the word to fly north and begin the actual work on the survey?

He was not going to get the answers staring up at the ceiling from Alison Booth's bed. And he was not going to make any telephone calls from his room.

He smiled as he thought about the "horrid little buggers" in his suitcase. Were there horrid little men crouched over dials in dark rooms waiting for sounds that never came?

There was a certain comfort in that.

"I can hear you thinking." Alison's voice was muffled in the pillow. "Isn't that remarkable."

"It's frightening."

She rolled over, her eyes shut, and smiled and reached under the blankets for him. "You also stretch quite sensually." She caressed the flatness of his stomach, and then his thighs, and then McAuliff knew the answers would have to wait. He pulled her to him; she opened her eyes and raised the covers so there was nothing between them.

The taxi let him off at Victoria's South Parade. The thoroughfare was aptly named, in the nineteenth-century sense. The throngs of people flowing in and out of the park's entrance were like crowds of brightly colored peacocks, strutting, half acknowledging, quickening steps only to stop and gape.

McAuliff walked into the park, doing his best to look like a strolling tourist. Intermittently he could feel the hostile, questioning glances as he made his way up the gravel path to the center of the park. It occurred to him that he had not seen a single other white person; he had not expected that. He had the distinct feeling that he was an object, to be tolerated but watched. Not essentially to be trusted.

He was a strange-toned outsider who had invaded the heart of this Man's playground. He nearly laughed when a young Jamaican mother guided a smiling child to the opposite side of the path as he approached. The child obviously had been fascinated by the tall, pinkish figure; the mother, quietly, efficiently, knew better. With dignity.

He saw the rectangular white sign with the brown lettering: QUEEN STREET, EAST. The arrow pointed to the right, at another, narrower gravel path. He started down it.

He recalled Holcroft's words: *Don't be in a hurry. Ever, if possible. And never when you are making a contact. There's nothing so obvious as a man in a rush in a crowd that's not; except a woman. Or that same man stopping every five feet to light the same cigarette over and over again, so he can peer around at everyone. Do the natural things, depending on the day, the climate, the surroundings . . .*

It was a warm morning . . . noon. The Jamaican sun was hot, but there were breezes from the harbor, less than a mile away. It would be perfectly natural for a tourist to sit down and take the sun and the breeze; to unbutton his collar, remove his jacket, perhaps. To look about with pleasant tourist curiosity.

There was a bench on the left; a couple had just gotten up. It was empty. He took off his jacket, pulled at his tie, and sat down. He stretched his legs and behaved as he thought was appropriate.

But it was not appropriate. For the most self-conscious of reasons: He was too free, too relaxed in this Man's playground. He felt it instantly, unmistakably. The discomfort was heightened by an old man with a cane who walked by and hesitated in front of him. He was a touch drunk, thought Alex; the head swayed slightly, the legs a bit unsteady. But the eyes were not unsteady. They conveyed mild surprise mixed with disapproval.

McAuliff rose from the bench and swung his jacket under his arm. He smiled blankly at the old man and was about to proceed down the path when he saw another man, difficult to miss. He was white—the only other white man in Victoria Park. At least, the only one he could see. He was quite far away, diagonally across the lawns, on the north-south path, about a hundred and fifty yards in the distance.

A young man with a slouch and a shock of untrained dark hair.

And he had turned away. He had been watching him, Alex was sure of that. Following him.

James Ferguson. The young man who had put on the

second-best performance of the night at the Courtleigh Manor last evening. The drunk who had the presence of mind to keep sharp eyes open for obstacles in a dimly lit room.

McAuliff took advantage of the moment and walked rapidly down the path, then cut across the grass to the trunk of a large palm. He was nearly two hundred yards from Ferguson now. He peered around the tree, keeping his body out of sight. He was aware that a number of Jamaicans sitting about on the lawn were looking at him; he was sure, disapprovingly.

Ferguson, as he expected, was alarmed that he had lost the subject of his surveillance. (It was funny, thought Alex. He could think the word "surveillance" now. He doubted he had used the word a dozen times in his life before three weeks ago.) The young botanist began walking rapidly past the brown-skinned strollers. Holcroft was right, thought McAuliff. A man in a hurry in a crowd that wasn't was obvious.

Ferguson reached the intersection of the Queen Street path and stopped. He was less than forty yards from Alex now; he hesitated, as if not sure whether to retreat back to the South Parade or go on.

McAuliff pressed himself against the palm trunk. Ferguson thrust forward, as rapidly as possible. He had decided to keep going, if only to get out of the park. The bustling crowds on Queen Street East signified sanctuary. The park had become unsafe.

If these conclusions were right—and the nervous expression on Ferguson's face seemed to confirm them— McAuliff realized that he had learned something else about this strange young man: He was doing what he was doing under duress and with very little experience.

Look for the small things, Holcroft had said. *They'll be there; you'll learn to spot them. Signs that tell you there is valid strength or real weakness . . .*

Ferguson reached the East Parade gate, obviously relieved. He stopped and looked carefully in all directions.

The unsafe field was behind him.

The young man checked his watch while waiting for the uniformed policeman to halt the traffic for pedestrians. The whistle blew, automobiles stopped with varying levels of screeches, and Ferguson continued down Queen Street.

Concealing himself as best he could in the crowd, Alex
followed. The young man seemed more relaxed now. He
wasn't as aggressive in his walk, in his darting glances. It
was as though, having lost the enemy, he was more concerned with explanations than with reestablishing contact.

But McAuliff wanted that contact reestablished. It was
as good a time as any to ask young Ferguson those questions he needed answered.

Alex started across the street, dodging the traffic, and
jumped over the curb out of the way of a Kingston taxi.
He made his way through the stream of shoppers to the
far side of the walk.

There was a side street between Mark Lane and Duke.
Ferguson hesitated, looked around, and apparently decided it was worth trying. He abruptly turned and entered.

McAuliff realized that he knew that street. It was a
free-port strip interspersed with bars. He and Sam Tucker
had been there late one afternoon a year ago, following a
Kaiser conference at the Sheraton. He remembered, too,
that there was a diagonally connecting alley that intersected the strip from Duke Street. He remembered because
Sam had thought there might be native saloons in the
moist, dark brick corridor, only to discover it was used
for deliveries. Sam had been upset; he was fond of back-
street native saloons.

Alex broke into a run. Holcroft's warning about
drawing attention would have to be disregarded. Tallon's
could wait; the man with arthritis could wait. This was the
moment to reach James Ferguson.

He crossed Queen Street again, now paying no attention
to the disturbance he caused, or the angry whistle from
the harassed Kingston policeman. He raced down the
block; there was the diagonally connecting alley. It
seemed even narrower than he remembered. He entered
and pushed his way past a half a dozen Jamaicans, mut-
tering apologies, trying to avoid the hard stares of those
walking in the opposite direction toward him—silent chal-
lenges, grown-up children playing king-of-the-road. He
reached the end of the passageway and stopped. He
pressed his back against the brick and peered around
the edge, up the side street. His timing was right.

James Ferguson, his expression ferretlike, was only ten
yards away. Then five.

And then McAuliff walked out of the alley and confronted him.

The young man's face paled to a deathly white. Alex gestured him against the stucco wall; the strollers passed in both directions, several complaining.

Ferguson's smile was false, his voice strained, "Well, hello, Alex . . . Mr. McAuliff. Doing a bit of shopping? This is the place for it."

"*Have* I been shopping, Jimbo-mon? You'd know if I had, wouldn't you?"

"I don't know what you . . . I wouldn't—"

"Maybe you're still drunk," interrupted Alex. "You had a lot to drink last night."

"Made a bloody fool of myself, I expect. Please accept my apologies."

"No apologies necessary. You stayed just within the lines. You were very convincing."

"Really, Alex, you're a bit much." Ferguson moved back. A Jamaican woman, basket balanced on her head, hurried past. "I said I was sorry. I'm sure you've had occasion to overindulge."

"Very often. As a matter of fact, I was a hell of a lot drunker than you last night."

"I don't know what you're implying, chap, and frankly, my head's too painful to play anagrams. Now, for the last time, I apologize."

"For the wrong sins, Jimbo-mon. Let's go back and find some real ones. Because I have some questions."

Ferguson awkwardly straightened his perennial slouch and whisked away the shock of hair on his forehead. "You're really quite abusive. I have shopping to do."

The young man started to walk around McAuliff. Alex grabbed his arm and slammed him back into the stucco wall. "Save your money. Do it in London."

"*No!*" Ferguson's body stiffened; the taut flesh around his eyes stretched further. "No, *please*," he whispered.

"Then let's start with the suitcases." McAuliff released the arm, holding Ferguson against the wall with his stare.

"I *told* you," the young man whined. "You were having trouble. I tried to help."

"You bet your ass I had trouble! And not only with Customs. Where did my luggage go? *Our* luggage? Who took it?"

"I don't know. I *swear* I don't!"

"Who told you to write that note?"

"*No* one told me! For God's sake, you're *crazy!*"

"Why did you put on that act last night?"

"What act?"

"You weren't drunk—you were sober."

"Oh, Christ Almighty, I wish you had my hangover. Really—"

"Not good enough, Jimbo-mon. Let's try again. Who told you to write that note?"

"You won't *listen* to me—"

"I'm listening. Why are you following me? Who told you to follow me this morning?"

"By God, you're insane!"

"By God, *you're fired!*"

"No! . . . You *can't*. *Please*." Ferguson's voice was frightened again, a whisper.

"What did you say?" McAuliff placed his right hand against the wall, over Ferguson's frail shoulder. He leaned into the strange young man. "I'd like to hear you say that again. What can't I do?"

"Please . . . don't send me back. I beg you." Ferguson was breathing through his mouth; spots of saliva had formed on his thin lips. "Not now."

"Send you back? I don't give a goddamn where you go! I'm not your keeper, little boy." Alex removed his hand from the wall and yanked his jacket from under his left arm. "You're entitled to return-trip airfare. I'll draw it for you this afternoon, and pay for one more night at the Courtleigh. After that, you're on your own. Go wherever the hell you please. But not with me; not with the survey."

McAuliff turned and abruptly walked away. He entered the narrow alleyway and took up his position in the line of laconic strollers. He knew the stunned Ferguson would follow. It wasn't long before he heard him. The whining voice had the quality of controlled hysteria. Alex did not stop or look back.

"McAuliff! Mr. McAuliff! *Please!*" The English tones echoed in the narrow brick confines, creating a dissonant counterpoint to the lilting hum of a dozen Jamaican conversations. "Please, *wait* . . . Excuse me, excuse me, please. I'm sorry, let me pass, please . . ."

"What you do, mon?! Don't push you."

The verbal objections did not deter Ferguson; the bodily obstructions were somewhat more successful. Alex kept moving, hearing and sensing the young man closing the gap slowly. It was eerily comic: a white man chasing another white man in a dark, crowded passageway that was exclusively—by civilized cautions—a native thoroughfare. McAuliff was within feet of the exit to Duke Street when he felt Ferguson's hand gripping his arm.

"Please. We have to talk . . . not here."

"Where?"

They emerged on the sidewalk. A long, horse-drawn wagon filled with fruits and country vegetables was in front of them at the curb. The sombreroed owner was arguing with customers by a set of ancient scales; several ragged children stole bananas from the rear of the vehicle. Ferguson still held McAuliff's arm.

"Go to the Devon House. It's a tourist—"

"I know."

"There's an outside restaurant."

"When?"

"Twenty minutes."

The taxi drove into the long entrance of Devon House, a Georgian monument to an era of English supremacy and white, European money. Circular floral gardens fronted the spotless columns; rinsed graveled paths wove patterns around an immense fountain. The small outdoor restaurant was off to the side, the tables behind tall hedges, the diners obscured from the front. There were only six tables, McAuliff realized. A very small restaurant; a difficult place in which to follow someone without being observed.

Perhaps Ferguson was not as inexperienced as he appeared to be.

"Well, hello, chap!"

Alex turned. James Ferguson had yelled from the central path to the fountain; he now carried his camera and the cases and straps and meters that went with it. "Hi," said McAuliff, wondering what role the young man intended to play now.

"I've got some wonderful shots. This place has quite a history, you know." Ferguson approached him, taking a second to snap Alex's picture.

"This is ridiculous," replied McAuliff quietly. "Who the hell are you trying to fool?"

"I know *exactly* what I'm doing. Please cooperate." And then Ferguson returned to his play-acting, raising his voice and his camera simultaneously. "Did you know that this old brick was the original courtyard? It leads to the rear of the house, where the soldiers were housed in rows of brick cubicles."

"I'm fascinated."

"It's well past elevenses, old man," continued an enthusiastic, loud Ferguson. "What say to a pint? Or a rum punch? Perhaps a spot of lunch."

There were only two other separate couples within the small courtyard restaurant. The men's straw hats and bulging walking shorts complemented the women's rhinestone sunglasses; they were tourists, obviously unimpressed with Kingston's Devon House. They would soon be talking with each other, thought McAuliff, making happier plans to return to the bar of the cruise ship or, at least, to a free-port strip. They were not interested in Ferguson or himself, and that was all that mattered.

The Jamaican rum punches were delivered by a bored waiter in a dirty white jacket. He did not hum or move with any rhythmic punctuation, observed Alex. The Devon House restaurant was a place of inactivity. Kingston was not Montego Bay.

"I'll tell you exactly what happened," said Ferguson suddenly, very nervously; his voice once more a panicked whisper. "And it's everything I know. I worked for the Craft Foundation, you knew all about that. Right?"

"Obviously," answered McAuliff. "I made it a condition of your employment that you stay away from Craft. You agreed."

"I didn't have a choice. When we got off the plane, you and Alison stayed behind; Whitehall and the Jensens went on ahead to the luggage pickup. I was taking some infrared photographs of the airport . . . I was in between, you might say. I walked through the arrival gate, and the first person I saw was Craft himself; the son, of course, not the old fellow. The son runs the foundation now. I tried to avoid him. I had every reason to; after all, he sacked me. But I couldn't. And I was amazed—he was positively effusive. Filled with apologies; what outstanding work I had done, how he personally had come to the airport to meet me when he heard I was with the survey." Ferguson swallowed a portion of his punch, darting his eyes around the brick courtyard. He seemed to have reached a block, as if uncertain how to continue.

"Go on," said Alex. "All you've described is an unexpected welcome wagon."

"You've *got to understand*. It was all so strange . . . as you say, unexpected. And as he was talking, this chap in uniform comes through the gate and asks me if I'm Ferguson. I say yes and he tells me you'll be delayed, you're tied up; that *you* want me to have your bags sent on to the hotel. I should write a note to that effect so B.O.A.C. will release them. Craft offered to help, of course. It all seemed minor, quite plausible, really, and everything happened so fast. I wrote the note and this chap said he'd take care of it. Craft tipped him. Generously, I believe."

"What kind of uniform was it?"

"I don't know. I didn't think. Uniforms all look alike when you're out of your own country."

"Go on."

"Craft asked me for a drink. I said I really couldn't. But he was adamant, and I didn't care to cause a scene, and you were delayed. You *do* see why I agreed, don't you?"

"Minor and plausible. Go on."

"We went to the lounge upstairs . . . the one that looks out over the field. It's got a name . . ."

" 'Observation.' "

"What?"

"It's called the 'Observation Lounge.' Please, go on."

"Yes. Well, I was concerned. I mean, I told him there were my own suitcases and Whitehall, the Jensens. And you, of course. I didn't want you wondering where I was . . . especially under the circumstances." Ferguson drank again; McAuliff held his temper and spoke simply.

"I think you'd better get to the point, Jimbo-mon."

"I hope that name doesn't stick. It was a bad evening."

"It'll be a worse afternoon if you don't go on."

"Yes . . . Craft told me you'd be in Customs for another hour and the chap in uniform would tell the others I was taking pictures; I was to go on to the Courtleigh. I mean, it was strange. Then he changed the subject—completely. He talked about the foundation. He said they were close to a major breakthrough in the baracoa fibers; that much of the progress was due to my work. And, for reasons ranging from the legal to the moral, they wanted me to come back to Craft. I was actually to be given a percentage of the market development . . . Do you realize what that could mean?"

"If this is what you had to tell me, you can join them today."

"Millions!" continued Ferguson, oblivious to Alex's interruption. "Actually *millions* . . . over the years, of course. I've never had any money. Stony, most of the time. Had to borrow the cash for my camera equipment, did you know that?"

"It wasn't something I dwelled on. But that's all over with. You're with Craft now . . ."

"*No.* Not yet. That's the point. After the survey. I *must* stay with the survey—stay with *you.*" Ferguson finished his rum punch and looked around for the waiter.

"Merely stay with the survey? With me? I think you've left out something."

"Yes. Actually." The young man hunched his shoulders over the table; he avoided McAuliff's eyes. "Craft said it was harmless, completely harmless. They only want to know the people you deal with in the government . . . which is just about everyone you deal with, because most everyone's *in* the government. I am to keep a log. That's all; simply a diary." Ferguson looked up at Alex, his eyes pleading. "You *do* see, don't you? It *is* harmless."

McAuliff returned the young man's stare. "That's why you followed me this morning?"

"Yes. But I didn't mean to do it this way. Craft suggested that I could accomplish a great deal by just . . . tagging along with you. Asking if I could join you when you went about survey business. He said I was embarrassingly curious and talked a lot anyway; it would be normal."

"Two points for Craft."

"What?"

"An obsolete American expression . . . Nevertheless, you followed me."

"I didn't mean to. I rang your room. Several times.

There was no answer. Then I called Alison . . . I'm sorry. I think she was upset."

"What did she say?"

"That she thought she heard you leave your room only minutes ago. I ran down to the lobby. And outside. You were driving away in a taxi. *Then* I followed you, in another cab."

McAuliff put his glass aside. "Why didn't you come up to me in Victoria Park? I saw you and you turned away."

"I was confused . . . and frightened. I mean, instead of asking to tag along, there I was, really following you."

"Why did you pretend you were so drunk last night?"

Ferguson took a long nervous intake of breath. "Because when I got to the hotel, I asked if your luggage had arrived. It hadn't. I panicked, I'm afraid . . . You see, before Craft left, he told me about your suitcases—"

"The bugs?" interrupted Alex angrily.

"The what?" Instantly, James understood. "No. *No!* I swear to you, *nothing* like that. Oh, God, how *awful.*" Ferguson paused, his expression suddenly pensive. "Yet, of course, it makes sense . . ."

No one could have rehearsed such a reversal of reactions, thought Alex. It was pointless to explode. "What about the suitcases?"

"What? . . . Oh, yes, Craft. At the very end of the conversation, he said they were checking your luggage— *checking,* that's all he said. He suggested, if anyone asked, that I say I'd taken it upon myself to write the note; that I saw you were having trouble. But I wasn't to worry, your bags would get to the hotel. But they weren't *there,* you see."

McAuliff did not see. He sighed wearily. "So you pretended to be smashed?"

"Naturally. I realized you'd have to know about the note; you'd ask me about it, of course, and be terribly angry if the luggage was lost; blame me for it . . . Well, it's a bit unsporting to be hard on a fellow who's squiffed and tried to do you a good turn. I mean, it is, really."

"You've got a very active imagination, Jimbo-mon. I'd go so far as to say convoluted."

"Perhaps. But you didn't get angry, did you? And here we are and nothing has changed. That's the irony: Nothing has changed."

"Nothing changed? What do you mean?"

Ferguson nervously smiled. "Well . . . I'm tagging along."

"I think something very basic has changed. You've told me about Craft."

"Yes. I would have anyway; that was my purpose this morning. Craft need never know; no way he could find out. I'll just tag along with you. I'll give you a portion of the money that's coming to me. I promise you that. I'll write it out, if you like. I've never had any money. It's simply a marvelous opportunity. You do see that, don't you?"

11

HE LEFT Ferguson at the Devon House and took a cab into Old Kingston. If he was being followed, he didn't give a damn. It was a time for sorting out thoughts again, not worrying about surveillance. He wasn't going anywhere.

He had conditionally agreed to cooperate with Ferguson. The condition was that theirs was a two-way street; the botanist could keep his log—freely supplied with controlled names—and McAuliff would be kept informed of this Craft's inquiries.

He looked up at the street signs; he was at the corner of Tower and Matthew, two blocks from the harbor. There was a coin telephone on a stanchion halfway down the sidewalk. He hoped it was operable.

It was.

"Has a Mr. Sam Tucker checked in?" he asked the clerk on the other end of the line.

"No, Mr. McAuliff. As a matter of fact, we were going over the reservations list a few minutes ago. Check-in time is three o'clock."

"Hold the room. It's paid for."

"I'm afraid it isn't, sir. Our instructions are only that you're responsible; we're trying to be of service."

"You're very kind. Hold it, nevertheless. Are there any messages for me?"

"Just one minute, sir. I believe there are."

The silence that ensued gave Alex the time to wonder about Sam. Where the hell *was* he? McAuliff had not been as alarmed as Robert Hanley over Tucker's disappearance. Sam's eccentricities included sudden wanderings, impulsive treks through native areas. There had been a time in Australia when Tucker stayed four weeks with an outback aborigine community, traveling daily in a Land Rover to the Kimberly survey site twenty-six miles away. Old Tuck was always looking for the unusual—generally associated with the customs and life styles of whatever country he was in. But his deadline was drawing near in Kingston.

"Sorry for the delay," said the Jamaican, his lilt denying the sincerity of the statement. "There are several messages. I was putting them in the order of their sequence.

"Thank you. What are—"

"They're all marked urgent, sir," interrupted the clerk. "Eleven fifteen is the first; from the Ministry of Education. Contact Mr. Latham as soon as possible. The next at 11:20 is from a Mr. Piersall at the Sheraton. Room 51. Then a Mr. Hanley called from Montego Bay at 12:06; he stressed the importance of your reaching him. His number is—"

"Wait a minute," said Alex, removing a pencil and a notebook from his pocket. He wrote down the names "Latham," "Piersall," "Hanley." "Go ahead."

"Montego exchange, 8227. Until five o'clock. Mr. Hanley said to call him in Port Antonio after 6:30."

"Did he leave that number?"

"No, sir. Mrs. Booth left word at 1:35 that she would be back in her room at 2:30. She asked that you ring through if you telephoned from outside. That's everything, Mr. McAuliff."

"All right. Thank you. Let me go back, please." Alex repeated the names, the jists of the messages, and asked for the Sheraton's telephone number. He had no idea who "Mr. Piersall" was. He mentally scanned the twelve contact names provided by Holcroft; there was no Piersall.

"Will that be all, sir?"

"Yes. Put me through to Mrs. Booth, if you please."

Alison's phone rang several times before she answered. "I was taking a shower," she said, out of breath. "Rather hoping you were here."

"Is there a towel around you?"

"Yes. I left it on the knob with the door open, if you must know. So I could hear the telephone."

"If I was there, I'd remove it. The towel, not the phone."

"I should think it appropriate to remove both." Alison laughed, and McAuliff could see the lovely half smile in the haze of the afternoon sun on Tower Street.

"You're right, you're parched. But your note said it was urgent. Is anything the matter?" There was a click within the interior of the telephone box; his time was nearly up. Alison heard it, too.

"Where are you? I'll call you right back," she said quickly.

The number had been deliberately, maliciously scratched off the dial's center. "No way to tell. How urgent? I've got another call to make."

"It can wait. Just don't speak to a man named Piersall until we talk. 'Bye now, darling."

McAuliff was tempted to call Alison right back; who was Piersall? But it was more important to reach Hanley in Montego. It would be necessary to call collect; he didn't have enough change.

It took the better part of five minutes before Hanley's phone rang and another three while Hanley convinced a switchboard operator at a less-than-chic hotel that he would pay for the call.

"I'm sorry, Robert," said Alex. "I'm in a coin box in Kingston."

"It's all right, lad. Have you heard from Tucker?" There was an urgency in Hanley's rapidly asked question.

"No. He hasn't checked in. I thought you might have something."

"I have, indeed, and I don't like it at all . . . I flew back to Mo'Bay a couple of hours ago, and these damn fools here tell me that two blacks picked up Sam's belongings, paid the bill, and walked out without a word."

"Can they do that?"

"This isn't the Hilton, lad. They had the money and they did it."

"Then where are *you?*"

"Goddamn it, I took the same room for the afternoon. In case Sam tries to get in touch, he'll start here, I figured. In the meantime, I've got some friends asking around town. You still don't want the police?"

McAuliff hesitated. He had agreed to Holcroft's command not to go to the Jamaican police for anything until he had checked with a contact first and received clearance. "Not yet, Bob."

"We're talking about an old friend!"

"He's still not overdue, Robert. I can't legitimately report him missing. And, knowing our old friend, I wouldn't want him embarrassed."

"I'd sure as hell raise a stink over two strangers picking up his belongings!" Hanley was angry, and McAuliff could not fault him for it.

"We're not sure they're strangers. You know Tuck; he hires attendants like he's the court of Eric the Red. Especially if he's got some money and he can spread it around the outback. Remember Kimberly, Bob." A statement. "Sam blew two months' wages setting up an agricultural commune, for Christ's sake."

Hanley chuckled. "Aye, lad, I do. He was going to put the hairy bastards in the wine business. He's a one-man Peace Corps with a vibrating crotch . . . All right, Alex. We'll wait until tomorrow. I have to get back to Port Antone'. I'll phone you in the morning."

"If he's not here by then, I'll call the police and you can activate your subterranean network—which I'm sure you've developed by now."

"Goddamn right. We old travelers have to protect ourselves. And stick together."

The blinding sun on the hot, dirty Caribbean street and the stench of the telephone mouthpiece was enough to convince McAuliff to return to Courtleigh Manor.

Later, perhaps early this evening, he would find the fish store called Tallon's and his arthritic contact.

He walked north on Matthew Lane and found a taxi on Barry Street; a half-demolished touring car of indeterminate make, and certainly not of this decade, or the last. As he stepped in, the odor of vanilla assaulted his nostrils. Vanilla and bay rum, the scents of black Jamaica; delightful in the evening, oppressive during the day under the fiery equatorial sun.

As the cab headed out of Old Kingston—harbor-front Kingston—where man-made decay and cascading tropical flora struggled to coexist, Alex found himself staring with uncomfortable wonder at the suddenly emerging new buildings of New Kingston. There was something obscene about the proximity of such bland, clean structures of stone and tinted glass to the rows of filthy, tin, corrugated shacks—the houses of gaunt children who played slowly, without energy, with bony dogs, and of pregnant young-old women hanging rags on ropes salvaged from the waterfront, their eyes filled with the bleak, hated prospects of getting through another day. And the new, bland, scrubbed obscenities were less than two hundred yards from even more terrible places of human habitation: rotted, rat-infested barges, housing those who had reached the last cellars of dignity. Two hundred yards.

McAuliff suddenly realized what these buildings were: banks. Three, four, five . . . six banks. Next to, and across from each other, all within an easy throw of a safe-deposit box.

Banks.

Clean, bland, tinted glass.

Two hundred yards.

Eight minutes later, the odd, ancient touring car entered the palm-lined drive of Courtleigh Manor. Ten yards in from the gates, the driver stopped, briefly, with a jerk. Alex, who was sitting forward, taking out his wallet, braced himself against the front seat as the driver quickly apologized. Then McAuliff saw what the Jamaican was doing. He was removing a lethal, thirty-inch machete from the worn felt next to him, and putting it under the seat. The driver grinned.

"I take a fare into old town, mon. Shack town. I keep long knife by me alla time there."

"Is it necessary?"

"Oh, mon! True, mon. Bad people; dirty people. Not Kingston, mon. Better to shoot alla dirty people. No good, mon. Put 'em in boats back to Africa. Sink boats; yes, mon!"

"That's quite a solution." The car pulled up to the curb, and McAuliff got out. The driver smiled obsequiously as he stated an inflated charge. Alex handed him the precise amount. "I'm sure you included the tip," he said as he dropped the bills through the window.

At the front desk, McAuliff took the messages handed to him; there was an addition. Mr. Latham of the Ministry of Education had telephoned again.

Alison was on the small balcony, taking the afternoon sun in her bathing suit. McAuliff entered the room from his connecting door.

She reached out and he took her hand. "Have you any idea what a lovely lady you are, lovely lady?"

"Thank you, lovely man."

He gently released her hand. "Tell me about Piersall," he said.

"He's at the Sheraton."

"I know. Room 51."

"You spoke to him." Alison obviously was concerned.

"No. That was his message. Phone him in room 51. Very urgent."

"He may be there now; he wasn't when you called."

"Oh? I got the message just before I talked to you."

"Then he must have left it downstairs. Or used a pay phone in the lobby. Within minutes."

"Why?"

"Because he was here. I talked with him."

"Do tell."

She did.

Alison had finished sorting out research notes she had prepared for the north coast, and was about to take her shower when she heard a rapid knocking from Alex's room. Thinking it was one of their party, Alison opened her own door and looked out in the corridor. A tall, thin man in a white Palm Beach suit seemed startled at her appearance. It was an awkward moment for both. Alison volunteered that she had heard the knocking and knew McAuliff was out; would the gentleman care to leave a message?

"He seemed very nervous. He stuttered slightly, and said he'd been trying to reach you since eleven o'clock. He asked if he could trust me. Would I speak only to you? He was really quite upset. I invited him into my room, but he said no, he was in a hurry. Then he blurted it out. He had news of a man named Sam Tucker. Isn't he the American who's to join us here?"

Alex did not bother to conceal his alarm. He bolted from his reclining position and stood up. "What about Tucker?"

"He didn't go into it. Just that he had word *from* him or *about* him. He wasn't really clear."

"Why didn't you tell me on the phone?"

"He asked me not to. He said I was to tell you when I saw you, *not* over the telephone. He implied that you'd be angry, but you should get in touch with him before you went to anyone else. Then he left . . . Alex, what the hell was he talking about?"

McAuliff did not answer; he was on his way to her telephone. He picked up the receiver, glanced at the connecting door, and quickly replaced the phone. He walked rapidly to the open door, closed it, and returned to the telephone. He gave the Sheraton's number and waited.

"Mr. Piersall, room 51, please."

The interim of silence was infuriating to McAuliff. It was broken by the soothing tones of a subdued English voice, asking first the identity of the caller and then whether the caller was a friend or, perhaps, a relative of Dr. Piersall's. Upon hearing Alex's replies, the unctuous voice continued, and as it did so, McAuliff remembered a cold night on a Soho street outside The Owl of Saint George. And the flickering of a neon light that saved his life and condemned his would-be killer to death.

Dr. Walter Piersall had been involved in a terrible, tragic accident.

He had been run down by a speeding automobile in a Kingston street.

He was dead.

12

WALTER PIERSALL, American, Ph.D., anthropologist, student of the Caribbean, author of a definitive study on Jamaica's first known inhabitants, the Arawak Indians, and the owner of a house called "High Hill" near Carrick Foyle in the parish of Trelawny.

That was the essence of the information supplied by the Ministry's Mr. Latham.

"A tragedy, Mr. McAuliff. He was an honored man, a titled man. Jamaica will miss him greatly."

"Miss him! Who killed him, Mr. Latham?"

"As I understand it, there is very little to go on; the vehicle sped away, the description is contradictory."

"It was broad daylight, Mr. Latham."

There was a pause on Latham's part. "I know, Mr. McAuliff. What can I say? You are an American; he was an American. I am Jamaican, and the terrible thing took place on a Kingston street. I grieve deeply for several reasons. And I did not know the man."

Latham's sincerity carried over the wire. Alex lowered his voice. "You say 'the terrible thing.' Do you mean more than an accident?"

"No. There was no robbery, no mugging. It was an accident. No doubt brought on by rum and inactivity. There is a great deal of both in Kingston, Mr. McAuliff. The men . . . or children who committed the crime are undoubtedly well into the hills now. When the rum wears off, the fear will take its place; they will hide. The Kingston police are not gentle."

"I see." McAuliff was tempted to bring up the name "Sam Tucker," but he held himself in check. He had told Latham only that Piersall had left a message for him. He would say no more for the time being. "Well, if there's anything I can do . . ."

"Piersall was a widower, he lived alone in Carrick Foyle. The police said they were getting in touch with a brother in Cambridge, Massachusetts . . . Do you know why he was calling you?"

"No idea."

"A great deal of the survey will take place in Trelawny Parish. Perhaps he had heard and was offering you hospitality."

"Perhaps . . . Mr. Latham, is it logical that he would know about the survey?" Alex listened intently to Latham's reply. Again, Holcroft: *Learn to spot the small things.*

"Logical? What is logical in Jamaica, Mr. McAuliff? It is a poorly kept secret that the Ministry—with the gracious help of our recent mother country—is undertaking an overdue scientific evaluation. A secret poorly kept is not really much of a secret. Perhaps it is not logical that Dr. Piersall knew; it is certainly possible, however."

No hesitations, no overly quick responses, no rehearsed words.

"Then I guess that's what he was calling about. I'm sorry."

"I grieve." Again Latham paused; it was not for effect. "Although it may seem improper, Mr. McAuliff, I should like to discuss the business between us."

"Of course. Go ahead."

"All of the survey permits came in late this morning . . . less than twenty-four hours. It generally takes the best part of a week . . ."

The processing was unusual, but Alex had come to expect the unusual with Dunstone, Limited. The normal barriers fell with abnormal ease. Unseen expeditors were everywhere, doing the bidding of Julian Warfield.

Latham said that the Ministry had anticipated more, rather than less, difficulty, as the survey team would be entering the territory of the Cock Pit, miles of uninhabited country—jungle, really. Escorts were required, guides trained in the treacherous environs. And arrangements had to be made with the recognized descendants of the Maroon people, who, by a treaty of 1739, controlled much of the territory. An arrogant, warlike people, brought to the islands as slaves, the Maroons knew the jungles far better than their white captors. The British sovereign, George the First, had offered the Maroons their independence, with a treaty that guaranteed the Cock Pit territories in perpetuity. It was a wiser course than continuing bloodshed. Besides, the territory was considered unfit for white habitation.

For over 235 years that treaty was often scoffed at but never violated, said Latham. Formal permission was still sought by Kingston from the "Colonel of the Maroons" for all those who wished to enter their lands.

The Ministry was no exception.

Yet the Ministry, thought McAuliff, was in reality Dunstone, Limited. So permissions were granted, permits obtained with alacrity.

"Your equipment was air-freighted to Boscobel," said Latham. "Trucks will transport it to the initial point of the survey."

"Then I'll leave tomorrow afternoon or, at the latest, early the next day. I'll be hiring out of Ocho Rios; the others can follow when I'm finished. It shouldn't take more than a couple of days."

"Your escort-guides, we call them 'runners,' will be available in two weeks. You will not have any need for them until then, will you? I assume you will be working the coast to begin with."

"Two weeks'll be fine . . . I'd like a choice of runners, please."

"There are not that many to choose from, Mr. McAuliff. It is not a career that appeals to many young people; the ranks are thinning. But I shall do what I can."

"Thank you. May I have the approved maps in the morning?"

"They will be sent to your hotel by ten o'clock. Good-bye, Mr. McAuliff. And again, my deeply felt regrets over Dr. Piersall."

"I didn't know him either, Mr. Latham," said Alex. "Good-bye."

He did not know Piersall, thought McAuliff, but he *had* heard the name "Carrick Foyle," Piersall's village. He could not remember where he had heard it, only that it was familiar.

Alex replaced the telephone and looked over at Alison, on the small balcony. She had been watching him, listening. She could not conceal her fear. A thin, nervous man in a white Palm Beach suit had told her—less than two hours ago—that he had confidential information, and now he was dead.

The late afternoon sun was a Caribbean orange, the shadows shafts of black across the miniature balcony. Be-

hind her was the near deep green of the high palms, behind them the awesome rise of the mountain range. Alison
Booth seemed to be framed within a tableau of chiaroscuro tropic colors. As though she were a target.

"He said it was an accident." Alex walked slowly to the
balcony doors. "Everyone's upset. Piersall was liked on
the island. Apparently, there's a lot of drunken hit-and-
runs in Kingston."

"And you don't believe him for an instant."

"I didn't say that." He lighted a cigarette; he did not
want to look at her.

"You don't have to. You didn't say one word about
your friend Tucker, either. Why not?"

"Common sense. I want to talk to the police, not an associate director of the Ministry. All he can do is babble
and create confusion."

"Then let's go to the police." Alison rose from the deck
chair. "I'll get dressed."

"No!" McAuliff realized as he said the word that he
was too emphatic. "I mean, I'll go. I don't want you involved."

"I spoke to the man. You didn't."

"I'll relay the information."

"They won't accept it from you. Why should they hear
it second-hand?"

"Because I say so." Alex turned away, ostensibly to find
an ashtray. He was not convincing, and he knew it. "Listen to me, Alison." He turned back. "Our permits came
in. Tomorrow I'm going to Ocho Rios to hire drivers and
carriers; you people will follow in a couple of days. While
I'm gone I don't want you—or any member of the
team—involved with the police or anybody else. Our job
here is the survey. That's my responsibility; you're my responsibility. I don't want delays."

She walked down the single step, out of the frame of
color, and stood in front of him. "You're a dreadful liar,
Alex. Dreadful in the sense that you're quite poor at it."

"I'm going to the police now. Afterwards, if it's not too
late, I may drop over to the Ministry and see Latham. I
was a little rough with him."

"I thought you ended on a very polite note."

It was Alison who spotted Holcroft's small things,
thought McAuliff. She was better than he was. "You only

heard me. You didn't hear him . . . If I'm not back by
seven, why not call the Jensens and have dinner with
them? I'll join you as soon as I can."

"The Jensens aren't here."

"What?"

"Relax. I called them for lunch. They left word at the
desk that since it was a day off, they were touring. Port
Royal, Spanish Town, Old Harbour. The manager set up
their tour."

"I hope they enjoy themselves."

He told the driver that he wanted a half-hour's tour of
the city. He had thirty minutes to kill before cocktails in
Duke Street—he'd spot the restaurant; he didn't know the
specific address—so the driver could do his imaginative
best within the time span.

The driver protested: Thirty minutes was barely sufficient to reach Duke Street from the Courtleigh in the afternoon traffic. McAuliff shrugged and replied that the
time was not absolute.

It was precisely what the driver wanted to hear. He
drove out Trafalgar, south on Lady Musgrave, into Old
Hope Road. He extolled the commercial virtues of New
Kingston, likening the progress to Olympian feats of mas-
ter planning. The words droned on, filled with idiomatic
exaggerations of the "alla time big American millions"
that were turning the tropical and human overgrowth that
was Kingston into a Caribbean financial mecca. It was understood that the millions would be German or English or
French, depending on the accent of the passenger.

It didn't matter. Within minutes, McAuliff knew that
the driver knew he was not listening. He was staring out
the rear window, watching the traffic behind them.

It was there.

A green Chevrolet sedan, several years old. It stayed
two to three cars behind, but whenever the taxi turned or
sped ahead of other vehicles, the green Chevrolet did the
same.

The driver saw it, too.

"You got trouble, mon?"

There was no point in lying. "I don't know."

"*I* know, mon. Lousy green car be'n d'ere alla time. It
stay in big parking lot at Courtleigh Manor. Two block
son of a bitch drivin'."

McAuliff looked at the driver. The Jamaican's last statement triggered his memory of Robert Hanley's words from Montego Bay. *Two blacks picked up Sam's things.* Alex knew the connection was far-fetched, coincidental at best in a black country, but it was all he had to go on. "You can earn twenty dollars, friend," he said quickly to the driver. "If you can do two things."

"You tell me, mon!"

"First, let the green car get close enough so I can read the license plate, and when I've got it, lose them. Can you do that?"

"You watch, mon!" The Jamaican swung the wheel to the right; the taxi veered briefly into the right lane, narrowly missing an oncoming bus, then lurched back into the left, behind a Volkswagen. McAuliff crouched against the seat, his head pressed to the right of the rear window. The green Chevrolet duplicated the taxi's movements, taking up a position two cars behind.

Suddenly the cab driver accelerated again, passing the Volks and speeding ahead to a traffic light that flashed the yellow caution signal. He swung the car into the left intersection; Alex read the street sign and the wording on the large shield-shaped sign beneath:

TORRINGTON ROAD
ENTRANCE
GEORGE VI MEMORIAL PARK

"We head into race course, mon!" shouted the driver. "Green son of a bitch have to stop at Snipe Street light. He come out'a d'ere fast. You watch good now!"

The cab sped down Torrington, swerving twice out of the left lane to pass three vehicles, and through the wide-gated entrance into the park. Once inside, the driver slammed on the brakes, backed the taxi into what looked like a bridle path, spun the wheel, and lurched forward into the exit side of the street.

"You catch 'em good now, mon!" yelled the Jamaican as he slowed the car down and entered the flow of traffic leaving the George VI Memorial Park.

Within seconds the green Chevrolet came into view, hemmed between automobiles entering the park. And then McAuliff realized precisely what the driver had done. It was early track time; George VI Memorial Park housed the sport of kings. Gambling Kingston was on the way to the races.

Alex wrote down the license number, keeping himself out of sight but seeing clearly enough to know that the two blacks in the Chevrolet did not realize that they had passed within feet of the car they were following.

"Them sons of bitches got to drive alla way 'round, mon! Them dumb block sons of bitches! . . . Where you want to go, mon? Plenty of time, now. They don't catch us."

McAuliff smiled. He wondered if the Jamaican's talents were listed in Holcroft's manual somewhere. "You just earned yourself an extra five dollars. Take me to the corner of Queen and Hanover streets, please. No sense wasting time, now."

"Hey, mon! You hire my taxi alla time in Kingston. I do what you say. I don't ask questions, mon."

Alex looked at the identification behind the dirty plastic frame above the dashboard. "This isn't a private cab . . . Rodney."

"You make a deal with me, mon; I make a deal with the taxi boss." The driver grinned in the rear-view mirror.

"I'll think about it. Do you have a telephone number?"

The Jamaican quickly produced an outsized business card and handed it back to McAuliff. It was the taxi company's card, the type that was left on hotel counters. Rodney's name was printed childishly in ink across the bottom. "You telephone company number, say you gotta have Rodney. Only Rodney, mon. I get the message real quick. All' time they know where Rodney is. I work hotels and Palisados. Them get me quick."

"Suppose I don't care to leave my name——"

"No, name, mon!" broke in the Jamaican, grinning in the mirror. "I got lousy son-of-a-bitch memory. Don't want no name! You tell taxi phone . . . you the fella at the race course. Give place; I get to you, mon."

Rodney accelerated south to North Street, left to Duke, and south again past the Gordon House, the huge new complex of the Kingston legislature.

Out on the sidewalk, McAuliff straightened his jacket and his tie and tried to assume the image of an average white businessman not entirely sure of which government entrance he should use. Tallon's was not listed in any telephone or shopping directory; Holcroft had indicated that it was below the row of government houses, which meant below Queen, but he was not specific.

As he looked for the fish store, he checked the people around him, across the street, and in the automobiles that seemed to go slower than the traffic allowed.

For a few minutes he felt himself in the pocket of fear again; afraid that the unseen had their eyes on him.

He reached Queen Street and hurried across with the last contingent making the light. On the curb he turned swiftly to watch those behind on the other side.

The orange sun was low on the horizon, throwing a corridor of blinding light from the area of Victoria Park several hundred yards to the west. The rest of the street was in dark, sharply defined shadows cast from the structures of stone and wood all around. Automobiles passed east and west, blocking a clear vision of those on the north corner. Corners.

He could tell nothing. He turned and proceeded down the block.

He saw the sign first. It was filthy, streaked with runny print that had not been refinished in months, if not years:

TALLON'S
FINE FISH & NATIVE DELICACIES
311-½ QUEEN'S ALLEY
1 BLOCK—DUKE ST. WEST

He walked the block. The entrance to Queen's Alley was barely ten feet high, cut off by grillwork covered with tropical flowers. The cobblestone passage did not go through to the next street. It was a dead end, a lightless cul-de-sac; the sort of hidden back street common to Paris and Rome and Greenwich Village. Although it was in the middle of a commercial market area, there was a personal quality about its appearance, as though an unwritten sign proclaimed this section private: residents only, keys required, not for public usage. All that was needed, thought McAuliff, was a gate.

In Paris and Rome and Greenwich Village, such wide alleys held some of the best restaurants in the world, known only to those who cared.

In Saigon and Macao and Hong Kong, they were the

recesses where anything could be had for a price.

In Kingston, this one housed a man with arthritis who worked for British Intelligence.

Queen's Alley was no more than fifty feet long. On the right was a bookstore with subdued lighting in the windows, illuminating a variety of wares from heavy academic leather to non-glossy pornography. On the left was Tallon's.

He had pictured casements of crushed ice supporting rows of wide-eyed dead fish, and men in soiled, cheap white aprons running around scales, arguing with customers.

The crushed ice was in the window; so were several rows of glassy-eyed fish. But what impressed him was the other forms of ocean merchandise placed artistically: squid, octopus, shark, and exotic shellfish.

Tallon's was no Fulton Market.

As if to add confirmation to his thoughts, a uniformed chauffeur emerged from Tallon's entrance carrying a plastic shopping bag, insulated, Alex was sure, with crushed ice.

The double doors were thick, difficult to open. Inside, the counters were spotless; the sawdust on the floor was white. The two attendants were just that: attendants, not countermen. Their full-length aprons were striped blue and white and made of expensive linen. The scales behind the chrome-framed glass cases had shiny brass trimmings. Around the shop, stacked on shelves lighted by tiny spotlights in the ceiling, were hundreds of tins of imported delicacies from all parts of the world.

It was not quite real.

There were three other customers: a couple and a single woman. The couple was at the far end of the store, studying labels on the shelves; the woman was ordering from a list, being overly precise, arrogant.

McAuliff approached the counter and spoke the words he had been instructed to speak.

"A friend in Santo Domingo told me you had north-coast trout."

The light-skinned black behind the white wall barely looked at Alex, but within that instant there was recognition. He bent down, separating shellfish inside the case, and answered casually. Correctly. "We have some fresh-water trout from Martha Brae, sir."

"I prefer salt-water trout. Are you sure you can't help me?"

"I'll see, sir." The man shut the case, turned, and walked down a corridor in the wall behind the counter, a passageway Alex assumed led to large refrigerated rooms.

When a man emerged from a side door within the corridor, McAuliff caught his breath, trying to suppress his astonishment. The man was black and slight and old; he walked with a cane, his right forearm stiff, and his head trembled slightly with age.

It was the man in Victoria Park: the old man who had stared at him disapprovingly in front of the bench on the Queen Street path.

He walked to the counter and spoke, his voice apparently stronger than his body. "A fellow salt-water trout lover," he said, in an accent more British than Jamaican, but not devoid of the Caribbean. "What are we to do with those fresh-water aficionados who cost me so much money? Come, it is nearly closing. You shall have your choice from my own selection."

A hinged panel of the butcher-block counter was lifted by the light-skinned black in the striped apron. Alex followed the arthritic old man down the short corridor and through a narrow door into a small office that was a miniature extension of the expensive outer design. The walls were paneled in fruitwood; the furniture was a single mahogany desk with a functional antique swivel chair, a soft leather couch against the wall, and an armchair in front of the desk. The lighting was indirect, from a lone china lamp on the desk. With the door closed, Alex saw oak file cabinets lined against the inner wall. Although the room was confining in size, it was eminently comfortable—the isolated quarters of a contemplative man.

"Sit, Mr. McAuliff," said the proprietor of Tallon's, indicating the armchair as he hobbled around the desk and sat down, placing his cane against the wall. "I've been expecting you."

"You were in Victoria Park this morning."

"I did not expect you then. To be quite frank, you startled me. I'd been looking at your photograph minutes before I took my stroll. From nowhere the face of this photograph was in front of my eyes in Victoria." The old man smiled and gestured with his palms up, signifying unexpected coincidence. "Incidentally, my name is 'Tallon.' Westmore Tallon. We're a fine old Jamaican family, as I'm sure you've been told."

"I hadn't, but one look at your . . . fish store would seem to confirm it."

"Oh, yes. We're frightfully expensive, very exclusive. Private telephone number. We cater only to the wealthiest on the island. From Savanna to Montego to Antonio and Kingston. We have our own delivery service—by private plane, of course . . . It's most convenient."

"I should think so. Considering your extracurricular activities."

"Which, of course, we must never consider to the point of discussion, Mr. McAuliff," replied Tallon quickly.

"I've got several things to tell you. I expect you'll transmit the information and let Holcroft do what he wants."

"You sound angry."

"On one issue, I am. Goddamned angry . . . Mrs. Booth. Alison Booth. She was manipulated here through Interpol. I think that smells. She made one painful—and dangerous—contribution. I should think you people would let her alone."

Tallon pushed his foot against the floor, turning the silent antique swivel to his right. He aimlessly reached over for his cane and fingered it. "I am merely a . . . liaison, Mr. McAuliff, but from what I understand, no pressure was exerted on you to employ Mrs. Booth. You did so freely. Where was the manipulation?"

Alex watched the small, arthritic man toy with the handle of the cane. He was struck by the thought that in some strange way Westmore Tallon was like an artist's composite of Julian Warfield and Charles Whitehall. The communion of elements was disturbing. "You people are very professional," he said quietly, a touch bitterly. "You're ingenious when it comes to presenting alternatives."

"She can't go home, Mr. McAuliff. Take my word for that."

"From a certain point of view, she might as well . . . The Marquis de Chatellerault is in Jamaica."

Tallon spun in the antique chair to face McAuliff. For an instant he seemed frozen. He stared at Alex, and when he blinked it was as though he silently rejected McAuliff's statement. "This is impossible," he said simply.

"It's not only possible, I don't even think it's a secret. Or if it is, it's poorly kept; and as somebody said about an hour ago, that's not much of a secret."

"Who gave you this information?" Tallon held onto his cane, his grasp visibly firmer.

"Charles Whitehall. At three o'clock this morning. He was invited to Savanna-la-Mar to meet Chatellerault."

"What were the circumstances?"

"The circumstances aren't important. The important fact is that Chatellerault is in Savanna-la-Mar. He is the houseguest of a family named Wakefield. They're white and rich."

"We know them," said Tallon, writing a note awkwardly with his arthritic hand. "They're customers. What else do you have?"

"A couple of items. One is extremely important to me, and I warn you, I won't leave here until something's done about it."

Tallon looked up from his notepaper. "You make pronouncements without regard for realistic appraisal. I have no idea whether I can do anything about anything. Your camping here would not change that. Please continue."

Alex described James Ferguson's unexpected meeting with Craft at the Palisados Airport and the manipulation that resulted in the electronic devices in his luggage. He detailed Craft's offer of money in exchange for information about the survey.

"It's not surprising. The Craft people are notoriously curious," said Tallon, writing painfully on his notepaper. "Shall we get to the item you say is so vital?"

"I want to summarize first."

"Summarize what?" Tallon put down his pencil.

"What I've told you."

Tallon smiled. "It's not necessary, Mr. McAuliff. I take notes slowly, but my mind is quite alert."

"I'd like us to understand each other . . . British Intelligence wants the Halidon. That was the purpose—the only purpose—of my recruitment. Once the Halidon could be reached, I was finished. Complete protection still guaranteed to the survey team."

"And so?"

"I think you've got the Halidon. Chatellerault and Craft."

Tallon continued to stare at McAuliff. His expression was totally neutral. "You have arrived at this conclusion?"

"Holcroft said this Halidon would interfere. Eventually try to stop the survey. Diagrams aren't necessary. The marquis and Craft fit the prints. Go get them."

"I see . . ." Tallon reached once more for his cane. His personal scepter, his sword Excaliber. "So, in one extraordinary simplification, the American geologist has solved the riddle of the Halidon."

Neither man spoke for several moments. McAuliff broke the silence with equally quiet anger. "I could get to dislike you, Mr. Tallon. You're a very arrogant man."

"My concerns do not include your approval, Mr. McAuliff. Jamaica is my passion—yes, my *passion*, sir. What you think is not important to me . . . except when you make absurd pronouncements that could affect my work . . . Arthur Craft, *père et fils*, have been raping this island for half a century. They subscribe to the belief that theirs is a mandate from God. They can accomplish too much in the name of Craft; they would not hide behind a symbol. And Halidon *is* a symbol, Mr. McAuliff . . . The Marquis de Chatellerault? You were quite correct. Mrs. Booth *was* manipulated—brilliantly, I think—into your survey. It was cross-pollination, if you like; the circumstances were optimum. Two kling-klings in a hibiscus, one inexorably forcing the other to reveal himself. She was bait, pure and simple, Mr. McAuliff. Chatellerault has long been suspected of being an associate of Julian Warfield. The marquis is with Dunstone, Limited." Tallon lifted his cane up laterally, placed it across his desk, and continued to gaze blankly at Alex.

McAuliff said finally, "You withheld information; you didn't tell me things I should have been told. Yet you expect me to function as one of you. That smells, Tallon."

"You exaggerate. There is no point in complicating further an already complicated picture."

"I should have been told about Chatellerault, instead of hearing his name from Mrs. Booth."

Tallon shrugged. "An oversight. Shall we proceed?"

"All right. There's a man named Tucker. Sam Tucker."

"Your friend from California? The soil analyst?"

"Yes."

McAuliff told Hanley's story without using Hanley's

name. He emphasized coincidence of the two blacks who had removed Tucker's belongings and the two Jamaicans who had followed his taxi in the green Chevrolet sedan. He described briefly the taxi owner's feats of driving skills in the racetrack park, and gave Tallon the license-plate number of the Chevrolet.

Tallon reached for his telephone and dialed without speaking to Alex. "This is Tallon," he said quietly into the phone. "I want M.V. information. It is urgent. The license is KYB-448. Call me back on this line." He hung up and shifted his eyes to McAuliff. "It should take no longer than five minutes."

"Was that the police?"

"Not in any way the police would know . . . I understand the Ministry received your permits today. Dunstone does facilitate things, doesn't it?"

"I told Latham I was leaving for Ocho Rios tomorrow afternoon. I won't if Tucker doesn't show up. That's what I want you to know."

Once again, Westmore Tallon reached for his cane, but not with the aggressiveness he had displayed previously. He was suddenly a rather thoughtful, even gentle, man. "If your friend was taken against his will, it would be kidnapping. A very serious crime, and insofar as he's American, the sort of headline attraction that would be an anathema. It doesn't make sense, Mr. McAuliff . . . You say he's due today, which could be extended to this evening, I presume?"

"Yes."

"Then I suggest we wait . . . I cannot believe the parties involved could—or would—commit such a gargantuan mistake. If Mr. Tucker is not heard from by . . . say ten o'clock, call me." Tallon wrote a number on a piece of paper and handed it to Alex. "Commit this to memory, please; leave the paper here."

"What are you going to do if Tucker doesn't show?"

"I will use perfectly legitimate connections and have the matter directed to the most authoritative officials in the Jamaican police. I will alert highly placed people in the government: the governor-general, if necessary. St. Croix has had its murders; tourism is now practically non-existent. Jamaica could not tolerate an American kidnapping . . . Does that satisfy you?"

"I'm satisfied." Alex crushed out his cigarette in the ashtray, and as he did so, he remembered Tallon's reaction to Chatellerault's appearance in Savanna-la-Mar. "You were surprised that Chatellerault was on the island. Why?"

"As of two days ago, he was registered at the George V in Paris. There's been no word of his leaving, which means he flew here clandestinely, probably by way of Mexico. It is disturbing. You must keep a close watch on Mrs. Booth . . . you have a weapon, I assume?"

"Two rifles in the equipment. An .030 Remington telescopic and a long-power .22 automatic. Nothing else."

Tallon seemed to debate with himself, then made a decision. He took a key ring from his pocket, selected a key, and opened a lower drawer of his desk. He removed a bulky manila envelope, opened the flap, and shook a pistol onto his blotter. A number of cartridges fell out with the gun. "This is a .38 Smith and Wesson, short barrel. All markings have been destroyed. It's untraceable. Take it, please; it's wiped clean. The only fingerprints will be yours. Be careful."

McAuliff looked at the weapon for several seconds before reaching out and slowing picking it up. He did not want it; there was a finality of commitment somehow attached to his having it. But again, there was the question of alternatives: Not having it might possibly be foolish, though he did not expect to use it for anything more than a show of force.

"Your dossier includes experience in small-arms fire. But it could be a long time. Would you care to refresh yourself at a pistol range? We have several, within minutes by plane."

"No, thank you," replied Alex. "Not too long ago, in Australia, it was the only diversion we had."

The telephone rang with a muted bell. Tallon picked it up and acknowledged with a simple "Yes?"

He listened without speaking to the party on the other end of the line. When he terminated the call, he looked at McAuliff.

"The green Chevrolet sedan is registered to a dead man. The vehicle's license is in the name of Walter Piersall. Residence: High Hill, Carrick Foyle, parish of Trelawny."

13

MCAULIFF spent another hour with Westmore Tallon, as the old Jamaican aristocrat activated his informational network. He had sources all over the island.

Before the hour was up, one important fact had been uncovered: The deceased, Walter Piersall of Carrick Foyle, parish of Trelawny, had in his employ two black assistants with whom he invariably traveled. The coincidence of the two men who had removed Sam Tucker's belongings from the hotel in Montego Bay and the two men who followed Alex in the green Chevrolet was no longer far-fetched. And since Piersall had brought up Sam's name with Alison Booth, the conclusion was now to be assumed.

Tallon ordered his own people to pick up Piersall's men. He would telephone McAuliff when they had done so.

Alex returned to Courtleigh Manor. He stopped at the desk for messages. Alison was at dinner; she hoped he would join her. There was nothing else.

No word from Sam Tucker.

"If there are any calls for me, I'll be in the dining room," he said to the clerk.

Alison sat alone in the middle of the crowded room, which was profuse with tropical plants and open-grilled windows. In the center of each table was a candle within a lantern, these were the only sources of light. Shadows flickered against the dark red and green and yellow foliage; the hum was the hum of contentment, rising but still quiet crescendos of laughter; perfectly groomed, perfectly dressed manikins in slow motion, all seemingly waiting for the nocturnal games to begin.

This was the manikins' good hour. When manners and studied grace and minor subtleties were important. Later it would be different; other things would become important . . . and too often ugly. Which is why James Ferguson knew his drunken pretense had been plausible last night.

And why Charles Whitehall arrogantly, quietly, had

thrown the napkin across the table onto the floor. To clean up the foreigner's mess.

"You look pensive. Or disagreeable," said Alison as he pulled out the chair to sit down.

"Not really."

"What happened? What did the police say? I half expected a call from them."

McAuliff had rehearsed his reply, but before delivering it he gestured at the cup of coffee and the brandy glass in front of Alison. "You've had dinner, I guess."

"Yes. I was famished. Haven't you?"

"No. Keep me company?"

"Of course. I'll dismiss the eunuchs."

He ordered a drink. "You have a lovely smile. It's sort of a laugh."

"No sidetracking. What happened?"

McAuliff lied quite well, he thought. Certainly better— at least more persuasively—than before. He told Alison he had spent nearly two hours with the police. Westmore Tallon had furnished him with the address and even described the interior of the main headquarters; it had been Tallon's idea for him to know the general details. One could never tell when they were important.

"They backed up Latham's theory. They say it's hit-and-run. They also hinted that Piersall had a diversion or two that was closeted. He was run down in a very rough section."

"That sounds suspiciously pat to me. They're covering themselves." The girl's eyebrows furrowed, her expression one of disbelief.

"They may be," answered Alex casually, sincerely. "But they can't tie him to Sam Tucker, and that's my only concern."

"He *is* tied. He told me."

"And *I* told *them.* They've sent men to Carrick Foyle, that's where Piersall lived. In Trelawny. Others are going over his things at the Sheraton. If they find anything, they'll call me." McAuliff felt that he was carrying off the lie. He was, after all, only bending the truth. The arthritic Westmore Tallon was doing these things.

"And you're satisfied with that? You're just going to take their word for it? You were awfully troubled about Mr. Tucker a few hours ago."

"I still am," said Alex, putting down his glass and look- ing at her. He had no need to lie now. "If I don't hear from Sam by late tonight . . . or tomorrow morning, I'm going to go to the American Embassy and yell like hell."

"Oh . . . all right. Did you mention the little buggers this morning? You never told me."

"The what?"

"Those bugs in your luggage. You said you were sup- posed to report them."

Again McAuliff felt a wave of inadequacy; it irked him that he wasn't keeping track of things. Of course, he hadn't seen Tallon earlier, had not received his instruc- tions, but that was no explanation. "I should have listened to you last night. I can just get rid of them; step on them, I guess."

"There's a better way."

"What's that?"

"Put them someplace else."

"For instance?"

"Oh, somewhere harmless but with lots of traffic. It keeps the tapes rolling and people occupied."

McAuliff laughed; it was not a false laugh. "That's very funny. And very practical. Where?"

Alison brought her hands to her chin; a mischievous lit- tle girl thinking mischievously. "It should be within a hun- dred yards or so—that's usually the range tolerance. And where there's a great deal of activity . . . Let's see. I complimented the headwaiter on the red snapper. I'll bet he'd bring me to the chef to get the recipe."

"They love that sort of thing," added Alex. "It's per- fect. Don't go away. I'll be right back."

Alison Booth, former liaison to Interpol, reported that two electronic devices were securely attached to the per- manent laundry hamper under the salad table in the Courtleigh Manor kitchen. She had slipped them in—and pushed them down—along with a soiled napkin, as an en- thusiastic chef described the ingredients of his Jamaican red snapper sauce.

"The hamper was long, not deep," she explained as McAuliff finished the last of his dinner. "I pressed rather hard; the adhesive will hold quite well, I think."

"You're incredible," said Alex, meaning it.

"No, just experienced," she replied, without much humor. "You were only taught one side of the game, my darling."

"It doesn't sound much like tennis."

"Oh, there are compensations. For example, do you have any idea how limitless the possibilities are? In that kitchen, for the next three hours or so, until it's tracked?"

"I'm not sure I know what you mean."

"Depending upon who's on the tapes, there'll be a mad scramble writing down words and phrases. Kitchen talk has its own contractions, its own language, really. It will be assumed you've taken your suitcase to a scheduled destination, for reasons of departure, naturally. There'll be quite a bit of confusion." Alison smiled, her eyes again mischievous, as they had been before he had gone upstairs to pry loose the bugs.

"You mean 'Sauce Béarnaise' is really a code for submachine gun? 'B.L.T.' stands for 'hit the beaches'?"

"Something like that. It's quite possible, you know."

"I thought that sort of thing only happened in World War Two movies. With Nazis screaming at each other, sending panzer divisions in the wrong directions." McAuliff looked at his watch. It was 9:15. "I have a phone call to make, and I want to go over a list of supplies with Ferguson. He's going to—"

He stopped. Alison had reached over, her hand suddenly on his arm. "Don't turn your head," she commanded softly, "But I think your little buggers provoked a reaction. A man just came through the dining room entrance very rapidly, obviously looking for someone."

"For us?"

"For you, to be precise, I'd say."

"The kitchen codes didn't fool them very long."

"Perhaps not. On the other hand, it's quite possible they've been keeping loose tabs on you and were double checking. It's too small a hotel for round-the-clock—"

"Describe him," interrupted McAuliff. "As completely as you can. Is he still facing this way?"

"He saw you and stopped. He's apologizing to the man on the reservations book, I think. He's white; he's dressed in light trousers, a dark jacket, and a white—no, a yellow shirt. He's shorter than you by a bit; fairly chunky—"

"What?"

"You know, bulky. And middle-young, thirties, I'd say.

His hair is long, not mod, but long. It's dark blond or light brown; it's hard to tell in this candlelight."

"You've done fine. Now I've got to get to a telephone."

"Wait till he leaves; he's looking over again," said Alison, feigning interested, intimate laughter. "Why don't you leer a little and signal for the check. Very casually, my darling."

"I feel like I'm in some kind of nursery school. With the prettiest teacher in town." Alex held up his hand, spotted the waiter, and made the customary scribble in the air. "I'll take you to your room, then come back downstairs and call."

"Why? Use the phone in the room. The buggers aren't there."

Damn! Goddamn! It had happened again; he wasn't prepared. The little things, always the little things. They were the traps. Holcroft said it over and over again . . . Holcroft. The Savoy. Don't make calls on the Savoy phone.

"I was told to use a pay telephone. They must have their reasons."

"Who?"

"The Ministry. Latham . . . the police, of course."

"Of course. The police." Alison withdrew her hand from his arm as the waiter presented the bill for Alex to sign. She didn't believe him; she made no pretense of believing him. Why should she? He was a rotten actor; he was caught . . . But it was preferable to an ill-phrased statement or an awkward response to Westmore Tallon over the phone while Alison watched him. And listened. He had to feel free in his conversation with the arthritic liaison; he could not have one eye, one ear on Alison as he talked. He could not take the chance that the name Chatellerault, or even a hint of the man, was heard. Alison was too quick.

"Has he left yet?"

"As you signed the check. He saw we were leaving." Her reply was neither angry nor warm, merely neutral.

They walked out of the candlelit dining room, past the cascading arcs of green foliage into the lobby, toward the bank of elevators. Neither spoke. The ride up to their floor continued in silence, made bearable by other guests in the small enclosure.

He opened the door and repeated the precautions he

had taken the previous evening—minus the scanner. He was in a hurry now; if he remembered, he would bless the room with electronic benediction later. He checked his own room and locked the connecting door from her side. He looked out on the balcony and in the bathroom. Alison stood in the corridor doorway, watching him.

He approached her. "Will you stay here until I get back?"

"Yes," she answered simply.

He kissed her on the lips, staying close to her, he knew, longer than she expected him to; it was his message to her. "You are a lovely lady."

"Alex?" She placed her hands carefully on his arms and looked up at him. "I know the symptoms. Believe me, I do. They're not easy to forget . . . There are things you're not telling me and I won't ask. I'll wait."

"You're overdramatizing, Alison."

"That's funny."

"What is?"

"What you just said. I used the words with David. In Malaga. He was nervous, frightened. He was so unsure of himself. And of me. And I said to him: David, you're being overly dramatic . . . I know now that it was at that moment he knew."

McAuliff held her eyes with his own. "You're not David and I'm not you. That's as straight as I can put it. Now, I have to get to a telephone. I'll see you later. Use the latch."

He kissed her again, went out the door, and closed it behind him. He waited until he heard the metallic sounds of the inserted bolt, then turned toward the elevators.

The doors closed; the elevator descended. The soft music was piped over the heads of assorted businessmen and tourists; the cubicle was full. McAuliff's thoughts were on his imminent telephone call to Westmore Tallon, his concerns about Sam Tucker.

The elevator stopped at an intermediate floor. Alex looked up at the lighted digits absently, vaguely wondering how another person could fit in the cramped enclosure. There was no need to think about the problem; the two men who waited by the parting doors saw the situation, smiled, and gestured that they would wait for the next elevator.

And then McAuliff saw him. Beyond the slowly closing panels, far down in the corridor. A stocky man in a dark jacket and light trousers. He had unlocked a door and was about to enter a room; as he did so, he pulled back his jacket to replace the key in his pocket. The shirt was yellow.

The door closed.

"Excuse me! Excuse me, please!" said McAuliff rapidly as he reached across a tuxedoed man near the panel of buttons and pushed the one marked 2, the next number in descent. "I forgot my floor. I'm terribly sorry."

The elevator, its thrust suddenly, electrically interrupted, jerked slightly as it mindlessly prepared for the unexpected stop. The panels opened and Alex sidled past the irritated but accommodating passengers.

He stood in the corridor in front of the bank of elevators and immediately pushed the *Up* button. Then he reconsidered. Where were the stairs?

The "EXIT—STAIRCASE" sign was blue with white letters. That seemed peculiar to him; exit signs were always red. It was at the far end of the hallway. He walked rapidly down the heavily carpeted corridor, nervously smiling at a couple who emerged from a doorway at midpoint. The man was in his fifties and drunk; the girl was barely in her twenties, sober and mulatto. Her clothes were the costume of a high-priced whore. She smiled at Alex; another sort of message. He acknowledged, his eyes telling her he wasn't interested but good luck, take the company drunk for all she could.

He pushed the crossbar on the exit door. Its sound was too loud; he closed it carefully, quietly, relieved to see there was a knob on the inside of the door.

He ran up the concrete stairs on the balls of his feet, minimizing the sound of his footsteps. The steel panel had the Roman numeral *III* stenciled in black over the beige paint. He twisted the knob slowly and opened the door onto the third-floor corridor.

It was empty. The nocturnal games had begun below; the players would remain in the competitive arenas until the prizes had been won or lost or forgotten in alcoholic oblivion. He had only to be alert for stragglers, or the over-anxious, like the pigeon on the second floor who was being maneuvered with such precision by the child-woman mulatto. He tried to recall at which door the man in the yellow shirt had stood. He had been quite far down the hallway, but not at the end. Not by the staircase; two-thirds of the way, perhaps. On the right; he had pulled back his jacket with his right hand, revealing the yellow shirt. That meant he was now inside a door on Alex's left. Reversing the viewpoint, he focused on three . . . no, four doors on his left that were possible. Beginning with the second door from the staircase, one-third the distance to the elevators.

Which one?

McAuliff began walking noiselessly on the thick carpet down the corridor, hugging the left wall. He paused before each door as he passed, his head constantly turning, his eyes alert, his ears listening for the sound of voices, the tinkling of glasses. For anything.

Nothing.

Silence. Everywhere.

He looked at the brass numbers. 218, 216, 214, 212. Even 210. Any farther would be incompatible with what he remembered.

He stopped at the halfway point and turned. Perhaps he knew enough. Enough to tell Westmore Tallon. Alison had said that the tolerance range for the electronic bugs was one hundred yards from first positioning to the receiving equipment. This floor, this section of the hotel, was well within that limit. Behind one of those doors was a tape recorder activated by a man in front of a speaker or with earphones clamped over his head.

Perhaps it was enough to report those numbers. Why should he look further?

Yet he knew he would. Someone had seen fit to intrude on his life in a way that filled him with revulsion. Few things caused him to react violently, but one of them was the actual, intended invasion of his privacy. And greed. Greed, too, infuriated him. Individual, academic, corporate.

Someone named Craft—because of his greed—had instructed his minions to invade Alex's personal moments.

Alexander Tarquin McAuliff was a very angry man.

He started back toward the staircase, retracing his steps, close to the wall, closer to each door, where he stopped and stood immobile. Listening.

212. 214. 216. 218 . . .

And back once again. It was a question of patience. Behind one of those doors was a man in a yellow shirt. He wanted to find that man.

He heard it.

Room 214.

It was a radio. Or a television set. Someone had turned up the volume of a television set. He could not distinguish the words, but he could hear the excitement behind the rapid bursts of dialogue from a clouded speaker, too loud to avoid distortion.

Suddenly, there was the sound of a harsh, metallic crack of a door latch. Inches away from McAuliff someone had pulled back the bolt and was about to open the door.

Alex raced to the staircase. He could not avoid noise, he could only reduce it as much as possible as he lurched into the dimly lit concrete foyer. He whipped around, pushing the heavy steel door closed as fast and as quietly as he could; he pressed the fingers of his left hand around the edge, preventing the door from shutting completely, stopping the sound of metal against metal at the last half second.

He peered through the crack. The man in the yellow shirt came out of the room, his attention still within it. He was no more than fifty feet away in the silent corridor—silent except for the sound of the television set. He seemed angry, and before he closed the door he looked inside and spoke harshly in a Southern drawl.

"Turn that fuckin' thing down, you goddamn ape!"

The man in the yellow shirt then slammed the door and walked rapidly toward the elevators. He remained at the end of the corridor, nervously checking his watch, straightening his tie, rubbing his shoes over the back of his trousers until a red light, accompanied by a soft, echoing bell, signaled the approach of an elevator. McAuliff watched from the stairwell two hundred feet away.

The elevator doors closed, and Alex walked out into the corridor. He crossed to Room 214 and stood motionless for a few moments. It was a decision he could abandon, he knew that. He could walk away, call Tallon, tell him the room number, and that would be that.

But it would not be very satisfying. It would not be satisfying at all. He had a better idea: He would take whoever was in that room to Tallon himself. If Tallon didn't like it, he could go to hell. The same for Holcroft. Since it was established that the electronic devices were planted by a man named Craft, who was in no way connected with the elusive Halidon, Arthur Craft could be taught a lesson. Alex's arrangements with Holcroft did not include abuses from third and fourth parties.

It seemed perfectly logical to get Craft out of the chess game. Craft clouded the issues, confused the pursuit.

McAuliff had learned two physical facts about Arthur Craft: He was the son of Craft the elder and he was American. He was also an unpleasant man.

It would have to do.

He knocked on the door beneath the numerals *214*.

"Yes, mon? Who is it, mon?" came the muffled reply from within.

Alex waited and knocked again. The voice inside came nearer the door.

"Who is it, please, mon?"

"Arthur Craft, you idiot!"

"Oh! Yes sir, Mr. Craft, mon!" The voice was clearly frightened. The knob turned; the bolt had not been inserted.

The door had opened no more than three inches when McAuliff slammed his shoulder against it with the full impact of his near two hundred pounds. The door crashed against the medium-sized Jamaican inside, sending him reeling into the center of the room. Alex gripped the edge of the vibrating door and swung it back into place, the slam of the heavy wood echoing throughout the corridor.

The Jamaican steadied himself, in his eyes a combination of fury and fear. He whipped around to the room's writing desk; there were boxed speakers on each side. Between them was a pistol.

McAuliff lurched forward, his left hand aiming for the gun, his right grabbing any part of the man it could reach. Their hands met above the warm steel of the pistol; Alex gripped the black's and dug his fingers into the man's throat.

The man shook loose; the gun went careening off the surface of the desk onto the floor. McAuliff lashed out

with the back of his fist at the black's face, instantane-
ously opening his hand and yanking forward, pulling the
man's head down by the hair. As the head went down,
Alex brought his left knee crashing up into the man's
chest, then into his face.

Voices from a millennium ago came back to him: *Use
your knees! Your feet! Grab! Hold! Slash at the eyes! The
blind can't fight! . . . Rupture!*

It was over. The voices subsided. The man collapsed at
his feet.

McAuliff stepped back. He was frightened; something
had happened to him. For a few terrifying seconds, he
had been back in the Korean hills. He looked down at the
motionless Jamaican beneath him. The head was turned,
flat against the carpet; blood was oozing from the pink
lips.

Thank God the man was breathing.

It was the gun. The goddamned *gun!* He had not expected a gun. A fight, yes. His anger justified that. But he
had thought of it as a scuffle—intense, over quickly. He
would confront, embarrass, forcibly make whoever was
monitoring the tapes go with him. To embarrass; to teach
an avaricious employer a lesson.

But not this.

This was deadly. This was the violence of survival.

The tapes. The *voices.* The excited voices kept coming
out of the speakers on the desk.

It was not a television set he had heard. The sounds
were the sounds of the Courtleigh Manor kitchen. Men
shouting, other men responding angrily; the commands of
superiors, the whining complaints of subordinates. All
frantic, agitated . . . mostly unintelligible. They must
have driven those listening furious.

Then Alex saw the revolving reels of the tape deck. For
some reason, it was on the floor, to the right of the desk.
A small, compact Wollensak recorder, spinning as if nothing had happened.

McAuliff grabbed the two speakers and crashed them
repeatedly against each other until the wood splintered
and the cases cracked open. He tore out the black shells
and the wires and threw them across the room. He
crossed to the right of the desk and crushed his heel into
the Wollensak, grinding the numerous flat switches until a

puff of smoke emerged from the interior and the reels stopped their movement. He reached down and ripped off the tape; he could burn it, but there was nothing of consequence recorded. He rolled the two reels across the floor, the thin strand of tape forming a narrow *V* on the carpet.

The Jamaican groaned; his eyes blinked as he swallowed and coughed.

Alex picked up the pistol on the floor, and squeezed it into his belt. He went into the bathroom, turned on the cold water, and threw a towel into the basin.

He pulled the drenched towel from the sink and walked back to the coughing, injured Jamaican. He knelt down, helped the man into a sitting position, and blotted his face. The water flowed down on the man's shirt and trousers . . . water mingled with blood.

"I'm sorry," said Alex. "I didn't mean to hurt you. I wouldn't have if you hadn't reached for that goddamned pistol."

"*Mon!*" The Jamaican coughed his interruption. "You *crazy-mon!*" The Jamaican held his chest and winced painfully as he struggled to his feet. "You break up . . . everyt'ing, mon!" said the injured man, looking at the smashed equipment.

"I certainly did! Maybe your Mr. Craft will get the message. If he wants to play industrial espionage, let him play in somebody else's backyard. I resent the intrusion . . . Come on, let's go." Alex took the man by the arm and began leading him to the door.

"No, mon!" shouted the black, resisting.

"*Yes,* mon," said McAuliff quietly. "You're coming with me."

"Where, mon?"

"To see a little old man who runs a fish store, that's all." Alex shoved him; the Negro gripped his side. His ribs were broken, thought McAuliff.

"Please, mon! No *police,* mon! I lose everyt'ing!" The Jamaican's dark eyes were pleading as he held his ribs.

"You went for a gun, mon! That's a very serious thing to do."

"Them not my gun. Them gun got no bullets, mon."

"*What?*"

"Look-see, mon! Please! I got good job . . . I don' hurt nobody . . ."

Alex wasn't listening. He reached into his belt for the pistol.

It was no weapon at all.

It was a starter's gun; the kind held up by referees at track meets.

"Oh, for Christ's sake . . ." Arthur Craft, Junior, played games—little boys' games with little boys' toys.

McAuliff looked at the panicked Jamaican.

"Okay, mon. You just tell your employer what I said. The next time, I'll haul him into court."

It was a silly thing to say, thought Alex, as he walked out into the corridor, slamming the door behind him. There'd be no courts; Julian Warfield or his adversary, R. C. Holcroft, was far more preferable. Alongside Dunstone, Limited, and British Intelligence, Arthur Craft was a cipher.

An unimportant intrusion that in all likelihood was no more.

He walked out of the elevator and tried to recall the location of the telephone booths. They were to the left of the entrance, past the front desk, he remembered.

He nodded to clerks while thinking of Westmore Tallon's private number.

"Mr. McAuliff, sir?" The speaker was a tall Jamaican with very broad shoulders, emphasized by a tight nylon jacket.

"Yes?"

"Would you come with me, please?"

Alex looked at the man. He was neat, the trousers pressed, a white shirt and a tie in evidence beneath the jacket. "No . . . why should I?"

"Please, we have very little time. A man is waiting for you outside. A Mr. Tucker."

"What? How did—"

"*Please,* Mr. McAuliff. I cannot stay here."

Alex followed the Jamaican out the glass doors of the entrance. As they reached the driveway, he saw the man in the yellow shirt—Craft's man—walking on the path from the parking lot; the man stopped and stared at him, as if unsure what to do.

"Hurry, please," said the Jamaican, several steps in front of McAuliff, breaking into a run. "Down past the gates. The car is waiting!"

They ran down the drive, past the stone gateposts.

The green Chevrolet was on the side of the road, its motor running. The Jamaican opened the back door for Alex.

"Get in!"

McAuliff did so.

Sam Tucker, his massive frame taking up most of the back seat, his shock of red hair reflecting the outside lights, extended his hand.

"Good to see you, boy!"

"Sam!"

The car lurched forward, throwing Alex into the felt. In the front seat, McAuliff saw that there were three men. The driver wore a baseball cap; the third man—nearly as large as Sam Tucker—was squeezed between the driver and the Jamaican who had met him inside the Courtleigh lobby. Alex turned back to Tucker.

"What *is* all this, Sam? Where the hell have you been?"

The answer, however, did not come from Sam Tucker. Instead, the black by the window, the man who had led Alex down the driveway, turned and spoke quietly.

"Mr. Tucker has been with us, Mr. McAuliff . . . If events can be controlled, we are your link to the Halidon."

14

THEY DROVE for nearly an hour. Always climbing, higher and higher, it seemed to McAuliff. The winding roads snaked upward, the turns sudden, the curves hidden by sweeping waterfalls of tropic greenery. There were stretches of unpaved road. The automobile took them poorly; the whining of the low gear was proof of the strain.

McAuliff and Sam Tucker spoke quietly, knowing their conversation was overheard by those in front. That knowledge did not seem to bother Tucker.

Sam's story was totally logical, considering his habits and life style. Sam Tucker had friends, or acquaintances, in many parts of the world no one knew about. Not that he intentionally concealed their identities, only that they were part of his personal, not professional, life.

One of these people had been Walter Piersall.

"I mentioned him to you last year, Alexander," said Tucker in the darkness of the back seat. "In Ocho Rios."

"I don't remember."

"I told you I'd met an academic fellow in Carrick Foyle. I was going to spend a couple of weekends with him."

That was it, thought McAuliff. The name "Carrick Foyle"; he *had* heard it before. "I remember now. Something about a lecture series at the Kingston Institute."

"That's right. Walter was a very classy type—an anthro man who didn't bore you to death. I cabled him I was coming back."

"You also got in touch with Hanley. He's the one who set off the alarms."

"I called Bob after I got into Montego. For a little sporting life. There was no way I could reach him later. We traveled fast, and when we got where we were going, there was no telephone. I figured he'd be mad as hell."

"He was worried, not mad. It was quite a disappearing act."

"He should know better. I have friends on this island, not enemies. At least, none either of us knows about."

"What happened? Where did you go?"

Tucker told him.

When Sam arrived in Montego Bay, there was a message from Piersall at the arrivals desk. He was to call the anthropologist in Carrick Foyle after he was settled. He did, but was told by a servant in Carrick Foyle that Piersall might not return until late that night.

Tucker then phoned his old friend Hanley, and the two men got drunk, as was their established custom at reunions.

In the morning, while Hanley was still sleeping, Sam left the hotel to pick up cigars.

"It's not the sort of place that's large on room service, boy."

"I gathered that," said Alex.

"Out on the street, our friends here—" Tucker gestured toward the front seat—"were waiting in a station wagon—"

"Mr. Tucker was being followed," interrupted the black by the window. "Word of this reached Dr. Piersall. He sent us to Mo'Bay to look after his friend. Mr. Tucker gets up early."

Sam grinned. "You know me. Even with the juice, I can't sleep long."

"I know," said Alex, remembering too many hotel rooms and survey campsites in which Tucker had wandered about at the first light of dawn.

"There was a little misunderstanding," continued Sam. "The boys here said Piersall was waiting for me. I figured, what the hell, the lads thought enough of me to stick out the night, I'd go with 'em straight off. Old Robert wouldn't be up for an hour or so . . . I'd call him from Piersall's house. But, goddamn it, we didn't go to Carrick Foyle. We headed for a bamboo camp down the Martha Brae. It took us damn near two hours to get there, a godforsaken place, Alexander."

When they arrived at the bamboo camp, Walter Piersall greeted Sam warmly. But within minutes Tucker realized that something had happened to the man. He was not the same person that Sam had known a year ago. There was a zealousness, an intensity not in evidence twelve months ago.

Walter Piersall was caught up in things Jamaican. The quiet anthropologist had become a fierce partisan in the battles being waged between social and political factions within Jamaica. He was suddenly a jealous guardian of the islanders' rights, an enemy of the outside exploiters.

"I've seen it happen dozens of times, Alexander," said Sam. "From the Tasman to the Caribbean; it's a kind of island fever. Possession . . . oneness, I think. Men migrate for taxes or climate or whatever the hell and they turn into self-proclaimed protectors of their sanctuaries . . . the Catholic convert telling the pope he's not with it . . ."

In his cross-island proselytizing, Piersall began to hear whispers of an enormous land conspiracy. In his own backyard in the parish of Trelawny. At first he dismissed them; they involved men with whom one might disagree, but whose integrity was not debated. Men of extraordinary stature.

The conspiratorial syndrome was an ever-present nuisance in any infant, growing government; Piersall understood that. In Jamaica it was given credence by the influx of foreign capital looking for tax havens, by a parliament ordering more reform programs than it could possibly control, and by a small, wealthy island aristocracy trying to protect itself—the bribe was an all-too-prevalent way of life.

Piersall had decided, once and for all, to put the whispered rumors to rest. Four months ago he'd gone to the Ministry of Territories and filed a Resolution of Intent to purchase by way of syndication twenty square miles of land on the north border of the Cock Pit. It was a harmless gesture, really. Such a purchase would take years in the courts and involve the satisfactory settling of historic island treaties; his point was merely to prove Kingston's willingness to accept the filing. That the land was not controlled by outsiders.

"Since that day, Alexander, Piersall's life was made a hell." Sam Tucker lit a thin native cigar; the aromatic smoke whipped out the open window into the onrushing darkness. "He was harassed by the police, pulled into the parish courts dozens of times for nonsense; his lectures were canceled at the university and the Institute; his telephone tapped—conversations repeated by government attorneys . . . Finally, the whispers he tried to silence killed him."

McAuliff said nothing for several moments. "Why was

Piersall so anxious to contact you?" he asked Tucker.

"In my cable I told him I was doing a big survey in Trelawny. A project out of London by way of Kingston. I didn't want him to think I was traveling six thousand miles to be his guest; he was a busy man, Alexander."

"But you were in Kingston tonight. Not in a bamboo camp on the Martha Brae. Two of these men"—McAuliff gestured front—"followed me this afternoon. In this car."

"Let me answer you, Mr. McAuliff," said the Jamaican by the window, turning and placing his arm over the seat. "Kingston intercepted Mr. Tuck's cable; they made kling-kling addition, mon. They thought Mr. Tuck was mixed up with Dr. Piersall in bad ways. Bad ways for them, mon. They sent dangerous men to Mo'Bay. To find out what Mr. Tuck was doing—"

"How do you know this?" broke in Alex.

For the briefest instant, the black by the window glanced at the driver. It was difficult to tell in the dim light and rushing shadows, but McAuliff thought the driver nodded imperceptibly.

"We took the men who came to Mo'Bay after Mr. Tuck. That is all you need to know, mon. What was learned caused Dr. Piersall much concern. So much, mon, that we flew to Kingston. To reach you, mon . . . Dr. Piersall was killed for that."

"Who killed him?"

"If we knew, there would be dead men hung in Victoria Park."

"What did you learn . . . from the men in Montego?"

Again, the black who spoke seemed to glance at the driver. In seconds he replied, "That people in Kingston believed Dr. Piersall would interfere further. When he went to find you, mon, it was their proof. By killing him they took a big sea urchin out of their foot."

"And you don't know who did it—"

"Hired niggers, mon," interrupted the black.

"It's insane!" McAuliff spoke to himself as much as to Sam Tucker. "People killing people . . . men following other men. It's goddamn crazy!"

"Why is it crazy to a man who visits Tallon's Fish Market?" asked the black suddenly.

"How did—" McAuliff stopped. He was confused; he had been so careful. "How did you know that? I lost you at the racetrack!"

The Jamaican smiled, his bright teeth catching the light from the careening reflections through the windshield. "Ocean trout is not really preferable to the fresh-water variety, *mon.*"

The counterman! The nonchalant counterman in the striped linen apron. "The man behind the counter is one of you. That's pretty good," said McAuliff quietly.

"We're *very* good. Westmore Tallon is a British agent . . . So like the English: Enlist the clandestine help of the vested interests. And so fundamentally stupid. Tallon's senile Etonian classmates might trust him; his countrymen do not."

The Jamaican removed his arm from the seat and turned front. The answer was over.

Sam Tucker spoke pensively, openly. "Alexander . . . now tell me what the hell is going on. What have you done, boy?"

McAuliff turned to Sam. The huge, vital, capable old friend was staring at him in the darkness, the rapid flashes of light bouncing across his face. Tucker's eyes held confusion and hurt. And anger.

What in hell *had* he done, thought Alex.

"Here we are, mon," said the driver in the baseball cap, who had not spoken throughout the trip.

McAuliff looked out the windows. The ground was flat now, but high in the hills and surrounded by them. Everything was sporadically illuminated by a Jamaican moon filtering through the low-flying clouds of the Blue Mountains. They were on a dirt road; in the distance, perhaps a quarter of a mile away, was a structure, a small cabinlike building. A dim light could be seen through a single window. On the right were two other . . . structures. Not buildings, not houses or cabins, nothing really definable; just free-form, sagging silhouettes . . . translucent? Yes . . . wires, cloth. Or netting . . . They were large tentlike covers, supported by numerous poles. And then Alex understood: beyond the tents the ground was matted flat and along the border, spaced every thirty or forty feet apart, were unlit cradle torches. The tents were camouflaged hangars; the ground a landing strip.

They were at an unmarked airfield in the mountains.

The Chevrolet slowed down as it approached what turned out to be a small farmhouse. There was an ancient tractor beyond the edge of the building; field tools—

plows, shoulder yokes, pitchforks—were scattered about carelessly. In the moonlight the equipment looked like stationary relics. Unused, dead remembrances only.

Camouflage.

As the hangars were camouflaged.

An airfield no map would indicate.

"Mr. McAuliff? Mr. Tucker? If you would come with me, please." The black spokesman by the window opened the door and stepped out. Sam and Alex did the same. The driver and the third Jamaican remained inside, and when the disembarked passengers stepped away from the car, the driver accelerated the motor and sped off down the dirt road.

"Where are they going?" asked McAuliff anxiously.

"To conceal the automobile," answered the black. "Kingston sends out ganga air patrols at night, hoping to find such fields as these. With luck to spot light aircraft on narcotics runs."

"This ganga country? I thought it was north," said Tucker.

The Jamaican laughed. "Ganga, weed, poppy . . . north, west, east. It is a healthy export industry, mon. But not ours . . . Come, let us go inside."

The door of the miniature farmhouse opened as the three of them approached. In the frame stood the light-skinned black whom Alex had first seen in a striped apron behind the counter at Tallon's.

The interior of the small house was primitive: wooden chairs, a thick round table in the center of the single room, an army cot against the wall. The jarring contradiction was a complicated radio set on a table to the right of the door. The light in the window was from the shaded lamp in front of the machinery; a generator could be heard providing what electricity was necessary.

All this McAuliff observed within seconds of entering. Then he saw a second man, standing in shadows across the room, his back toward the others. The body—the cut of the coat, the shoulders, the tapered waist, the tailored trousers—was familiar.

The man turned around; the light from the table lamp illuminated his features.

Charles Whitehall stared at McAuliff and then nodded once, slowly.

* * *

The door opened, and the driver of the Chevrolet entered with the third black. He walked to the round table in the center of the room and sat down. He removed his baseball cap, revealing a large shaven head.

"My name is Moore. Barak Moore, Mr. McAuliff. To ease your concerns, the woman, Alison Booth, has been called. She was told that you went down to the Ministry for a conference."

"She won't believe that," replied Alex.

"If she cares to check further, she will be informed that you are with Latham at a warehouse. There is nothing to worry about, mon."

Sam Tucker stood by the door; he was relaxed but curious. And strong; his thick arms were folded across his chest, his lined features—tanned by the California sun—showed his age and accentuated his leathery strength. Charles Whitehall stood by the window in the left wall, his elegant, arrogant face exuding contempt.

The light-skinned black from Tallon's Fish Market and the two Jamaican "guerrillas" had pulled their chairs back against the far right wall, away from the center of attention. They were telegraphing the fact that Barak Moore was their superior.

"Please, sit down." Barak Moore indicated the chairs around the table. There were three. Tucker and McAuliff looked at each other; there was no point in refusing. They walked to the table and sat down. Charles Whitehall remained standing by the window. Moore glanced up at him. "Will you join us?"

"If I feel like sitting," answered Whitehall.

Moore smiled and spoke while looking at Whitehall. "Charley-mon finds it difficult to be in the same room with me, much less at the same table."

"Then why is he here?" asked Sam Tucker.

"He had no idea he was going to be until a few minutes before landing. We switched pilots in Savanna-la-Mar."

"His name is Charles Whitehall," said Alex, speaking to Sam. "He's part of the survey. I didn't know he was going to be here either."

"What's your field, boy?" Tucker leaned back in his chair and spoke to Whitehall.

"Jamaica . . . *boy*."

"I meant no offense, son."

"You are offensive" was Whitehall's simple reply.

"Charley and me," continued Barak Moore, "we are at the opposite poles of the politic. In your country, you have the term 'white trash'; he considers me 'black garbage.' For roughly the same reasons: He thinks I'm too crude, too loud, too unwashed. I am an uncouth revolutionary in Charley-mon's eyes . . . he is a graceful rebel, you see." Moore swept his hand in front of him, balletically, insultingly. "But our rebellions are different, *very* different, mon. I want Jamaica for *all* the people. He wants it for only a few."

Whitehall stood motionless as he replied. "You are as blind now as you were a decade ago. The only thing that has changed is your name, Bramwell Moore." Whitehall sneered vocally as he continued. *"Barak* . . . as childish and meaningless as the social philosophy you espouse; the sound of a jungle toad."

Moore swallowed before he answered. "I'd as soon kill you,· I think you know that. But it would be as counterproductive as the solutions you seek to impose on our homeland. We have a common enemy, you and I. Make the best of it, *fascisti-mon.*"

"The vocabulary of your mentors. Did you learn it by rote, or did they make you read?"

"Look!" McAuliff interrupted angrily. "You can fight or call names, or kill each other for all I give a damn, but I want to get back to the hotel!" He turned to Barak Moore. "Whatever you have to say, get it over with."

"He has a point, Charley-mon," said Moore. "We come later . . . I will, as they say, summarize. It is a brief summary, mon . . . That there are development plans for a large area of the island—plans that exclude the people—is now established. Dr. Piersall's death confirms it. That your geological survey is tied to those plans, we logically assume; therefore, the Ministry and the Royal Society are—knowingly or unknowingly—concealing the identity of the financial interests. Furthermore, Mr. McAuliff here is not unaware of these facts, because he deals with British Intelligence through the despicable Westmore Tallon . . . That is the summary. Where do we go?" Moore stared at Alex, his eyes small black craters in a huge mountain of dark skin. "We have a right to go somewhere, Mr. McAuliff."

"Before you shove him against the wall, boy," interjected Sam Tucker, to Alex's surprise, "remember, I'm no part of you. I don't say I won't be, but I'm not now."

"I should think you'd be as interested as we are, Tucker." The absence of the "Mister," McAuliff thought, was Moore's hostile response to Sam's use of the word "boy." Moore did not realize that Tucker used the term for everyone.

"Don't mistake me," added Sam. "I'm interested. Just don't go running off too fast at the mouth . . . I think you should say what you know, Alex."

McAuliff looked at Tucker, then Moore, then over at Whitehall. Nothing in Holcroft's instructions included such a confrontation. Except the admonition to *keep it simple; build on part of the truth.*

"The people in British Intelligence—and everything they represent—want to stop this development as much as you do. But they need information. They think the Halidon has it. They want to make contact with the Halidon. I'm supposed to try and make that contact."

Alex wasn't sure what to expect from his statement, but certainly not what happened. Barak Moore's blunt features, grotesque under the immense shaven head, slowly changed from immobility to amusement, from amusement to the pinched flesh of outright mirth; it was a humor based in cruelty, however. His large mouth opened, and a coughing, malevolent laugh emerged.

From the window there was another sound, another laugh: higher and jackal-like. Charles Whitehall's elegant neck was stretched back, his head tilted toward the ceiling, his arms folded across his tailored jacket. He looked like some thin, black Oriental priest finding amusement in a novice's ignorance.

The three Jamaicans in the row of chairs, their white teeth gleaming in the shadows, were smiling, their bodies shaking slightly in silent laughter.

"What's so goddamn funny?" asked McAuliff, annoyed by the undefined humiliation.

"Funny, mon? Many times more than *funny*. The mongoose chases the deadly snake, so the snake wants to make friends?" Moore laughed his hideous laugh once again. "It is not in any law of nature, mon!"

"What Moore is telling you, Mr. McAuliff," broke in Whitehall, approaching the table, "is that it's preposterous to think the Halidon would cooperate with the English. It is inconceivable. It is the Halidons of this island that drove the British from Jamaica. Put simply, M.I.5 is not to be trusted."

"What *is* the Halidon?" Alex watched the black scholar, who stood motionless, his eyes on Barak Moore.

"It is a force," said Whitehall quietly.

McAuliff looked at Moore; he was returning Whitehall's stare. "That doesn't say very much, does it?"

"There is no one in this room who can tell you more, mon." Barak Moore shifted his gaze to Alex.

Charles Whitehall spoke. "There are no identities, McAuliff. The Halidon is an unseen curia, a court that has no chambers. No one is lying to you. Not about this . . . This small contingent here, these three men; Moore's elite corps, as it were—"

"Your words, Charley-mon! We don't use them! *Elite!*" Barak spat out the word.

"Immaterial," continued Whitehall. "I venture to say there are no more than five hundred people in all Jamaica who have heard of the Halidon. Less than fifty who know for certain any of its members. Those that do would rather face the pains of Obeah than reveal identities."

"*Obeah!*" Sam Tucker's comment was in his voice. He had no use for the jingoistic diabolism that filled thousands upon thousands of native minds with terror—Jamaica's counterpart of the Haitian voodoo. "Obeah's horseshit, boy! The sooner your hill and village people learn that, the better off they'll be!"

"If you think it's restricted to the hills and the villages, you are sadly mistaken," said Whitehall. "We in Jamaica do not offer Obeah as a tourist attraction. We have too much respect for it."

Alex looked up at Whitehall. "Do *you* have respect for it? Are *you* a believer?"

Whitehall leveled his gaze at McAuliff, his eyes knowing—with a trace of humor. "Yes, Mr. McAuliff, I have respect for Obeah. I have traced its strains to its origins in Mother Africa. I have seen what it's done to the veldt, in the jungles. Respect; I do not say commitment or belief."

"Then the Halidon is an organization." McAuliff took out his cigarettes. Barak Moore reached over to accept one; Sam Tucker leaned forward in his chair. Alex continued. "A secret society that has a lot of clout. Why? . . . Obeah?"

"Partly, mon," answered Moore, lighting his cigarette like a man who does not smoke often. "It is also very rich. It is whispered that it possesses wealth beyond anyone's thinking, mon."

Suddenly, McAuliff realized the obvious. He looked back and forth between Charles Whitehall and Barak Moore.

"Christ Almighty! You're as anxious to reach the Halidon as I am! As British Intelligence is!"

"That is so, mon." Moore crushed out his barely smoked cigarette on the surface of the table.

"Why?" asked Alex.

Charles Whitehall replied. "We are dealing with two giants, Mr. McAuliff. One black, one white. The Halidon must win."

15

THE MEETING in the isolated farmhouse high in the hills
of the Blue Mountains lasted until two o'clock in the
morning.

The common objective was agreed to: contact with the
Halidon.

And since Barak Moore's and Charles Whitehall's judgment that the Halidon would not deal directly with British
Intelligence was convincing, McAuliff further agreed to
cooperate with the two black antagonists. Barak and his
"elite" guerrillas would provide additional safety for the
survey team. Two of the three men sitting against the wall
of the farmhouse would fly to Ocho Rios and be hired as
carriers.

If the Jamaicans suspected he knew more than he was
telling them, they did not press him, thought Alex. They
accepted his story—now told twice to Whitehall—that initially he had taken the survey as an investment for future
work. From Kingston. M.I.5 was a complication thrust
upon him.

It was as if they understood he had his own concerns,
unrelated to theirs. And only when he was sure those concerns were not in conflict would he be completely open.

Insane circumstances had forced him into a war he
wanted no part of, but one thing was clear above all other
considerations: the safety of those he had brought to the
island.

. . . Two things.

One million dollars.

From either enemy. Dunstone, Limited, or British Intelligence.

"M.I.5 has not told you, then, who is behind this land
rape," said Barak Moore—not asking a question—continuing immediately. "It goes beyond the Kingston flunkies,
mon."

"If the British reach the Halidon, they'll tell them what
they know," said McAuliff. "I'm sure of that. They want
to pool their information, that much they've told me."

"Which means the English assume the Halidon know a

great deal," added Whitehall pensively. "I wonder if that is so."

"They have their reasons," said Alex cautiously. "There was a previous survey team."

The Jamaicans knew of it. Its disappearance was either proof of the Halidon's opposition or an isolated act of theft and murder by a roving band of primitive hill people in the Cock Pit.

There was no way to tell.

Circles within circles.

What of the Marquis de Chatellerault? Why had he insisted upon meeting with Whitehall in Savanna-la-Mar?

"The marquis is a nervous man," said Whitehall. "He claims to have widespread interests on the island. He smells bad fish with this survey."

"Has it occurred to you that Chatellerault is himself involved?" McAuliff spoke directly to the black scholar. "M.I.5 thinks so. Tallon told me that this afternoon."

"If so, the marquis does not trust his colleagues."

"Did Chatellerault mention anyone else on the team?" asked Alex, afraid of the answer.

Whitehall looked at McAuliff and replied simply. "He made several allusions, and I told him that I wasn't interested in side issues. They were not pertinent; I made that clear."

"Thank you."

"You're welcome."

Sam Tucker raised his scraggy eyebrows, his expression dubious. "What the hell *was* pertinent? What did he want?"

"To be kept informed of the survey's progress. Report all developments."

"Why did he think you'd do that?" Sam leaned forward in the chair.

"I would be paid handsomely, to begin with. And there could be other areas of interest, which, frankly, there are not."

"*Ha,* mon!" interjected Moore. "You see, they believe Charley-mon can be bought! They know better with Barak Moore!"

Whitehall looked at the revolutionary, dismissing him. "There is little to pay you for." He opened his silver cigarette case; Moore grinned at the sight of it. Whitehall closed it slowly, placed it at his right, and lighted his cigarette with a match. "Let's get on. I'd rather not be here all night."

"Okay, mon." Barak glanced at each man quickly. "We want the same as the English. To reach the Halidon." Moore pronounced the word in the Jamaican dialect: *hollydawn*. "But the Halidon must come to us. There must be a strong reason. We cannot cry out for them. They will not come into the open."

"I don't understand a damn thing about any of this," said Tucker, lighting a thin cigar, "but if you wait for them, you could be sitting on your asses a long goddamn time."

"We think there is a way. We think Dr. Piersall provided it." Moore hunched his shoulders, conveying a sense of uncertainty, as if he was not sure how to choose his words. "For months Dr. Piersall tried to . . . define the Halidon. To seek it out, to understand. He went back into Caribe history, to the Arawak, to Africa. To find meaning." Moore paused and looked at Whitehall. "He read your books, Charley-mon. I told him you were a bad liar, a diseased goat. He said you did not lie in your books . . . From many small things, Dr. Piersall put together pieces of the puzzle, he called it. His papers are in Carrick Foyle."

"Just a minute." Sam Tucker was irritated. "Walter talked a goddamned streak for two days. On the Martha Brae, in the plane, at the Sheraton. He never mentioned any of this. Why didn't he?" Tucker looked over at the Jamaicans against the wall, at the two who had been with him since Montego Bay.

The black who had spoken in the Chevrolet replied. "He would have, mon. It was agreed to wait until McAuliff was with you. It is not a story one repeats often."

"What did the puzzle tell him?" asked Alex.

"Only part, mon," said Barak Moore. "Only part of the puzzle was complete. But Dr. Piersall arrived at several theories. To begin with, Halidon is an offshoot from the Coromanteen tribe. They isolated themselves after the Maroon wars, for they would not agree to the treaties that called upon the Maroon nation—the Coromantees—to run down and capture runaway slaves for the English.

The Halidon would not become bounty hunters of brother Africans. For decades they were nomadic. Then, perhaps two hundred, two hundred and fifty years ago, they settled in one location. Unknown, inaccessible to the outside world. But they did not divorce themselves from the outside world. Selected males were sent out to accomplish what the elders believed should be accomplished. To this day it is so. Women are brought in to bear children so that the pains of inbreeding are avoided . . . And two final points: The Halidon community is high in the mountains where the winds are strong, of that Piersall was certain. And last, the Halidon has great riches . . . These are the pieces of the puzzle; there are many missing."

No one spoke for a while. Then Tucker broke the silence.

"It's a hell of a story," said Sam "but I'm not sure where it gets us. Our knowing it won't bring them out. And you said we can't go after them. Goddamn! If this . . . tribe has been in the mountains for two hundred years and nobody's found them, we're not likely to, boy! Where is 'the way' Walter provided?"

Charles Whitehall answered. "If Dr. Piersall's conclusions are true, the *way* is in the knowledge of them, Mr. Tucker."

"Would you explain that?" asked Alex.

In an unexpected show of deference, the erudite scholar turned to the rough-hewn guerrilla. "I think . . . Barak Moore should amplify. I believe the key is in what he said a few minutes ago. That the Halidon must have a strong reason to contact us."

"You are not mistaken, mon. Dr. Piersall was certain that if word got to the Halidon that their existence—and their great wealth—had been confirmed by a small band of responsible men, they would send an emissary. They guard their wealth above all things, Piersall believed. But they have to be convinced beyond doubt . . . That is the way."

"Who do you convince?" asked Alex.

"Someone must travel to Maroon Town, on the border of the Cock Pit. This person should ask for an audience with the Colonel of the Maroon people, offer to pay much, much money. It was Dr. Piersall's belief that this man, whose title is passed from one generation to the next within the same tribal family, is the only link to the Halidon."

"The story is told him, then?"

"No, McAuliff, mon! Not even the Colonel of the Maroons is to be so trusted. At any rate, it would be meaningless to him. Dr. Piersall's studies hinted that the Halidon kept open one perpetual line to the African brothers. It was called 'nagarro'—"

"The Akwamu tongue," broke in Whitehall. "The language is extinct, but derivations exist in the Ashanti and Mossai-Grusso dialects. 'Nagarro' is an abstraction, best translated to mean 'a spirit materialized.'"

"A spirit . . ." Alex began to repeat the phrase, then stopped. "Proof . . . proof of something real."

"Yes," replied Whitehall.

"Where is it?" asked McAuliff.

"The proof is in the meaning of another word," said Barak Moore. "The meaning of the word 'Halidon.'"

"What is it?"

"I do not know—"

"Goddamn!" Sam Tucker exploded. Barak Moore held up his hand, silencing him.

"Piersall found it. It is to be delivered to the Colonel of the Maroon people. For him to take up into the mountains."

McAuliff's jaws were tense; he controlled himself as best he could. "We can't deliver what we don't have."

"You will have it, mon." Barak settled his gaze on Alexander. "A month ago Dr. Piersall brought me to his home in Carrick Foyle. He gave me my instructions. Should anything happen to him, I was to go to a place in the forests of his property. I have committed this place to memory, mon. There, deep under the ground, is an oil-cloth packet. Inside the packet is a paper; on it is written the meaning of the Halidon."

The driver on the ride back to Kingston was the Jamaican who was obviously Barak Moore's second-in-command, the black who had done the talking on the trip out to the airfield. His name was Floyd. Charles Whitehall sat in the front seat with him; Alex and Sam Tucker sat in back.

"If you need stories to say where you were," said Floyd

to all of them, "there was a long equipment meeting at a Ministry warehouse. On Crawford Street, near the docks. It can be verified."

"Who were we meeting with?" asked Sam.

"A man named Latham. He is in charge—"

"*Latham?*" broke in Alex, recalling all too vividly his telephone conversation with the ministry man that afternoon. "He's the one—"

"We know," interrupted Floyd, grinning in the rearview mirror at McAuliff. "He's one of us, mon."

He let himself into the room as quietly as possible. It was nearly 3:30; the Courtleigh Manor was quiet, the nocturnal games concluded.

He closed the door silently and started across the soft carpet. A light was on in Alison's room, the door open perhaps a foot. His own room was dark. Alison had turned off all the lamps; they had been on when he left her five hours ago.

Why had she done that?

He approached the slightly open door, removing his jacket as he did so.

There was a click behind him. He turned. A second later, the bedside lamp was snapped on, flooding the room with its dim light, harsh only at the source.

Alison was sitting up in his bed. He could see that her right hand gripped the small deadly weapon "issued by the London police"; she was placing it at her side, obscuring it with the covers.

"Hello, Alex."

"Hello."

It was an awkward moment.

"I stayed here because I thought your friend Tucker might call. I might not have heard the telephone."

"I could think of better reasons." He smiled and approached the bed. She picked up the cylinder and twisted it. There was the same click he had heard seconds ago. She placed the strange weapon on the night table.

"Also, I wanted to talk."

"You sound ominous." He sat down. "I wasn't able to call you . . . everything happened so fast. Sam showed up; he just walked through the goddamn lobby doors and wondered why I was so upset . . . Then, as he was registering, the call came from Latham. He was really in a hurry. I think I threw him with Ocho Rios tomorrow. There was a lot of equipment that hadn't been shipped to Boscobel—"

"Your phone didn't ring," interrupted Alison quietly.

"What?"

"Mr. Latham didn't ring through to your room."

McAuliff was prepared; he had remembered *a little thing*. "Because I'd left word we were having dinner. They were sending a page to the dining room."

"That's very good, Alex."

"What's the matter with you? I told the clerk to call you and explain. We *were* in a hurry; Latham said we had to get to the warehouse . . . down on Crawford Street, by the docks . . . before they closed the check-in books for the night."

"That's not very good. You can do better."

McAuliff saw that Alison was deadly serious. And angry. "Why do you say that?"

"The front desk did not call me; there was no explaining *clerk* . . ." Alison pronounced the word "clerk" in the American fashion, exaggerating the difference from English speech. It was insulting. "An 'assistant' of Mr. Latham's telephoned. He wasn't very good, either. He didn't know what to say when I asked to speak to Latham; he didn't expect that . . . Did you know that Gerald Latham lives in the Barbican district of Kingston? He's listed right in the telephone book."

The girl stopped; the silence was strained. Alex spoke softly as he made the statement. "He was home."

"He was home," replied Alison. "Don't worry. He didn't know who called him. I spoke to a woman first, and when he got on the phone I hung up."

McAuliff inhaled a deep breath and reached into his shirt pocket for his pack of cigarettes. He wasn't sure there was anything to say. "I'm sorry."

"So am I," she said quietly. "I'll write you out a proper letter of resignation in the morning. You'll have to accept a promissory note for the airfare and whatever other expenses I'm liable for. I'll need what money I have for a while. I'm sure I'll find a situation."

"You can't do that." McAuliff found himself saying the words with strength, in utter conviction. And he knew why. Alison was perfectly willing to leave the survey; she was *going* to leave it. If her motive—or motives—for coming to Jamaica were not what she had said they were, she would not do that. "For Christ's sake, you can't resign because I lied about a few hours! Damn it, Alison, I'm not accountable to you!"

"Oh, stop behaving like a pompous, wounded ass! You don't do that very well, either . . . I will *not* go through the labyrinth again; I'm sick to death of it. No more, do you hear!" Suddenly her voice fell and she caught her breath—and the fear was in her eyes. "I can't stand it any longer."

He stared at her. "What do you mean?"

"You elaborately described a long interview with the Jamaican police this afternoon. The station, the district, the officers . . . very detailed, Alex. I called them after I hung up on Latham. They'd never heard of you."

16

HE KNEW he had to go back to the beginning—to the very beginning of the insanity. He had to tell her the truth. There was relief in sharing it.

All of it. So it made sense, what sense there was to make.

He did.

And as he told the story, he found himself trying to understand all over again. He spoke slowly, in a monotone actually; it was the drone of a man speaking through the mists of confusion.

Of the strange message from Dunstone, Limited, that brought him to London from New York, and a man named "Julian Warfield." Of a "financial analyst" at the Savoy Hotel whose plastic card identified him as "Holcroft, R. C., British Intelligence." The pressurized days of living in two worlds that denied their own realities—the covert training, the secret meetings, the vehicle transfers, the hiring of survey personnel under basically false pretenses. Of a panicked, weak James Ferguson, hired to spy on the survey by a man named "Arthur Craft the Younger," who was not satisfied being one of the richest men in Jamaica. Of an arrogant Charles Whitehall, whose brilliance and scholarship could not lift him above a fanatic devotion to an outworn, outdated, dishonored concept. Of an arthritic little islander, whose French and African blood had strained its way into the Jamaican aristocracy and M.I.5 by way of Eton and Oxford.

Of Sam Tucker's odd tale of the transformation of Walter Piersall, anthropologist, converted by "island fever" into a self-professed guardian of his tropic sanctuary.

And finally of a shaven-headed guerrilla revolutionary named "Barak Moore." And everyone's search for an "unseen curia" called "the Halidon."

Insanity. But all very, very real.

The sun sprayed its shafts of early light into the billowing gray clouds above the Blue Mountains. McAuliff sat in the frame of the balcony door; the wet scents of the Jamaican dawn came up from the moist grounds and down from the tall palms, cooling his nostrils and so his skin.

He was nearly finished now. They had talked—he had talked—for an hour and forty-five minutes. There remained only the Marquis de Chatellerault.

Alison was still in the bed, sitting up against the pillows. Her eyes were tired, but she did not take them off him.

He wondered what she would say—or do—when he mentioned Chatellerault. He was afraid.

"You're tired; so am I. Why don't I finish in the morning?"

"It is morning."

"Later, then."

"I don't think so. I'd rather hear it all at once."

"There isn't much more."

"Then I'd say you saved the best for last. Am I right?" She could not conceal the silent alarm she felt. She looked away from him, at the light coming through the balcony doors. It was brighter now, that strange admixture of pastel yellow and hot orange that is peculiar to the Jamaican dawn.

"You know it concerns you . . ."

"Of course I know it. I knew it last night." She returned her eyes to him. "I didn't want to admit it to myself . . . but I knew it. It was all too tidy."

"Chatellerault," he said softly. "He's here."

"Oh, *God*," she whispered.

"He can't touch you. Believe me."

"He followed me. Oh my God . . ."

McAuliff got up and crossed to the bed. He sat on the edge and gently stroked her hair. "If I thought he could harm you, I never would have told you. I'd simply have him . . . removed." *Oh, Christ*, thought Alex. How easily the new words came. Would he soon be using *kill*, or *eliminate?*

"Right from the very start, it was all programmed. *I* was programmed." She stared at the balcony, allowing his hand to caress the side of her face, as if oblivious to it. "I should have realized; they don't let you go that easily."

"Who?"

"All of them, my darling," she answered, taking his hand, holding it to her lips. "Whatever names you want to give them, it's not important. The letters, the numbers, the official-sounding nonsense . . . I was warned, I can't say I wasn't."

"How?" He pulled her hand down, forcing her to look at him. "How were you warned? Who warned you?"

"In Paris one night. Barely three months ago. I'd finished the last of my interviews at the . . . underground carnival, we called it."

"Interpol?"

"Yes. I met a chap and his wife. In a waiting room, actually. It's not supposed to happen; isolation is terribly important, but someone got their rooms mixed up . . . They were English. We agreed to have a late supper together . . . He was a Porsche automobile dealer from Macclesfield. He and his wife were at the end of their tethers. He'd been recruited because his dealership—the cars, you see—were being used to transport stolen stock certificates from European exchanges. Every time he thought he was finished, they found reasons for him to continue—more often than not, without telling him. It was almost three years; he was about out of his mind. They were going to leave England. Go to Buenos Aires."

"He could always say no. They couldn't force him."

"Don't be naive, darling. Every name you learn is another hook, each new method of operation you report is an additional notch in your expertise." Alison laughed sadly. "You've traveled to the land of the informer. You've got a stigmata all your own."

"I'll tell you again: Chatellerault can't touch you."

She paused before acknowledging his words, his anxiety. "This may sound strange to you, Alex. I mean, I'm not a brave person—no brimfuls of courage for me—but I have no great fear of him. The appalling thing . . . the fear is *them*. They wouldn't let me go. No matter the promises, the agreements, the guarantees. They couldn't resist. A file somewhere, or a computer, was activated and came up with *his* name; automatically mine appeared in a data bank. That was it: factor X plus factor Y, subtotal—your life is not your own. It never stops. You live with the fear all over again."

Alex took her by the shoulders. "There's no law, Alison. We can pack; we can leave."

"My darling, my darling . . . You *can't*. Don't you see?

Not that way. It's what's behind you: the agreements, the countless files filled with words, your words . . . you can't deny them. You cross borders, you need papers; you work, you need references. You drive a car or take a plane or put money in a bank . . . They have all the weapons. You can't hide. Not from them."

McAuliff let go of her and stood up. He picked up the smooth, shiny cylinder of gas from the bedside table and looked at the printing and the inked date of issue. He walked aimlessly to the balcony doors and instinctively breathed deeply; there was the faint, very faint, aroma of vanilla with the slightest trace of a spice.

Bay rum and vanilla.

Jamaica.

"You're wrong, Alison. We don't have to hide. For a lot of reasons, we have to finish what we've started; you're right about that. But you're wrong about the conclusion. It does stop. It will stop." He turned back to her. "Take my word for it."

"I'd like to. I really would. I don't see how."

"An old infantry game. Do unto others before they can do unto you. The Holcrofts and the Interpols of this world use us because we're afraid. We know what they can do to what we think are our well-ordered lives. That's legitimate; they're bastards. And they'll admit it . . . But have you ever thought about the magnitude of disaster we can cause *them?* That's also legitimate, because we can be bastards, too. We'll play this out—with armed guards on all our flanks. And when we're finished, we'll *be* finished. With them."

Charles Whitehall sat in the chair, the tiny glass of Pernod on the table beside him. It was six o'clock in the morning; he had not been to bed. There was no point in trying to sleep; sleep would not come.

Two days on the island and the sores of a decade ago were disturbed. He had not expected it; he had expected to control everything. Not *be* controlled.

His enemy now was not the enemy—enemies—he had waited ten years to fight: the rulers in Kingston; worse, perhaps, the radicals like Barak Moore. It was a new enemy, every bit as despicable, and infinitely more powerful, because it had the means to control his beloved Jamaica.

Control by corruption; ultimately own . . . by possession.

He had lied to Alexander McAuliff. In Savanna-la-Mar, Chatellerault openly admitted that he was part of the Trelawny Parish conspiracy. British Intelligence was right. The marquis's wealth was intrinsic to the development of the raw acreage on the north coast and in the Cock Pit, and he intended to see that his investment was protected. Charles Whitehall was his first line of protection, and if Charles Whitehall failed, he would be destroyed. It was as simple as that. Chatellerault was not the least obscure about it. He had sat opposite him and smiled his thin Gallic smile and recited the facts . . . and names . . . of the covert network Whitehall had developed on the island over the past decade.

He had capped his narrative with the most damaging information of all: the timetable and the methods Charles and his political party expected to follow on their road to power in Kingston.

The establishment of a military dictatorship with one, non-military leader to whom all were subservient—the Praetorian of Jamaica was the title, Charles Whitehall the man.

If Kingston knew these things . . . well, Kingston would react.

But Chatellerault made it clear that their individual objectives were not necessarily in conflict. There were areas—philosophical, political, financial—in which their interests might easily be merged. But first came the activity on the north coast. That was immediate; it was the springboard to everything else.

The marquis did not name his partners—Whitehall got the distinct impression that Chatellerault was not entirely sure who they all were—but it was manifestly clear that he did not trust them. On one level he seemed to question motives, on another it was a matter of abilities. He spoke briefly about previous interference and/or bungling, but did not dwell on the facts.

The facts obviously concerned the first survey.

What had happened?

Was the Halidon responsible?

Was the Halidon *capable* of interference?

Did the Halidon really exist?

The Halidon.

He would have to analyze the anthropologist Piersall's papers; separate a foreigner's exotic fantasies from island reality. There was a time, ten years ago, when the Ras Tafarians were symbols of African terror, before they were revealed to be children stoned on grass with mud-caked hair and a collective desire to avoid work. And there were the Pocomanians, with their bearded high priests inserting the sexual orgy into the abstract generosities of the Christian ethic: a socio-religious excuse for promiscuity. Or the Anansi sects—inheritors of the long-forgotten Ashanti belief in the cunning of the spider, on which all progress in life was patterned.

There were so many. So often metaphysically paranoid; so fragmented, so obscure.

Was the Halidon—Hollydawn—any different?

At this juncture, for Charles Whitehall it didn't really matter. What mattered was his own survival and the survival of his plans. His aims would be accomplished by keeping Chatellerault at bay and infiltrating the structure of Chatellerault's financial hierarchy.

And working with his first enemy, Barak Moore.

Working with both enemies.

Jamaica's enemies.

James Ferguson fumbled for the light switch on the bedside lamp. His thrusts caused an ashtray and a glass to collide, sending both crashing to the floor. Light was coming through the drawn curtains; he was conscious of it in spite of the terrible pain in his eyes and through his head, from temple to temple. Pain that caused flashes of darkness to envelope his inner eye. He looked at his watch as he shaded his face from the dim spill of the lamp. It was 6:15.

Oh, Christ! His head hurt so, tears welled in the far corners of his eyes. Shafts of pain—sharp, immobilizing—shot down into his neck and seemed to constrict his shoulders, even his arms. His stomach was in a state of tense, muscular suspension; if he thought about it, he knew he would be sick and vomit.

There was no pretense regarding the amount of alcohol he had consumed last night. McAuliff could not accuse him of play-acting now. He had gotten drunk. Very drunk. And with damn good reason.

He had been elated.

Arthur Craft had telephoned him in panic. In *panic!*

Craft the Younger had been caught. McAuliff had found the room where the taping was being done and beaten someone up, *physically beaten* him *up!* Craft had yelled over the telephone, demanding where McAuliff had gotten his name.

Not from him! Certainly not from Jimbo-mon. He had said nothing.

Craft had roared, swearing at the goddamned nigger on the tape machine, convinced the black fucker had confessed to McAuliff, adding that the goddamned nigger would never get near a courtroom.

"If it came to that."

If it came to that.

"You never *saw* me," Craft the Younger had screamed. "We never talked! We didn't meet! You get that absolutely clear, you shaky son of a bitch!"

"Of course . . . of course, Mr. Craft," he had replied. "But then, sir . . . we *did* talk, didn't we? This doesn't have to change anything."

He had been petrified, but he had said the words. Quietly, with no great emphasis. But his message had been clear.

Arthur Craft, Junior, was in an awkward position. Craft the Younger should not be yelling; he should be polite. Perhaps even solicitous.

After all, they *had* talked . . .

Craft understood. The understanding was first indicated by his silence, then confirmed by his next statement.

"We'll be in touch."

It had been so simple. And if Craft the Younger wanted it different, wanted things as they were not, well, Craft controlled an enormously wealthy foundation. Certainly he could find something for a very, *very* talented botanist.

When he hung up the telephone last night, James had felt a wave of calm come over him. The sort of quiet confidence he experienced in a laboratory, where his eye and mind were very sure indeed.

He would have to be cautious, but he could do it.

He had gotten drunk when he realized that.

And now his head and stomach were in pain. But he could stand them; they were bearable now. Things were going to be different.

He looked at his watch. His goddamn Timex. It was 6:25. A cheap watch, but accurate.

Instead of a Timex there might be a Piaget Chronometer in his future. And new, very expensive camera equipment. And a real bank balance.

And a new life.

If he was cautious.

The telephone rang on Peter Jensen's side of the bed, but his wife heard it first.

"Peter . . . Peter! For heaven's sake, the *phone*."

"What? . . . What, old girl?" Peter Jensen blinked his eyes; the room was dark, but there was daylight beyond the drawn curtains.

The telephone rang again. Short bursts of bell; the kind of rapid blasts hotel switchboards practice. Nimble fingers, irritated guests.

Peter Jensen reached over and switched on the light. The traveling clock read ten minutes to eight.

Again the shrill bell, now steady.

"Damn!" sputtered Peter as he realized the instrument was beyond the lamp, requiring him to reach farther. "Yes, *yes?* Hello?"

"Mr. Peter Jensen, please?" said the unfamiliar male voice.

"Yes. What is it? This is Jensen."

"Cable-International, Mr. Jensen. A wire arrived for you several minutes ago. From London. Shall I read it? It's marked urgent, sir."

"No!" replied Peter quickly, firmly. "No, don't do that. I've been expecting it; it's rather long, I should think."

"Yes, sir, it is."

"Just send it over right away, if you please. Can you do that? The Courtleigh Manor. Room 401. It won't be necessary to stop at the desk."

"I understand, Mr. Jensen. Right away. There'll be a charge for an unscheduled—"

"Of course, of course," interrupted Peter. "Just send it over, please."

"Yes, sir."

Twenty-five minutes later, the messenger from Cable-International arrived. Moments before, room service had wheeled in a breakfast of melon, tea, and scones. Peter Jensen opened the two-page cablegram and spread it out over the linen cloth on his side of the table. There was a pencil in his hand.

Across from him, Ruth held up a page of paper, scanning it over the rim of her cup. She, too, had a pencil, at the side of the saucer.

"The company name is 'Parkhurst,' " said Peter.

"Check," said Ruth, putting down her tea. She placed the paper alongside, picked up the pencil, and made a mark on the page.

"The address is 'Sheffield By The Glen.' " Peter looked over at her.

"Go ahead," replied Ruth, making a second notation.

"The equipment to be inspected is microscopes."

"Very well." Ruth made a third mark on the left of the page, went back to her previous notes, and then darted her eyes to the bottom right. "Are you ready?"

"Yes."

Ruth Wells Jensen, paleontologist, proceeded to recite a series of numbers. Her husband started at the top of the body of the cablegram and began circling words with his pencil. Several times he asked his wife to repeat a number. As she did so, he counted from the previous circle and circled another word.

Three minutes later, they had finished the exercise. Peter Jensen swallowed some tea and reread the cablegram to himself. His wife spread jam on two scones and covered the teapot with the cozy.

"Warfield is flying over next week. He agrees. McAuliff has been reached."

THREE

The North Coast

17

HOLCROFT'S WORDS kept coming back to McAuliff: *You'll find it quite acceptable to operate on different levels. Actually, it evolves rather naturally, even instinctively. You'll discover that you tend to separate your concentrations.*

The British Intelligence agent had been right. The survey was in its ninth day, and Alex found that for hours at a time he had no other thoughts but the immediate work at hand.

The equipment had been trucked from Boscobel Airfield straight through to Puerto Seco, on Discovery Bay. Alex, Sam Tucker, and Alison Booth flew into Ocho Rios ahead of the others and allowed themselves three days of luxury at the San Souci while McAuliff ostensibly hired a crew—two of the five of which had been agreed upon in an isolated farmhouse high in the hills of the Blue Mountains. Alex found—as he'd expected—that Sam and Alison got along extremely well. Neither was difficult to like; each possessed an easy humor, both were professionals. And there was no reason to conceal from Sam the fact that they were lovers. As Tucker phrased it: "I'd be shocked if you weren't, Alexander."

Sam's approval was important to McAuliff. For at no time was Alison to be left alone when he was away. Under no circumstances. Ever.

Sam Tucker was the ideal protective escort. Far superior to himself, Alex realized. Tuck was the most resourceful man he had ever known, and just about the hardest. He had within him an aggressiveness that when called upon was savage. He was not a man to have as an enemy. Alison was as safe as a human being could be in his care.

The fourth day had been the first day of the survey work. The team was housed halfway between Puerto Seco and Rio Bueno Harbour, in a pleasant beach motel called Bengal Court. Work began shortly after six in the morning. The initial objective of the survey was to plot the coastline definitely. Alex and Sam Tucker operated the equipment.

Azimuths were shot along the shoreline, recorded by

transit cameras. The angular degree demarcations were correlated with the coastal charts provided by the Jamaican Institute. By and large, these charts were sectional and imperfect, acceptable for the details of road maps and small-craft navigation, but inadequate for geophysical purposes. To set up accurate perimeters, McAuliff employed sonic geodometers which bounced sound waves back and fourth between instruments, giving what amounted to perfect bearings. Each contour, each elevation was recorded on both sonic graphs and transit cameras.

These chores were dull, laborious, and sweat-provoking under the hot sun. The single relief was the constant presence of Alison, as much as she herself objected to it. Alex was adamant, however. He instructed Barak Moore's two men to stay within a hundred yards of her at all times, and then commanded Alison not to stroll out of his sight.

It was an impossible demand, and McAuliff realized he could not prolong it more than a few days. Alison had work to do; minor over the coastal area, a great deal once they started inland. But all beginnings were awkward under pressure; he could not separate this particular concentration that easily, nor did he wish to.

Very rapidly your own personal antennae will be activated automatically. Their function will be second nature, as it were. You will fall into a rhythm, actually. It is the connecting link between your divided objectives. You will recognize it and build a degree of confidence in the process.

Holcroft.

But not during the first few days; there was no confidence to speak of. He did grant, however, that the fear was lessening . . . partially, imperceptibly. He thought this was due to the constant physical activity and the fact that he *could* require such men as Sam and Barak Moore's "special forces" to take up posts around Alison. And at any given moment he could turn his head and there she was—on the beach, in a small boat—chipping rocks, instructing one of the crew in the manipulation of a drill bore.

But, again, were not all these his antennae? And was not the lessening of fear the beginnings of confidence?

R. C. Holcroft. Supercilious son of a bitch. Manipulator. Speaker of truths.

But not the whole truth.

The areas bordering Braco Beach were hazardous. Sheets of coral overlay extended hundreds of yards out into the surf. McAuliff and Sam Tucker crawled over the razor-sharp miniature hills of ocean polyps and set up their geodometers and cameras. Both men incurred scores of minor cuts, sore muscles, and sorer backs.

That was the third day, marked by the special relief of Alison's somehow commandeering a fisherman's flat-bottom boat and, with her two "escorts," bringing a picnic lunch of cold chicken out to the reef.

It was a comfortable hour on the most uncomfortable picnic grounds imaginable.

The black revolutionary, Floyd, who had guided the boat into its precarious coral mooring, succinctly observed that the beach was flatter and far less wet.

"But then they'd have to crawl all the way out here again," Alison had replied, holding onto her wide-brimmed cloth sun hat.

"Mon, you have a good woman!" This observation came from Floyd's companion, the huge, quiet Negro named Lawrence.

The five of them perched—there was no other description—on the highest ridges of the coral jetty, the spray cascading up from the base of the reef, creating faint rainbow prisms of color in its mist. Far out on the water two freighters were passing each other, one heading for the open sea, the second aiming for the bauxite docks east of Runaway Bay. A luxurious cabin cruiser rigged for deep-sea fishing sliced through the swells several hundred yards in front of them, the passengers pointing in astonishment at the strange sight of five humans picnicking on a reef.

McAuliff watched the others respond to the cruiser's surprised riders. Sam Tucker stood up, gestured at the coral, and yelled, "Diamonds!"

Floyd and Lawrence, their black, muscular bodies bared to the waist, roared at Sam's antics. Lawrence pried loose a coral stone and held it up, then chucked it to Tucker, who caught it and shouted again, "Twenty carats!"

Alison, her bluejeans and light field blouse drenched with the spray, joined in the foolish game. She elaborately accepted the coral stone, presented by Sam, and held it on top of her outstretched hand as though it were a jeweled ring of great value. A short burst of breeze whipped across the reef; Alison dropped the stone in an effort to hold her hat, whose brim had caught the wind. She was not successful; the hat glided off and disappeared over a small mound of coral. Before Alex could rise and go after it, Lawrence was on his feet, dashing sure-footedly over the rocks and down toward the water. Within seconds he had the hat, now soaked, and effortlessly leaped back up from the water's edge and handed it to Alison.

The incident had taken less than ten seconds.

"You keep the hat on the head, Miss *Aleesawn*. Them sun very hot; roast skin like cooked chicken, mon."

"Thank you, Lawrence," said Alison gratefully, securing the wet hat over her head. "You run across this reef as though it were a golf green!"

"Lawrence is a fine caddy, Miss Alison," said Floyd smiling, still sitting. "At the Negril Golf Club he is a favorite, is that not so, Lawrence?"

Lawrence grinned and glanced at McAuliff knowingly. "Eh, mon. At Negril they alla time ask for me. I cheat good, mon. Alla time I move them golf balls out of bad places to the smooth grass. I think everybody know. Alla time ask for Lawrence."

Sam Tucker chuckled as he sat down again. "Alla time big goddamn tips, I'd say."

"Plenty good tips, mon," agreed Lawrence.

"And probably something more," added McAuliff, looking at Floyd and remembering the exclusive reputation of the Negril Golf Club. "Alla time plenty of information."

"Yes, mon." Floyd smiled conspiratorially. "It is as they say: The rich Westmorelanders talk a great deal during their games of golf."

Alex fell silent. It seemed strange, the whole scene. Here they were, the five of them, eating cold chicken on a coral reef three hundred yards from shore, playing children's games with passing cabin cruisers and joking casually about the surreptitious gathering of information on a golf course.

Two black revolutionaries—recruits from a band of hill country guerrillas. A late-middle aged "soldier of fortune." (Sam Tucker would object to the cliché, but if it was ever applicable, he was the applicant.) A strikingly handsome . . . lovely English divorcée whose background just happened to include undercover work for an international police organization. And one thirty-eight year old ex-infantryman who six weeks ago flew to London thinking he was going to negotiate a geological survey contract.

The five of them. Each knowing that he was not what he appeared to be; each doing what he was doing . . . she was doing . . . because there were no alternatives. Not really.

It wasn't strange; it was insane.

And it struck McAuliff once again that he was the least qualified among these people, under these circumstances. Yet because of the circumstances—having nothing to do with qualifications—he was their leader.

Insanity.

By the seventh day, working long hours with few breaks, Alex and Sam had charted the coastline as far as Burwood, five miles from the mouth of the Martha Brae, their western perimeter. The Jensens and James Ferguson kept a leisurely parallel pace, setting up tables with microscopes, burners, vials, scales, and chemicals as they went about their work. None found anything exceptional, nor did they expect to in the coastal regions. The areas had been studied fairly extensively for industrial and resort purposes; there was nothing of consequence not previously recorded. And since Ferguson's botanical analyses were closely allied with Sam Tucker's soil evaluations, Ferguson volunteered to make the soil tests, freeing Tucker to finish the topographics with Alex.

These were the geophysical concerns. There was something else, and none could explain it.

It was first reported by the Jensens.

A sound. Only a sound. A low wail or cry that seemed to follow them throughout an entire afternoon.

When they first heard it, it came from the underbrush beyond the dunes. They thought that perhaps it was an animal in pain. Or a small child in some horrible anguish, an agony that went beyond a child's tears.

In a very real sense, it was terrifying.

So the Jensens raced beyond the dunes into the underbrush, thrashing at the tangled foliage to find the source of the dreadful, frightening cry.

They had found nothing.

The animal, or the child, or whatever it was, had fled.

Shortly thereafter—late in the same afternoon—James Ferguson came running down to the beach, his face an expression of bewildered panic. He had been tracing a giant mollusk fern to its root source; the trek had taken him up into a rocky precipice above the shore. He had been in the center of the overhanging vines and macca-fats when a vibration—at first a vibration—caused his whole body to tremble. There followed a wild, piercing screech, both high-pitched yet full, that pained his ears beyond—he said—endurance.

He had gripped the vines to keep from plummeting off the precipice.

Terrified, he had scrambled down hysterically to firmer ground and raced back to the others.

James had not been more than a few hundred yards away.

Yet none but he had heard the terrible thing.

Whitehall had another version of the madness. The black scholar had been walking along the shoreline, half sand, half forest, of Bengal Bay. It was an aimless morn-ing constitutional; he had no destination other than the point, perhaps.

About a mile east of the motel's beach, he rested briefly on a large rock overlooking the water. He heard a noise from behind, and so he turned, expecting to see a bird or a mongoose fluttering or scampering in the woods.

There was nothing.

He turned back to the lapping water beneath him, when suddenly there was an explosion of sound—sustained, hol-lowlike, a dissonant cacophony of wind.

And then it stopped.

Whitehall had gripped the rock and stared into the for-est. At nothing.

Aware only that he was afflicted with a terrible pain in his temples.

But Charles was a scholar, and a scholar was a skeptic. He had concluded that, somewhere in the forest, an enor-mous unseen tree had collapsed from the natural weight of ages. In its death fall, the tons of ripping, scraping wood-against-wood within the huge trunk had caused the phenomenon.

And none was convinced.

As Whitehall told his story, McAuliff watched him. He

did not think Charles believed it himself.

Things not explicable had occurred, and they were all—if nothing else—scientists of the physical. The explainable.

Perhaps they all took comfort in Whitehall's theory of sonics. Alexander thought so; they could not dwell on it. There was work to do.

Divided objectives.

Alison thought she had found something, and with Floyd's and Lawrence's help she made a series of deep bores arcing the beaches and coral jetties. Her samplings showed that there were strata of soft lignite interspersed throughout the limestone beds on the ocean floor. Geologically it was easily explained: Hundreds of thousands of years ago, volcanic disturbances swallowed whole land masses of wood and pulp. Regardless of explanations, however, if there were plans to sink pilings for piers or even extended docks, the construction firms were going to have to add to their base supports.

Alison's concentrations were a relief to McAuliff. She was absorbed, and so complained less about his restrictions, and, more important, he was able to observe Floyd and Lawrence as they went about the business of watching over her. The two blacks were extremely thorough. And gracefully subtle. Whenever Alison wandered along the beach or up into the shore grass, one or both had her flanked or preceded or followed. They were like stalking panthers prepared to spring, yet they did not in their tracking call attention to themselves. They seemed to become natural appendages, always carrying something— binoculars, sampling boxes, clipboards . . . whatever was handy—to divert any zeroing in on their real function.

And during the nights, McAuliff found a protective bonus he had neither asked for nor expected: Floyd and Lawrence alternated patrols around the lawns and in the corridors of the Bengal Court motel. Alex discovered this on the night of the eighth day, when he got up at four in the morning to get himself a plastic bucket of ice from the machine down the hall. He wanted ice water.

As he turned the corner into the outside alcove where the machine was situated, he was suddenly aware of a figure behind the latticework that fronted the lawn. The fig-

ure had moved quickly; there had been no sound of footsteps.

McAuliff rapidly scooped the cubes into the small
bucket, closed the metal door, and walked back around
the corner into the hallway. The instant he was out of
sight, he silently placed the ice at his feet and pressed his
back against the wall's edge.

There was movement.

McAuliff whipped around the corner, with every intention of hurling himself at whoever came into view. His
fists were clenched, his spring accurate; he lunged into
the figure of Lawrence. It was too late to regain his
footing.

"Eh, *mon!*" cried the black softly as he recoiled and fell
back under Alex's weight. Both men rolled out of the alcove onto the lawn.

"Christ!" whispered McAuliff, next to Lawrence on the
ground. "What the hell are you doing here?"

Lawrence smiled in the darkness; he shook his hand,
which had been pinned by Alex under his back. "You're a
big fella, mon! You pretty quick, too."

"I was pretty damned excited . . . What *are* you doing
out here?"

Lawrence explained briefly, apologetically. He and
Floyd had made an arrangement with the night watch-
man, an old fisherman who prowled around at night with
a shotgun neither guerrilla believed he knew how to use.
Barak Moore had ordered them to stand evening patrols;
they would have done so whether commanded to or not,
said Lawrence.

"When do you sleep?"

"Sleep *good,* mon," replied Lawrence. "We take turns
alla time."

Alex returned to his room. Alison sat up in bed when
he closed the door.

"Is everything all right?" she asked apprehensively.

"Better than I expected. We've got our own miniature
army. We're fine."

On the afternoon of the ninth day, McAuliff and
Tucker reached the Martha Brae River. The geodometer
charts and transit photographs were sealed hermetically
and stored in the cool vaults of the equipment truck. Peter Jensen gave his summary of the coastal ore and mineral deposits; his wife, Ruth, had found traces of plant

fossils embedded in the coral, but her findings were of little value, and James Ferguson, covering double duty in soil and flora, presented his unstartling analyses. Only Alison's discovery of the lignite strata was unexpected.

All reports were to be driven into Ocho Rios for duplication. McAuliff said he would do this himself; it had been a difficult nine days, and the tenth was a day off. Those who wanted to go into Ochee could come with him; the others could go to Montego or laze around the Bengal Court beach, as they preferred. The survey would resume on the morning of the eleventh day.

They made their respective plans on the river bank, with the inevitable picnic lunches put up by the motel. Only Charles Whitehall, who had done little *but* lie around the beach, knew precisely what he wanted to do, and he could not state it publicly. He spoke to Alex alone.

"I really *must* see Piersall's papers. Quite honestly, McAuliff, it's been driving me crazy."

"We wait for Moore. We agreed to that."

"When? For heaven's sake, when will he show up? It will be ten days tomorrow; he said ten days."

"There were no guarantees. I'm as anxious as you. There's an oilcloth packet buried somewhere on his property, remember?"

"I haven't forgotten for an instant."

Separation of concentrations; divided objectives.
Holcroft.

Charles Whitehall was as concerned academically as he was conspiratorially. Perhaps more so, thought Alex. The black scholar's curiosity was rooted in a lifetime of research.

The Jensens remained at Bengal Court. Ferguson requested an advance from McAuliff and hired a taxi to drive him into Montego Bay. McAuliff, Sam Tucker, and Alison Booth drove the truck to Ocho Rios. Charles Whitehall followed in an old station wagon with Floyd and Lawrence; the guerrillas insisted that the arrangements be thus.

Barak Moore lay in the tall grass, binoculars to his eyes. It was sundown; rays of orange and yellow light filtered through the green trees above him and bounced off the white stone of Walter Piersall's house, four hundred yards away. Through the grass he saw the figures of the Trelawny Parish police circling the house, checking the windows and the doors; they would leave at least one man on watch. As usual.

The police had finished the day's investigation, the longest investigation, thought Barak, in the history of the parish. They had been at it nearly two weeks. Teams of civilians had come up from Kingston: men in pressed clothes, which meant they were more than police.

They would find nothing, of that Barak Moore was certain.

If Walter Piersall had accurately described his caches.

And Barak could not wait any longer. It would be a simple matter to retrieve the oilcloth packet—he was within a hundred and fifty yards of it at the moment—but it was not that simple. He needed Charles Whitehall's total cooperation—more than Whitehall realized—and that meant he had to get inside Piersall's house and bring out the rest of Piersall's legacy. The anthropologist's papers.

The papers. They were cemented in the wall of an old, unused cistern in Piersall's basement.

Walter Piersall had carefully removed several cistern blocks, dug recesses in the earth beyond, and replaced the stones. It was in one of these recesses that he had buried his studies of the Halidon.

Charles Whitehall would not help unless he saw those papers. Barak needed Charley-mon's help.

The Trelawny police got into their vehicles; a single uniformed guard waved as the patrol cars started down the road.

He, Barak, the people's revolutionary, had to work with Whitehall, the political criminal. Their own war—perhaps a civil war—would come later, as it had in so many new lands.

First, there was the white man. And his money and his companies and his unending thirst for the sweat of the black man. That was first, very much first, mon!

Barak's thoughts had caused him to stare blindly into the binoculars. The guard was nowhere in sight now. Moore scanned the area, refocusing the Zeiss Ikon lenses as he covered the sides and the sloping back lawn of Piersall's house. It was a comfortable white man's home, thought Barak.

It was on top of a hill, the entrance road a long climb

from George's Valley to the west and the Martha Brae to the east. Mango trees, palms, hibiscus, and orchids lined the entrance and surrounded the one-and-a-half-storied white stone structure. The house was long, most of the wide, spacious rooms on the first floor. There was black iron grillwork everywhere, across the windows and over the door entrances. The only glass was in the second-floor bedrooms; all the windows had teak shutters.

The rear of High Hill, as the house was called, was the most striking. To the east of the old pasture of high grass, where Barak lay, the gently sloping back lawn had been carved out of the forests and the fields, seeded with a Caribbean fescue that was as smooth as a golf course; the rocks, painted a shiny white, gave the appearance of whitecaps in a green sea.

In the center of the area was a medium-sized pool, installed by Piersall, with blue and white tiles that reflected the sun as sharply as the blue-green water in it. Around the pool and spreading out over the grass were tables and chairs—white wrought iron—delicate in appearance, sturdy in design.

The guard came into view again, and Moore caught his breath, as much in astonishment as in anger. The guard was playing with a dog, a vicious-looking Doberman. There had been no dogs before. It was a bad thing, thought Barak . . . yet, perhaps, not so bad. The presence of the dog probably meant that this policeman would stay alone at his post longer than the normal time span. It was a police custom to leave dogs with men for two reasons: because the district they patrolled was dangerous, or because the men would remain for a relatively long time at their watches. Dogs served several purposes; they were alarms, they protected, and they helped pass the hours.

The guard threw a stick; the Doberman raced beyond the pool, nearly crashing into a wrought-iron table, and snatched it up in his mouth. Before the dog could bring it back the policeman threw another stick, bewildering the Doberman, who dropped the first retrieval and went after the second.

He is a stupid man, thought Barak, watching the laughing guard. He did not know animals, and a man who did not know animals was a man who could be trapped.

He would be trapped tonight.

18

IT WAS a clear night. The Jamaican moon—three-quarters of it—shone brightly between the high banks of the river. They had poled a stolen bamboo raft down the rushing waters of the Martha Brae until they had reached the point of shortest distance to the house in Carrick Foyle. They maneuvered the raft into a pitch-black recess and pulled it out of the water, hiding it under cascading umbrellas of full-leaved mangroves and maiden palms.

They were the raiding party: Barak, Alex, Floyd and Whitehall. Sam Tucker and Lawrence had stayed at Bengal Court to protect Alison.

They crept up the slope through the dense, ensnaring foliage. The slope was steep, the traveling slow and painfully difficult. The distance to the High Hill property was no more than a mile—perhaps a mile and a quarter—but it took the four of them nearly an hour to reach it. Charles Whitehall thought the route was foolish. If there was one guard and one dog, why not drive to the road below the winding, half-mile entrance and simply walk up to the outer gates?

Barak's reasoning held more sophistication than Whitehall conceded to the Trelawny police. Moore thought it possible that the parish authorities had set up electronic tripwires along the entrance drive. Barak knew that such instruments had been in use in Montego Bay, Kingston, and Port Antonio hotels for months. They could not take the chance of setting one off.

Breathing heavily, they stood at the southern border of Piersall's sloping lawn and looked up at the house called "High Hill." The moon's illumination on the white stone made the house stand out like an alabaster monument, still, peaceful, graceful, and solid. Light spilled out of the teak shutters in two areas of the house: the downstairs back room opening onto the lawn and the center bedroom on the second floor. All else was in darkness.

Except the underwater spotlights in the pool. A slight breeze caused ripples on the water; the bluish light danced from underneath.

"We must draw him out," said Barak. "Him and the dog, mon."

"Why? What's the point?" asked McAuliff, the sweat from the climb rolling down into his eyes. "He's one, we're four."

"Moore is right," answered Charles Whitehall. "If there are electronic devices outside, then certainly he has the equivalent within."

"He would have a police radio, at any rate, mon," interjected Floyd. "I know those doors; by the time we broke one down, he would have time—easy to reach others."

"It's a half hour from Falmouth; the police are in Falmouth," pressed Alex. "We'd be in and out by then."

"Not so, mon," argued Barak. "It will take us a while to select and pry loose the cistern stones . . . We'll dig up the oilcloth packet first. Come!"

Barak Moore led them around the edge of wooded property, to the opposite side, into the old grazing field. He shielded the glass of his flashlight with his fingers and raced to a cluster of breadfruit trees at the northern end of the rock-strewn pasture. He crouched at the trunk of the farthest tree; the others did the same. Barak spoke—whispered.

"Talk quietly. These hill winds carry voices. The packet is buried in the earth forty-four paces to the right of the fourth large rock on a northwest diagonal from this tree."

"He was a man who knew Jamaica," said Whitehall softly.

"How do you mean?" McAuliff saw the grim smile on the scholar's face in the moonlight.

"The Arawak symbols for a warrior's death march were in units of four, always to the right of the setting sun."

"That's not very comforting," said Alex.

"Like your American Indians," replied Whitehall, "the Arawaks were not comforted by the white man."

"Neither were the Africans, Charley-mon." Barak locked eyes with Whitehall in the moonlight. "Sometimes I think you forget that." He addressed McAuliff and Floyd. "Follow me. In a line."

They ran in crouched positions through the tall grass behind the black revolutionary, each man slapping a large prominent rock as he came upon it. One, two, three, four.

At the fourth rock, roughly a hundred and fifty yards from the base of the breadfruit tree, they knelt around the stone. Barak cupped his flashlight and shone it on the top. There was a chiseled marking, barely visible. Whitehall bent over it.

"Your Dr. Piersall had a progressive imagination; progressive in the historical sense. He's jumped from Arawak to Coromantee. See?" Whitehall traced his index finger over the marking under the beam of the flashlight and continued softly. "This twisted crescent is an Ashanti moon the Coromantees used to leave a trail for members of the tribe perhaps two or three days behind in a hunt. The chips on the convex side of the crescent determine the direction: one—to the left; two—to the right. Their placement on the rim shows the angle. Here: two chips, dead center; therefore, directly to the right of the stone facing the base of the crescent." Whitehall gestured with his right hand northeast.

"As Piersall instructed." Barak nodded his head; he did not bother to conceal his pique at Charley-mon's explanation. Yet there was respect in that pique, thought McAuliff, as he watched Moore begin pacing off the forty-four steps.

Piersall had disguised the spot chosen for burial. There was a thicket of mollusk ferns spreading out in a free-form spray within the paced-off area of the grass. They had been rerooted expertly; it was illogical to assume any sort of digging had taken place there in years.

Floyd took a knapsack shovel from his belt, unfolded the stem, and began removing the earth. Charles Whitehall bent down on his knees and joined the revolutionary, clawing at the dirt with his bare hands.

The rectangular black box was deep in the ground. Had not the instructions been so precise, the digging might have stopped before reaching it. The depth was over three feet. Whitehall suspected it was exactly four feet when deposited. The Arawak unit of four.

The instant Floyd's small shovel struck the metal casing, Whitehall lashed his right hand down, snatched the box out of the earth, and fingered the edges, trying to pry it apart. It was not possible, and Whitehall realized it within seconds. He had used this type of receptacle perhaps a thousand times: It was a hermetically sealed archive case whose soft, rubberized edges created a vacuum within. It had two locks, one at each end, with separate keys; once the keys were inserted and turned, air was allowed in, and after a period of minutes the box could be forced open. It was the sort of repository used in the most heavily endowed libraries to house old manuscripts, manuscripts that were studied by scholars no more than once every five years or so and thus preserved with great care. The name "archive case" was well suited for documents in archives for a millennium.

"Give me the keys!" whispered Charles urgently to Barak.

"I have no keys, mon. Piersall said nothing about keys."

"Damn!"

"Keep quiet!" ordered McAuliff.

"Put that dirt back," said Moore to Floyd. "So it is not so obvious, mon. Push back the ferns."

Floyd did as he was told; McAuliff helped him. Whitehall stared at the rectangular box in his hands; he was furious.

"He was paranoid!" whispered the scholar, turning to Barak. "You said it was a packet. An oilcloth packet! Not this. This will take a blowtorch to open!"

"Charley's got a point," said Alex, shoveling in dirt with his hands, realizing that he had just called Whitehall "Charley." "Why did he go to this trouble? Why didn't he just put the box with the rest of the papers in the cistern?"

"You ask questions I cannot answer, mon. He was very concerned, that's all I can tell you."

The dirt was back in the hole. Floyd smoothed out the surface and pushed the roots of the mollusk ferns into the soft earth. "That will do, I think, mon," he said, folding the stem of the shovel and replacing it in his belt.

"How are we going to get inside?" asked McAuliff. "Or get the guard outside?"

"I have thought of this for several hours," replied Barak. "Wild pigs, I think."

"Very *good,* mon!" interrupted Floyd.

"In the pool?" added Whitehall knowingly.

"Yes."

"What the hell are you talking about?" Alex watched the faces of the three blacks in the moonlight.

Barak answered. "In the Cock Pit there are many wild

pigs. They are vicious and troublesome. We are perhaps ten miles from the Cock Pit's borders. It is not unusual for pigs to stray this far . . . Floyd and I will imitate the sounds. You and Charley-mon throw rocks into the pool."

"What about the dog?" asked Whitehall. "You'd better shoot it."

"No shooting, mon! Gunfire would be heard for miles. I will take care of the dog." Moore withdrew a small anesthetizing dart gun from his pocket. "Our arsenal contains many of these. Come."

Five minutes later McAuliff thought he was part of some demonic children's charade. Barak and Floyd had crept to the edge of the tall grass bordering the elegant lawn. On the assumption that the Doberman would head directly to the first human smell, Alex and Whitehall were in parallel positions ten feet to the right of the revolutionaries, a pile of stones between them. They were to throw the rocks as accurately as possible into the lighted pool sixty feet away at the first sounds emanating from Moore and his comrade.

It began.

The shrieks intruded on the stillness of the night with terrible authenticity. They were the bellows of panicked beasts, shrill and somehow horrible.

"*Eeeowahhee . . . gnnrahha, gnnrahhaaa . . . eeaww, eeaww . . . eeeowahhee . . .*"

McAuliff and Whitehall lobbed rocks into the pool; the splashes were interspersed with the monstrous shrieks. A weird cacophony filled the air.

The shutters from the first floor room were thrown open. The guard could be seen behind the grillwork, a rifle in his hand.

Suddenly a stone hit Alex's cheek: The blow was gentle, not stunning. He whipped his head toward the direction of the throw. Floyd was waving his arm in the tall grass, commanding McAuliff to stop hurling the rocks. Alex grabbed Whitehall's hand. They stopped.

The shrieks then became louder, accompanied by blunt thuds of pounding earth. Alex could see Barak and Floyd in the moonlight. They were slapping the ground like crazed animals; the horrible noises coming from their shaking heads reached a crescendo.

Wild pigs fighting in the high grass.

The door of Piersall's house crashed open. The guard, rifle in hand, released the dog at his side. The animal lurched out onto the lawn and raced toward the hysterical sounds and all-too-human odors.

McAuliff knelt, hypnotized by what followed in the Jamaican moonlight. Barak and Floyd scrambled back into the field without raising their bodies above the grass and without diminishing the pitch of their animal screams. The Doberman streaked across the lawn and sprang head-long over the border of the field and into the tall grass.

The continuing shrieks and guttural roars were joined by the savage barking of the vicious dog. And, amid the terrible sounds, Alex could distinguish a series of spits; the dart gun was being fired repeatedly.

A yelping howl suddenly drowned out the man-made bellowing; the guard ran to the edge of the lawn, his rifle raised to fire. And before McAuliff could absorb or understand the action, Charles Whitehall grabbed a handful of rocks and threw them toward the lighted pool. And then a second handful hard upon the first.

The guard spun around to the water; Whitehall slammed Alex out of the way, raced along the edge of the grass, and suddenly leaped out on the lawn at the black patrolman.

McAuliff watched, stunned.

Whitehall, the elegant academic—the delicately boned Charley-mon—lashed his arm out into the base of the guard's neck, crashed his foot savagely into the man's midsection, and seized a wrist, twisting it violently so that the rifle flew out of the guard's hands; the man jerked off his feet, spun into the air, and whipped to the ground. As the guard vibrated off the grass, Whitehall took swift aim and crashed his heel into the man's skull below his fore-head.

The body contorted, then lay still.

The shrieking stopped; all was silent.

It was over.

Barak and Floyd raced out from the high grass onto the lawn. Barak spoke.

"Thank you, Charley-mon. Indiscriminate gunfire might have found us."

"It was necessary," replied Whitehall simply. "I must see those papers."

"Then let us go," said Barak Moore. "Floyd, take this real pig inside; tie him up somewhere."

"Don't waste time," countered Whitehall, starting for the house, the receptacle under his arm. "Just throw him into the grass. He's dead."

Inside, Floyd led them to the cellar stairs and down into Piersall's basement. The cistern was in the west section, about six feet deep and five wide. The walls were dry; cobwebs laced the sides and the top. Barak brushed aside the filmy obstructions and lowered himself into the pit.

"How do you know which are the blocks?" asked Whitehall urgently, the black rectangular box clasped in his hand.

"There is a way; the Doctor explained," replied Moore, taking out a small box of safety matches. He struck one and started at the north center line, revolving slowly clock-wise, holding the lighted match against the cracks in the blocks on the lower half of the pit.

"Ground phosphorus," stated Whitehall quietly. "Packed into the concrete edges."

"Yes, mon. Not much; enough to give a little flame, or a sputter, perhaps."

"You're wasting time!" Whitehall spat out the words. "Swing to your *left,* toward the northwest point! Not to your right."

The three men looked abruptly at the scholar. *"What,* Charley-mon?" Barak was bewildered.

"Do as I say! . . . Please."

"The Arawak symbols?" asked McAuliff. "The . . . odyssey to death, or whatever you called it? To the right of the setting sun?"

"I'm glad you find it amusing."

"I don't, Charley-mon. Not one goddamn bit," answered Alex softly.

"Ayee . . ." Barak whistled as tiny spits of flame burst out of the cistern's cracks. "Charley, you got brains, mon! Here they are . . . Floyd, mon, give me the tools."

Floyd reached into his field jacket and produced a five-inch stone chisel and an all-metal folding hammer. He handed them down to his superior. "You want help?" he asked.

"There is not room for two," replied Barak as he started hammering along the cracks.

Three minutes later Moore had managed to dislodge the first block from its surrounding adhesive; he tugged at it, pulling it slowly out of the cistern wall. Whitehall held the flashlight now, his eyes intent on Moore's manipulations. The block came loose; Floyd reached down and took it from Barak's hands.

"What's behind?" Whitehall pierced the beam of light into the gaping hole.

"Space, mon. Red dirt and space," said Moore. "And I think the top of another box. A larger box."

"For God's sake, *hurry!*"

"Okay, Charley-mon. There is no dinner engagement at the Mo'Bay Hilton, mon." Barak chuckled. "Nothing will be rewritten by a hidden mongoose."

"Relax." McAuliff did not look at Whitehall when he spoke. He did not want to. "We have all night, don't we? You killed a man out there. He was the only one who could have interfered. And you decided he had to die for that."

Whitehall turned his head and stared at McAuliff. "I killed him because it was necessary." Whitehall transferred his attention back to Barak Moore. The second block came loose with far less effort than the first. Barak reached into the space and rocked the stone until the cracks widened and it slid out. Floyd took the block and placed it carefully to one side.

Whitehall crouched opposite the hole, shining the flashlight into it. "It's an archive case. Let me have it." He handed Floyd the flashlight and reached across the pit as Barak pulled the receptacle out of the dirt and gave it to him. "Extraordinary!" said Charles, fingering the oblong box, his knee pressed against the top of the first receptacle on the floor beside him. Whitehall was not going to let either out of his possession.

"The case you mean, mon?" asked Moore.

"Yes." Whitehall turned the box over, then held it up as Floyd shone the beam of light on it. "I don't think any of you understand. Without the keys or proper equipment, these bloody things take hours to open. Watertight, airtight, vacuumed, and crushproof. Even a starbit drill could not penetrate the metal . . . Here! See." The scholar pointed to some lettering on the bottom surface. "Hitchcock Vault Company. Indianapolis. The finest in the world. Museums, libraries . . . government archives everywhere use Hitchcock. Simply extraordinary."

When the sound came, it had the impact of an earth-shattering explosion, although the noise was distant—that of the whining low gear of an automobile racing up the long entrance drive from the road below.

And then another.

The four men looked back and forth at one another. They were stunned. Outside there was an intrusion that was not to be. *Could* not be.

"Oh my *God, Jesus, mon!*" Barak jumped out of the pit.

"Take those tools, you damn fool!" cried Whitehall. "Your fingerprints!"

Floyd, rather than Barak, leaped into the cistern, grabbed the hammer and chisel, and put them into the pockets of his field jacket. "There is only the staircase, mon! No other way!"

Barak ran to the stairs. McAuliff reached down for the first receptacle at Whitehall's side; simultaneously, Whitehall's hand was on it.

"You can't carry both, Charley-mon," said Alex in answer to Whitehall's manic stare. "This one's mine!" He grabbed the box, jerked it out from under Whitehall's grip, and followed Moore to the stairs. The automobiles, in grinding counterpoint, were getting nearer.

The four men leaped up the stairs in single file and raced through the short corridor into the darkened, rug-less living room. The beams of headlights could be seen shining through the slits in the teak shutters. The first car had reached the compact parking area; the sounds of doors opening could be heard. The second vehicle roared in only seconds behind. In the corner of the room could be seen, in the strips of light, the cause for the instrusion: an open-line portable radio. Barak ran to it and, with a single blow of his fist into the metal, smashed the front and then tore off the back antennae.

Men outside began shouting. Predominately one name:

"Ray*mond!*"

"*Ray*mond!"

"Raymond! Where you at, mon!"

Floyd assumed the lead and raced to the rear center door. "This way! Quick, mon!" he whispered to the others. He yanked the door open and held it as they all gathered. McAuliff could see in the reflection of the pool's light that Floyd held a pistol in his free hand. Floyd spoke to Barak. "I will deflect them, mon. To the west. I know the property good, mon!"

"Be careful! You two," said Barak to Whitehall and McAuliff. "Go straight into the woods; we'll meet at the raft. One-half hour from now. No more. Whoever is there, leave. Pole down, mon. The Martha Brae is no good without a raft, mon. *Go!*" He shoved Alex through the door.

Outside, McAuliff started across the strangely peaceful lawn, with the blue-green light of the pool illuminating the stately wrought-iron furniture. He could hear the shouts from behind. Men had raced up from the entrance drive to the sides of the house. Alex wondered if they could see him; he was running as fast as he could toward the seemingly impenetrable wall of forest beyond the sloping lawn. He gripped the oblong receptacle under his right arm.

He got his answer instantly.

The insanity had started.

Gunshot!

Bullets cracked above him; abrupt detonations spaced erratically behind him.

Men were firing pistols indiscriminately.

Oh, Jesus; he was back there again!

Long-forgotten instructions returned once more. Diagonals; make diagonals. *Short, quick spurts; but not too short. Just enough to give the enemy a half second to assume position-aim.*

He had given those instructions. To scores of men in the Korean hills.

The shouting became an overlapping chorus of hysteria: and then a single scream pierced the symphony.

McAuliff hurled himself into the air, into the sudden growth of dense foliage that bordered the lawn. He fell into a thicket and rolled to his left.

On the ground, out of sightlines, roll! Roll for all you're worth into a second position!

Basics.

Fundamentals.

He was positive he would see men coming after him down the hill.

There weren't.

Instead, what he saw hypnotized him, as he had been hypnotized watching the two black revolutionaries in the high grass pretending to be wild pigs.

Up by the house—to the west of it, actually—Floyd was reeling around and around, the light of the pool catching the dull green of his field jacket. He was allowing himself to be an open target, firing a pistol, pinning the police to the sides of the house. He ran out of ammunition, reached into his pocket, withdrew another gun, and started firing again—now racing to the edge of the pool, in full sacrificial view.

He had been hit. Repeatedly. Blood was spreading throughout the cloth of the field jacket and all over the trousers covering his legs. The man had at least a half dozen bullets in him, ebbing away his life, leaving him only moments to live.

"McAuliff!" The whispered shout was from his right. Barak Moore, his grotesque shaven head glistening with sweat in the filtered moonlight, threw himself down beside Alex. "We get out of here, mon! Come!" He tugged at McAuliff's drenched shirt.

"For God's sake! Can't you see what's happening up there? That man's dying!"

Barak glanced up through the tangled overgrowth. He spoke calmly. "We are committed till death. In its way, it is a luxury. Floyd knows that."

"For *what*, for Christ's sake? For goddamn stinking *what*? You're goddamn madmen!"

"Let us *go!*" commanded Moore. "They will follow us in seconds. Floyd is giving us this chance, you white shit, mon!"

Alex grabbed Barak's hand, which was still gripping his shirt, and threw it off. "That's it, isn't it? I'm a white shit. And Floyd has to die because you think so. And that guard had to die because Whitehall thinks so! . . . You're sick."

Barak Moore paused. "You are what you are, mon. And you will not take this island. Many, many will die, but this island will not be yours . . . You will be dead, too, if you do not run with me." Moore suddenly stood up and ran into the forest darkness.

McAuliff looked after him, holding the black oblong box to his chest. Then he rose from the ground and followed the black revolutionary.

They waited at the water's edge, the raft bobbing up and down in the onrushing current. They were waist deep in the river, Barak checking his wristwatch, Alex shifting his feet in the soft mud to hold the bamboo sides of the raft more firmly.

"We cannot wait much longer, mon," said Barak. "I can hear them in the hills. They come closer!"

McAuliff could not hear anything but the sounds of the rushing river and the slapping of water against the raft. And Barak. "We can't leave him here!"

"No choice. You want your head blown off, mon?"

"No. And it *won't* be. We stole papers from a dead man. At his instructions. That's no call for being shot at. Enough's enough, goddamn it!"

Barak laughed. "You have a short memory, mon! Up in the tall grass there is a dead policeman. Without doubt, Floyd took at least one other life with him; Floyd was an expert shot . . . Your head will be blown off; the Falmouth police will not hesitate."

Barak Moore was right. *Where the hell was Whitehall?*

"Was he shot? Do you know if he was wounded?"

"I think not, mon. I cannot be sure . . . Charley-mon did not do as I told him. He ran southwest into the field."

A single shaft of light was seen a hundred yards upstream, streaking down through the overgrown banks.

"Look!" cried Alex. Moore turned.

There was a second, then a third beam. Three dancing columns of light, wavering toward the river below.

"No time now, mon! Get in and pole fast!"

The two of them shoved the raft toward the center current and jumped onto the bamboo-rodded surface.

"I get in front, mon!" yelled Moore, scrambling over the platformed, high-backed seat used by tourists viewing the beauty of the Martha Brae. "You stay in the rear, mon! Use the pole and when I tell you, stop and put your legs over the backside!"

McAuliff focused his eyes in the moonlight, trying to

distinguish which was the loose pole among the strapped cylinders of bamboo. It was wedged between the low railing and the deck; he picked it up and plunged it into the waters, into the mud below.

The raft entered the rapids and began careening downstream. Moore stood up in the bow and used his pole as a deflector, warding the racing bamboo float off the treacherous series of flesh-cutting rocks that broke the surface of the water. They were approaching a bend in the river. Barak shouted.

"Sit on the backside, mon! Put your feet into the water. *Quick, mon!*"

Alex did as he was ordered; he soon understood. The drag created by his weight and his feet gave Moore the slightly slower speed he needed to navigate the raft through a miniature archipelago of hazardous rocks. The bamboo sides crashed back and forth, into and over the mounds of jagged stone; twice McAuliff thought the raft would list right out of the water.

It was the sound of the harsh scrapings and his concentration on the rapids that caused Alex to delay his realization of the gunshots. And then that realization was complete with the stinging, searing pain in his left arm. A bullet had grazed his flesh; the blood trickled down his sleeve in the moonlight.

There was a staccato burst of gunfire.

"You get down, mon!" yelled Barak. "Get flat! They cannot follow us; we get around the bend, there is a grotto. Many caves. They lead up to the Brae Road, mon. . . . *Ayeee!*"

Moore buckled; he let go of the pole, grabbed his stomach, and fell onto the bamboo deck. Alex reached down for the oblong archive case, crammed it into his belt, and crawled as fast as he could to the front of the raft. Barak Moore was writhing; he was alive.

"How bad are you hurt?"

"Pretty bad, mon! . . . Stay *down!* If we get stuck, jump out and push us off . . . Around bend, mon."

Barak was unconscious. The bamboo raft plunged over a shallow, graveled surface and then into the final curve of the bend, where the water was deep, the current powerful and faster than before. the sounds of gunfire stopped; they were out of sight of the Trelawny police.

McAuliff raised his shoulders; the archive case was cutting into his skin beneath his belt, his left arm stung with pain. The river now became a huge flat pool, the waters rushing under the surface. There were stone cliffs diagonally across, rising sharply out of the river bank.

Suddenly Alex saw the beam of a lone flashlight, and the terrible pain of fear pierced his stomach. The enemy was not behind—he was waiting.

Involuntarily, he reached into his pocket for his gun. The Smith & Wesson given him by Westmore Tallon. He raised it as the raft steered itself toward the stone cliffs and the flashlight.

He lowered himself over the unconscious body of Barak Moore and waited, his arm outstretched, the pistol aimed at the body beyond the flashlight.

He was within forty yards of the silent figure. He was about to squeeze the trigger and take a life.

"Barak, mon!" came the words.

The man on the river bank was Lawrence.

Charles Whitehall waited in the high grass by the cluster of breadfruit trees. The archive case was securely under his arm; he knelt immobile in the moonlight and watched Piersall's house and grounds two hundred yards away. The body of the dead guard had not been found. Floyd's corpse had been carried into the house for the light necessary for a complete search of the dead body.

One man remained behind. The others had all raced into the eastern forests and down to the Martha Brae in pursuit of Moore and McAuliff.

That was precisely what Charles Whitehall thought would happen. And why he had not done as Barak Moore commanded.

There was a better way. If one acted alone.

The single Trelawny policeman was fat. He waddled back and forth by the wooded border of the lawn; he was pacing nervously, as if afraid to be alone. He carried a rifle in his hands, jerking it toward every sound he heard or thought he heard.

Suddenly there was gunfire far below in the distance, down at the river. It was full, rapid. Either much ammunition was being wasted, or Moore and McAuliff were having a bad time of it.

But it was *his* moment to move. The patrolman was hugging the edge of the forest, peering down. The gunfire was both his protection and the source of his fear. He cradled his rifle and nervously lighted a cigarette.

Charles got up and, clutching the archive case, raced through the tall grass behind the west flank of the field. He then turned right and ran toward Piersall's house, through the diminishing woods to the border of the entrance drive.

The two patrol cars stood peacefully in the moonlight, in front of the wide stone steps to High Hill. Whitehall emerged from the woods and crossed to the first vehicle. One door was open—the driver's door. The dim interior light shone over the black leather.

The keys were in the ignition. He removed them and then reached under the dashboard radio and ripped every wire out of the panel. He closed the door silently, ran to the second car, and saw that its keys were also in place. He walked rapidly back to the first car and as quietly as possible unlatched the hood. He yanked off the distributor cap and tugged at the rubber lid until it sprang loose from the wires.

He returned to the second vehicle, got in, and placed the archive case beside him. He pressed the accelerator several times. He checked the gearshift mechanism and was satisfied.

He turned the key in the ignition. The motor started instantly.

Charles Whitehall backed the patrol car out of the parking area, swung the wheel, and sped off down the drive.

19

THE DOCTOR closed the patio door and walked out onto the terrace that connected Alison's and McAuliff's rooms. Barak Moore was in Alison's bed. She had insisted; no comments were offered, the decision was not debated.

Alex's upper left arm was bandaged; the wound was surface, painful, and not serious. He sat with Alison on the waist-high terrace sea wall. He did not elaborate on the night raid; there would be time later. Sam Tucker and Lawrence had taken positions at each end of the patio in order to keep any wanderers from coming into the small area.

The doctor, a black from Falmouth whom Lawrence had contacted at midnight, approached McAuliff. "I have done what I can. I wish I felt more confident."

"Shouldn't he be in a hospital?" Alison's words were as much a rebuke as a question.

"He should be," agreed the doctor wearily. "I discussed it with him; we concluded it was not feasible. There is only a government clinic in Falmouth. I think this is cleaner."

"Barak is wanted," explained Alex quietly. "He'd be put in prison before they got the bullet out."

"I sincerely doubt they would take the trouble to remove the bullet, Mr. McAuliff."

"What do you think?" asked Alex, lighting a cigarette.

"He will have a chance if he remains absolutely still. But only a chance. I have cauterized the abdominal wall; it could easily rerupture. I have replaced blood . . . yes, my office has a discreet file of certain individuals' blood classifications. He is extremely weak. If he survives two or three days, there is hope."

"But you don't think he will," stated McAuliff.

"No. There was too much internal bleeding. My . . . portable operating kit is not that good. Oh, my man is cleaning up. He will take out the sheets, clothing, anything that has been soiled. Unfortunately, the odor of ether and disinfectant will remain. Keep the outside doors open when you can. Lawrence will make sure no one enters."

Alex slid off the wall and leaned against it. "Doctor? I gather you're part of Barak's organization, if that's the word."

"It is too precise at this juncture."

"But you know what's going on."

"Not specifically. Nor do I wish to. My function is to be available for medical purposes. The less involvement otherwise, the better for everyone."

"You can get word to people, though, can't you?"

The doctor smiled. "By 'people' I assume you mean Barak's followers."

"Yes."

"There are telephone numbers . . . public telephones, and specific hours. The answer is yes."

"We're going to need at least one other man. Floyd was killed."

Alison Booth gasped. Her eyes riveted on Alex; her hand reached out for his arm. He covered it gently. "Oh my God," she whispered.

The doctor looked at Alison but did not comment on her reaction. He turned back to McAuliff. "Barak told me. There may be a problem; we do not know yet. The survey is being watched. Floyd was part of it, and the police will find out. You will be questioned, of course. Naturally, you know absolutely nothing; wear long sleeves for a while—a few days, until the wound can be covered with a large plaster. To replace Floyd now with one of our men could be a self-induced trap."

Reluctantly, Alex nodded. "I see," he said softly. "But I need another man. Lawrence can't do triple duty . . ."

"May I make a suggestion?" asked the doctor with a thin smile and a knowing look in his eyes.

"What's that?"

"Use British Intelligence. You really should not ignore them."

"Get some sleep, Sam. Lawrence, you do the same," said Alex to the two men on the terrace. The doctor had left; his assistant remained with Barak Moore. Alison had gone into McAuliff's room and shut the door. "Nothing will happen tonight, except possibly the police . . . to ask me questions about a crewman I haven't seen since early afternoon."

"You know what to say, mon?" Lawrence asked the question with authority, as if he would provide the answer.

"The doctor explained; Barak told him."

"You must be angry, mon! Floyd alla time a nigger thief from Ochee. Now you know: supplies stolen. You drum-drum angry, mon!"

"It doesn't seem fair, does it?" said Alex sadly.

"Do as he says, lad," countered Sam Tucker. "He knows what he's talking about . . . I'll nap out here. Hate the goddamn bed, anyway."

"It isn't necessary, Sam."

"Has it occurred to you, boy, that the police may just come here without announcing themselves? I'd hate like hell for them to get the rooms mixed up."

"Oh Lord . . ." McAuliff spoke with weariness. It was the exhaustion of inadequacy, the pressure of continually being made aware of it. "I didn't think about that."

"Neither did the goddamn doctor," replied Sam. "Lawrence and I have, which is why we'll stand turns."

"Then I'll join you."

"You do enough tonight, mon," said Lawrence firmly. "You have been hurt . . . Maybe policemen do not come so quick. Floyd carry no papers. Early morning Sam Tuck and me take Barak away."

"The doctor said he was to stay where he is."

"The doctor is a kling-kling, mon! Two, three hours Barak will sleep. If he is not dead, we take him to Braco Beach. The ocean is still before sunrise; a flat-bottom is very gentle, mon. We take him away."

"He makes sense again, Alex." Tucker gave his approval without regret. "Our medical friend notwithstanding, it's a question of alternatives. And we both know most wounded men can travel gentle if you give 'em a couple of hours."

"What'll we do if the police come tonight? And search?"

Lawrence answered, again with authority. "I tell Tuck, mon. The person in that room has Indie Fever. The bad smell helps us. Falmouth police plenty scared of Indie Fever."

"So is everybody else," added Sam, chuckling.

"You're inventive," said McAuliff. And he meant it. "Indie Fever" was the polite term for a particularly nasty offshoot of encephalitis, infrequent but nevertheless very much a reality, usually found in the hill country. It could swell a man's testicles many times their size and render him impotent as well as a figure of grotesque ridicule.

"You go get sleep now, McAuliff, mon . . . please."

"Yes. Yes, I will. See you in a few hours." Alex looked at Lawrence for a moment before turning to go inside. It was amazing. Floyd was dead, Barak barely alive, and the grinning, previously carefree youngster who had seemed so naive and playful in comparison to his obvious superiors was no longer the innocent. He had, in a matter of hours, become the leader of his faction, lord of his pack. A hard authority had been swiftly developed, although he still felt the need to qualify that authority.

Get sleep now . . . please.

In a day or two the "please" would be omitted. The command would be all.

So forever the office made the man.

Sam Tucker smiled at McAuliff in the bright Jamaican moonlight. He seemed to be reading Alex's thoughts. Or was Sam remembering McAuliff's first independent survey? Tucker had been there. It had been in the Aleutians, in springtime, and a man had died because Alex had not been firm enough in his disciplining the team regarding the probing of ice fissures.

Alexander Tarquin McAuliff had matured quickly that springtime in the Aleutians.

"See you later, Sam."

Inside the room, Alison lay in bed, the table lamp on. By her side was the archive case he had carried out of Carrick Foyle. She was outwardly calm, but there was no mistaking the intensity beneath the surface. McAuliff removed his shirt, threw it on a chair, and crossed to the dial on the wall that regulated the overhead fan. He turned it up; the four blades suspended from the ceiling accelerated, the whirr matching the sound of the distant surf outside. He walked to the bureau, where the bucket of ice had melted halfway. Cubes were bunched together in the water, enough for drinks.

"Would you like a Scotch?" he asked without looking at her.

"No thank you," she replied in her soft British accent. Soft, but laced—as all British speech was laced—with that core of understated, superior rationality.

"I would."

"I should think so."

He poured the whisky into a hotel glass, threw in two ice cubes, and turned around. "To answer you before you ask, I had no idea tonight would turn out the way it did."

"Would you have gone had you known?"

"Of course not . . . But it's over. We have what we need now."

"This?" Alison touched the archive case.

"Yes."

"From what you've told me . . . on the word of a dying savage. Told to him by a dead fanatic."

"I think those descriptions are a little harsh." McAuliff went to the chair by the bed and sat down facing her. "But I won't defend either one yet. I'll wait. I'll find out what's in here, do what they say I should do, and see what happens."

"You sound positively confident, and I can't imagine why. You've been shot at. A bullet came within five inches of killing you. Now you sit here calmly and tell me you'll simply bide your time and see what happens? Alex! For God's sake, what are you doing?"

McAuliff smiled and swallowed a good deal of whisky. "What I never thought was possible," he said slowly, abruptly serious. "I mean that . . . And I've just seen a boy grow up into a man. In one hour. The act cost a terrible price, but it happened . . . and I'm not sure I can understand it, but I saw it. That transformation had something to do with belief. We haven't got it. We act out of fear or greed or both . . . all of us. He doesn't. He does what he does, becomes what he becomes, because he believes . . . And, strangely enough, so does Charley-mon."

"What in heaven's name are you talking about?"

McAuliff lowered his glass and looked at her. "I have an idea we're about to turn this war over to the people who should be fighting it."

Charles Whitehall exhaled slowly, extinguished the acetylene flame, and removed his goggles. He put the torch down on the long narrow table and took off the asbestos gloves. He noted with satisfaction that his every movement was controlled; he was like a confident surgeon, no motion wasted, his mind ahead of his every muscle.

He rose from the stool and stretched. He turned to see that the door of the small room was still bolted. A foolish thing to do, he thought; he had bolted the door. He was alone.

He had driven over back roads nearly forty miles away from Carrick Foyle, to the border of Saint Anne's. He had left the police car in a field and walked the last mile into town.

Ten years ago St. Anne's was a meeting place for those of the Movement between Falmouth and Ocho Rios. The "nigger rich," they had called themselves, with good-sized fields in Drax Hall, Chalky Hill, and Davis Town. Men of property and certain wealth, which they had forced from the earth and were not about to turn over to the Commonwealth sycophants in Kingston. Charles Whitehall remembered names, as he remembered most things—a necessary discipline—and within fifteen minutes after he reached St. Anne's, he was picked up by a man in a new Pontiac, who cried at seeing him.

When his needs were made known, he was driven to the house of another man in Drax Hall, whose hobby was machinery. The introductions were brief; this second man embraced him, held on to him for such a length of time—silently—that Charles found it necessary to disengage him.

He was taken to a tool shack at the side of the house, where everything he had requested was laid out on the long narrow table that butted against the wall, a sink at midpoint. Besides the overhead light, there was a goosenecked lamp, whose bright illumination could be directed at a small area. Charles was amused to see that along with these requirements was a bowl of fresh fruit and a huge pewter tankard filled with ice.

A messiah had returned.

And now the archive case was open. He stared down at the severed end, the metal edges still glowing with dying orange, then yellow—lingering—soon to be black again. Inside he could see the brown folds of a document roll— the usual encasement for folded papers, each sheet against the imperceptibly moist surface of the enveloping shield.

In the earth a living vault. Precise for a thousand years.

Walter Piersall had buried a rock for many ages in the event his own overlooked it.

He was a professional.

As a physician might with a difficult birth, Charles reached in and pulled the priceless child from its womb. He unraveled the document and began reading.

Acquaba.

The tribe of Acquaba.

Walter Piersall had gone back into the Jamaican archives and found the brief allusion in the records pertaining to the Maroon Wars.

On January 2, 1739 a descendant of the Coromanteen tribal chieftains, one Acquaba, led his followers into the mountains. The tribe of Acquaba would not be a party to the Cudjoe treaty with the British, insofar as said treaty called upon the Africans to recapture slaves for the white garrisons . . .

There was the name of an obscure army officer who had supplied the information to His Majesty's Recorder in Spanish Town, the colony's capital.

Middlejohn, Robt. Maj. W.I. Reg. 641.

What made the name of "Middlejohn, Robt." significant was Piersall's discovery of the following.

His Majesty's Recorder. Spanish Town. February 9-1739. [*Docm'ts. recalled. Middlejohn. W. I. Reg.* 641.]

And . . .

His Majesty's Recorder. Spanish Town. April 20-1739. [*Docm'ts. recalled. R.M. W. I. Reg.* 641]

Robert Middlejohn. Major. West Indian Regiment 641, in the Year of Our Lord 1739, had been significant to someone.

Who?

Why?

It took Walter Piersall weeks at the Institute to find the next clue. A second name.

But not in the eighteenth century; instead, 144 years later, in the year 1883.

Fowler, Jeremy. Clerk, Foreign Service.

One Jeremy Fowler had removed several documents from the archives in the new capital of Kingston on *the instructions of Her Majesty's Foreign Offiice, June 7, 1883. Victoria Regina.*

The colonial documents in question were labeled simply "Middlejohn papers." 1739.

Walter Piersall speculated. Was it possible that the *Middlejohn papers* continued to speak of the Tribe of Acquaba, as the first document had done? Was the retention of that first document in the archives an oversight? An omission committed by one Jeremy Fowler on June 7, 1883?

Piersall flew to London and used his academic credentials to gain access to the Foreign Office's West Indian Records. Since he was dealing in matters of research nearly a hundred years old, the F.O. had no objections. The archivists were most helpful.

And there were no transferred documents from Kingston in the year 1883.

Jeremy Fowler, clerk of the Foreign Service, had stolen the *Middlejohn papers*.

If there was a related answer, Walter Piersall now had two specifics to go on: the name "Fowler" and the year 1883 in the colony of Jamaica.

Since he was in London, he traced the descendants of Jeremy Fowler. It was not a difficult task.

The Fowlers—sons and uncles—were proprietors of their own brokerage house on the London Exchange. The patriarch was Gordon Fowler, Esquire, great-great-grandson of Jeremy Fowler, clerk, Foreign Service, colony of Jamaica.

Walter Piersall interviewed old Fowler on the premise that he was researching the last two decades of Victoria's rule in the Jamaica; the Fowler name was prominent. Flattered, the old gentleman gave him access to all papers, albums, and documents relative to Jeremy Fowler.

These materials told a not unfamiliar story of the times: a young man of "middle breeding" entering the Colonial Service, spending a number of years in a distant outpost, only to return to England far richer than when he left.

Sufficiently rich to be able to buy heavily into the Exchange during the last decade of the nineteenth century. A propitious time; the source of the current Fowler wealth.

One part of the answer.

Jeremy Fowler had made his connection in the Colonial Service.

Walter Piersall returned to Jamaica to look for the second part.

He studied, day by day, week by week, the recorded history of Jamaica for the year 1883. It was laborious.

And then he found it. May 25, 1883.

A disappearance that was not given much attention insofar as small groups of Englishmen—hunting parties—were constantly getting lost in the Blue Mountains and tropic jungles, usually to be found by scouting parties of blacks led by other Englishmen.

As this lone man had been found.

Her Majesty's Recorder, Jeremy Fowler.

Not a clerk, but the official Crown Recorder.

Which was why his absence justified the space in the papers. The Crown Recorder was not insignificant. Not landed gentry, of course, but a person.

The ancient newspaper accounts were short, imprecise, and strange.

A Mr. Fowler had last been observed in his government office on the evening of May 25, a Saturday. He did not return on Monday and was not seen for the rest of the work week. Nor had his quarters been slept in.

Six days later, Mr. Fowler turned up in the garrison of Fleetcourse, south of the impenetrable Cock Pit, escorted by several Maroon Negroes. He had gone on horseback . . . alone . . . for a Sunday ride. His horse had bolted him; he had gotten lost and wandered for days until found by the Maroons.

It was illogical. In those years, Walter Piersall knew, men did not ride alone into such territories. And if one did, a man who was sufficiently intelligent to be Her Majesty's Recorder would certainly know enough to take a left angle from the sun and reach the south coast in a matter of hours, at best a day.

And one week later Jeremy Fowler stole the *Middlejohn papers* from the archives. The documents concerning a sect led by a Coromanteen chieftan named Acquaba . . . that had disappeared into the mountains 144 years before.

And six months later he left the Foreign—Colonial—Service and returned to England a very, very wealthy man.

He had discovered the Tribe of Acquaba.

It was the only logical answer. And if that were so, there was a second, logical speculation: Was the Tribe of Acquaba . . . the Halidon?

Piersall was convinced it was. He needed only current proof.

Proof that there was substance to the whispers of the incredibly wealthy sect high in the Cock Pit mountains. An isolated community that sent its members out into the world, into Kingston, to exert influence.

Piersall tested five men in the Kingston government, all in positions of trust, all with obscure backgrounds. Did any of them belong to the Halidon?

He went to each, telling each that he alone was the recipient of his startling information: *the Tribe of Acquaba. The Halidon.*

Three of the five were fascinated but bewildered. They did not understand.

Two of the five disappeared.

Disappeared in the sense of being removed from Kingston. Piersall was told one man had retired suddenly to an island in the Martinique chain. The other was transferred out of Jamaica to a remote post.

Piersall had his current proof.

The Halidon was the Tribe of Acquaba.

It existed.

If he needed further confirmation, final proof, the growing harassment against him was it. The harassment now included the selected rifling and theft of his files and untraceable university inquiries into his current academic studies. Someone beyond the Kingston government was concentrating on him. These acts were not those of concerned bureaucrats.

The Tribe of Acquaba . . . Halidon.

What was left was to reach the leaders. A staggeringly difficult thing to do. For throughout the Cock Pit there were scores of insulated sects that kept to themselves; most of them poverty-stricken, scraping an existence off the land. The Halidon would not proclaim its self-sufficiency; which one was it?

The anthropologist returned once again to the volumes of African minutiae, specifically seventeenth-and eighteenth-century Coromanteen. The key had to be there.

Piersall had found the key; he had not footnoted its source.

Each tribe, each offshoot of a tribe, had a *single sound applicable to it only. A whistle, a slap, a word. This symbol was known only within the highest tribal councils, understood by only a few, who communicated it to their out-tribal counterparts.*

The symbol, the sound, the word . . . was 'Halidon.'

Its meaning.

It took him nearly a month of sleepless days and nights, using logarithmic charts of phonetics, hieroglyphs, and African symbols of daily survival.

When he was finished, he was satisfied. He had broken the ancient code.

It was too dangerous to include it in this summary. For in the event of his death—or murder—this summary might fall into the wrong hands. Therefore, there was a second archive case containing the secret.

The second without the first was meaningless.

Instructions were left with one man. To be acted upon in the event he was no longer capable of doing so himself.

Charles Whitehall turned over the last page. His face and neck were drenched with sweat. Yet it was cool in the shack. Two partially opened windows in the south wall let in the breezes from the hills of Drax Hall, but they could not put out the nervous fires of his anxiety.

Truths had been learned. A greater, overwhelming truth was yet to be revealed.

That it would be now, he was certain.

The scholar and the patriot were one again.

The Praetorian of Jamaica would enlist the Halidon.

20

JAMES FERGUSON was exhilarated. It was the feeling he had when momentous things happened in the lens of a microscope and he knew he was the first observer—or, at least, the first witness who recognized a causal effect for what it was.

Like the baracoa fiber.

He was capable of great imagination when studying the shapes and densities of microscopic particles. A giant manipulating a hundred million infinitesimal subjects.

It was a form of total control.

He had control now. Over a man who did not know what it was like to have to protest too loudly over the inconsequential because no one paid attention; to be forever down to his last few quid in the bank because none paid him the value of his work.

All that was changing. He could think about a great many things that were preposterous fantasies only yesterday: his own laboratories with the most expensive equipment—electronic, computerized, databanked; throwing away the little budget pads that told him whom he had last borrowed from.

A Maserati. He would buy a Maserati. Arthur Craft had one, why shouldn't he?

Arthur Craft was paying for it.

Ferguson looked at his watch—his goddamned inexpensive Timex—and signaled the bartender to total his bill.

When the bartender did not come over in thirty seconds, Ferguson reached for the tab in front of him and turned it over. It was simple enough to add: a dollar and fifty cents, twice.

James Ferguson then did what he had never done in his life. He took out a five-dollar bill, crumpled it up in his hand, got off the bar stool, and threw the wadded bill toward the cash register several yards in front of him. The bill bounced off the bottles on the lighted shelf and arced to the floor.

He started for the entrance.

There was *machismo* in his gesture; that was the word, that was the feeling.

In twenty minutes, he would meet the emissary from Craft the Younger. Down off Harbour Street, near Parish Wharf, on Pier Number Six. The man would be obsequious—he had no choice—and give him an envelope containing one thousand dollars.

One thousand dollars.

In a single envelope; not saved in bits and pieces over months of budgeting, nor with the tentacles of Inland Revenue or debtors-past reaching out to cut it in half. It was his to do with as he pleased. To squander, to throw away on silly things, to pay a girl to get undressed and undress him and do things to him that were fantasies . . . only yesterday.

He had borrowed—taken a salary advance, actually—from McAuliff. Two hundred dollars. There was no reason to repay it. Not now. He would simply tell McAuliff . . . "Alex"; from now on it would be "Alex," or perhaps "Lex"—very informal, very sure . . . to deduct the silly money from his paycheck. All at once, if he felt like it. It was inconsequential; it didn't really matter.

And it certainly didn't, thought Ferguson.

Every month Arthur Craft would give him an envelope. The agreed-upon amount was a thousand dollars in each envelope, but that was subject to change. Related to the increased cost of living, as it were. Increased as his appetites and comforts increased.

Just the beginning.

Ferguson crossed St. James Square and proceeded toward the waterfront. It was a warm night, with no breeze, and humid. Fat clouds, flying low and threatening rain, blocked the moon; the antiquated street lamps threw a subdued light in counterpoint to the gaudy neons of white and orange that announced the diversions of Montego Bay night life.

Ferguson reached Harbour Street and turned left. He stopped under a street lamp and checked his watch again. It was ten minutes past midnight; Craft had specified 12:15. In five minutes, he would have a thousand dollars.

Pier Six was directly ahead on his right, across the street. There was no ship in the dock, no activity within the huge loading area beyond the high linked fence; only a large naked bulb inside a wire casing that lit up the sign:

PIER SIX
HAMMOND LINES

He was to stand under the lamp, in front of the sign, and wait for a man to drive up in a Triumph sportscar. The man would ask him for identification. Ferguson would show him his passport and the man would give him the envelope.

So simple. The entire transaction would take less than thirty seconds. And change his life.

Craft had been stunned; speechless, actually, until he had found his voice and screamed a torrent of abuse . . . until, again, he realized the futility of his position. Craft the Younger had gone too far. He had broken laws and would be an object of scorn and embarrassment. James Ferguson could tell a story of airport meetings and luggage and telephone calls and industrial espionage . . . and promises.

Such promises.

But his silence could be purchased. Craft could buy his confidence for a first payment of one thousand dollars. If Craft did not care to do so, Ferguson was sure the Kingston authorities would display avid interest in the details of his story.

No, he had not spoken to anyone . . . yet. But things had been written down. (Lies Craft could not trace, of course.) That did not mean he was incapable of finding the spoken words; such capability was very much within his province . . . as the first payment was within Craft's province. One canceled the other; which would it be?

And so it was.

Ferguson crossed Harbour Street and approached the wire-encased light and the sign. A block and a half away, crowds of tourists swelled into the street, a one-way flow toward the huge passenger terminal and the gangplanks of a cruise ship. Taxis emerged out of side streets and alleys from the center of Montego Bay, blowing their horns anxiously, haltingly making their way to the dock. Three bass-toned whistles filled the air, vibrating the night, signifying that the ship was giving a warning: All passengers were to be on board.

He heard the Triumph before he saw it. There was the gunning of an engine from the darkness of a narrow side street diagonally across from Pier Six. The shiny, red, low-slung sportscar sped out of the dark recess and coasted to a stop in front of Ferguson. The driver was another Craft employee, one he recognized from a year ago. He did not recall the man's name; only that he was a quick, physical person, given to arrogance. He would not be arrogant now.

He wasn't. He smiled in the open car and gestured Ferguson to come over. "Hello, *Fergy!* It's been a long time."

Ferguson hated the nickname "Fergy"; it had dogged him for most of his life. Just when he had come to think it was part of a schoolboy past, someone—always someone unpleasant, he reflected—used it. He felt like correcting the man, reminding him of his messenger status, but he did not. He simply ignored the greeting.

"Since you recognize me, I assume there's no need to show you my identification," said James, approaching the Triumph.

"Christ, no! How've you been?"

"Well, thank you. Do you have the envelope? I'm in a hurry."

"Sure. Sure, I do, Fergy . . . Hey, you're a pistol, buddy! Our friend is pissing rocks! He's half out of his skull, you know what I mean?"

"I know what you mean. He should be. The envelope, please."

"Sure." The driver reached into his jacket and withdrew an envelope. He then leaned over and handed it to Ferguson. "You're supposed to count it. If it's all there, just give me back the envelope . . . make any kind of mark on it you like. Oh, here's a pen." The man opened the glove compartment and took out a ballpoint pen and held it up for Ferguson.

"That's not necessary. He wouldn't try to cheat me."

"Hey, come on, Fergy! It's my ass that'll be in a sling! Count it, mark it; what's the difference?"

Ferguson opened the bulky envelope. The denominations were all tens and fives, over a hundred bills. He had not asked for small denominations; it was convenient, though, he had to admit that. Less suspicious than hundreds or fifties or even twenties.

He started counting the bills.

Twice Craft's man interrupted him with insignificant

questions, causing James to lose his count. He had to start over again both times.

When he had finished, the driver suddenly handed him a wrapped package. "Oh, because our friend wants to show there's no bad feeling—he's a sport, you know what I mean?—he sent you one of those new Yashica .35 millimeters. He remembered you're crazy about photography."

Ferguson saw the Yashica label on the top of the package. A seven-hundred-dollar instrument! One of the very best! Craft the Younger was indeed a frightened man. "Thank . . . Arthur for me. But tell him this isn't deductible from any future payments."

"Oh, I'll tell him . . . Now, I'm going to tell you something, Fergy-baby. You're on fuckin' *Candid Camera*." The driver spoke quietly.

"What are you talking about?"

"Right behind you, Fergy-baby."

Ferguson whipped around toward the high linked fence and the deserted area beyond. There were two men in the shadows of a doorway. They came out slowly, perhaps thirty yards away from him. And one of the men carried a tripod with a camera attached. "What have you done?"

"Just a little insurance, Fergy-baby. Our friend is contract-conscious, you know what I mean? Infrared film, babe. I think you know what that is. And you just gave a terrific performance counting out money and taking Christ knows what from a guy who hasn't been seen in public north of Caracas for over six months. You see, our friend flew me out of Rio just to get my picture taken . . . with you."

"You can't do this! Nobody would believe this!"

"Why not, babe? You're a hungry little prick, you know what I mean? Hungry little pricks like you get hung easy . . . Now, you listen to me, asshole. You and Arthur, you're one on one. Only his one is a little heavier. That film would raise a lot of questions you couldn't find any answers for. I'm a very unpopular man, Fergy. You'd get thrown off the island . . . but probably you'd get thrown into the can first. You wouldn't last fifteen minutes with those social rejects, you know what I mean? They'd peel your white skin, babe, layer by layer . . . Now, you be a good boy, Fergy. Arthus says for you to keep the thousand. You'll probably earn it." The man held up the empty envelope. "Two sets of prints on this.

Yours and mine . . . Ciao, baby. I've got to get out of here and back to non-extradition country."

The driver gunned the engine twice and slapped the gearshift effortlessly. He swung the Triumph expertly in a semicircle and roared off into the darkness of Harbour Street.

Julian Warfield was in Kingston now. He had flown in three days ago and used all of Dunstone's resources to uncover the strange activities of Alexander McAuliff. Peter Jensen had followed instructions to the letter; he had kept McAuliff under the closest scrutiny, paying desk clerks and doormen and taxi drivers to keep him informed of the American's every move.

And always he and his wife were out of sight, in no way associated with that scrutiny.

It was the least he could do for Julian Warfield . . . He would do anything Julian asked, anything Dunstone, Limited, demanded. He would deliver nothing but his best to the man and the organization that had taken him and his wife out of the valley of despair and given them a world with which they could cope and in which they could function.

Work they loved, money and security beyond the reach of most academic couples. Enough to forget.

Julian had found them nearly twenty years ago, beaten, finished, destroyed by events . . . impoverished, with nowhere and no one to return to. He and Ruth had been caught; it was a time of madness, of Klaus Fuchs and Guy Burgess and convictions born of misplaced zeal. He and his wife had supplemented their academic income by working for the government on covert geological operations—oil, gold, minerals of value. And they had willingly turned over everything in the classified files to a contact at the Soviet Embassy.

Another blow for equality and justice.

And they were caught.

But Julian Warfield came to see them.

Julian Warfield offered them their lives again . . . in exchange for certain assignments he might find for them. Inside the government and out; on the temporary staffs of companies . . . within England and without; always in the highest professional capacities, pursuing their professional labors.

All charges were dropped by the Crown. Terrible mistakes had been made against most respected members of the academic community. Scotland Yard had apologized. Actually *apologized*.

Peter and Ruth never refused Julian; their loyalty was unquestioned.

Which was why Peter was now on his stomach in the cold, damp sand while the light of a Caribbean dawn broke over the eastern horizon. He was behind a mound of coral rock with a perfect view of McAuliff's oceanside terrace. Julian's last instructions had been specific.

Find out who comes to see him. Who's important to him. Get identities, if you can. But for God's sake, stay in the background. We'll need you both in the interior.

Julian had agreed that McAuliff's disappearances—into Kingston, into taxis, into an unknown car at the gates of the Courtleigh Manor—all meant that he had interests in Jamaica other than Dunstone, Limited.

It had to be assumed that he had broken the primary article of faith. Secrecy.

If so, McAuliff could be transferred . . . forgotten without difficulty. But before that happened, it was essential to discover the identity of Dunstone's island enemy.

Or enemies.

In a very real sense, the survey itself was secondary to that objective. Definitely secondary. If it came down to it, the survey could be sacrificed if, by that sacrifice, identities were revealed.

And Peter knew he was nearer those identities now . . . in this early dawn on the beach of Bengal Court.

It had begun three hours ago.

Peter and Ruth had retired a little past midnight. Their room was in the east wing of the motel, along with Ferguson's and Charles Whitehall's. McAuliff, Alison, and Sam Tucker were in the west wing, the division signifying only old friends, new lovers, and late drinkers.

They heard it around one o'clock: an automobile swerving into the front drive, its wheels screeching, then silent, as if the driver had heard the noise and suddenly become alarmed by it.

It had been strange. Bengal Court was no kind of nightclub, no "drum-drum" watering hole that catered to the swinging and/or younger tourist crowds. It was quiet, with very little to recommend it to the image of fast drivers. As a matter of fact, Peter Jensen could not remember having heard *any* automobiles drive into Bengal Court after nine o'clock in the evening since they had been there.

He had risen from the bed and walked out on the terrace, and had seen nothing. He had walked around the east end of the motel to the edge of the front parking lot, where he did see something; something extremely alarming, barely visible.

In the far section of the lot, in shadows, a large black man—he believed he was black—was lifting the unconscious figure of another man out of the rear seat of an automobile. Then, farther beyond, a white man ran across the lawn from around the corner of the west wing. It was Sam Tucker. He approached the black carrying the unconscious form, gave instructions—pointing to the direction from which he had come—and continued to the automobile, silently closing the rear door.

Sam Tucker was supposed to be in Ocho Rios with McAuliff. It seemed unlikely that he would have returned to Bengal Court alone.

And as Jensen pondered this, there was the outline of another figure on the west lawn. It was Alison Booth. She gestured to the black man; she was obviously excited, trying to remain in control of herself. She led the large black man into the darkness around the far corner.

Peter Jensen suddenly had a sinking feeling. Was the unconscious figure Alexander McAuliff? Then he rethought the immediate visual picture. He could not be sure—he could barely see, and everything was happening so rapidly—but as the black passed under the dim spill of a parking light, the bobbing head of his charge extended beyond his arms. Peter had been struck by the oddness of it. The head appeared to be completely bald . . . as if shaven.

Sam Tucker looked inside the automobile, seemed satisfied, then raced back across the west lawn after the others.

Peter remained crouched in his concealed position after the figure had disappeared. It was extraordinary. Tucker and Alison Booth were not in Ocho Rios; a man had been hurt, apparently quite seriously, and instead of taking him directly inside the motel's front entrance, they furtively carried him in, smuggled him in. And it might be conceivable that Sam Tucker would come back to Bengal Court without McAuliff; it was inconceivable that Alison Booth would do so.

What were they doing? What in heaven's name had happened . . . was happening?

The simplest way to find out, thought Peter, was to get dressed, return to the tiny bar, and, for reasons he had not yet created, call McAuliff for a drink.

He would do this alone. Ruth would remain in their room. But first Peter would walk down to the beach, to the water's edge, where he would have a full view of the motel and the oceanside terraces.

Once in the miniature lounge, Peter invented his reason to phone McAuliff. It was simple to the point of absurdity. He had been unable to sleep, taken a stroll on the beach, seen a light beyond the drawn curtains in Alexander's room, and gathered he had returned from Ocho Rios. Would he and Alison be his guests for a nightcap?

Jensen went to the house phone at the end of the bar. When McAuliff answered, his voice was laced with the frustration of a man forced to be civil in the most undesirable of circumstances. And McAuliff's lie was apparent.

"Oh, Jesus, Peter, thanks but we're *beat*. We just got settled at the Sans Souci when Latham called from the Ministry. Some damned bureaucratic problem with our interior permits; we had to drive all the way back for some kind of goddamned . . . inspection first thing in the morning. . . . inoculation records, medical stuff. Crew, mainly."

"Terribly inconsiderate, old boy. Nasty bastards, I'd say."

"They are . . . We'll take a raincheck, though. Perhaps tomorrow."

Peter had wanted to keep McAuliff on the phone a bit longer. The man was breathing audibly; each additional moment meant the possibility of Jensen's learning something. "Ruth and I thought we'd hire a car and go to Dunn's Falls around noon tomorrow. Surely you'll be finished by then. Care to come along?"

"Frankly, Peter," said McAuliff haltingly, "we were hoping to get back to Ochee, if we could."

"Then that would rule out Dunn's Falls, of course. You've seen it, though, haven't you? Is it all they say?"

"Yes . . . yes, it certainly is. Enjoy yourselves—"

"You *will* be back tomorrow night, then?" interjected Jensen.

"Sure . . . Why?"

"Our raincheck, old boy."

"Yes," said McAuliff slowly, carefully. "We'll be back tomorrow night. Of course we'll be back tomorrow night . . . Good night, Peter."

"Good night, chap. Sleep well." Jensen hung up the house phone. He carried his drink slowly back to a table in the corner, nodding pleasantly to the other guests, giving the impression he was waiting for someone, probably his wife. He had no wish to join anyone; he had to think out his moves.

Which was why he was now lying in the sand behind a small mound of surfaced coral on the beach, watching Lawrence and Sam Tucker talking.

He had been there for nearly three hours. He had seen things he knew he was not supposed to see: two men arriving—one obviously a doctor with the inevitable bag, the other some sort of assistant carrying a large trunklike case and odd-shaped paraphernalia.

There had been quiet conferences between McAuliff, Alison, and the doctor, later joined by Sam Tucker and the black crewman, Lawrence.

Finally, all left the terrace but Tucker and the black. They stayed outside.

On guard.

Guarding not only Alexander and the girl, but also whoever was in that adjoining room. The injured man with the oddly shaped head who had been carried from the automobile.

Who was he?

The two men had stayed at their posts for three hours now. No one had come or gone. But Peter knew he could not leave the beach. Not yet.

Suddenly, Jensen saw the black crewman, Lawrence, walk down the terrace steps and start across the dunes toward the beach. Simultaneously, Tucker made his way over the grass to the corner of the building. He stood immobile on the lawn; he was waiting for someone. Or watching.

Lawrence reached the surf, and Jensen lay transfixed as the huge black man did a strange thing. He looked at his

watch and then proceeded to light two matches, one after
the other, holding each aloft in the breezeless dawn air for
several seconds and throwing each into the lapping water.

Moments later, the action was explained. Lawrence
cupped his hand over his eyes to block the blinding,
head-on light of the sun as it broke the space above the
horizon, and Peter followed his line of sight.

Across the calm ocean surface, in the massive land
shadows by the point, there were two corresponding flick-
ers of light. A small boat had rounded the waters of the
cove's entrance, its gray-black hull slowly emerging in the
early sunlight.

Its destination was that section of the beach where
Lawrence stood.

Several minutes later, Lawrence struck another match
and held it up until there was an acknowledgment from
the approaching craft, at which instant both were extinguished and the black crewman started running back over
the sand toward Bengal Court.

On the lawn, by the corner of the building, Sam Tucker
turned and saw the racing Lawrence. He walked to the
stairs in the sea wall and waited for him. The black man
reached the steps; he and Tucker spoke briefly, and together they approached the terrace doors of the adjoining
room—Alison Booth's room. Tucker opened them, and
the two men went inside, leaving the double doors ajar.

Peter kept shifting his eyes from the motel to the
beach. There was no visible activity from the terrace; the
small boat plodded its way over the remarkably still
waters toward the beach, now only three or four hundred
yards from shore. It was a long, flat-bottom fishing boat,
propelled by a muffled engine. Sitting in the stern was a
black man in what appeared to be ragged clothes and a
wide straw sun hat. Hook poles shot up from the small
deck, nets were draped over the sides of the hull; the effect was that of a perfectly normal Jamaican fisherman
out for the dawn catch.

When the boat came within several hundred feet of the
shore, the black skipper lit a match, then extinguished it
quickly. Jensen looked up at the terrace. In seconds, the
figure of Sam Tucker emerged from the darkness beyond
the open doors. He held one end of a stretcher on which a
man lay wrapped in blankets; Lawrence followed, holding
the other end.

Gently but swiftly, the two men ran—glided—the stretcher across the terrace, down the sea-wall steps, over the sand, and toward the beach. The timing was precise, not a moment wasted. It seemed to Jensen that the instant the boat hit shallow water, Tucker and Lawrence waded into the calm surf with the stretcher and placed it carefully over the sides onto the deck. The nets were swung over on top of the blanketed man and the fishing boat was immediately pushed back into the water by Sam Tucker as Lawrence slid onto the bow slat. Seconds later, Lawrence had removed his shirt and from some recess in the boat lifted out a torn, disheveled straw hat, clamped it on his head, and yanked a hook pole from its clasp. The transformation was complete. Lawrence the conspirator was now a lethargic native fisherman.

The small flat-bottom craft turned, rippling the glasslike surface of the water, and headed out. The motor chugged a bit louder than before; the skipper wanted to get away from the beach with his concealed human cargo.

Sam Tucker waved; Lawrence nodded and dipped the hook pole. Tucker came out of the miniature surf and walked swiftly back toward Bengal Court.

Peter Jensen watched as the fishing boat veered in open water toward the point. Several times Lawrence leaned forward and down, fingering nets but obviously checking the condition of the man on the stretcher. Intermittently, he seemed to be issuing quiet commands to the black at the engine tiller. The sun had now cleared the edge of the Jamaican horizon. It would be a hot day.

Up at the terrace Peter saw that the double doors of Alison Booth's room remained open. With the additional light, he could also see that there was new acitivity inside. Sam Tucker came out twice, carrying two tan plastic bags, which he left on the patio. Then a second man—the doctor's assistant, Peter realized—emerged, holding a large cylinder by its neck and a huge black suitcase in his other hand. He placed them on the stone, bent down below them on the sea wall, and stood up moments later with two elongated cans—aerosol cans, thought Jensen—and handed one to Tucker as he came through the door. The two men talked briefly and then went back inside the room.

No more than three minutes had elapsed when Tucker and the doctor's aide were seen again, this time somewhat comically as they backed into the door frame simultaneously. Each held his arm outstretched; in each hand was an aerosol can, clouds of mist spewing from both.

Tucker and the black aide had systematically sprayed the interior of the room.

Once finished, they crossed to the plastic bags, the case, and the large cylinder. They picked up the objects, spoke briefly again, and started for the lawn.

Out on the water, the fishing boat was halfway to the point of the cove. But something had happened. It had stopped; it bobbed gently on the calm surface, no longer traveling forward. Peter could see the now tiny figure of Lawrence standing up in the bow, then crouching, then standing up again. The skipper was gesturing, his movements excited.

The boat pushed forward once more, only to turn slowly and change direction. It did not continue on its course—if the point was, indeed, its course. Instead, it headed for the open sea.

Jensen lay on the moist sand for the next fifteen minutes, watching the small craft progressively become a black dot within a gray-black ocean splashed with orange sunlight. He could not read the thoughts of the two Jamaicans; he could not see the things that were happening on that boat so illogically far out on the water. But his knowledge of tides and currents, his observations during the last three hours, led his conclusions to one end.

The man on the stretcher had died. His corpse would soon be stripped of identification, weighted down with net lead, and thrown into the water, eventually to be carried by floor currents far away from the island of Jamaica. Perhaps to be washed ashore weeks or months from now on some Cayan reef or, more fortuitously, torn apart and devoured by the predators of the deep.

Peter knew it was time to call Julian, meet with Julian. Immediately.

McAuliff rolled over on his side, the sharp pain in his shoulder suddenly surging through his chest. He sat up quickly, momentarily bewildered. He focused his thoughts; it was morning; the night before had been a series of terrifying confusions. The pieces would have to be put back together, plans made.

He looked down at Alison, beside him. She was breathing deeply, steadily, in complete sleep. If the evening had been a nightmare for him, it had been no less a torment for her. Perhaps worse. At least he had been in motion, constant, unceasing movement. She had been waiting, thinking; he had had no time for thoughts.

It was worse to wait. In some ways.

Slowly, as silently as he could, he swung his legs over the side of the bed and stood up. His whole body was stiff; his joints pained him, especially his kneecaps.

It was understandable. The muscles he had used last night were dormant strings of an unused instrument, called into play by a panicked conductor. The allusion was proper, thought Alex—about his thoughts. He nearly smiled as he conjured up the phrase: so out of tune.

Everything was out of tune.

But the notes *were* forming recognizable chords . . . somewhere. In the distance. There was a melody of sorts that could be vaguely distinguished.

Yet not *distinguished*. Hardly noble.

Not yet.

An odor assaulted his nostrils. It was not the illusion of spice and vanilla, but nevertheless sweet. If there was an association, it was south Oriental . . . Java, the Sunda Trench, pungent, a bit sickening. He crossed quietly to the terrace door, about to open it, when he realized he was naked. He walked silently to a chair by the curtained window, where he had thrown a pair of swimming trunks several days ago. He removed them from the wooden rim and put them on.

"I hope they're not wet," said Alison from the bed. "The maid service here is a touch lacking, and I didn't hang them up."

"Go back to sleep," Alex replied. "You were asleep a moment ago. Very much alseep."

"I'm very much awake now . . . Good heavens, it's a quarter past eight."

"And?"

"Nothing, really . . . I just didn't think we'd sleep this long."

"It's not long. We didn't get to bed until after three. Considering everything that happened, noon would have been too early."

"How's your arm? The shoulder?"

"A little sore . . . like most of me. Not crippling."

"What *is* that terrible smell?" Alison sat up; the sheet fell away, revealing a curiously prim nightgown, opaque cotton with buttons. She saw Alex's gaze, the beginning of a smile on his lips. She glanced down and laughed. "My granny nightshirt. I put it on after you feel asleep. It was chilly, and you hadn't the slightest interest in anything but philosophical discourse."

He walked to the edge of the bed and sat down beside her. "I was long-winded, wasn't I?"

"I couldn't shut you up; there was simply no way. You drank a great deal of Scotch—how's your head, incidentally?"

"Fine. As though I'd had Ovaltine . . ."

". . . straight alcohol couldn't have stayed with you. I've seen that before, too . . . Sorry. I forgot you object to my British pronouncements."

"I made a few myself last night. I withdraw my objections."

"Do you still believe them? Your pronouncements? As they say . . . in the cold logic of the morning?"

"I think I do; the thrust of my argument being that no one fights better for his own turf than he who lives on it, depends on it . . . Yes, I believe it. I'd feel more confident if Barak hadn't been hurt."

"Strange name, Barak."

"Strange man. And very strong. He's needed, Alison. Boys can become men quickly, but they're still not seasoned. His ken is needed."

"By whom?"

McAuliff looked at her; at the lovely way her eyebrows rose quizzically above her clear, light blue eyes. "By his own side," he answered simply.

"Which is not Charles Whitehall's side." There was no question implied.

"No. They're very different. And I think it's necessary . . . at this point, under these circumstances . . . that Barak's faction be as viable as Charley-mon's."

"That concern strikes me as dangerously close to interference, darling."

"I know. It's just that everything seems so complicated to me. But it doesn't to Whitehall. And it doesn't to Barak Moore. They see a simple division muddled up by second and third parties . . . Don't you see? They're not distracted. They first go after one objective, then another, and another; knowing ultimately they'll have to deal with each other. Neither one loses sight of that. Each stores his apples as he goes along."

"What?" Alison leaned back on the pillow, watching McAuliff as he stared blankly at the wall. "I don't follow that."

"I'm not sure I can explain it. A wolf pack surrounds its victims, who huddle in the center. The dogs set up an erratic rhythm of attack, taking turns lunging in and out around the circle until the quarry's confused to the point of exhaustion. Then the wolves close in." Alex stopped; he was uncertain.

"I gather Charles and this Barak are the victims," said Alison, trying to help him.

"Jamaica's the victim, and they're Jamaica. The wolves—the enemies—are Dunstone and all it represents: Warfield and his crowd of . . . global manipulators—the Chatelleraults of this world; British Intelligence, with its elitists, like Tallon and *his* crowd of colonial opportunists; the Crafts of this island . . . internal bleeders, you could call them. Finally, maybe even this Halidon, because you can't control what you can't find; and even if you find it, it may not be controllable . . . There are a lot of wolves."

"There's a lot of confusion," added Alison.

McAuliff turned and looked at her. "For *us*. Not for *them*. That's what's remarkable. The victims have worked out a strategy: Take each wolf as it lunges. Destroy it."

"What's that got to do with . . . apples?"

"I jumped out of the circle and went into a straight line."

"Aren't we abstract," stated the girl.

"It's valid. As any army—and don't kid yourself, Charles Whitehall and Barak Moore have their armies— as any army moves forward, it maintains its lines of supply. In this case, support. Remember. When all the wolves have been killed, they face each other. Whitehall and Moore both are piling up apples . . . support." McAuliff stopped again and got up from bed. He walked to the window to the right of the terrace doors, pulled the curtain, and looked out at the beach. "Does any of this make sense to you?" he asked softly.

"It's very political, I think, and I'm not much at that

sort of thing. But you're describing a rather familiar pattern, I'd say—"

"You bet your *life* I am," interrupted Alex, speaking slowly and turning from the windows. "Historical precedents unlimited . . . and *I'm* no goddamn historian. Hell, where do you want to start? Caesar's Gaul? Rome's Ferrara? China in the thirties? The Koreas, the Vietnams, the Cambodias? Half a dozen African states? The words are there, over and over again. Exploitation from outside, inside revolt—insurgence and counterinsurgence. Chaos, bloodbath, expulsion. Ultimately reconstruction in so-called compromise. That's the pattern. That's what Barak and Charley-mon expect to play out. And each knows that while he's joining the other to kill a wolf, he's got to entrench himself further in the turf at the same time. Because when the compromise comes . . . as it must . . . he wants it more *his* way than less."

"What you're saying—getting away from circles and straight lines—is that you don't approve of Barak's 'army' being weakened. Is that it?"

"Not *now*. Not at this moment."

"Then you *are* interfering. You're an outsider taking an inside position. It's not your . . . turf, my darling."

"But I brought Charley here. I gave him his respectability, his cover. Charley's a son of a bitch."

"Is Barak Moore a saint?"

"Not for a second. He's a son of a bitch, too. And it's important that he is." McAuliff returned to the window. The morning sun was striking the panes of glass, causing tiny modules of condensation. It was going to be a hot day.

"What are you going to do?" Alison sat forward, prepared to get up as she looked over at Alex.

"Do?" he asked quietly, his eyes concentrating on something outside the window. "What I was sent here to do; what I'm being paid one million dollars to do. Complete the survey or find this Halidon. Whichever comes first. Then get us out of here . . . on our terms."

"That sounds reasonable," said Alison, rising from the bed. "What *is* that sickening odor?"

"Oh? I forgot to tell you. They were going to spray down your room, get rid of the medicine smells." McAuliff stepped closer to the window and shaded his eyes from the rays of the morning sun.

"The ether or disinfectant or whatever it was was far more palatable. My bathing suit's in there. May I get it?"

"What?" Alex was not listening, his attention on the object of his gaze outside.

"My bathing suit, darling. It's in my room."

McAuliff turned from the window, oblivious to her words. "Wait here. I'll be right back." He walked rapidly to the terrace door, opened it, and ran out.

Alison looked after him, bewildered. She crossed to the window to see what Alex had seen. It took several seconds to understand; she was helped by watching McAuliff run across the sand toward the water.

In the distance, down at the beach, was the lone figure of a large black man staring out at the ocean. It was Lawrence.

Alex approached the tall Jamaican, wondering if he should call out. Instinctively, he did not. Instead, he cleared his throat when he was within ten yards; cleared it loud enough to be heard over the sound of the lapping small waves.

Lawrence turned around. Tears were in his eyes, but he did not blink or change the muscles of his face. He was a child-man accepting the agonies of a very personal torment.

"What happened?" asked McAuliff softly, walking up to the shirtless boy-giant.

"I should have listened to you, mon. Not to him. He was wrong, mon."

"Tell me what happened," repeated Alex.

"Barak is dead. I did what he ordered me to do and he is dead. I listened to him and he is dead, mon."

"He knew the risk; he had to take it. I think he was probably right."

"No . . . He was wrong because he is dead. That makes him wrong, mon."

"Floyd's gone . . . Barak. Who is there now?"

Lawrence's eyes bore into McAuliff's; they were red from silent weeping, and beyond the pride and summoned strength, there was the anguish of a child. And the pleading of a boy. "You and me, mon. There is no one else . . . You will help me, mon?"

Alex returned the rebel's stare; he did not speak.

Welcome to the seat of revolution, McAuliff thought to himself.

21

THE TRELAWNY POLICE made Floyd's identification at 7:02
in the morning. The delay was caused by the lack of any
print facilities in Falmouth and the further lack of cooperation on the part of several dozen residents who were
systematically routed from their beds during the night to
observe the corpse. The captain was convinced that any
number of them recognized the bullet-pierced body, but it
was not until two minutes past seven when one old
man—a gardener from Carrick Foyle—had reacted sufficiently to the face of the bloody mess on the table for the
captain to decide to apply sterner methods. He held a
lighted cigarette millimeters in front of the old man's left
eye, which he stretched open with his free hand. He told
the trembling black that he would burn the gelatine of his
eyeball unless he told the truth.

The ancient gardener screamed and told the truth. The
man who was the corpse on the table had worked for
Walter Piersall. His name was Floyd Cotter.

The captain then telephoned several parish precincts for
further information on one Cotter, Floyd. There was
nothing; they had never heard of him. But the captain had
persisted; Kingston's interest in Dr. Walter Piersall, before
and after his death, was all-inclusive. Even to the point of
around-the-clock patrols at the house on the hill in Carrick Foyle. The captain did not know why; it was not his
province to question, much less analyze, Kingston's commands. That they were was enough. Whatever the motives
that resulted in the harassment of the white scholar before
his death, and the continued concern about his residence
after, was Kingston's bailiwick, not his. He simply followed orders. He followed them well, even enthusiastically. That was why he was the prefect captain of the parish police in Falmouth.

And that was why he kept making telephone calls about
one Floyd Cotter, deceased, whose corpse lay on the table
and whose blood would not stop oozing out of the punc-
tures on his face and in his chest and stomach and legs;
blood that dried on the pages of The Gleamer, hastily
scattered about the floor.

At five minutes to eight, as the captain was about to lift the receiver off its base and call the precinct in Sherwood Content, the telephone rang. It was his counterpart in Puerto Seco, near Discovery Bay, whom he had contacted twenty minutes ago. The man said that after their conversation, he had talked with his deputies on the early shift. One of the men reported that there was a Floyd with a survey team, headed by an American named McAuliff, that had begun work about ten days ago on the shoreline. The survey had hired a carrier crew out of Ocho Rios. The Government Employment Office had been involved.

The captain then woke up the director of the G.E.O. in Ochee. The man was thoroughly awake by the time he got on the line, because he had no telephone and consequently had had to leave his house and walk to a Johnny Canoe store, where he—and most of the neighborhood—took calls. The employment chief recalled that among the crewmen hired by the American named McAuliff, there *had* been a Floyd, but he did not remember the last name. This Floyd had simply shown up with other applicants who had heard of the available work from the Ochee grapevine. He had not been listed in the employment files; neither had one or two others eventually hired.

The captain listened to the director, thanked him, and said nothing to contradict or enlighten him. But after hanging up the phone, he put in a call to Gordon House in Kingston. To the inspector who headed the search teams that had meticulously gone over Piersall's house in Carrick Foyle.

The inspector's conclusion was the same as the captain's: The deceased Floyd Cotter—former employee of Walter Piersall—had returned with friends to loot the house and been interrupted.

Was anything missing?

Digging in the cellar? In an old cistern out of use for years?

The inspector would fly back to Falmouth by noon. In the meantime, the captain might discreetly interrogate Mr. McAuliff. If nothing else, ascertain his whereabouts.

At twenty minutes past nine, the captain and his first deputy drove through the gates of Bengal Court.

Alexander was convincingly agitated. He was appalled —and naturally sorry—that Floyd Cotter had lost his life, but goddamn it, the episode answered several questions. Some very expensive equipment was missing from the supply truck, equipment that could bring high prices in a thieves' market. This Floyd Cotter obviously had been the perpetrator; he was a thief, had been the thief.

Did the captain want a list of the missing items? There was a geodometer, a water scope, half a dozen jeweled compasses, three Polaroid filter screens, five brand-new medicine kits in Royal Society cases, a Rolleiflex camera, and a number of other things of lesser value—but not inexpensive. The captain's deputy wrote as rapidly as he could on a notepad as Alex rattled off the "missing" items. Twice he asked for spellings; once the point of his pencil broke. It was a harried few minutes.

After the interview was over, the captain and his deputy shook hands with the American geologist and thanked him for his cooperation. McAuliff watched them get into the police car and waved a friendly good-bye as the vehicle sped out of the parking lot through the gates.

A quarter of a mile down the road, the captain braked the patrol car to a stop. He spoke quietly to his deputy.

"Go back through the woods to the beach, mon. Find out who he is with, who comes to see him."

The deputy removed his visor cap and the creased khaki shirt of his uniform with the yellow insignias of his rank, and reached into the back for a green T-shirt. He slipped it over his head and got out of the car. He stood on the tarred pavement, unbuckled his belt, and slid his holster off the leather strip. He handed it through the window to the captain.

The captain reached down below the dashboard and pulled out a rumpled black baseball cap that was discolored with age and human sweat. He gave it to the deputy and laughed.

"We all look alike, mon. Aren't you the fella who alla time sell *cocoruru?*"

"Alla time John Crow, mon. Mongoose him not."

The deputy grinned and started toward the woods beyond the bank of the pavement, where there was a rusty, torn wire fence. It was the demarcation of the Bengal Court property.

The patrol car roared off down the road. The prefect captain of the Falmouth police was in a hurry. He had to drive to Halfmoon Bay and meet a seaplane that was flying in from Kingston.

* * *

Charles Whitehall stood in the tall grass on a ridge overlooking the road from Priory-on-the-Sea. Under his arm was the black archive case, clamped shut and held together with three-inch strips of adhesive. It was shortly after twelve noon, and McAuliff would be driving up the road soon.

Alone.

Charles had insisted on it. That is, he had insisted before he had heard McAuliff's words—spoken curtly, defensively—that Barak Moore was dead.

Barak dead.

Bramwell Moore, schoolboy chum from so many years ago in Savanna-la-Mar, dead from Jamaican bullets.

Jamaican bullets.

Jamaican *police* bullets. That was better. In adding the establishmentarian, there was a touch of compassionate logic—a contradiction in terms, thought Whitehall; logic was neither good nor evil, merely logic. Still, words defined logic and words could interpreted—thus the mendacity of all official statistics: self-serving logic.

His mind was wandering, and he was annoyed with himself. Barak had known, as he knew, that they were not playing chicken-in-de-kitchen any longer. There was no bandana-headed mother wielding a straw broom, chasing child and fowl out into the yard, laughing and scolding simultaneously. This was a different sort of insurgence. Bandana-headed mothers were replaced by visor-capped men of the state; straw brooms became high-powered rifles. The chickens were ideas . . . far more deadly to the uniformed servants of the state than the loose feathers were to the bandana-headed servants of the family.

Barak dead.

It seemed incredible. Yet not without its positive effect. Barak had not understood the problems of their island; therefore, he had not understood the proper solutions. Barak's solutions were decades away.

First there had to be strength. The many led by a very strong, militant few.

Perhaps one.

In the downhill distance there was a billow of dust; a station wagon was traveling much too fast over the old dirt road.

McAuliff was anxious too.

246 / JONATHAN RYDER

Charles started back across the field to the entrance drive of the house. He had requested that his Drax Hall host be absent between the hours of twelve and three. No explanations were given, and no questions were asked.

A messiah had returned. That was enough.

"Here it is," said McAuliff, standing in front of Whitehall in the cool toolshed, holding the smaller archive case in his left hand. "But before you start fiddling around, I want a couple of things clear."

Charles Whitehall stared at the American. "Conditions are superfluous. We both know what must be done."

"What's not superfluous," countered Alex, "is that you understand there'll be no . . . unilateral decisions. This isn't your private war, *Charley-mon.*"

"Are you trying to sound like Barak?"

"Let's say I'm looking after his interests. And mine."

"Yours I can comprehend. Why his? They're not compatible, you know."

"They're not even connected."

"So why concern yourself?" Whitehall shifted his eyes to the archive case. He realized that his breathing had become audible; his anxiety was showing, and again he was annoyed with himself. "Let me have that, please."

"You asked me a question. I'm going to answer it first," replied McAuliff. "I don't trust you, Charley. You'll use anyone. Anything. Your kind always does. You make pacts and agreements with anything that moves. And you do it very well. You're so flexible you meet yourself around corners. But all the time it's *sturm-und-drang,* and I'm not much for that."

"Oh, I see. You subscribe to Barak's canefield paratroopers. The chaos of the Fidelisti, where the corporals spit and chew cigars and rape the generals' daughters so society is balanced. Three-year plans and five-year plans and crude uneducated bullies managing the affairs of state. Into disaster, I might add. Don't be a fool, McAuliff. You're better than that."

"Cut it out, Charley. You're not on a podium addressing your chiefs of staff," said Alex wearily. "I don't believe in that oversimplification any more than I believe in your two-plus-two solutions. Pull in your hardware. I'm still the head of this survey. I can fire you in a minute. Very publicly. Now, that might not get you off the island, but your situation won't be the same."

"What guarantee do I have that you won't force me out?"

"Not much of one. You'll just have to take my word that I want those bastards off my back as badly as you do. For entirely different reasons."

"Somehow I think you're lying."

"I wouldn't gamble on that."

Whitehall searched McAuliff's eyes. "I won't. I said this conversation was superfluous, and it is. Your conditions are accepted because of what must be done . . . Now, may I have that case, please?"

Sam Tucker sat on the terrace, alternately reading the newspaper and glancing over the sea wall to the beach, where Alison and James Ferguson were in deck chairs near the water. Every now and then, when the dazzling Caribbean sun had heated their skin temperatures sufficiently, Alison and the young botanist waded into the water. They did not splash or jump or dive; they simply fell onto the calm surface, as though exhausted. It seemed to be an exercise of weariness for both of them.

There was no joy *sur la plage,* thought Sam, who nevertheless picked up a pair of binoculars whenever Alison began paddling about and scanned the immediate vicinity around which she swam. He focused on any swimmer who came near her; there were not many, and all were recognizable as guests of Bengal Court.

None was a threat, and that's what Sam Tucker was looking for.

Ferguson had returned from Montego Bay a little before noon, just after Alex had driven off to Drax Hall. He had wandered onto the connecting terraces, startling Sam and the temporarily disoriented Lawrence, who had been sitting on the sea wall talking quietly about the dead Barak Moore. They had been stunned because Ferguson had been expansive about his day-off plans in Mo'Bay.

Ferguson arrived looking haggard, a nervous wreck. The assumption was that he had overindulged and was hung to his fuzzy-cheeked gills; the jokes were along this line, and he accepted them with a singular lack of humor. But Sam Tucker did not subscribe to the explanation. James Ferguson was not ravaged by the whiskey input of the night before; he was a frightened young man who had not slept. His fear, thought Sam, was not anything he cared to discuss; indeed, he would not even talk about his night in Montego, brushing it off as a dull, unrewarding interlude. He appeared only to want company, as if there was immediate security in the familiar. He seemed to cling to the presence of Alison Booth, offering to fetch and carry . . . A schoolboy's crush or a faggot's devotion? Neither fit, for he was neither.

He was afraid.

Very inconsistent behavior, concluded Sam Tucker.

Tucker suddenly heard the quiet, rapid footsteps behind him and turned. Lawrence, fully clothed now, came across the terrace from the west lawn. The black revolutionary walked over to Sam and knelt—not in fealty, but in a conscious attempt to conceal his large frame behind the sea wall. He spoke urgently.

"I don't like what I see and hear, mon."

"What's the matter?"

"John Crow hide wid' block chicken!"

"We're being watched?" Tucker put down the newspaper and sat forward.

"Yes, mon. Three, four hours now."

"Who?"

"A digger been walking on the sand since morning. Him keep circling the west-cove beach too long for tourist leave-behinds. I watch him good. His trouser pants rolled up, look too new, mon. I go behind in the woods and find his shoes. Then I know the trouser pants, mon. Him policeman."

Sam's gnarled features creased in thought. "Alex spoke with the Falmouth police around 9:30. In the lobby . . . He said there were two: a chief and an Indian."

"What, mon?"

"Nothing . . . That's what you saw. What did you hear?"

"Not all I saw." Lawrence looked over the sea wall, east toward the center beach. Satisfied, he returned his attention to Sam. "I follow the digger to the kitchen alley, where he waits for a man to come outside to speak with him. It is the clerk from the lobby desk. Him shake his head many times. The policeman angry, mon."

"But what did you *hear*, boy?"

"A porter-fella was plenty near, cleaning snapper in his buckets. When the digger-policeman left I ask him hard, mon. He tell me this digger kep' asking where the American fella went, who had telephoned him."

"And the clerk didn't know."

"That's right, mon. The policeman was angry."

"Where is he now?"

"Him wait down at the east shore." Lawrence pointed over the sea wall, across the dunes to a point on the other side of the central beach. "See? In front of the sunfish boats, mon."

Tucker picked up the binoculars and focused on the figure near the shallow-bottomed sailboats by the water. The man and boats were about four hundred yards away. The man was in a torn green T-shirt and rumpled baseball cap; the trousers *were* a contradiction. They were rolled up to the knees, like most scavengers of the beach wore them, but Lawrence was right, they were creased, too clean. The man was chatting with a *cocoruru* peddler, a thin, very black Jamaican who rolled a wheelbarrow filled with coconuts up and down the beach, selling them to the bathers, cracking them open with a murderous-looking machete. From time to time the man glanced over toward the west-wing terraces, directly into the binoculars, thought Sam. Tucker knew the man did not realize he was being observed; if he did, the reaction would appear on his face. The only reaction was one of irritation, nothing else.

"We'd better supply him with the proper information, son," said Sam, putting down the binoculars.

"What, mon?"

"Give him something to soothe that anger . . . So he won't think about it too much."

Lawrence grinned. "We make up a story, eh, mon?"

"Eh, mon," replied Sam smiling. "A casual, very believable kind of story."

"McAuliff went shopping at Ochee, maybe? Ochee is six, seven miles from Drax Hall, mon. Same road."

"Why didn't Mrs. Booth . . . Alison go with him?"

"Him buy the lady a present. Why not, mon?"

Sam looked at Lawrence, then down at the beach, where Alison was standing up, prepared to go back into the water. "It's possible, boy. We should make it a little festive, though." Tucker got out of the chair and walked to the sea wall. "I think Alison should have a birthday."

The telephone rang in McAuliff's room. The doors were closed against the heat, and the harsh bell echoed from beyond the slatted panels. Tucker and Lawrence looked at each other, each knowing the other's thoughts. Although McAuliff had not elaborated on his late-morning departure from Bengal Court, neither had he concealed it. Actually, he had asked the desk for a road map, explaining only that he was going for a drive. Therefore, the front desk knew that he was not in his room.

Tucker crossed rapidly to the double doors, opened them, and went inside to the telephone.

"Mr. McAuliff?" The soft, precise Jamaican voice answered Sam's question with the obvious explanation. It was that of the switchboard operator.

"No, Mr. McAuliff is out. May I give him a message?"

"Please, sir, I have a call from Kingston. From a Mr. Latham. Will you hold the line, please?"

"Certainly. Tell Mr. Latham you've got Sam Tucker on the phone. He may want to speak with me."

Sam held the telephone under his wrinkled chin as he struck a match to a thin cigar. He had barely drawn the first smoke when he heard the double click of the connecting line. The voice was now Latham's. Latham, the proper bureaucrat from the Ministry who was also committed to the cause of Barak Moore. As Latham spoke, Tucker made the decision not to tell him of Barak's death.

"Mr. Tucker?"

"Yes, Mr. Latham. Alex drove into Ocho Rios."

"Very well. You can handle this, I'm sure. We were able to comply with McAuliff's request. He's got his interior runners several days early. They're in Duanvale and will be driving on Route 11 into Queenhythe later this afternoon."

"Queenhythe's near here, isn't it?"

"Three or four miles from your motel, that's all. They'll telephone when they get in."

"What are their names?"

"They're brothers. Marcus and Justice Hedrik. They're Maroons, of course. Two of the best runners in Jamaica; they know the Cock Pit extremely well, and they're trustworthy."

"That's good to hear. Alexander will be delighted."

Latham paused but obviously was not finished. "Mr. Tucker . . . ?"

"Yes, Mr. Latham?"

"McAuliff's altered the survey's schedule, it would appear. I'm not sure we understand . . ."

"Nothing to understand, Mr. Latham. Alex decided to work from a geographical midpoint. Less room for error that way; like bisecting a triangle from semicircular coordinates. I agree with him." Tucker inhaled on his thin cigar while Latham's silence conveyed his bewilderment. "Also," continued Sam, "it gives everyone a lot more to do."

"I see . . . The reasons, then, are quite compatible with . . . let us say, professional curiosity?"

"Very professional, Mr. Latham." Tucker realized that Latham would not speak freely on the telephone. Or felt he could not. "Beyond criticism, if you're worried about the Ministry's concerns. Actually, Alexander could be saving you considerable sums of money. You'll get a lot more data much quicker."

Latham paused again, as though to telegraph the importance of the following statement. "Naturally, we're always interested in conserving funds . . . And I assume you *all* agree with the decision to go in so quickly. Into the Cock Pit, that is."

Sam knew that Latham's statement could be translated into the question: *Does Barak Moore agree?*

"We *all* agree, Mr. Latham. We're all professionals."

"Yes . . . Well, that's splendid. One last item, Mr. Tucker."

"Yes, Mr. Latham?"

"We want Mr. McAuliff to use all the resources provided him. He's not to stint in an effort to save money; the survey's too important for that."

Tucker again translated Latham's code easily: *Alex was to maintain contact with British Intelligence liaisons. If he avoided them, suspicions would be aroused.*

"I'll tell him that, Mr. Latham, but I'm sure he's aware of it. These past two weeks have been very routine, very dull—simple coastline geodometrics. Not much call for equipment. Or resources."

"As long as he knows our feelings," said Latham rapidly, now anxious to terminate the conversation. "Good-bye, Mr. Tucker."

"Goodbye, Mr. Latham." Sam held his finger down on the telephone button for several moments, then released it and waited for the switchboard. When the operator came on the line, Tucker asked for the front desk.

"Bengal Court, good afternoon."

"This is Mr. Tucker, west wing 6, Royal Society survey."

"Yes, Mr. Tucker?"

"Mr. McAuliff asked me to make arrangements for tonight. He didn't have time this morning; besides, it was awkward. Mrs. Booth was with him." Sam paused, letting his words register.

The clerk automatically responded. "Yes, Mr. Tucker. What can we do for you?"

"It's Mrs. Booth's birthday. Do you think the kitchen could whip up a little cake? Nothing elaborate, you understand."

"Of course! We'd be *delighted,* sir." The clerk was effusive. "Our pleasure, Mr. Tucker."

"Fine. That's very kind of you. Just put it on Mr. McAuliff's bill—"

"There'll be no charge," interrupted the clerk, fluidly subservient.

"Very kind indeed. We'll be dining around 8:30, I guess. Our usual table."

"We'll take care of everything . . ."

"That is, it'll be 8:30," continued Sam, "if Mr. McAuliff finds his way *back* in time . . ." Tucker paused again, listening for the clerk's appropriate response.

"Oh? Is there a problem, Mr. Tucker?"

"Well, the damn fool drove south of Ocho Rios, around Fern Gully, I think, to locate some stalactite sculpture. He told me there were natives who did that sort of thing down there."

"That's true, Mr. Tucker. There are a number of stalactite craftsmen in the Gully. However, there are government restrictions—"

"Oh Lord, son!" interrupted Sam defensively. "He's just going to find Mrs. Booth a little present, that's all."

The clerk laughed, softly and obsequiously. "Please don't mistake me, Mr. Tucker. Government interference is often most unwarranted. I only meant that I hope Mr. McAuliff is successful. When he asked for the petrol map, he should have mentioned where he was going. I might have helped him."

"Well . . ." drawled Sam conspiratorially, "he was probably embarrassed, if you know what I mean. I wouldn't mention it; he'd be mad as hell at me."

"Of course."

"And thanks for the cake tonight. That's really very nice of you, son."

"Not at all, sir."

The good-byes were rapid, more so on the clerk's part. Sam replaced the telephone and walked back out onto the terrace. Lawrence turned from peering over the wall and sat on the flagstone deck, his back against the sea wall, his body hidden from the beach.

"Mrs. Booth and Jimbo-mon are out of water," said the black revolutionary. "They are in chairs again."

"Latham called. The runners will be here this afternoon . . . And I talked with the front desk. Let's see if our information gets transmitted properly." Tucker lowered himself on the chair slowly and reached for the binoculars on the table. He picked up the newspaper and held it next to the binoculars as he focused on the swimming-pool patio fronting the central beach of Bengal Court.

Within ten seconds he saw the figure of a man dressed in a coat and tie come out of the rear entrance of the motel. It was the front-desk clerk. He walked around the edge of the pool, past a group of wooden, padded sun chairs, nodding to guests, chatting with several. He reached the stone steps leading to the sand and stood there several moments, surveying the beach. Then he started down the steps and across the white, soft sand. He walked diagonally to the right, to the row of sun-fish sail-boats.

Sam watched as the clerk approached the digger-police-man in the sloppy baseball cap and the *cocoruru* peddler. The *cocoruru* man saw him coming, picked up the handles of his wheelbarrow, and rolled it on the hard sand near the water to get away. The digger-policeman stayed where he was and acknowledged the clerk.

The magnified features in the glass conveyed all that was necessary to Sam Tucker. The policeman's features

contorted with irritation. The man was apparently la-
menting his waste of time and effort, commodities not
easily expended on such a hot day.

The clerk turned and started back across the sand
toward the patio. The digger-policeman began walking
west, near the water's edge. His gait was swifter now;
gone was the stooped posture indigenous to a scavenger of
the beach.

He wasn't much of an undercover man, thought Sam
Tucker as he watched the man's progress toward the
woods of Bengal Court's west property. On his way to his
shoes and the egress to the shore road, he never once
looked down at the sand for tourist leave-behinds.

McAuliff stood looking over Charles Whitehall's left
shoulder as the black scholar ridged the flame of the
acetylene torch across the seamed edge of the archive
case. The hot point of flame bordered no more than an
eighth of an inch behind the seam, at the end of the
case.

The top edge of the archive case cracked. Charles extinguished the flame quickly and thrust the end of the case
under the faucet in the sink. The thin stream of water
sizzled into vapor as it touched the hot steel. Whitehall
removed his tinted goggles, picked up a miniature hammer, and tapped the steaming end.

It fell off, cracking and sizzling, into the metal sink.
Within the case could be seen the oilcloth of a packet. His
hands trembling slightly, Charles Whitehall pulled it out.
He got off the stool, carrying the rolled-up oilcloth to a
deserted area of the bench, and untied the nylon laces. He
unwound the packet until it was flat, unzipped the inner
lining, and withdrew two sheets of single-spaced typing.
As he reached for the bench lamp, he looked at McAuliff.

Alex was fascinated by what he saw. Whitehall's eyes
shone with a strange intensity. It was a fever. A messianic
fever.

A kind of victory rooted in the absolute.

A fanatic's victory, thought McAuliff.

Without speaking, Whitehall began to read. As he finished the first page, he slid it across the bench to Alex.

The word "Halidon" was in reality three words—or
sounds—from the African Ashanti, so corrupted by later

phonetics as to be hardly traceable. (Here Piersall included hieroglyphs that were meaningless to Alex.) The root word, again a hieroglyph, was in the sound *leedaw*, translated to convey the picture of a hollowed-out piece of wood that could be held in the hand. The *leedaw* was a primitive instrument of sound, a means of communication over distances in the jungles and hills. The pitch of its wail was controlled by the breath of the blower and the placement of his hand over slits carved through the surface—the basic principle of the woodwind.

The historical parallel had been obvious to Walter Piersall. Whereas the Maroon tribes, living in settlements, used an *abeng*—a type of bugle made from the horns of cattle—to signal their warriors or spread the alarm of an approaching white enemy, the followers of Acquaba were nomadic and could not rely on animal products with any certainty. They returned to the African custom of utilizing the most prolific material of their surroundings: wood.

Once having established the root symbol as the primitive horn, it remained for Piersall to specify the modification of the accompanying sounds. He went back to the Ashanti-Coromanteen studies to extract compatible noun roots. He found the final syllable, or sound, first. It was in the hieroglyph depicting a deep river current, or undertow, that periled man or animal in the water. Its sonic equivalent was a bass-toned wail or cry. The phonetic spelling was *nwa*.

The pieces of the primitive puzzle were nearly joined.

The initial sound was the symbol *hayee*, the Coromanteen word meaning the council of their tribal gods.

Hayee—leedaw—nwa.

The low cry of a jungle horn signifying peril, a supplication to the council of the gods.

Acquaba's code. The hidden key that would admit an outsider into the primitive tribal sect.

Primitive and not primitive at all.

Halidon. Hollydawn. A wailing instrument whose cry was carried by the wind to the gods.

This, then, was Dr. Walter Piersall's last gift to his island sanctuary. The means to reach, enlist, and release a powerful force for the good of Jamaica. To convince "it" to accept its responsibility.

There remained only to determine which of the isolated

communities in the Cock Pit mountains was the Halidon.
Which would respond to the code of Acquaba?

Finally, the basic skepticism of the scholar inserted itself into Piersall's document. He did not question the existence of the Halidon; what he did speculate on was its
rumored wealth and commitment. Were these more myth
than current fact? Had the myth grown out of proportion
to the conceivably diminished resources?

The answer was in the Cock Pit.

McAuliff finished the second page and looked over at
Charles Whitehall. The black fascist had walked from the
workbench to the small window overlooking the Drax
Hall fields. Without turning, he spoke quietly, as though
he knew Alex was staring at him, expecting him to speak.

"Now we know what must be done. But we must proceed cautiously, sure of every step. A wrong move on our
part and the cry of the Halidon will vanish with the
wind."

22

THE CARAVEL prop plane descended on its western approach to the small Boscobel airfield in Oracabessa. The motors revved in short bursts to counteract the harsh wind and rain of the sudden downpour, forcing the aircraft to enter the strip cleanly. It taxied to the far end, turned awkwardly, and rolled back toward the small, one-level concrete passenger terminal.

Two Jamaican porters ran through the low gates to the aircraft, both holding umbrellas. Together they pushed the metal step unit to the side of the plane, under the door; the man on the left then knocked rapidly on the fuselage.

The door was slapped open by a large white man who immediately stepped out, waving aside the offer of the two umbrellas. He jumped from the top level to the ground and looked around in the rain.

His right hand was in his jacket pocket.

He turned up to the aircraft door and nodded. A second large white man disembarked and ran across the muddy space toward the concrete terminal. His right hand, too, was in his pocket. He entered the building, glanced around, and proceeded out the exit to the parking area.

Sixty seconds later the gate by the luggage depot was swung open by the second man and a Mercedes 660 limousine drove through toward the Caravel, its wheels spinning frequently in the drenched earth.

The two Jamaicans remained by the step unit, their umbrellas waiting.

The Mercedes pulled alongside the plane, and the tiny, ancient figure of Julian Warfield was helped down the steps, his head and body shielded by the blacks. The second white man held the door of the Mercedes; his large companion was in front of the automobile, scanning the distance and the few passengers who had come out of the terminal.

When Warfield was enclosed in the back seat, the Jamaican driver stepped out and the second white man got behind the wheel. He honked the horn once; his companion turned and raced around to the left front door and climbed in.

The Mercedes's deep-throated engine roared as the limousine backed up beyond the tail assembly of the Caravel, then belched forward and sped through the gate.

With Julian Warfield in the back seat were Peter Jensen and his wife, Ruth.

"We'll drive to Peale Court, it's not far from here," said the small, gaunt financier, his eyes alive and controlled. "How long do you have? With reasonable caution."

"We rented a car for a trip to Dunns Falls," replied Peter. "We left it in the lot and met the Mercedes outside. Several hours, at least."

"Did you make it clear you were going to the Falls?"

"Yes. I invited McAuliff."

Warfield smiled. "Nicely done, Peter."

The car raced over the Oracabessa road for several miles and turned into a gravel drive flanked by two white stone posts. On both were identical brass plaques reading "PEALE COURT." They were polished to a high gloss, a rich mixture of gold and black.

At the end of the drive was a long parking area in front of a longer, one-story white stucco house with expensive wood in the doors, and many windows. It was perched on top of a steep incline above the beach.

Warfield and the Jensens were admitted by a passive, elderly black woman in a white uniform, and Julian led the way to a veranda overlooking the waters of Golden Head Bay.

The three of them settled in chairs, and Warfield politely asked the Jamaican servant to bring refreshments. Perhaps a light rum punch.

The rain was letting up; streaks of yellow and orange could be seen beyond the gray sheets in the sky.

"I've always been fond of Peale Court," said Warfield. "It's so peaceful."

"The view is breathtaking," added Ruth. "Do you own it, Julian?"

"No, my dear. But I don't believe it would be difficult to acquire. Look around, if you like. Perhaps you and Peter might be interested."

Ruth smiled and, as if on cue, rose from her chair. "I think I shall."

She walked back through the veranda doors into the larger living room with the light brown marble floor. Peter watched her, then looked over at Julian. "Are things that serious?"

"I don't want her upset," replied Warfield.

"Which, of course, gives me my answer."

"Possibly. Not necessarily. We've come upon disturbing news. M.I.5."

Peter reacted as though he'd been jolted unnecessarily. "I thought we had that area covered. *Completely*. It was passive."

"On the island, perhaps. Sufficient for our purposes. Not in London. Obviously." Warfield paused and took a deep breath, pursing his narrow, wrinkled lips. "Naturally, we'll take steps immediately to intercede, but it may have gone too far. Ultimately, we can control the Service . . . if we must, right out of the Foreign Office. What bothers me now is the current activity."

Peter Jensen looked out over the veranda railing. The afternoon sun was breaking through the clouds. The rain had stopped.

"Then we have two adversaries. This Halidon—whatever in blazes it is. And British Intelligence."

"Precisely. What is of paramount importance, however, is to keep the two separate. Do you see?"

Jensen returned his gaze to the old man. "Of course. Assuming they haven't already joined forces."

"They have not."

"You're sure of that, Julian?"

"Yes. Don't forget, we first learned of this Halidon through M.I.5 personnel—specialist level. Dunstone's payrolls are diverse. If contact had been made, we'd know it."

Again Jensen looked out at the waters of the bay, his expression pensive and questioning. "Why? *Why?* The man was offered a million dollars . . . There is nothing, *nothing* in his dossier that would give an *inkling* of this. McAuliff is suspect of *all* governmental interferences . . . quite rabid on the subject, actually. It was one of the reasons I proposed him."

"Yes," said Warfield noncommittally. "McAuliff was your idea, Peter . . . Don't mistake me, I am not holding you responsible, I concurred with your choice . . . Describe what happened last night. This morning."

Jensen did so, ending with the description of the fishing boat veering off into open water and the removal of the medical equipment from the motel room. "If it was an M.I.5 operation, it was crude, Julian. Intelligence has too many facilities available to be reduced to motels and fishing boats. If we only knew what happened."

"We do. At least, I think we do," replied Warfield. "Late last night the house of a dead white man, an anthropologist named Piersall, was broken into; ten, twelve miles from the coast. There was a skirmish. Two men were killed that we know of; others could have been wounded. They officially called it a robbery, which, of course, it wasn't really. Not in the sense of larceny."

"I know the name 'Piersall'——"

"You should. He was the university radical who filed that insane Letter of Intent with the Department of Territories."

"Of course! He was going to purchase half the Cock Pit! That was months ago. He was a lunatic." Jensen lighted his pipe; he gripped the bowl as he did so, he did not merely hold it. "So there is a third intruder," he said, his words drifting off quietly, nervously.

"Or one of the first two, Peter."

"How? What do you mean?"

"You just ruled out M.I.5. It could be the Halidon."

Jensen stared at Warfield. "If so, it would mean McAuliff is working with both camps. And if Intelligence has not made contact, it's because McAuliff has not permitted it."

"A very complicated young man." The old financier placed his glass down carefully on a tiled table next to his chair. He turned slightly to look through the veranda doors; the voice of Ruth Jensen could be heard chatting with the Jamaican maid inside the house. Warfield looked back at Peter. He pointed his thin, bony finger to a black leather case on a white wicker table across the open porch. "That is for you, Peter. Please get it."

Jensen rose from his chair, walked to the table, and stood by the case. It was smaller than the attaché variety. And thicker. Its two hasps were secured by combination locks. "What are the numbers?"

"The left lock is three zeros. The right, three fives. You may alter the combinations as you wish." Peter bent down and began manipulating the tiny vertical dials. Warfield continued. "Tomorrow you will start into the interior. Learn everything you can. Find out who comes to see him, for certainly he will have visitors. And the minute you establish the fact that he is in actual contact, and whom with, send out Ruth on some medical pretext with the information . . . Then, Peter, you must kill him. McAuliff is a keystone. His death will panic both camps, and we shall know all we need to know."

Jensen lifted the top of the black leather case. Inside, recessed in the green felt, was a brand-new Luger pistol. Its steel glistened, except for a dull space below the trigger housing where the serial number had been removed. Below the weapon was a five-inch cylinder, one end grooved.

A silencer.

"You've never asked this of me, Julian. Never . . . You mustn't." Jensen turned and stared at Warfield.

"I am not asking, Peter. I am demanding. Dunstone, Limited, has given you everything. And now it needs you in a way it has not needed you before. You must, you see."

FOUR

The Cock Pit

23

THEY BEGAN at midpoint of the western perimeter, two and a half miles south of Weston Favel, on the edge of the Cock Pit range. They made base camp on the bank of a narrow offshoot of the Martha Brae. All but the runners, Marcus and Justice Hedrik, were stunned by the seemingly impenetrable walls of jungle that surrounded them.

Strange, contradictory forests that were filled with the wet verdancy of tropic growth and the cold massiveness of sky-reaching black and green associated with northern climates. Dense macca-fat palms stood next to silk-cotton, or ceiba, trees that soared out of sight, their tops obscured by the midgrowth. Mountain cabbage and bull thatch, orchid and moss, fungi and eucalyptus battled for their individual rights to coexist in the Oz-like jungle primeval.

The ground was covered with ensnaring spreads of fern and pteridophyte, soft, wet and treacherous. Pools of swamplike mud were hidden in the thick, crowded sprays of underbrush. Sudden hills rose out of nowhere, remembrances of Oligocene upheavals, never to be settled back into the cradle of the earth.

The sounds of the screeching bat and parrot and tanager intruded on the forest's undertones; jungle rats and the mongoose could be heard intermittently in their unseen games of death. Every now and then there was the scream of a wild pig, pursuing or in panic.

And far in the distance, in the clearing of the river bank, were the mountains, preceded by sudden stretches of untamed grassland. Strangely gray with streaks of deep green and blue and yellow—rain and hot sunlight in an unceasing interchange.

All this fifteen minutes by air from the gaudy strips of Montego.

Unbelievable.

McAuliff had made contact with the north-coast contacts of British Intelligence. There were five, and he had reached each one.

They had given him another reason to consign R. C. Holcroft to the despised realm of the manipulator. For the Intelligence people were of small comfort. They stated perfunctorily their relief at his reporting, accepted his explanations of routine geographic chores that kept him occupied, and assured him—with more sound than conviction—that they were at his beck and call.

One man, the M.I.5 contact from Port Maria, drove down the coast to Bengal Court to meet with Alex. He was a portly black merchant who limited his identification to the single name of "Garvey." He insisted on a late-night rendezvous in the tiny bar of the motel, where he was known as a liquor distributor.

It did not take McAuliff long to realize that Garvey, ostensibly there to assure him of total cooperation and safety, was actually interrogating him for a report that would be sent back to London. Garvey had the stench and sight of a practiced informer about him. The stench was actual: The man suffered from body odor, which could not be concealed by liberal applications of bay rum. The sight was in his eyes—ferretlike, and a touch bloodshot. Garvey was a man who sought out opportunities and enjoyed the fruits thereof.

His questions were precise, McAuliff's answers apparently not satisfactory. And all questions led to the one question, the only one that mattered: Any progress concerning the Halidon?

Anything?

Unknown observers, strangers in the distance . . . a signal, a sign—no matter how remote or subtle?

Anything?

"Absolutely nothing" was a hard reply for Garvey to accept.

What about the blacks in the green Chevrolet who had followed him in Kingston? Tallon had traced them to the anthropologist Walter Piersall. Piersall had been a white agitator . . . common knowledge. Piersall had telephoned McAuliff . . . the Courtleigh switchboard cooperated with M.I.5. What did Piersall want?

Alex claimed he did not—could not—know, as Piersall had never reached him. An agitator, white *or* black, was an unpredictable bearer of unpredictable news. Predictably, this agitator had had an accident. It might be presumed—from what little McAuliff had been told by Tallon and others—that Piersall had been closing in on Dunstone, Limited; without a name, of course. If so, he McAuliff, was a logical person to reach. But this was conjecture; there was no way to confirm it as fact.

What had happened to the late-arriving Samuel Tucker? Where had he been?

Drinking and whoring in Montego Bay. Alex was sorry he had caused so much trouble about Sam; he should have known better. Sam Tucker was an incorrigible wanderer, albeit the best soil analyst in the business.

The perspiring Garvey was bewildered, frustrated by his confusion. There was too much activity for McAuliff to remain so insulated.

Alex reminded the liaison in short, coarse words that there was far too much survey activity—logistical, employment, above all government paperwork—for him not to be insulated. What the hell did Garvey think he had been doing?

The interview lasted until 1:30 in the morning. Before leaving, the M.I.5 contact reached into his filthy briefcase and withdrew a metallic object the size of a pen-and-pencil case, with its approximate thickness. It was a miniaturized radio-signal transmitter, set to a specific frequency. There were three thick, tiny glass lights across the top of the small panel. The first, explained Garvey, was a white light that indicated sufficient power for sending when turned on—not unlike the illuminated filigree of a strobe light. The second, a red light, informed the operator that his signal was being transmitted. The third, a green light, confirmed the reception of the signal by a corresponding device within a radius of twenty-five miles. There would be two simple codes, one for normal conditions, one for emergency. Code One was to be transmitted twice daily, once every twelve hours. Code Two, when aid was needed.

The receiving set, said Garvey, was capable of defining the signal within a diameter of one thousand yards by means of an attached radarscope with terrain coordinates. Nothing was left to chance.

Unbelievable.

The incredible assumption, therefore, was that the Intelligence men would never be more than twenty-five miles away, and Holcroft's "guaranteed" safety factor was the even more ridiculous assumption that the jungle distance could be traversed and the exact location pinpointed within a time period that precluded danger.

R. C. Holcroft was a winner, thought McAuliff.

"Is this everything?" McAuliff asked the sweating Garvey. "This goddamn metal box is our protection?"

"There are additional precautions," Garvey replied enigmatically. "I told you, nothing is left to chance—"

"What the hell does that mean?"

"It means you are protected. I am not authorized to speak further. As a matter of fact, mon, I do not *know* anything further. I am, like you, merely an employee. I do what I am told to do, say what I am told to say . . . And now I have said enough. I have an uncomfortable drive back to Port Maria."

The man named Garvey rose from the table, picked up his tattered briefcase, and waddled toward the door of the dimly lit room. Before leaving, however, he could not help himself. He stopped at the bar, where one of the motel's managers was standing, and solicited an order of liquor.

McAuliff shook his thoughts loose as he heard the voices of Ruth and Peter Jensen behind him. He was sitting on a dried mud flat above the river bank; the Jensens were talking as they walked across the clearing from their bivouac tent. It amazed Alex—*they* amazed him. They walked so casually, so normally, over the chopped Cock Pit ground cover; one might think they had entered Regent's Park for a stroll.

"Majestic place in its way, rather," said Peter, removing the ever-present pipe from between his teeth.

"It is the odd combination of color and substance, don't you think, Alex?" Ruth had her arm linked through her husband's. A noonday walk down the Strand. "One is so very sensuous, the other so massive and intricate."

"You make the terms sound contradictory, darling. They're not, you know." Peter chuckled as his wife feigned minor exasperation.

"He has an incorrigibly pornographic mind, Alex. Pay no attention. Still, he's right. It is majestic. And positively *dense*. Where's Alison?"

"With Ferguson and Sam. They're testing the water."

"Jimbo-mon's going to use up all of his film, I dare say," muttered Peter as he helped his wife to sit down next to McAuliff. "That new camera he brought back from Montego has consumed him."

"Frightfully expensive, I should think." Ruth smoothed the un-smoothable cloth of her bivouac slacks, like a woman not used to being without a skirt. Or a woman who was nervous. "For a boy who's always saying he's bone-stony, quite an extravagance."

"He didn't buy it; he borrowed it," said Alex. "From a friend he knew last year in Port Antonio."

"That's right, I forgot." Peter relit his pipe as he spoke. "You were all here last year, weren't you?"

"Not all, Peter. Just Sam and me; we worked for Kaiser. And Ferguson. He was with the Craft Foundation. No one else."

"Well, Charles is Jamaican," intruded Ruth nervously. "Surely he flies back and forth. Heaven knows, he must be rich enough."

"That's a rather brass speculation, luv."

"Oh, come off it, Peter. Alex knows what I mean."

McAuliff laughed. "I don't think he worries about money. He's yet to submit his bills for the survey outfits. I have an idea they're the most expensive in Harrod's Safari Shop."

"Perhaps he's embarrassed," said Peter, smiling. "He looks as though he had jumped right off the cinema screen. The black hunter; very impressive image, if somewhat contrived."

"Now you're the one who's talking brass, luv. Charles *is* impressive." Ruth turned to Alex. "My overage Lochinvar is green with envy."

"That camera's damn well new . . . not the sort of thing one lends, I shouldn't think." Peter looked at McAuliff as he spoke the non sequitur.

"Depends on the friend, I guess," replied Alex, aware that Peter was implying something beyond his words. "Ferguson can be a likable guy."

"*Very,*" added Ruth. "And so helpless, somehow. Except when he's over his equipment. Then he's positively a whiz."

"Which is all I really care about." McAuliff addressed

this judgment to Peter. "But then, you're all whizzes, cameras and fancy clothes and aromatic pipes notwithstanding." Alex laughed.

"Got me there, chap." Peter removed his pipe and shook his head. "Dreadful habit."

"Not at all," said McAuliff. "I like the smell, I really do. I'd smoke one myself but my tongue burns. Then stings."

"There are preventive measures, but it's a dull subject . . . What's fascinating is this jungle laboratory we're in. Have you decided on crew assignments?"

"Vaguely," answered Alex. "Doesn't make an awful lot of difference. Who do you want?"

"One of those brothers for me," said Ruth. "They seem to know *exactly* where they are. I'd be lost in half a mo'! . . . Of course, that's selfish; my work is least important . . ."

"We still don't want to lose you, do we, Peter?" McAuliff leaned forward.

"Not as long as she behaves."

"Take your pick," said Alex. "Marcus or Justice?"

"What marvelously dotty names!" cried Ruth. "I choose Justice." She looked at her husband. "Always justice."

"Yes, of course, my dear."

"All right," agreed McAuliff. "Then Marcus'll be with me. One of them has to. And Alison asked for Lawrence, if you don't mind, Peter."

"Not at all, chap. Sorry his friend . . . what was his name? Floyd? Yes, Floyd. Sorry he jumped ship, as it were. Did you ever find out what happened to him?"

"No," replied Alex. "He just disappeared. Unreliable guy. Something of a thief, too, according to Lawrence."

"Pity . . . He seemed rather intelligent."

"*That's* condescending, darling. Worse than brassy." Ruth Jensen picked up a tiny stone and chucked it into the narrow river offshoot.

"Then just pick out a stout fellow who'll promise to lead me back to camp for meals and sleep."

"Fine. I'll do that. We'll work four-hour field sessions, staying in touch by radio. I don't want anyone going beyond a sonic mile from camp for the first few days."

"*Beyond!*" Ruth looked at McAuliff, her voice having risen an octave. "*Dear* Alex, if I stumble more than twenty feet into that maze of overgrowth, commit me!"

"Rubbish," countered her husband, "when you start cracking rocks, you lose time *and* distance . . . Speaking of which, Alex, old boy, I presume there'll be a fairly steady flow of visitors. To observe our progress; that sort of thing."

"Why?" McAuliff was now aware that both husband and wife were sending out abstract, perhaps unconscious, signals. Peter less than Ruth. He was subtler, surer of himself than she was. But not completely sure. "We'll bring out field reports every ten days or so. Rotate days off that way. That'll be good enough."

"Well, we're not exactly at the end of nowhere; although I grant you, it looks like it. I should think the moneymen would want to check up on what they're paying for."

Peter Jensen had just made a mistake, and McAuliff was suddenly alarmed. "What moneymen?"

Ruth Jensen had picked up another stone, about to throw it into the brackish river. Arm poised, she froze for a second before hurling it.

The moment was not lost on any of them. Peter tried to minimize it.

"Oh . . . some Royal Society titans or perhaps a few of these buggers from the Ministry. I know the R. S. boys, and God knows the Jamaicans have been less than cordial. I just thought . . . Oh, well, perhaps I'm off-center."

"Perhaps," said Alex quietly, "you're ahead of me. Onsite inspectors aren't unusual. I was thinking about the convenience. Or lack of it. It took us nearly a day to get here. Of course, we had the truck and the equipment . . . Still, it seems like a lot of trouble."

"Not really." Peter Jensen tapped his pipe on his boots. "I've been checking the maps, looking about from the river clearing. The grasslands are nearer than we think. Less than a couple of miles, I'd say. Light planes could easily land."

"That's a good point. I hadn't thought of it." McAuliff leaned forward once again to engage Peter, but Peter did not look at him now. "I mean if we needed . . . equipment or supplies, we could get them much quicker than I'd anticipated. Thanks, Peter."

"Oh, don't *thank* him." Ruth spoke with a nervous giggle. "Don't *cater* to him." She looked briefly at her husband; McAuliff wished he could have seen her eyes. "Peter just wants to convince himself he's a hop-skip from a pub."

"Rubbish. Just idle conversation, old girl . . ."

"I think he's bored with us, Ruth," said Alex laughing softly, almost intimately. "I think he wants to see new faces."

"As long as it's not new bodies, my dear, the tolerance is possible," retorted Ruth Jensen with throated caricature.

The three of them laughed out loud.

McAuliff knew the humor was forced. Mistakes had been made, and the Jensens were afraid.

Peter *was* looking for new faces . . . or a new face. A face he believed Alex expected.

Who was it?

Was it possible . . . remotely possible that the Jensens were not what they seemed?

There was the sound of whistling from a path in the north bush. Charles Whitehall emerged into the clearing, his safari uniform pressed and clean, in counterpoint to the rumpled clothes of Marcus Hedrik, the older brother of the two Cock Pit runners. Marcus remained a respectful distance behind Whitehall, his passive black face inscrutable.

McAuliff rose from the ground and spoke to the Jensens. "It's Charley. There's a hill community several miles west of the river; he was going to try to hire a couple of hands."

Ruth and Peter took their cue, because they very much wanted to. "Well, we've still got some equipment sorting to do," said the husband, rising quickly.

"Indeed we do! Help me up, luv."

The Jensens waved to Charles Whitehall and rapidly started for their tent.

McAuliff met Whitehall at the midpoint of the clearing. The black scholar dismissed Marcus Hedrik, instructing him to issue preparation orders to the rest of the crew about the evening patrols. Alex was fascinated to watch and listen to Charley-mon speaking to the runner. He fell easily into the hill country patois—damn near indecipherable to McAuliff—and used his hands and eyes in gestures and looks that were absolutely compatible with the obtuse speech.

"You do that very well," said Alex as the runner trudged out of hearing.

"I should. It's what you hired me for. I am the best there is."

"That's one of the things I like about you, Charley. You take compliments so gracefully."

"You did not hire me for my graces. They are a bonus you don't deserve." Whitehall allowed himself a slight smile. "You enjoy calling me 'Charley,' McAuliff?" added the elegant black.

"Do you object?"

"Not really. Because I understand. It is a defense mechanism; you Americans are rife with them. 'Charley' is an idiomatic leveler, peculiarly indigenous to the sixties and seventies. The Vietcong were 'Charley,' so too the Cambodians and the Laotians; even your man on the American street. It makes you feel superior. Strange that the name should be Charley, is it not?"

"It happens to be *your* name."

"Yes, of course, but I think that is almost beside the point." The black looked away briefly, then back at Alex. "The name 'Charles' is Germanic in origin, actually. Its root meaning is 'full grown' or possibly—here scholars differ—'great size.' Is it not interesting that you Americans take just such a name and reverse its connotation?"

McAuliff exhaled audibly and spoke wearily. "I accept the lesson for the day and all its subtle anti-colonialism. I gather you'd prefer I call you 'Charles,' or 'Whitehall,' or perhaps 'Great Black Leader.' "

"Not for a moment. 'Charley' is perfectly fine. Even amusing. And, after all, it is better than 'Rufus.' "

"Then what the hell is this all about?"

Whitehall smiled—again, only slightly—and lowered his voice. "Until ten seconds ago, Marcus Hedrik's brother has been standing behind the lean-to on our left. He was trying to listen to us. He is gone now."

Alex whipped his head around. Beyond the large tarpaulin lean-to, erected to cover some camp furniture against a forest shower, Justice Hedrik could be seen walking slowly toward two other crewmen across the clearing. Justice was younger than his brother Marcus, perhaps in his late twenties, and stockily muscular.

"Are you sure? I mean, that he was listening to us?"

"He was carving a piece of ceiba wood. There is too much to do to waste time carving artifacts. He was listening. Until I looked over at him."

"I'll remember that."

"Yes. Do. But do not give it undue emphasis. Runners are splendid fellows when they are taking in tourist groups; the tips are generous. I suspect neither brother is too pleased to be with us. Our trip is professional—worse, academically professional. There is not much in it for them. So there will be some hostility."

McAuliff started to speak, then hesitated. He was bewildered. "I . . . I may have missed something. What's that got to do with his listening?"

Whitehall blinked slowly, as if patiently explaining to an inept pupil—which, obviously, he felt was the case. "In the primitive intelligence, hostility is usually preceded by an overt, blunt curiosity."

"Thank you, Dr. Strangelove." Alex did not hide his irritation. "Let's get off this. What happened over in the hill community?"

"I sent a messenger to Maroon Town. I asked for a very private meeting with the Colonel of the Maroons. He will listen; he will accept."

"I wasn't aware a meeting was that tough to get. If I remember what Barak said, and I do, we just offer money."

"We do not want a tourist audience, McAuliff. No tribal artifacts or Afro-Carib beads bought for an extra two-dollah-Jamaican. Our business is more serious than tourist trade. I want to prepare the Colonel psychologically; make him think."

Alex paused; Whitehall was probably right. If what Barak Moore had said had validity. If the Colonel of the Maroons was the sole contact with the Halidon, the decision to make that contact would not be lightly arrived at; a degree of psychological preparation would be preferable to none at all. But not so much as to make him run, avoid the decision.

"How do you think you accomplished that?" asked McAuliff.

"I hired the leader of the community to act as courier.

I gave him one hundred dollars, which is like offering either of us roughly a quarter of a million. The message requests a meeting in four days, four hours after the sun descends over the mountains—"

"The Arawak symbols?" interrupted Alex.

"Precisely. Completed by specifying that the meeting should take place to the right of the Coromanteen crescent, which I would presume to be the Colonel's residence. The Colonel was to send back the exact location with our courier . . . Remember, the Colonel of the Maroon Tribes is an ancestral position; he is a descendant and, like all princes of the realm, schooled in its traditions. We shall know soon enough if he perceives us to be quite out of the ordinary."

"How?"

If the location he chooses is in some unit of four. Obviously."

"Obviously . . . So for the next few days we wait."

"Not just wait, McAuliff. We will be watched, observed very closely. We must take extreme care that we do not appear as a threat. We must go about our business quite professionally."

"I'm glad to hear that. We're being paid to make a geological survey."

24

WITH THE FIRST penetration into the Cock Pit, the work of the survey consumed each member of the team. Whatever their private fears or foreign objectives, they were professionals, and the incredible laboratory that was the Cock Pit demanded their professional attentions.

Portable tables, elaborately cased microscopes, geoscopes, platinum drills, sediment prisms, and depository vials were transported by scientist and carrier alike into the barely penetrable jungles and into the grasslands. The four-hour field sessions were more honored in the breach; none cared to interrupt his experiments or analyses for such inconveniences as meals and routine communications. The disciplines of basic precautions were swiftly consigned to aggravating nuisances. It took less than a full working day for the novelty of the ever-humming, ever-irritating walkie-talkies to wear off. McAuliff found it necessary to remind Peter Jensen and James Ferguson angrily that it was mandatory to leave the radio receiving switches on, regardless of the intermittent chatter between stations.

The first evenings lent credence to the wisdom of Charles Whitehall's purchases at Harrod's Safari Shop: The team sat around the fires in canvas chairs, as though recuperating from the day's hunt. But instead of talk of cat, horn, spore, and bird, other words flew around, spoken with no less enthusiasm. *Zinc, manganese* and *bauxite; ochers, gypsum,* and *phosphate . . . Cretaceous, Eocene, shale,* and *igneous; wynne grass, tamarind, bloodwood; guano, gros-michel,* and *woman's tongue . . . arid* and *acid* and *peripatus; water runoffs, gas pockets,* and *layers of vesicular lava—honeycombs of limestone.*

The overriding generalization was shared by everyone: The Cock Pit was an extraordinarily fruitful land mass with abundant reserves of rich soil, available water, and unbelievable deposits of gases and ores.

All this was accepted as fact before the morning of the third day. McAuliff listened as Peter Jensen summed it up with frightening clarity.

"It's inconceivable that no one's gone in and developed. I dare say Brasilia couldn't hold a candle! Three-quarters of the life force is right here, waiting to be used!"

The reference to the city carved out of the Brazilian jungles made Alex swallow and stare at the enthusiastic, middle-aged, pipe-smoking mineral expert.

We're going to build a city . . . Julian Warfield's words.

Unbelievable.

And viable.

It did not take great imagination to understand Dunstone, Limited, now. The project was sound, taking only gigantic sums of capital to set it in motion; sums available to Dunstone. And once set in motion, the entire island could be tied to the incredible development . . . Armies of workers, communities, *one source.*

Ultimately, the government.

Kingston could not, *would* not turn it off. Once in motion—*one source*—the benefits would be overwhelming and undeniable. The enormity of the cash flow alone could subvert the parliament.

Slices of the gigantic pie.

Economically and psychologically, Kingston would become dependent on Dunstone, Limited.

So complicated, yet so basically, ingeniously simple.

Once they have Kingston, they have the laws of the land in their vaults. To shape as they will. Dunstone will own a nation . . . R. C. Holcroft's words.

It was nearly midnight; the couriers were banking the fires under the scrutiny of the two runners, Marcus and Justice Hedrik. The black revolutionary, Lawrence, was playing his role as one of the crew, subservient and pleasant, but forever scanning the forests beyond, never allowing himself to be too far away from Alison Booth.

The Jensens and Ferguson had gone to their tents. McAuliff, Sam Tucker, and Alison sat around a small bivouac table, the light of the dying fires flickering across their faces as they talked quietly.

"Jensen's right, Alexander," said Tucker, lighting a thin cigar. "Those behind this know exactly what they're doing. I'm no ore expert, but one strike, one hint of a mother lode, and you couldn't stop the speculation money."

"It's a company named Dunstone."

"What is?"

"Those behind . . . the company's called Dunstone; the man's name is Warfield. Julian Warfield. Alison knows."

Sam held the cigar between his fingers and looked at McAuliff. "They hired you." Tucker's statement was spoken slowly, a touch gruffly.

"He did," replied Alex. "Warfield did."

"Then this Royal Society grant . . . the Ministry, and the Institute, *are* covers."

"Yes."

"And you knew it from the beginning."

"So does British Intelligence. I wasn't just acting as an informer, Sam. They trained me . . . as best they could over a couple of weeks."

"Was there any particular reason why you kept it a secret, Alexander?" Tucker's voice—especially as capped with McAuliff's name—was not comforting. "I think you should have told me. Especially after that meeting in the hills. We've been together a long time, boy . . . No, I don't think you acted properly."

"He was generously proper, Sam," said Alison, with a combination of precision and warmth. "For your benefit. I speak from experience. The less you're aware of, the better your prospects. Take my word for it."

"Why should I?" asked Tucker.

"Because I've been there. And because I was there, I'm here now."

"She's tied in against Chatellerault. That's what I couldn't tell you. She worked for Interpol. A data bank picked out her name; it was made to look so completely logical. She wanted to get out of England—"

"*Had* to get out, my darling . . . Do you see, Sam? The computer was Interpol's; all the intelligence services are first cousins, and don't let anyone tell you otherwise. M.I.5 ran a cross-reference, and here I am. Valuable bait, another complication . . . Don't be anxious to learn too much. Alex was right."

The ensuing silence was artificial. Tucker inhaled on his thin cigar, the unasked questions more pronounced by their absence. Alison whisked strands of hair, let down for the evening, off her forehead. McAuliff poured himself a small quantity of Scotch. Finally Sam Tucker spoke.

"It's fortunate I trust you, Alexander."

"I know that. I counted on it."

"But *why?*" continued Sam quietly. "Why in hell did you *do* it? You're not that hungry. Why did you work for *them?*"

"For whom? Or which? Dunstone or British Intelligence?"

Tucker paused, staring at Alex before he replied. "*Jesus,* I don't know. Both, I guess, boy."

"I accepted the first before the second showed up. It was a good contract, the best I'd ever been offered. Before I realized it, I was locked in. I was convinced I couldn't get out . . . by both sides. At one point, it was as simple as staying alive . . . Then there were guarantees and promises . . . and more guarantees and more promises." McAuliff stared across the clearing; it was strange. Lawrence was crouched over the embers of a fire, looking at them. "Before you know it, you're in some kind of crazy cell block, hurtling through space, bouncing off the walls . . . that's not a very sane picture."

"Move and counter-move, Sam," interrupted Alison. "They're experts."

"Who? Which?" Tucker leaned forward in his chair, holding Alison with his old eyes.

"Both," answered the girl firmly. "I saw what Chatellerault did to my husband. I know what Interpol did to me."

The silence returned once more, less strained than before. And once again, Sam Tucker broke it softly.

"You've got to define your enemies, Alexander. I get the feeling you haven't done that . . . present company excepted as allies, I sincerely hope."

"I've defined them as best I can. I'm not sure those definitions will hold. It's complicated; at least for me."

"Then simplify, boy. When you're finished, who wants you hanged the quickest?"

McAuliff looked at Alison. "Again, both. Dunstone literally; M.I.5 figuratively. One dead, the other dependent—subject to recall. A name in a data bank. That's very real."

"I agree," said Tucker, relighting his thin cigar. "Now, let's reverse the process. Who can *you* hang the quickest? The surest?"

Alex laughed quietly, joined by Alison. The girl spoke. "My Lord, you *do* think alike."

"Answer my question, son."

"I can protect myself . . . ourselves . . . with what I know, what I've pieced together. Both, I guess."

"That doesn't answer the question. Who the quickest?"

"Dunstone, I imagine. At the moment, it's more vulnerable. Warfield made a mistake; he thinks I'm *really* hungry. He thinks he bought me because he made me a part of them. They fall, I fall . . . I'd have to say Dunstone."

"All right," replied Sam, assuming the mantle of a soft-spoken attorney. "Enemy number one defined as Dunstone. You can extricate yourself by simple blackmail: third-person knowledge, documents tucked away in lawyers' offices. Agreed?"

"Yes."

"That leaves enemy number two: Her Majesty's Intelligence boys. Let's define them. What's their hook into you?"

"Protection. It's supposed to be protection."

"Not noticeably successful, would you say, son?"

"Not noticeably successful," said Alex in agreement. "But we're not finished yet."

"We'll get to that; don't rush . . . what's *your* hook into *them?*"

McAuliff paused in thought. "Their methods . . . and their contacts, I think. Exposing their covert operations."

"Really the same as with Dunstone, isn't it?" Tucker was zeroing in on his target.

"Again, yes."

"Let's go back a second. What does Dunstone offer?"

"Money. A great deal of money. They need this survey."

"Are you prepared to lose it?"

"Hell, yes! But I may not have to—"

"That's immaterial. I assume that's part of the 'guarantees and promises.' "

"That's right."

"But it's not a factor. You haven't stolen from the thieves. In any way can they get you indicted as one of them?"

"Christ, no! They may think so, but they're wrong."

"Then there are your answers. Your definitions. Eliminate the hooks and the offers. Theirs. The money and the protection. Lose one—the money; make the other un-necessary—the protection. You're dealing from strength, with your own hooks. *You* make whatever offers you wish."

"You jumped, Sam," said McAuliff slowly. "Or you forgot. We're not finished; we may need the protection. If we take it, we can't deny it. We'd be a joke. The Water-gate syndrome. Worms crawling over each other."

Sam Tucker put down his thin cigar in the ashtray on the table and reached for the bottle of Scotch. He was about to speak, but was interrupted by the sight of Charles Whitehall walking out of a jungle path into the clearing. Whitehall looked around, then crossed rapidly to Lawrence, who was still over the coals of the banked fire, the orange glow coloring his skin a bronzed black. The two men spoke. Lawrence stood up, nodded once, and started toward the jungle path. Whitehall watched him briefly, then turned and looked over at McAuliff, Sam, and Alison.

With urgency, he began walking across the clearing to them.

"There's your protection, Alexander," said Sam quietly as Whitehall approached. "The two of them. They may despise each other, but they've got a common hate that works out fine for you. For all of us, goddamn it . . . Bless their beautiful black hides."

"The courier has returned." Charles Whitehall adjusted the light of the Coleman lantern in his tent. McAuliff stood inside the canvas flap of the doorway—Whitehall had insisted that Alex come with him; he did not wish to speak in front of Alison and Sam Tucker.

"You could have told the others."

"That will be a . . . multilateral decision. Personally, I would not subscribe to it."

"Why not?"

"We must be extremely careful. The less that is known by the more, the better."

McAuliff pulled out a pack of cigarettes and walked to the single nylon-strapped chair in the center of the tent. He sat down, knowing that Charley-mon would not; the black was too agitated, trying almost comically to remain calm. "That's funny. Alison used the same words a little while ago. For different reasons . . . What's the message from Maroon Town?"

"Affirmative! The Colonel will meet with us. What's more important—*so* much more important—is that his reply was in units of four!"

Whitehall approached the chair, his eyes filled with that messianic anxiety Alex had seen in Drax Hall. "He made a counter-proposal for our meeting. Unless he hears otherwise, he will assume it is acceptable . . . He asks for eight days. And rather than four hours after sundown, he requests the same four hours after two in the morning. *Two* in the *morning!* Diagramatically to the *right* of the setting sun. Don't you see? He *understands,* McAuliff. He understands! Piersall's first step is confirmed!"

"I thought it would be," replied Alex lamely, not quite sure how to handle Whitehall's agitation.

"It doesn't matter to you, does it?" The Jamaican stared at McAuliff incredulously. "A scholar had made an extraordinary discovery. He'd followed elusive threads in the archives going back over two hundred years. His work proved out; it could have enormous academic impact. The story of Jamaica might well have to be rewritten . . . Can't you *see?*"

"I can see you're excited, and I can understand that. You should be . . . But right now, I'm concerned with a less erudite problem. I don't like the delay."

Whitehall silently exploded in exasperation. He looked up at the canvas ceiling, inhaled deeply, and quickly regained his composure. The judgment he conveyed was obvious: The blunt mind in front of him was incapable of being reached. He spoke with condescending resignation. "It's good. It indicates progress."

"Why?"

"I did not tell you, but I included a message with our request for a meeting. It was admittedly a risk but I felt—unilaterally—that it was worth taking. It could expedite our objective with greater speed. I told the courier to say the request came from . . . new believers of Acquaba."

McAuliff tensed; he was suddenly angry with Whitehall, but had the presence to minimize his anger. The horrible memory of the fate of the first Dunstone survey came to mind. "For such a brilliant guy, I think that was pretty stupid, Charley-*mon*."

"Not stupid. A calculated risk. If the Halidon decides to make contact on the strength of Piersall's code, it will arrive at that decision only after it learns more about us. It will send out for information; it will see that *I* am part of the unit. The elders of the Halidon will know of my credentials, my scholarship, my contributions to the Jamaican story. These will be in our favor."

Alex leaped out of the chair and spoke quietly, viciously. "You egomaniacal son of a bitch! Has it occurred to you that your . . . *other* credentials may *not* be favorable? You could be the one piece of rotten meat!"

"Impossible!"

"You arrogant prick! I won't have the lives of this team jeopardized by your inflated opinion of yourself! I want protection, and I'm going to get it!"

There was a rustling outside the tent. Both men whipped around toward the canvas flap of the entrance. The canvas parted, and the black revolutionary, Lawrence, walked in slowly, his hands in front of him, bound by rope. Behind Lawrence was another man. It was the runner Marcus Hedrik. In his hand was a gun. It was jabbed into the flesh of his prisoner.

Hedrik spoke quietly. "Do not go for your weapons. Don't make noise. Just stay exactly where you are."

"Who are you?" asked McAuliff, amazed that Hedrik's voice had lost the hesitant, dull tones he had heard for the better part of a week.

"For the moment, that is not important."

"Garvey!" whispered Alex. "Garvey said it! He said there were others . . . he didn't know who. You're with British Intelligence!"

"No," replied Marcus Hedrik softly, even politely. "Two of your couriers were English agents. They're dead. And the obese Garvey had an accident on the road to Port Maria. He is dead also."

"Then—"

"It is not you who will ask the questions, Mr. McAuliff. It is I. You will tell me . . . you new believers . . . what you know of Acquaba."

25

THEY TALKED for several hours, and McAuliff knew that for the time being he had saved their lives. At one point Sam Tucker interrupted, only to receive and acknowledge the plea in Alexander's eyes: Sam *had* to leave them alone. Tucker left, making it clear that he would be with Alison. He expected Alex to speak with them before retiring. Sam did not notice the ropes on Lawrence's hands in the shadowed corner, and McAuliff was grateful that he did not.

"Marcus Hedrik" was not the runner's name. Marcus and Justice Hedrik had been replaced; where they were was of no consequence insisted this unnamed member of the Halidon. What was of paramount consequence was the whereabouts of the Piersall document.

Always leave something to trade off . . . in the last extremity. The words of R. C. Holcroft.

The documents.

McAuliff's ploy.

The Halidonite probed with infinite care every aspect of Piersall's conclusions as related by Charles Whitehall. The black scholar traced the history of the Acquaba sect, but he would not reveal the *nagarro:* the meaning of the Halidon. The "runner" neither agreed nor disagreed; he was simply an interrogator. He was also a perceptive and cautious man.

Once satisfied that Charles Whitehall would tell him no more, he ordered him to remain inside his tent with Lawrence. They were not to leave; they would be shot if they tried. His fellow "runner" would stay on guard.

The Halidonite recognized the intransigence of McAuliff's position. Alex would tell him nothing. Faced with that, he ordered Alex under gunpoint to walk out of the campsite. As they proceeded up a path toward the grasslands, McAuliff began to understand the thoroughness of the Halidon—that small part of it to which he was exposed. Twice along the alley of dense foliage, the man with the weapon commanded him to stop. There followed a brief series of guttural parrot calls, responded to in kind. Alex heard the softly spoken words of the man with the gun.

"The bivouac is surrounded, Mr. McAuliff. I'm quite sure Whitehall and Tucker, as well as your couriers, know that now. The birds we imitate do not sing at night."

"Where are we going?"

"To meet with someone. My superior, in fact. Continue, please."

They climbed for another twenty minutes; a long jungle hill suddenly became an open grassland, a field that seemed extracted from some other terrain, imposed on a foreign land surrounded by wet forests and steep mountains.

The moonlight was unimpeded by clouds; the field was washed with dull yellow. And in the center of the wild grass stood two men. As they approached, McAuliff saw that one of the men was perhaps ten feet behind the first, his back to them. The first man faced them.

The Halidonite facing them was dressed in what appeared to be ragged clothes, but with a loose field jacket and boots. The combined effect was a strange, unkempt paramilitary appearance. Around his waist was a pistol belt and holster. The man ten feet away and staring off in the opposite direction was in a caftan held together in the middle by a single thick rope.

Priestlike. Immobile.

"Sit on the ground, Dr. McAuliff," instructed the strangely ragged paramilitary man, in clipped tones used to command.

Alex did so. The use of the title "Doctor" told him the unfamiliarity was more his than theirs.

The subordinate who had marched him up from the camp approached the priest figure. The two men fell into quiet conversation, walking slowly into the grass while talking. The two figures receded over a hundred yards into the dull yellow field.

They stopped.

"Turn around, Dr. McAuliff." The order was abrupt; the black man above him had his hand on his holster. Alex pivoted in his sitting position and faced the descending forest from which he and the runner had emerged.

The waiting was long and tense. Yet McAuliff understood that his strongest weapon—perhaps his only viable strength—was calm determination.

He was determined; he was not calm.

He was frightened in the same way he had experienced fear before. In the Korean hills; alone, no matter the number of troops; waiting to witness his own single annihilation.

Pockets of fear.

"It is an extraordinary story, is it not, Dr. McAuliff?"

That voice. My God! He knew that voice.

He pressed his arms against the ground and started to whip his head and body around.

His temple crashed into the hard steel of a pistol; the agonizing pain shot through his face and chest. There was a series of bright flashes in front of his eyes as the pain reached a sensory crescendo.

It subsided to a numbing ache, and he could feel a trickle of blood on his neck.

"You will remain the way you are while we talk," said the familiar voice.

Where had he heard it before?

"I know you."

"You don't *know* me, Dr. McAuliff."

"I've heard your voice . . . somewhere."

"Then you have remarkable recall. So much has happened . . . I shall not waste words. Where are Piersall's documents? I am sure it is unnecessary to tell you that your life and the lives of those you brought to Jamaica depend on our having them."

"How do you know they'd do you any good? What if I told you I had copies made?"

"I would say you were lying. We know the placement of every Xerox machine, every photostat copier, every store, hotel, and individual that does such work along the coast. Including Bueno, the Bays, and Ocho Rios. You have had no copies made."

"You're not very bright, Mr. Halidon . . . It is Mr. Halidon, isn't it?" There was no response, so Alex continued. "We photographed them."

"Then the films are not developed. And the only member of your team possessing a camera is the boy, Ferguson. He is hardly a confidant . . . But this is immaterial, Dr. McAuliff. When we say documents, we assume any and all reproductions thereof. Should any surface

. . . *ever* . . . there will be, to put it bluntly, a massacre of innocents. Your survey team, their families, children . . . all those held dear by everyone. A cruel and unnecessary prospect."

. . . *to the last extremity.* R. C. Holcroft.

"It would be the Halidon's last action, wouldn't it?" McAuliff spoke slowly but sharply, stunned by his own calm. "A kind of final . . . *beau geste* before extinction. If you want it that way, I don't give a damn."

"*Stop it, McAuliff!*" The voice suddenly screamed, a piercing shriek over the blades of wild grass, its echo muted by the surrounding jungles.

Those words . . . They were the *words* he had heard before!

Stop it. Stop it . . . stop it . . .

Where? For God's sake, where had he heard them?

His mind raced; images were blurred with blinding colored lights, but he could not focus.

A man. A black man—tall and lithe and muscular . . . A man following orders. A man commanding but not with his own commands. The voice that had just roared was the same voice from the past . . . *following orders.* In panic . . . as before.

Something . . .

"You said we would talk. Threats are one-sided conversations; you take turns, you don't talk. I'm not on anybody's side. I want your . . . superiors to know that." Alex held his breath during the silence that followed.

The quiet reply came with measured authority . . . and a small but recognizable trace of fear. "There *are* no superiors as far as you are concerned. My temper is short. These have been difficult days . . . You should realize that you are very close to losing your life."

The man with the pistol had moved slightly; Alex could see him now out of the corner of his eye. And what he saw convinced him he was on the track of an immediate truth. The man's head had snapped up at the priest figure; the man with the weapon dangling in his hand was questioning the priest figure's words.

"If you kill me . . . or any member of the team, the Halidon will be exposed in a matter of hours."

Again silence. Again the measured authority; again the now unmistakable undertone of fear. "And how is this remarkable exposure going to take place, Dr. McAuliff?"

Alex drew a deep breath silently. His right hand was clasping his left wrist; he pressed his fingers into his own flesh as he replied.

"In my equipment there is a radio signaling device. It is standard and operates on a frequency that rides above interference. It's functional within a radius of twenty-five miles . . . Every twelve hours I send out one of two codes; a light on the miniature panel confirms reception *and* pinpoints location-identification. The first code says everything's normal, no problems. The second says something else. It instructs the man on the receiving end to implement two specific orders: fly the documents out and send help in. The absence of transmission is the equivalent of the second code, only more so. It alerts all the factions in Kingston, including British Intelligence. They'll be forced in; they'll start with our last location and fan out. The Cock Pit will be swarming with planes and troops . . . I'd better transmit the code, Mr. Halidon. And even when I do, you won't know which one I'm sending, will you?" McAuliff stopped for precisely three seconds. And then he said quietly, "Checkmate, Mr. Bones."

A macaw's screech could be heard in the distance. From somewhere in the wet forests a pride of wild pigs was disturbed. The warm breeze bent the reeds of the tall grass ever so slightly; crickets were everywhere. All these were absorbed by Alex's senses. And he understood, too, the audible, trembling intake of breath from the darkness behind him. He could feel the mounting, uncontrollable pitch of anger.

"No, mon!" The man with the pistol cried out, lunging forward.

Simultaneously, McAuliff felt the rush of air and heard the rustle of cloth that precedes the instant of impact from behind. Too late to turn; defense only in crouching, hugging the earth.

One man tried to stop the priest figure as he lunged forward; the weight of two furious bodies descended on Alex's shoulders and back. Arms were thrashing, fingers spastically clutched; hard steel and soft cloth and warm flesh enveloped him. He reached above and grasped the first objects his hands touched, yanked with all his strength, and rolled forward.

The priest figure somersaulted over his back; Alex crashed his shoulders downward, rising on one knee for greater weight, and threw himself on the coarse cloth of the caftan. As he pinned the priest, he felt himself instantly pulled backward, with such force that the small of his back ached in pain.

The two Halidonites locked his arms, stretching his chest to the breaking point; the man with the pistol held the barrel to his temple, digging it into his skin.

"That will be *enough,* mon."

Below him on the ground, the yellow moonlight illuminating a face creased with fury, was the priest figure.

McAuliff instantly understood the bewildering, unfocused images of blinding, colored lights his mind had associated with the panicked words *stop it, stop it.*

He had last seen this "priest" of the Halidon in London's Soho. During the psychedelic madness that was The Owl of Saint George. The man lying on the ground in a caftan had been dressed in a dark suit then, gyrating on the crowded dance floor. He had screamed at McAuliff to *Stop . . . stop it!* He had delivered a crushing fist into Alex's midsection; he had disappeared into the crowds, only to show up an hour later in a government car on the street by a public telephone.

This "priest" of the Halidon was an agent of British Intelligence.

"You said your name was Tallon." McAuliff strained his speech through the pain, the words interrupted by his lack of breath. "In the car that night you said your name was Tallon. And . . . when I called you on it, you said you were . . . testing me."

The priest figure rolled over and slowly began to rise. He nodded to the two Halidonites to relax their grips and addressed them. "I would not have killed him. You know that."

"You were angry, mon," said the man who had taken Alex out of the camp.

"Forgive us," added the man who had cried out and lunged at the priest figure. "It was necessary."

The "priest" smoothed his cassock and tugged at the thick rope around his waist. He looked down at McAuliff. "Your recollection is sharp, Doctor. I sincerely hope your ability to think clearly is equally acute."

"Does that mean we talk?"

"We talk."

"My arms hurt like hell. Will you tell your sergeants to let go of me?"

The "priest" nodded once again, and flicked his wrist in accord. Alex's arms were released; he shook them.

"My sergeants, as you call them, are more temperate men than I. You should be grateful to them."

The man with the pistol belt demurred, his voice respectful. "Not so, mon. When did you last sleep?"

"That does not matter. I should have more control . . . My friend refers to a hectic several weeks, McAuliff. Not only did I have to get myself out of England, avoiding Her Majesty's Service, but also a colleague who had disappeared in a Bentley around a Soho corner . . . A West Indian in London has a thousand hiding places."

Alex remembered vividly. "That Bentley tried to run me down. The driver wanted to kill me. Only someone else was killed . . . because of a neon light."

The priest figure stared at McAuliff. He, too, seemed to recall the evening vividly. "It was a tragedy born of the instant. We thought a trap had been set, the spring caught at the last moment."

"Three lives were lost that night. Two with cyanide—"

"We are committed," interrupted the Halidonite, who looked at his two companions and spoke gently. "Leave us alone, please."

In warning, both men removed the weapons from their belts as they pulled Alex to his feet. As ordered, they retreated into the field. McAuliff watched them. A ragged-clothed twosome with the unlikely jackets and pistol belts. "They not only do as you say, they protect you from yourself."

The priest figure also looked at his retreating subordinates. "When we are in our formative years, we are all given batteries of tests. Each is assigned areas of instruction and future responsibility from the results. I often think grave errors are made." The man tugged at his caftan and turned to McAuliff. "We must deal now with each other, must we not? . . . As I am sure you have surmised, I was an impermanent member of M.I.5."

"An 'infiltrator' is the word that comes to mind."

"A very successful one, Doctor. Holcroft himself twice recommended me for citations. I was one of the best West

Indian specialists . . . I was reluctant to leave. You—and those maneuvering you—created the necessity."

"How?"

"Your survey suddenly contained too many dangerous components. We could live with several, but when we found out that your closest associate on the geological team—Mr. Tucker—was apparently a friend of Walter Piersall, we knew we had to keep you under a microscope . . . Obviously, we were too late."

"What were the other components?"

The priest figure hesitated. He touched his forehead, where a grass burn had developed from his fall to the ground. "Do you have a cigarette? This very comfortable sheet has one disadvantage: There are no pockets."

"Why do you wear it?"

"It is a symbol of authority, nothing more."

McAuliff reached into his pocket, withdrew a pack of cigarettes, and shook one up for the Halidonite. As he lighted it for him, he saw that the black hollows in the very black skin beneath the eyes were stretched in exhaustion. "What were the dangerous components?"

"Oh, come, Doctor, you know them as well as I do."

"Maybe I don't; enlighten me. Or is that dangerous, too?"

"Not now. Not at this point. The *reality* is the danger. Piersall's documents are the reality. The . . . components are inconsequential."

"Then tell me."

The priest figure inhaled on his cigarette and blew the smoke into the soft breeze of the dull yellow light. "The woman you know about. There are many who fear her on the Continent. Among those, one of the Dunstone hierarchy . . . the Marquis de Chatellerault. Where she is, so is an arm of the Intelligence service. The boy, Ferguson, is deep with the Craft interests; actually, they fear him. Or did. And rightly so. He never understood the calamitous economic potential of his fiber work."

"I think he did," interrupted Alex. "And does. He expects to make money out of Craft."

The Halidonite laughed quietly. "They will never let him. But he is a component. Where does Craft stand? Is he part of Dunstone? Nothing happens in Jamaica that the soiled hand of Craft has not touched . . . Samuel Tucker I have told you about: his association with the suddenly vital Walter Piersall. Whose summons did he answer? Is he on the island because of his old friend McAuliff? Or his new friend Piersall? Or is it coincidence?"

"It is coincidence," said Alex. "You'd have to know Sam to understand that."

"But we do not, you see. We only understand that among the first telephone calls he made was to a man who was disturbing us profoundly. Who was walking around Kingston with the secrets of two hundred years in his brain . . . and somewhere on paper." The priest figure looked at McAuliff—stared at him, really. His eyes in the moonlight conveyed a supplication for Alex to understand. He looked away and continued. "Then there is Charles Whitehall. A very . . . *very* dangerous and unpredictable component. You must know his background; Holcroft certainly did. Whitehall feels his time on the island has come. His is the hot mysticism of the fanatic. The black Caesar come to ride up Victoria Park on nigger-Pompei's horse. He has followers throughout Jamaica. If there is anyone who might expose Dunstone—wittingly or otherwise—it could well be Whitehall and his fascists."

"Holcroft didn't know that," protested McAuliff. "He made it clear that you . . . the Halidon . . . were the only ones who could stop Dunstone."

"Holcroft is a professional. He creates internal chaos, knowing that his breakthrough can come at any instant during the panic. Would it surprise you to know that Holcroft is in Kingston now?"

Alex thought for a moment. "No . . . I'm surprised he hasn't let me know it."

"There is a sound reason. He doesn't want you to fall back on him. He wants the forces to remain on collision courses. He flew in when word was received that Chatellerault was in Savanna-la-Mar . . . You knew *that*, didn't you?"

"*He* knows it because I told Westmore Tallon."

"And then there are the Jensens. That charming, devoted couple. So normal, so lovable, really . . . who send back word to Julian Warfield of every move you make, of every person you make contact with; who bribe Jamaicans to spy on you . . . The Jensens made a huge mistake once, years ago. Dunstone, Limited, stepped in and recruited them. In exchange for obliterating that mistake."

McAuliff looked up at the clear night sky. A single

elongated cloud was drifting from a distant mountain toward the yellow moon. He wondered if the condensation would disappear before it reached the shining satellite, or blur it from beneath . . . envelop it from the ground.

As he was so enveloped.

"So those are the components," said Alex aimlessly. "The Halidon knows a lot more than anyone else, it seems. And I'm not sure what that means."

"It means, Doctor, that we are the silent caretakers of our land."

"I don't recall any election. Who gave you the job?"

"To quote an American writer: 'It comes with the territory.' It is our heritage. We do not swim in the political rivers, however. We leave those to the legitimate competitors. We *do* try out best to keep the pollution to a minimum." The priest figure finished his cigarette and crushed the burning end under his sandaled foot.

"You're killers," said McAuliff simply. "I know that. I think that's the worst kind of human pollution."

"Are you referring to Dunstone's previous survey?"

"I am."

"You don't know the circumstances. And I'm not the one to define them. I am here only to persuade you to give me Piersall's documents."

"I won't do that."

"Why?" The Halidonite's voice rose in anger, as before. His black eyes above the black hollows pierced into McAuliff's.

"Mon?" came the shouted query from the field. The priest figure waved his arm in dismissal.

"This is not your business, McAuliff. Understand that and get out. Give me the documents and take your survey off the island before it is too late."

"If it was that simple, I would. I don't *want* your fight, goddamn it. It has no appeal for me . . . On the other hand, I don't relish being chased all over the globe by Julian Warfield's guns. Can't *you* understand *that?"*

The priest figure stood immobile. His eyes softened; his lips parted in concentration as he stared at Alexander. He spoke slowly; he was barely audible. "I warned them that it might come to this. Give me the *nagarro,* doctor. What is the meaning of the Halidon?"

McAuliff told him.

26

THEY RETURNED to the river campsite, McAuliff and the runner who had assumed the name and function of "Marcus Hedrik." There was no pretense now. As they neared the bivouac area, black men in rags could be seen in the bush, the early dawn light shafting through the dense foliage, intermittently reflecting off the barrels of their weapons.

The survey camp was surrounded, the inhabitants prisoners of the Halidon.

A hundred yards from the clearing, the runner—now preceding Alex on the narrow jungle path, pistol secure in his field jacket belt—stopped and summoned a Halidon patrol. He did so by snapping his fingers repeatedly until a large black man emerged from between the trees.

The two men spoke briefly, quietly, and when they were finished the patrol returned to his post in the tropic forest. The runner turned to McAuliff.

"Everything is peaceful. There was a skirmish with Charles Whitehall, but it was anticipated. He severely wounded the guard, but others were nearby. He is bound and back in his tent."

"What about Mrs. Booth?"

"The woman? She is with Samuel Tucker. She was asleep a half hour ago . . . That Tucker, he will not sleep. He sits in the chair in front of his tent, a rifle in his hands. The others are quiet. They will be rising soon."

"Tell me," said Alex while the runner still faced him, "what happened to all that Arawak language? The Maroon Colonel, the units of four, the eight days?"

"You forgot, Doctor. I led the Whitehall-mon to his courier. The Colonel of the Maroons never got the message. The reply you received came from us." The runner smiled. Then he turned, gesturing for Alex to follow him into the clearing.

Under the eyes of the runner, McAuliff waited for the white light of the miniature panel to reach full illumination. When it did, he pressed the signal-transmitter button, holding his left hand over his fingers as he did so. He knew the concealment was unnecessary; he would not radio for aid. He would not jam the frequency with cries of emergency. It had been made clear that at the first sight of hostile forces, each member of the survey would be shot through the head, Alison Booth and Sam Tucker the first to be executed.

The remainder of the understanding was equally clear. Sam Tucker would continue to send the signals every twelve hours. Alexander would return with the runner into the grassland. From there, with the "priest" he would be taken to the hidden community of the Halidon. Until he returned, the team was a collective hostage.

Alison, Sam, Charles Whitehall and Lawrence would be told the truth. The others would not. The Jensens, James Ferguson and the crew would be given another explanation, a bureaucratic one readily acceptable to professional surveyors: During the night a radio message from Kingston had been relayed by Falmouth; the Ministry of the Interior required McAuliff's presence in Ocho Rios; there were difficulties with the Institute. It was the sort of complication to which survey directors were subjected. Field work was constantly interrupted by administrative foulups.

When the priest figure suggested the time of absence be no less than three full days, Alex demanded to know the reason for so long a period.

"I can't answer that, McAuliff."

"Then why should I agree to it?"

"It is only time. Then, too, are we not at checkmate . . . Mr. Bones? We fear exposure perhaps more than you fear for your lives."

"I won't concede that."

"You do not know us. Give yourself the margin to learn. You will not be disappointed."

"You were told to say three days, then?"

"I was."

"Which presumes that whoever told you to say it expected you to bring me to them."

"It was a distinct probability."

Alexander agreed to three full days.

The black revolutionary, Lawrence, was rubbing a penicillin salve over Charles Whitehall's bare back. The rope burns were deep; whoever had lashed Charley-mon had done so in fever-pitch anger. The ropes on both men had been removed after McAuliff's talk with them.

Alexander had made it clear he would brook no further interference. Their causes were expendable.

"Your arrogance is beyond understanding, McAuliff!" said Charles Whitehall, suppressing a grimace as Lawrence touched a sensitive burn.

"I accept the rebuke. You're very qualified in that department."

"You are not *equipped* to deal with these people. I have spent my life, my *entire life,* stripping away the layers of Jamaican—Caribbean—history!"

"Not your entire life, Charley-mon," replied Alex, calmly but incisively. "I told you last night. There's the little matter of your extra-scholastic activity. 'The black Caesar riding up Victoria Park on nigger-Pompei's horse . . .'"

"*What?*"

"They're not my words, Charley."

Lawrence suddenly pressed his fist into a raw lash mark on Whitehall's shoulder. The scholar arched his neck back in pain. The revolutionary's other hand was close to his throat. Neither man moved; Lawrence spoke.

"You don't ride no nigger horse, mon. You den walk like everybody else."

Charles Whitehall stared over his shoulder at the blur of the brutal, massive hand poised for assault. "You play the fool, you know. Do you think any political entity with a power structure based in wealth will tolerate *you?* Not for a minute, you egalitarian jackal. You will be crushed."

"You do not seek to crush us, mon?"

"I seek only what is best for Jamaica. Everyone's energies will be used to that end."

"You're a regular Pollyanna," broke in Alex, walking toward the two men.

Lawrence looked up at McAuliff, his expression equal parts of suspicion and dependence. He removed his hand and reached for the tube of penicillin salve. "Put on your shirt, mon. Your skin is covered," he said, twisting the small cap onto the medicine tube.

"I'm leaving in a few minutes," said McAuliff, standing in front of Whitehall. "Sam will be in charge; you're to do as he says. Insofar as possible, the work is to continue

normally. The Halidon will stay out of sight . . . at least
as far as the Jensens and Ferguson are concerned."

"How can that be?" asked Lawrence.

"It won't be difficult," answered Alex. "Peter is drilling
for gaspocket sediment a mile and a half southwest. Ruth
is due east in a quarry; the runner we know as 'Justice'
will be with her. Ferguson is across the river working
some fern groves. All are separated, each will be
watched."

"And me?" Whitehall buttoned his expensive cotton
safari shirt as though dressing for a concert at Covent
Garden. "What do you propose for me?"

"You're confined to the clearing, Charley-mon. For
your own sake, don't try to leave it. I can't be responsible
if you do."

"You think you have any say about anything now,
McAuliff?"

"Yes, I do. They're as much afraid of me as I am of
them. Just don't try to upset the balance, either one of
you. I buried a man on an Alaskan job a number of years
ago. Sam will tell you. I know the standard prayers."

Alison stood on the river bank, looking down at the
water. The heat of the early sun was awakening the late
sleepers of the forest. The sounds were those of combative
foraging; flyer against flyer, crawler fighting crawler. The
green vines dangling from the tall macca-fat palms glistened with the moisture rising from below; fern and moss
and matted cabbage growth bordered the slowly flowing
currents of the Martha Brae offshoot. The water was
morning-clear, bluish-green.

"I went to your tent," said McAuliff, walking up to her.
"Sam said you were out here."

She turned and smiled. "I wasn't really disobeying, my
darling. I'm not running anywhere."

"Nowhere to go . . . You'll be all right . . . The runner's waiting for me."

Alison took two steps and stood in front of him. She
spoke quietly, barely above a whisper. "I want to tell you
something, Alexander T. McAuliff. And I refuse to be
dramatic or tearful or anything remotely theatrical . . .
because those are crutches . . . And both of us can walk
without them. Six weeks ago I was running. Quite desper-

ately, trying my goddamnedest to convince myself that by
running I was escaping—which I knew underneath was
absurd. In Kingston I told you how absurd it was. They
can find you. Anywhere. The computers, the data banks,
the horrid, complicated tracers they have in their cellars
and in their hidden rooms are too real now. Too thorough. And there is no life underground, in remote places,
always wondering . . . I don't expect you to understand
this, and, in a way, it's why what you're doing is right
. . . 'Do unto others *before* they do unto you.' That's
what you said. I believe that's a terrible way to think. And
I also believe it's the only way we're going to have a life
of our own."

McAuliff touched her face with his fingers. Her eyes
were bluer than he had ever seen them. "That sounds dangerously like a proposal."

"My wants are simple, my expressions uncomplicated.
And, as you said once, I'm a damned fine professional."

" 'McAuliff and Booth. Surveyors. Offices: London and
New York.' That'd look good on the letterhead."

"You wouldn't consider 'Booth and McAuliff'? I mean,
alphabetically—"

"No, I wouldn't," he interrupted gently as he put his
arms around her.

"Do people always say silly things when they're afraid?"
she asked, her face buried in his chest.

"I think so," he replied.

Peter Jensen reached down into the full pack and felt
his way among the soft articles of clothing. The canvas
was stuffed. Jensen winced as he slid the object of his
search up the sides of the cloth.

It was the Luger. It was wrapped in plastic, the silencer
detached, tied to the barrel and in plastic also.

His wife stood by the entrance flap of their tent, the slit
folded back just sufficiently for her to look outside. Peter
unwrapped both sections of the weapon and put the
silencer in the pocket of his field jacket. He pressed the
release, slid out the magazine, and reached into his other
pocket for a box of cartridges. Methodically he inserted
the shells until the spring of the magazine was taut, the
top bullet ready for chamber insertion. He slid the magazine back into the handle slot and cracked it into position.

Ruth heard the metallic click and turned around. "Do you have to do this?"

"Yes. Julian was very clear. McAuliff was my selection, his concurrence a result of that choice. McAuliff's made contact. With whom? With what? I must find out." Peter pulled open his jacket and shoved the Luger down between a triangle of leather straps sewn into the lining. He buttoned the field jacket and stood up straight. "Any bulges, old girl? Does it show?"

"No."

"Good. Hardly the fit of Whitehall's uniform, but I dare say a bit more comfortable."

"You will be careful? It's so dreadful out there."

"All that camping you dragged me on had a purpose. I see that now, my dear." Peter smiled and returned to his pack, pushing down the contents, pulling the straps into buckling position. He inserted the prongs, tugged once more, and slapped the bulging outsides. He lifted the canvas sack by the shoulder harness and let it fall to the dirt. "There! I'm set for a fortnight if need be."

"How will I know?"

"When I don't come back with my carrier. If I pull it off right, he might even be too petrified to return himself." Peter saw the tremble on his wife's lips, the terrible fear in her eyes. He motioned for her to come to him, which she did. Rushing into his arms.

"Oh, God, *Peter*—"

"Please, Ruth. *Shhh.* You mustn't," he said, stroking her hair. "Julian has been everything to us. We both know that. And Julian thinks we'd be very happy at Peale Court. Dunstone will need many people in Jamaica, he said. Why not us?"

When the unknown carrier came into camp, James Ferguson could see that the runner, Marcus Hedrik, was as angry as he was curious. They were all curious. McAuliff had left early that morning for the coast; it seemed strange that the carrier had not met him on the river. The carrier insisted he had seen no one but wandering hill people, some fishing, some hunting—no white man.

The carrier had been sent by the Government Employment Office, a branch in Falmouth that knew the survey was looking for additional hands. The carrier was familiar with the river offshoot, having grown up in Weston Favel, and was anxious for work. Naturally, he had the proper papers, signed by some obscure functionary at G.E.O., Falmouth.

At 2:30 in the afternoon, James Ferguson, having rested after lunch, sat on the edge of his cot, prepared to gather up his equipment and head back into the field. There was a rustling outside his tent. He looked up, and the new carrier suddenly slapped open the flap and walked in. He was carrying a plastic tray.

"I say—"

"I pick up dishes, mon," said the carrier rapidly. "Alla time be very neat."

"I have no dishes here. There's a glass or two need washing . . ."

The carrier lowered his voice. "I got message for Fergu-mon. I give it to you. You read it quick." The black reached into his pocket and withdrew a sealed envelope. He handed it to Ferguson.

James ripped the back and pulled out a single page of stationery. It was the stationery of The Craft Foundation, and Ferguson's eyes were immediately pulled to the signature. It was known throughout Jamaica—the scrawl of Arthur Craft, Senior, the semiretired but all-powerful head of the Craft enterprises.

My dear James Ferguson:

Apologies from a distance are always most awkward and often the most sincere. Such is the present case.

My son has behaved badly, for which he, too, offers his regrets. He sends them from the South of France where he will be residing for an indeterminate—but long—period of time.

To the point: your contributions in our laboratories on the baracoa experiments are immense. They led the way to what we believe can be a major breakthrough that can have a widespread industrial impact. We believe this breakthrough can be accelerated by your immediate return to us. Your future is assured, young man, in the way all genius should be rewarded. You will be a very wealthy man.

However, time is of the essence. Therefore I recommend that you leave the survey forthwith—the messenger will explain the somewhat odd fashion of departure but you may be assured that I have appraised Kingston of my wishes and they are in full agreement. (The baracoa is for *all* Jamaica.) We are also in mutual agreement that it is unnecessary to involve the survey director, Dr. McAuliff, as his immediate interests are rightfully in conflict with ours. A substitute botanist will join the survey within a matter of days.

I look forward to renewing our acquaintance.

Very truly yours,
Arthur Craft, Senior

James Ferguson held his breath in astonishment as he reread the letter.

He had done it.

He had really done it.

Everything.

He looked up at the carrier, who smiled and spoke softly.

"We leave late afternoon, mon. Before dark. Come back early from your work. I will meet you on the river bank and we will go."

27

THE PRIEST FIGURE identified himself by the single name
of "Malcolm." They traveled south on hidden routes that
alternated between steep rocky climbs, winding grottos,
and dense jungle. The Halidonite in the ragged clothes
and the field jacket led the way, effortlessly finding concealed paths in the forests and covered openings that led
through long dark tunnels of ancient stone—the dank
smell of deep grotto waters ever present, the bright reflection of stalactites, suspended in alabaster isolation, caught
in the beams of flashlights.

It seemed to McAuliff that at times they were descending into the cellars of the earth, only to emerge from the
darkness of a grotto onto higher ground. A geological
phenomenon, tunneled caves that inexorably progressed
upward, evidence of oceanic-terrestrial upheavals that be-
spoke an epoch of incredible geophysical combustion. The
cores of mountains rising out of the faults and trenches,
doing infinite battle to reach the heat of the sun.

Twice they passed hill communities by circling above
them on ridges at the edge of the forest. Malcolm both
times identified the sects, telling of their particular beliefs
and the religious justification for their withdrawal from
the outside world. He explained that there were approximately twenty-three Cock Pit communities dedicated to
isolation. The figure had to be approximate, for there was
ever-present the rebellion of youth who found in their intermittent journeys to the marketplace temptations out-
weighing the threats of Obeah. Strangely enough, as one
community, or two or three, disintegrated, there were always others that sprang up to take their places . . . and
often their small villages.

"The 'opiate of the people' is often an escape from simple hardship and the agonizing pointlessness of the coastal
towns."

"Then eliminate the pointlessness." Alex remembered
the sights of Old Kingston, the corrugated-tin shacks
across from the abandoned, filthy barges peopled by out-
casts; the emaciated dogs, the bone-thin cats, the eyes of

numbed futility on the young-old women. The men with no teeth praying for the price of a pint of wine, defecating in the shadows of dark alleys.

And three blocks above, the shining, immaculate banks with their shining, tinted windows.

Shining, immaculate, and obscene in their choice of location.

"Yes, you are right," replied Malcolm the Halidonite. "It is the pointlessness that erodes the people most rapidly. It is so easy to say 'give meaning.' And so difficult to know how. So many complications."

They continued their journey for eight hours, resting after difficult sections of jungle and steep clifflike inclines and endless caves. McAuliff judged that they had gone no farther than seventeen, perhaps eighteen miles into the Cock Pit country, each mile more treacherous and enervating than the last.

Shortly after five in the afternoon, while high in the Flagstaff Range, they came to the end of a mountain pass. Suddenly in front of them was a plateau of grassland about a half-mile long and no more than five hundred yards wide. The plateau fronted the banks of a mountain cliff, at three-quarters altitude. Malcolm led them to the right, to the western edge. The slope of the plateau descended into thick jungle, as dense and forbidding as any McAuliff had ever seen.

"That is called the Maze of Acquaba," said Malcolm, seeing the look of astonishment on Alex's face. "We have borrowed a custom from ancient Sparta. Each male child, on his eleventh birthday, is taken into the core and must remain for a period of four days and nights."

"Units of four . . ." McAuliff spoke as much to himself as to Malcolm as he stared down at the unbelievably cruel density of jungle beneath. "The odyssey of death."

"We're neither that Spartan nor Arawak," said Malcolm, laughing softly. "The children do not realize it, but there are others with them . . . Come."

The two Halidonites turned and started toward the opposite ledge of the plateau. Alex took a last look at the Maze of Acquaba and joined them.

At the eastern edge, the contradictory effect was immediate.

Below was a valley no more than a half a mile in

length, perhaps a mile wide, in the center of which was a quiet lake. The valley itself was enclosed by hills that were the first inclines of the mountains beyond. On the north side were mountain streams converging into a high waterfall that cascaded down into a relatively wide, defined avenue of water.

On the far side of the lake were fields—pastures, for there were cattle grazing lazily. Cows, goats, a few burrows, and several horses. This area had been cleared and seeded—generations ago, thought McAuliff.

On the near side of the lake, below them, were thatched huts, protected by tall ceiba trees. At first glance, there seemed to be seventy or eighty such dwellings. They were barely visible because of the trees and arcing vines and dense tropical foliage that filled whatever spaces might have been empty with the bright colors of the Caribbean. A community roofed by nature, thought Alex.

Then he pictured the sight from the air. Not as he was seeing it, on a vertical-diagonal, but from above, from a plane. The village—and it was a village—would look like any number of isolated hill communities with thatched roofs and nearby grazing fields. But the difference was in the surrounding mountains. The plateau was an indentation formed at high altitude. This section of the Flagstaff Range was filled with harsh updrafts and uncontrollable wind variants; jets would remain at a six-thousand-foot minimum, light aircraft would avoid direct overhead. The first would have no place to land, the second would undoubtedly crash if it attempted to do so.

The community was protected by natural phenomena above it and by a torturous passage on the ground that could never be defined on a map.

"Not very prepossessing, is it?" Malcolm stood next to McAuliff. A stream of children were running down a bordered path toward the lake, their shouts carried on the wind. Natives could be seen walking around the huts; larger groups strolled by the avenue of water that flowed from the waterfall.

"It's all . . . very neat." It was the only word McAuliff could think of at the moment.

"Yes," replied the Halidonite. "It's orderly. Come, let's go down. There is a man waiting for you."

The runner-guide led them down the rocky slope. Five

minutes later the three of them were on the western level of the thatched community. From above Alex had not fully realized the height of the trees that were on all sides of the primitive dwellings. Thick vines sloped and twisted, immense ferns sprayed out of the ground and from within dark recesses of the underbrush.

Had the view from the plateau above been fifty feet higher, thought McAuliff, none of what he had seen would have been visible.

Roofed by nature.

The guide started across a path that seemed to intersect a cluster of huts within the junglelike area.

The inhabitants were dressed, like most Jamaican hill people, in a variety of soft, loose clothing, but there was something different that McAuliff could not at first discern. There was a profusion of rolled-up khaki trousers and dark-colored skirts and white cotton shirts and printed blouses—all normal, all seen throughout the island. Seen really in all outback areas—Africa, Australia, New Zealand—where the natives had taken what they could—stolen what they could—of the white invaders' protective comforts. Nothing unusual . . . But something was very different, and Alex was damned if he could pinpoint that difference.

And then he did so. At the same instant that he realized there was something else he had been observing.

Books.

A few—three or four or five, perhaps—of the dozens of natives within this jungle community were carrying books. Carrying *books* under their arms and in their hands.

And the clothing was *clean*. It was as simple as that. There were stains of wetness, of sweat, obviously, and the dirt of field work and the mud of the lake . . . but there was a cleanliness, a neatness, that was *not* usual in the hill or outback communities. Africa, Australia, New Guinea, or Jacksonville, Florida.

It was a normal sight to see clothing worn by natives in varying stages of disrepair—torn, ripped, even shredded. But the garments worn by these hill people were whole, untorn, unripped.

Not castoffs, not ill-fitting stolen property.

The Tribe of Acquaba was deep within a jungle primeval but it was not—like so many of the isolated hill peo-

ple—a wornout race of poverty-stricken primitives
scratching a bare subsistence from the land.

Along the paths and around the dwellings Alex could
see strong black bodies and clear black eyes, the elements
of balanced diets and sharp intelligences.

"We shall go directly to Daniel's," said Malcolm to the
guide. "You are relieved now. And thank you."

The guide turned right down a dirt path that seemed to
be tunneled under a dense web of thick jungle vines. He
was removing his pistol belt, unbuttoning his field jacket.
The commando was home, reflected McAuliff. He could
take off his costume—so purposely ragged.

Malcolm gestured, interrupting Alex's thoughts. The
path on which they had been walking under an umbrella
of macca-fats and ceibas veered left into a clearing of
matted spider grass. This open area extended beyond the
conduit of rushing water that shot out from the base of
the high waterfall streaming down the mountain. On the
other side of the wide, banked gulley the ground sloped
toward a barricade of rock; beyond were the grazing fields
that swung right, bordering the eastern shore of the lake.

In the huge pasture, men could be seen walking with
staffs toward the clusters of livestock. It was late afternoon, the heat of the sun was lessening. It is time to shelter the cattle for the night, thought McAuliff.

He had been absently following Malcolm, more concerned with observing everything he could of the strange,
isolated village, when he realized where the Halidonite
was leading them.

Toward the base of the mountain and the waterfall.

They reached the edge of the lake-feeding channel and
turned left. Alex saw that the conduit of water was deeper
than it appeared from a distance. The banks were about
eight feet in height; the definition he had seen from the
plateau was a result of carefully placed rocks, imbedded
in the earth of the embankments. This natural phenomenon had been controlled by man, like the seeded fields
generations ago.

There were three crossings of wooden planks with
waist-high railings, each buttressed into the sides of the
embankments, where there were stone steps . . . placed
decades ago. The miniature bridges were spaced about
fifty yards apart.

Then McAuliff saw it; barely saw it, as it was concealed behind a profusion of tall trees, immense giant-fern, and hundreds of flowering vines at the base of the mountain.

It was a wooden structure. A large cabinlike dwelling whose base straddled the channel, the water rushing out from under the huge pilings that supported the hidden edifice. On each side of the pilings were steps—again in stone, again placed generations ago—that led up to a wide catwalk fronting the building. In the center of the planked catwalk was a door. It was closed.

From any distance—certainly from the air—the building was completely concealed.

Its length was perhaps thirty feet; its width impossible to determine, as it seemed to disappear into the jungle and the crashing waterfall.

As they approached the stone steps, McAuliff saw something else, which so startled him that he had to stop and stare.

On the west side of the building, emerging from within and scaling upward into the tangling mass of foliage, were thick black cables.

Malcolm turned and smiled at Alex's astonishment. "Our contact with the outside, McAuliff. Radio signals that are piped into telephone trunk lines throughout the island. Not unlike the radio-phones in taxis and private automobiles. Generally much clearer than the usual telephone service. All untraceable, of course. Now let us see Daniel."

"Who is Daniel?"

"He is our Minister of Council. His is an elective office. Except that his term is not guided by the calendar."

"Who elects him?"

The Halidonite's smile faded somewhat. "The council."

"Who elects *it?*"

"The tribe."

"Sounds like regular politics."

"Not exactly," said Malcolm enigmatically. "Come. Daniel's waiting."

The Halidonite opened the door, and McAuliff walked into a large high-ceilinged room with windows all around the upper wall. The sounds of the waterfall could be heard; these were mingled with the myriad noises of the jungle outside.

There were wooden chairs—chairs fashioned by hand, not machinery. In the center of the back wall, in front of a second, very large, thick door was a table, at which sat a black girl in her late twenties. On her "desk" were papers, and at her left was an office typewriter on a regulation typewriter table. The incongruity of such equipment in such a place caused Alex to stare.

And then he swallowed as he saw a telephone—a regular, pushbutton telephone—on a stand to the girl's right.

"This is Jeanine, Dr. McAuliff. She works for Daniel."

The girl stood, her smile brief and tenuous. She acknowledged Alex with a hesitant nod; her eyes were concerned as she spoke to Malcolm. "Was the trip all right?"

"Since I brought back our guest, I cannot say it was wildly successful."

"Yes," replied Jeanine, her expression of concern now turned to fear. "Daniel wants to see you right away. This way . . . Dr. McAuliff."

The girl crossed to the door and rapped twice. Without waiting for a reply, she twisted the knob and opened it. Malcolm came alongside Alex and gestured him inside. McAuliff walked hesitantly through the door frame and into the office of the Halidon's Minister of Council.

The room was large, with a single, enormous leaded glass window taking up most of the rear wall. The view was both strange and awesome. Twenty feet beyond the glass was the midsection of a waterfall; it took up the entire area; there was nothing but endless tons of crashing water, its sound muted but discernible. In front of the window was a long, thick hatch table, its dark wood glistening. Behind it stood the man named Daniel, Minister of Council.

He was a black Jamaican with sharp Afro-European features, slightly more than medium height and quite slender. His shoulders were broad, however; his body tapered like that of a long-distance runner. He was in his early forties, perhaps. It was difficult to tell; his face had lean youth, but his eyes were not young.

He smiled—briefly, cordially, but not enthusiastically—at McAuliff and came around the table, his hand extended.

As he did so, Alex saw that Daniel wore white casual slacks and a dark blue shirt open at the neck. Around his throat was a white silk kerchief, held together by a gold ring. It was a kind of uniform, thought Alex. As Malcolm's robes were a uniform.

"Welcome, Doctor. I will not ask you about your trip, I have made it too many times myself. It is a bitch."

Daniel shook McAuliff's hand. "It is a bitch," said Alex warily.

The minister abruptly turned to Malcolm. "What's the report? I can't think of any reason to give it privately. Or is there?"

"No . . . Piersall's documents are valid. They're sealed, and McAuliff has them ready to fly out from a location within a twenty-five-mile radius of the Martha Brae base camp. Even he doesn't know where . . . We have three days, Daniel."

The minister stared at the priest figure. Then he walked slowly back to his chair behind the hatch table without speaking. He stood immobile, his hands on the surface of the wood, and looked up at Alex.

"So by the brilliant persistence of an expatriate island fanatic we face . . . castration. Exposure renders us impotent, you know, Dr. McAuliff. We will be plundered. Stripped of our possessions. And the responsibility is yours . . . *You.* A geologist in the employ of Dunstone, Limited. And a most unlikely recruit in the service of British Intelligence." Daniel looked over at Malcolm. "Leave us alone, please. And be ready to start out for Montego."

"When?" asked Malcolm.

"That will depend on our visitor. He will be accompanying you."

"I *will?*"

"Yes, Dr. McAuliff. If you are alive."

28

"THERE IS but a single threat one human being can make against another that must be listened to. That threat is obviously the taking of life." Daniel had walked to the enormous window framing the cascading, unending columns of water. "In the absence of overriding ideological issues, usually associated with religion or national causes, I think you will agree."

"And because I'm not motivated religiously or nationally, you expect the threat to succeed." McAuliff remained standing in front of the long, glistening hatch table. He had not been offered a chair.

"Yes," replied the Halidon's Minister of Council, turning from the window. "I am sure it has been said to you before that Jamaica's concerns are not your concerns."

"It's . . . 'not my war' is the way it was phrased."

"Who said that to you? Charles Whitehall or Barak Moore?"

"Barak Moore is dead," said Alex.

The minister was obviously surprised. His reaction, however, was a brief moment of thoughtful silence. Then he spoke quietly. "I am sorry. His was a necessary check to Whitehall's thrust. His faction has no one else, really. Someone will have to be brought up to take his place . . ." Daniel walked to the table, reached down for a pencil, and wrote a note on a small pad. He tore off the page and put it to the side.

McAuliff saw without difficulty the words the minister had written. They were: "Replace Barak Moore." In this day of astonishments, the implication of the message was not inconsiderable.

"Just like that?" asked Alex, nodding his head in the direction of the page of notepaper.

"It will not be simple, if that is what you mean," replied Daniel. "Sit down, Dr. McAuliff. I think it is time you understood. Before we go further . . ."

Alexander Tarquin McAuliff, geologist, with a company on 38th Street in New York City, United States of America, sat down in a native-made chair in an office room high in the inaccessible mountains of the Flagstaff Range, deep within the core of the impenetrable Cock Pit country on the island of Jamaica, and listened to a man called Daniel, Minister of Council for a covert sect with the name of Halidon.

He could not think any longer. He could only listen.

Daniel covered the initial groundwork rapidly. He asked Alex if he had read Walter Piersall's papers. McAuliff nodded.

The minister then proceeded to confirm the accuracy of Piersall's studies by tracing the Tribe of Acquaba from its beginnings in the Maroon Wars in the early eighteenth century.

"Acquaba was something of a mystic, but essentially a simple man. A Christ figure without the charity or extremes of mercy associated with the Jesus beliefs. After all, his forebears were born to the violence of the Coromanteen jungles. But his ethics were sound . . ."

"What is the source of your wealth?" asked Alex, his faculties returning. "If there *is* wealth. And a source."

"Gold," replied Daniel simply.

"Where?"

"In the ground. On our lands."

"There is no gold in Jamaica."

"You are a geologist. You know better than that. There are traces of crystalline deposit in scores of minerals throughout the island—"

"Infinitesimal," broke in McAuliff. "Minute, and so impacted with worthless ores as to make any attempt at separation prohibitive. More expensive than the product."

"But . . . gold, nevertheless."

"Worthless."

Daniel smiled. "How do you think the crystalline traces became impacted? I might even ask you—theoretically, if you like—how the island of Jamaica came to be."

"As any isolated land mass in the oceans. Geologic upheavals—" Alex stopped. The theory was beyond imagination, made awesome because of its simplicity. A section of a vein of gold, millions upon millions of years ago, exploding out of the layers of earth beneath the sea, impacting deposits throughout the mass that was disgorged out of the waters. "My God . . . there's a vein . . ."

"There is no point in pursuing this," said Daniel. "For

centuries the colonial law of Jamaica spelled out an absolute: All precious metals discovered on the island were the possession of the Crown. It was the primary reason no one searched."

"*Fowler,*" said McAuliff softly. "Jeremy Fowler . . ."

"I beg your pardon?"

"The Crown Recorder in Kingston. Almost a hundred years ago . . ."

Daniel paused. "Yes. In 1883, to be exact . . . so that was Piersall's fragment." The minister of the Halidon wrote on another page of notepaper. "It will be removed."

"This Fowler," asked Alex softly. "Did he know?"

Daniel looked up from the paper, tearing it off the pad as he did so. "No. He believed he was carrying out the wishes of a dissident faction of Maroons conspiring with a group of north-coast landowners. The object was to destroy the records of a tribal treaty so thousands of acres could be cleared for plantations. It was what he was told and what he was paid for."

"The family in England still believes it."

"Why not? It was"—the minister smiled—"*Colonial Service.* Shall we return to more currently applicable questions? You see, Dr. McAuliff, we want you to understand. *Thoroughly.*"

"Go ahead."

According to Daniel, the Halidon had no ambitions for political power. It never had such ambitions; it remained outside the body politic, accepting the historical view that order emerges out of the chaos of different, even conflicting ideologies. Ideas were greater monuments than cathedrals, and a people must have free access to them. That was the lesson of Acquaba. Freedom of mobility, freedom of thought . . . freedom to do battle, if need be. The religion of the Halidon was essentially humanist, its jungle gods symbols of continuously struggling forces battling for the mortals' freedom. Freedom to survive in the world in the manner agreed upon within the tribe, without imposing that manner on the other tribes.

"Not a bad premise, is it?" asked Daniel confidently, again rapidly.

"No," answered McAuliff. "And not particularly original, either."

"I disagree," said the minister. "The thought may have

a hundred precedents, but the practice is almost unheard of . . . Tribes, as they develop self-sufficiency, tend to graduate to the point where they are anxious to impose themselves on as many other tribes as possible. From the Pharaohs to Caesar; from the Empire—several empires, Holy Roman, British, et cetera—to Adolf Hitler; from Stalin to your own conglomeratized government of self-righteous proselytizers. Beware the pious believers, Mc-Auliff. They were all pious in their fashions. Too many are still."

"But you're not." Alex looked over at the enormous leaded glass window and the rushing, plummeting water beyond. "You just decide who is . . . and act accordingly. Free to 'do battle,' as you call it."

"You think that is a contradiction of purpose?"

"You're goddamned right I do. When 'doing battle' includes killing people . . . because they don't conform to *your* idea of what's acceptable."

"Who have we killed?"

Alex shifted his gaze from the waterfall to Daniel. "I can start with last night. Two carriers on the survey who were probably picking up a few dollars from British Intelligence; for what? Keeping their eyes open? Reporting what we had for dinner? Who came to see us? Your runner, the one I called 'Marcus,' said they were agents; he killed them. And a fat pig named Garvey, who was a pretty low-level, uninformed liaison and I grant you, smelled bad. But I think a fatal accident on the road to Port Maria was a bit drastic." McAuliff paused for a moment and leaned forward in the chair. "You massacred an entire survey team—every member—and for all you know, they were hired by Dunstone the same way I was: just looking for work. Now, maybe you can justify all those killings, but neither you nor anyone else can justify the death of Walter Piersall . . . Yes. Mr. High and Mighty Minister, I think you're pretty violently pious yourself."

Daniel had sat down in the chair behind the hatch table during Alex's angry narrative. He now pushed his foot against the floor, sending the chair gently to his right, toward the huge window. "Over a hundred years ago, this office was the entire building. One of my early predecessors had it placed here. He insisted that the minister's room—'chamber,' it was called then—overlook this section of our waterfall. He claimed the constant movement and the muffled sound forced a man to concentrate, blocked out small considerations . . . That long-forgotten rebel proved right. I never cease to wonder at the different bursts of shapes and patterns. And while wondering, the mind really concentrates."

"Is that by way of telling me those who were killed were . . . small considerations?"

Daniel pushed the chair back in place and faced McAuliff. "No, Doctor. I was trying to think of a way to convince you. I shall tell you the truth, but I am not sure you will believe it. Our runners, our guides—our infiltrators, if you will—are trained to use *effect* whenever possible. Fear, McAuliff, is an extraordinary weapon. A nonviolent weapon; not that we are necessarily nonviolent . . . Your carriers are not dead. They were taken prisoner, blindfolded, led to the outskirts of Weston Favel, and released. They were not hurt, but they were frightened severely. They will not work for M.I.5 again. Garvey *is* dead, but we did not kill him. Your Mr. Garvey sold anything he could get his hands on, including women, especially young girls. He was shot on the road to Port Maria by a distraught father, the motive obvious. We simply took the credit . . . You say we massacred the Dunstone survey. Reverse that, Doctor. Three of the four white men tried to massacre our scouting party. They killed six of our young men after asking them into the camp for a conference."

"One of those . . . white men was a British agent."

"So Malcolm tells us."

"I don't believe a trained Intelligence man would kill indiscriminately."

"Malcolm agrees with you. But the facts are there. An Intelligence agent is a man first. In the sudden pitch of battle, a man takes sides. This man, whichever one he was, chose his side . . . He did not have to choose the way he did."

"The fourth man? He was different, then?"

"Yes." Daniel's eyes were suddenly reflective. "He was a good man. A Hollander. When he realized what the others were doing, he objected violently. He ran out to warn the rest of our party. His own men shot him."

For several moments, neither spoke. Finally McAuliff asked, "What about Walter Piersall? Can you find a story for that?"

"No." said Daniel. "We do not know what happened. Or who killed him. We have ideas, but nothing more. Walter Piersall was the last man on earth we wanted dead. Especially under the circumstances. And if you do not understand that, then you're stupid."

McAuliff got out of the chair and walked aimlessly to the huge window. He could feel Daniel's eyes on him. He forced himself to watch the crashing streams of water in front of him. "Why did you bring me here? Why have you told me so much? About you . . . and everything else."

"We had no choice. Unless you lied or unless Malcolm was deceived, neither of which I believe . . . And we understand your position as well as your background. When Malcolm flew out of England, he brought with him M.I.5's complete dossier on you. We are willing to make you an offer."

Alex turned and looked down at the minister. "I'm sure it's one I can't refuse."

"Not readily. Your life. And, not incidentally, the lives of your fellow surveyors."

"Piersall's documents?"

"Somewhat more extensive, but those, too, of course," answered Daniel.

"Go on." McAuliff remained by the window. The muted sound of the waterfall was his connection to the outside somehow. It was comforting.

"We know what the British want: the list of names that comprise the Dunstone hierarchy. The international financiers that fully expect to turn this island into an economic sanctuary, another Switzerland. Not long ago, a matter of weeks, they gathered here on the island from all over the world. In Port Antonio. A few used their real names, most did not. The timing is propitious. The Swiss banking institutions are breaking down their traditional codes of account-secrecy one after another. They are under extraordinary pressures, of course . . . We have the Dunstone list. We will make an exchange."

"It for our lives? And the documents . . ."

Daniel laughed, neither cruelly nor kindly. It was a genuine expression of humor. "Doctor, I am afraid it is you who are obsessed with small considerations. It is true we place great value on Piersall's documents, but the British do not. We must think as our adversaries think. The British want the Dunstone list above all things. And above all things, we want British Intelligence, and everything it represents, out of Jamaica. That is the exchange we offer."

McAuliff stood motionless by the window. "I don't understand you."

The minister leaned forward. "We demand an end to English influence . . . as we demand an end to the influence of all other nations—*tribes,* if you wish, Doctor— over this island. In short words, Jamaica is to be left to the Jamaicans."

"Dunstone wouldn't leave it to you," said Alex, groping. "I'd say its influence was a hell of a lot more dangerous than anyone else's."

"Dunstone is *our* fight; we have our *own* plans. Dunstone was organized by financial geniuses. But once confined in our territory, our alternatives are multiple. Among other devices, expropriation . . . But these alternatives take time, and we both know the British do not have the time. England cannot afford the loss of Dunstone, Limited."

McAuliff's mind raced back to the room in the Savoy Hotel . . . and R. C. Holcroft's quiet admission that *economics were a factor. A rather significant one.*

Holcroft the manipulator.

Alex walked back to the armchair and sat down. He realized Daniel was allowing him the time to think, to absorb the possibilities of the new information. There were so many questions; most, he knew, could not be answered, but several touched him. He had to try.

"A few days ago," he began awkwardly, "when Barak Moore died, I found myself concerned that Charles Whitehall had no one to oppose him. So did you. I saw what you wrote down—"

"What is your question?" asked Daniel civilly.

"I was right, wasn't I? They're the two extremes. They have followers. They're not just hollow fanatics."

"Whitehall and Moore?"

"Yes."

"Hardly. They're the charismatic leaders. Moore *was,*

Whitehall *is*. In all new emerging nations there are generally three factions: right, left, and the comfortable middle—the entrenched holdovers who have learned the daily
functions. The middle is eminently corruptible; it continues the same dull, bureaucratic chores with sudden new
authority. It is the first to be replaced. The healthiest way
is by an infusion of the maturest elements from both extremes. Peaceful balance."

"And that's what you're waiting for? Like a referee? An
umpire?"

"Yes. That's very good, Doctor. There's merit in the
struggle, you know; neither side is devoid of positive factors . . . Unfortunately, Dunstone makes our task more
difficult. We must observe the combatants carefully."

The minister's eyes had strayed again; and, again, there
was that brief, nearly imperceptible reflection. "Why?"

Daniel seemed at first reluctant to answer. And then he
sighed audibly. "Very well . . . Barak Moore's reaction to
Dunstone would be violent. A bloodbath . . . chaos.
Whitehall's would be equally dangerous. He would seek
temporary collusion, the power base being completely financial. He could be used as many of the German indus-
trialists honestly believed they were using Hitler. Only the
association feeds on absolute power . . . absolutely."

McAuliff leaned back in the chair. He was beginning to
understand. "So if Dunestone's out, you're back to the
. . . what was it . . . the healthy struggle?"

"Yes," said Daniel quietly.

"Then you and the British want the same thing. How
can you make conditions?"

"Because our solutions are different. We have the time
and the confidence of final control. The English . . . and
the French and the Americans and the Germans . . . do
not have either. The economic disasters they would suffer
could well be to our advantage. And that is all I will say
on the subject . . . We have the Dunstone list. You will
make the offer."

"I go with Malcolm to Montego—"

You will be escorted, and guarded," interrupted Daniel
harshly. "The members of your geological survey are
hostages. Each will be summarily executed should there be
the slightest deviation from our instructions."

"Suppose British Intelligence doesn't believe you? What

the hell am I supposed to do then?"

Daniel stood up. "They will believe you, McAuliff. For your trip to Montego Bay is merely part of news that will soon be worldwide. There will be profound shock in several national capitals. And you will tell British Intelligence that this is our proof. It is only the tip of the Dunstone iceberg . . . Oh, they will believe you, McAuliff. Precisely at noon, London time. Tomorrow."

"That's all you'll tell me?"

"No. One thing more. When the acts take place, the panicked giant—Dunstone—will send out its killers. Among others, you will be a target."

McAuliff found himself standing up in anger. "Thank you for the warning," he said.

"You are welcome," replied Daniel. "Now, if you will come with me."

Outside the office, Malcolm, the priest figure, was talking quietly with Jeanine. At the sight of Daniel, both fell silent. Jeanine blocked Daniel's path and spoke.

"There is news from the Martha Brae."

Alex looked at the minister and then back at the girl. "Martha Brae" had to mean the survey's campsite. He started to speak, but was cut off by Daniel.

"Whatever it is, tell us both."

"It concerns two men. The young man, Ferguson, and the ore specialist, Peter Jensen . . ."

Alex breathed again.

"What happened?" asked Daniel. "The young man first."

"A runner came into camp bringing him a letter from Arthur Craft, Senior. In it Craft made promises, instructing Ferguson to leave the survey, come up to Port Antonio, to the Foundation. Our scouts followed and intercepted them several miles down the river. They are being held there, south of Weston Favel."

"Craft found out about his son," said Alex. "He's trying to buy off Ferguson."

"The purchase might well be to Jamaica's advantage. And Ferguson is not a hostage high on your scale of values."

"I brought him to the island. He is valuable to me," answered Alex coldly.

"We shall see." Daniel turned to the girl. "Tell the

scouts to stay where they are. Hold Ferguson and the runner; instructions will follow. What about the Jensen man?"

"He is all right. The scouts are tracking him."

"He left camp?"

"He's pretending to be lost, our men think. Early this morning, soon after Dr. McAuliff left, he had his carrier stretch what is called an . . . azimuth line. He had the man walk quite a distance while he reeled out the nylon string. The signals were by tugs, apparently—"

"And Jensen cut the line and tied his end to a sapling," interrupted Alex in a rapid monotone. "With a loop around a nearby limb."

"How do you know this?" Daniel seemed fascinated.

"It's a very old, unfunny trick in the field. A distasteful joke. It's played on green recruits."

Daniel turned again to the girl. "So his carrier could not find him. Where is Jensen now?"

"He tried to pick up Malcolm's trail," replied the secretary. "The scouts say he came very close. He gave up and circled back to the west hill. From there he can watch the entire campsite. All means of entrance."

"He will wait the full three days, starving and trapped by cats, if he thinks it will help him. He does not dare go back to Warfield without something." Daniel looked at Alex. "Did you know you were *his* choice to direct the survey?"

"*I* was *his* . . ." McAuliff did not finish the statement. There was no point, he thought.

"Tell our people to stay with him," ordered the minister. "Get close, but don't take him . . . unless he uses a radio that could reach the coast. If he does, kill him."

"What the hell are you saying?" demanded McAuliff angrily. "Goddamn it, you have no right!"

"We have every right, Doctor. You adventurers come to this island! Soil it with your *filth!* Don't speak to me of *rights*, McAuliff!" And then, as suddenly as he had raised his voice, he lowered it. He spoke to the girl. "Convene the Council."

29

DANIEL LED McAuliff down the steps into the matted grass on the left bank of the miniature channel of rushing water. Neither man spoke. Alex looked at his watch; it was nearly eight o'clock. The rays of the twilight sun shot up from behind the western mountains in spectral shafts of orange; the intercepting hills were silhouetted in brownish black, emphasizing their incredible height, their fortress-immensity. The lake was a huge sheet of very dark glass, polished beyond the ability of man, reflecting the massive shadows of the mountains and the streaks of the orange sun.

They walked down the slope of the clearing to the stone fence bordering the grazing fields. At the far left was a gate; Daniel approached it, unlatched the large single bolt, and swung it open. He gestured McAuliff to go through.

"I apologize for my outburst," said the minister as they walked into the field. "It was misdirected. You are a victim, not an aggressor. We realize that."

"And what are you? Are you a victim? Or an aggressor?"

"I am the Minister of Council. And *we* are neither. I explained that."

"You explained a lot of things, but I still don't know anything about you," said McAuliff, his eyes on a lone animal approaching them in the darkening field. It was a young horse, and it whinnied and pranced hesitantly as it drew near.

"This colt is forever breaking out," laughed Daniel as he patted the neck of the nervous animal. "He will be difficult to train, this one . . . *Hyee! Hyee!*" cried the Halidonite as he slapped the colt's flank, sending it kicking and prancing and snorting toward the center of the field.

"Maybe that's what I mean," said Alex. "How do you train . . . people? Keep them from breaking out?"

Daniel stopped and looked at McAuliff. They were alone in the large pasture, awash with the vivid colors of the dying Jamaican sun. The light silhouetted the minister and caused McAuliff to shield his face. He could not see

Daniel's eyes, but he could feel them.

"We are an uncomplicated people in many ways," said the Halidonite. "What technology we require is brought in, along with our medical supplies, basic farm machinery, and the like. Always by our own members, using untraceable mountain routes. Other than these, we are self-sufficient on our lands. Our training—as you call it—is a result of understanding the immense riches we possess. Our isolation is hardly absolute. As you will see."

From childhood, Daniel explained, the Halidonite was told he was privileged and must justify his birthright by his life's actions. The ethic of contribution was imbued in him early in his education; the need to use his potential to the fullest. The outside world was shown in all its detail—its simplicities, its complications, its peace and its violence; its good and its evil. Nothing was concealed; exaggeration was not left to young imaginations. Realistic temptation was balanced—perhaps a bit strongly, admitted Daniel—with realistic punishment.

As near to his or her twelfth birthday as possible, the Halidonite was tested extensively by teachers, the Elders of the Council, and finally by the minister himself. On the basis of these examinations, individuals were selected for training for the outside world. There followed three years of preparation, concentrating on specific skills or professions.

When he or she reached sixteen, the Halidonite was taken from the community and brought to a family residence on the outside, where the father and mother were members of the tribe. Except for infrequent returns to the community and reunions with his own parents, the outside family would be the Halidonite's guardians for a number of years to come.

"Don't you have defections?" asked Alex.

"Rarely," replied Daniel. "The screening process is most thorough."

"What happens if it isn't thorough enough? If there are—"

"That is an answer I will not give you," interrupted the minister. "Except to say the Maze of Acquaba is a threat no prison can compete with. It keeps offenders—within and without—to a minimum. Defections are extremely rare."

From the tone of Daniel's voice, Alex had no desire to pursue the subject. "They're brought back?"

Daniel nodded.

The population of the Halidon was voluntarily controlled. Daniel claimed that for every couple that wanted more children, there invariably was a couple that wanted fewer or none. And, to McAuliff's astonishment, the minister added: "Marriages take place between ourselves and those of the outside. It is, of course, unavoidable and, by necessity, desirable. But it is a complicated procedure taking place over many months and with stringent regulations."

"A reverse screening process?"

"The harshest imaginable. Controlled by the guardians."

"What happens if the marriage doesn't . . ."

"That answer, too, is not in bounds, doctor."

"I have an idea the penalties are stiff," said Alex softly.

"You may have all the ideas you like," said Daniel, starting up again across the field. "But what is of the greatest importance is that you understand that we have scores . . . hundreds of guardians—halfway houses— throughout the countries of the world. In every profession, in all governments, in dozens of universities and institutions everywhere . . . You will never know who is a member of the Halidon. And that is our threat, our ultimate protection."

"You're saying that if I reveal what I know, you'll have me killed?"

"You and every member of your family. Wife, children, parents . . . in the absence of the formal structure, lovers, closest associates, every person who was or is an influence on your life. Your identity, even your memory, will be erased."

"You can't know every person I talk to, every telephone call I make. Where I am every minute. *No* one can! I could mount an army; I could find you!"

"But you will not," said Daniel quietly, in counterpoint to McAuliff's outburst. "For the same reason others have not . . . Come. We are here."

They were standing now on the edge of the field. Beyond was the tentacled foliage of the Cock Pit forest, in shadowed blackness.

Suddenly, startlingly, the air was filled with a penetrating sound of terrible resonance. It was a wailing, inhuman lament. The tone was low, breathless, enveloping everything and echoing everywhere. It was the sound of a giant woodwind, rising slowly, receding into a simple, obscure theme and swelling again to the plaintive cry of the higher melody.

It grew louder and louder, the echoes now picking up the bass tones and hurling them through the jungles, crashing them off the sides of the surrounding mountains until the earth seemed to vibrate.

And then it stopped, and McAuliff stood transfixed as he saw in the distance the outlines of figures walking slowly, purposefully, in measured cadence, across the fields in the chiaroscuro shadows of the early darkness. A few carried torches, the flames low.

At first there were only four or five, coming from the direction of the gate. Then there were some from the south bank of the black, shining lake; others from the north, emerging out of the darkness. Flat-bottomed boats could be seen crossing the surface of the water, each with a single torch.

Within minutes there were ten, then twenty, thirty . . . until McAuliff stopped counting. From everywhere. Dozens of slowly moving bodies swaying gently as they walked across the darkened fields.

They were converging toward the spot where Alex stood with Daniel.

The inhuman wailing began again. Louder—if possible—than before, and McAuliff found himself bringing his hands up to his ears; the vibrations in his head and throughout his body were causing pain—actual *pain*.

Daniel touched him on the shoulder; Alex whipped around as if he had been struck violently. For an instant he thought he had been, so severe were the agonizing sensations brought on by the deafening sound of the horrible lament.

"Come," said Daniel gently. "The *hollydawn* can injure you."

McAuliff heard him accurately; he knew that. Daniel had pronounced the word: not "halidon" but "hollydawn." As though the echoing, deafening sound had caused him to revert to a more primitive tongue.

Daniel walked rapidly ahead of Alex into what McAuliff thought was a wall of underbrush. Then the Halidonite suddenly began to descend into what appeared to be a trench dug out of the jungle. Alex ran to catch up, and nearly plummeted down a long, steep corridor of steps carved out of rock.

The strange staircase widened, flaring out more on both sides the deeper it went, until McAuliff could see that they had descended into a primitive amphitheater, the walls rising thirty or forty feet to the surface of the earth.

What was the staircase became an aisle, the curving rock on both sides forming rows of descending seats.

And suddenly the deafening, agonizing sound from above was no more. It had stopped. Everything was silent.

The amphitheater, carved out of some kind of quarry, blocked out all other sound.

McAuliff stood where he was and looked down at the single source of light: a low flame that illuminated the wall of rock at the center rear of the amphitheater. In that wall was embedded a slab of dull yellow metal. And on that slab of metal was a withered corpse. In front of the corpse was a latticework of thin reeds made of the same yellow substance.

McAuliff needed to go no closer to realize what the substance was: gold.

And the withered, ancient body—once huge—was that of the mystic descendant of the Coromanteen chieftans.

Acquaba.

The preserved remains of the progenitor . . . spanning the centuries. The true cross of the Tribe of Acquaba. For the believers to see. And sense.

"Down here." Daniel's words were whispered, but Alex heard them clearly. "You will sit with me. Please, hurry."

McAuliff walked down the remaining staircase to the floor of the quarry shell and over to the Halidonite on the right side of the primitive stage. Jutting out from the wall were two stone blocks; Daniel pointed to one: the seat nearest the corpse of Acquaba, less than eight feet away.

McAuliff lowered himself on to the hard stone, his eyes drawn to the open catafalque of solid and webbed gold. The leathered corpse was dressed in robes of reddish black; the feet and hands were bare . . . and huge, as the head was huge. Allowing for the contraction of two centuries, the man must have been enormous—nearer seven feet than six.

The single torch below the coffin of gold shot flickering

shadows against the wall; the thin reeds crisscrossing the front of the carved-out casket picked up the light in dozens of tiny reflections. The longer one stared, thought Alex, the easier it would be to convince oneself this was the shell of a god lying in state. A god who had walked the earth and worked the earth—two hundred years could not erase the signs on the enormous hands and feet. But this god, this man did not toil as other men . . .

He heard the sounds of muted steps and looked up into the small amphitheater. Through the entrance, hidden in darkness, and down the staircase they came, a procession of men and women separating and spreading throughout the lateral stone aisles, taking their seats.

In silence.

Those with torches stood equidistant from each other on graduating levels against oppostie walls.

All eyes were on the withered body beyond the latticework of gold. Their concentration was absolute; it was as if they drew sustenance from it.

In silence.

Suddenly, without warning, the sound of the *hollydawn* shattered the stillness with the impact of an explosion. The thunderous, wailing lament seemed to burst from the bowels of rock-covered earth, crashing upward against the stone, thrusting out of the huge pit that was the grave of Acquaba.

McAuliff felt the breath leaving his lungs, the blood rushing to his head. He buried his face between his knees, his hands clamped over his ears, his whole body shaking.

The cry reached a crescendo, a terrible screaming rush of air that swelled to a pitch of frenzy. *No human ears could stand it!* thought Alex as he trembled . . . as he had never before trembled in his life.

And then it was over and the silence returned.

McAuliff slowly sat up, lowering his hands, gripping the stone beneath him in an effort to control the violent spasms he felt shooting through his flesh. His eyes were blurred from the blood which had raced to his temples; they cleared slowly, in stages, and he looked out at the rows of Halidonites, at these chosen members of the Tribe of Acquaba.

They were—each one, all—still staring, eyes fixed on the ancient, withered body behind the golden reeds.

Alex knew they had remained exactly as they were throughout the shattering madness that had nearly driven him out of his mind.

He turned to Daniel; involuntarily he gasped. The Minister of Council, too, was transfixed, his black eyes wide, his jaw set, his face immobile. But he was different from all the others; there were tears streaming down Daniel's cheeks.

"You're mad . . . all of you," said Alex quietly. "You're insane . . ."

Daniel did not respond. Daniel could not hear him. He was in a hypnotic state.

They all were. Everyone in that carved-out shell beneath the earth. Nearly a hundred men and women inextricably held by some force beyond his comprehension.

Autosuggestion. Self-somnipathy. Group hypnosis. Whatever the catalyst, each individual in that primitive amphitheater was mesmerized beyond reach. On another plane . . . time and space unfamiliar.

Alexander felt himself an intruder; he was observing a ritual too private for his eyes.

Yet he had not asked to be here. He had been forced in—ripped out of place—and made to bear witness.

Still, the witnessing filled him with sorrow. And he could not understand. So he looked over at the body that was once the giant, Acquaba.

He stared at the shriveled flesh of the once-black face. At the closed eyes, so peaceful in death. At the huge hands folded so strongly across the reddish black robe.

Then back at the face . . . the eyes . . . the eyes . . .

Oh, my God! Oh, Christ!

The shadows were playing tricks . . . terrible, horrible tricks.

The body of Acquaba moved.

The eyes opened; the fingers of the immense hands spread, the wrists turned, the arms raised . . . inches above the ancient cloth.

In supplication.

And then there was nothing.

Only a shriveled corpse behind a latticework of gold.

McAuliff pressed himself back against the wall of stone, trying desperately to find his sanity. He closed his eyes and breathed deeply, gripping the rock beneath him.

He did not know how long it was—a minute, an hour, a decade of terror—until he heard Daniel's words.

"You saw it." A statement made gently. "Do not be afraid. We shall never speak of it again. There is no harm. Only good."

"I . . . I . . ." Alexander could not talk. The perspiration rolled down his face. And the carved-out council ground was cool.

Daniel stood up and walked to the center of the platform of rock. Instead of addressing the Tribe of Acquaba, he turned to McAuliff. His words were whispered, but, as before, they were clear and precise, echoing off the walls.

"The lessons of Acquaba touch all men, as the lessons of all prophets touch all men. But few listen. Still, the work must go on. For those who can do it. It is really as simple as that. Acquaba was granted the gift of great riches . . . beyond the imaginations of those who will never listen; who will only steal and corrupt . . . So we go out into the world without the world's knowledge. And we do what we can . . . It must ever be so, for if the world knew, the world would impose itself and the Halidon, the Tribe of Acquaba, and the lessons of Acquaba would be destroyed . . . We are not fools, Dr. McAuliff. We know with whom we speak, with whom we share our secrets. And our love . . . But do not mistake us. We can kill; we *will* kill to protect the vaults of Acquaba. In that we are dangerous. In that we are absolute. We will destroy ourselves *and* the vaults if the world outside interferes with us.

"I, as Minister of Council, ask you to rise, Dr. McAuliff. And turn yourself away from the Tribe of Acquaba, from this Council of the Halidon, and face the wall. What you will hear, staring only at stone, are voices, revealing locations and figures. As I mentioned, we are not fools. We understand the specifics of the marketplace. But you will not see faces, you will never know the identities of those who speak. Only know that they go forth bearing the wealth of Acquaba.

"We dispense vast sums throughout the world, concentrating as best we can on the areas of widespread human suffering. Pockets of famine, displacement . . . futility. Untold thousands are helped daily by the Halidon. Daily. In practical ways.

"Please rise and face the wall, Dr. McAuliff."

Alexander got up from the block of stone and turned. For a brief instant his eyes fell on the corpse of Acquaba. He looked away and stared at the towering sheet of rock.

Daniel continued. "Our contributions are made without thought of political gain or influence. They are made because we have the concealed wealth and the commitment to make them. The lessons of Acquaba.

"But the world is not ready to accept our ways, Acquaba's ways. The global mendacity would destroy us, cause us to destroy ourselves, perhaps. And that we cannot permit.

"So understand this, Dr. McAuliff. Beyond the certainty of your own death, should you reveal what you know of the Tribe of Acquaba, there is another certainty of far greater significance than your life: the work of the Halidon will cease. That is our ultimate threat . . ."

One by one, the voices recited their terse statements:

"Afro axis. Ghana. Fourteen thousand bushels of grain. Conduit: Smythe Brothers, Capetown. Barclay's Bank . . ."

"Sierra Leone. Three tons medical supplies. Conduit: Baldazi Pharmaceuticals, Algiers. Bank of Constantine . . ."

"Indo-China axis. Vietnam, Mekong, Quan Tho provinces. Radiology and laboratory personnel and supplies. Conduit: Swiss Red Cross. Bank of America . . ."

"Southwest Hemisphere axis. Brazil. Rio de Janiero. Typhoid serum. Conduit: Surgical Salizar. Banco Terceiro, Rio . . ."

"Northwest Hemisphere axis. West Virginia. Appalachia. Twenty-four tons food supplies. Conduit: Atlantic Warehousing. Chase Manhattan, New York . . ."

"India axis. Dacca. Refugee camps. Inoculation serums, medicals. Conduit: International Displacement Organization. World Bank, Burma . . ."

The voices of men and women droned on, the phrases clipped, yet somehow gentle. It took nearly an hour, and McAuliff began to recognize that many spoke twice, but always with different information. Nothing was repeated.

Finally there was silence.

A long period of silence. And then Alexander felt a hand on his shoulder. He turned, and Daniel's eyes bore in on him.

"Do you understand?"

"Yes, I understand," McAuliff said.

They walked across the field toward the lake. The sounds of the forest mingled with the hum of the mountains and the crashing of the waterfall nearly a mile to the north.

They stood on the embankment, and Alex bent down, picked up a small stone, and threw it into the black, shining lake that reflected the light of the moon. He looked at Daniel.

"In a way, you're as dangerous as the rest of them. One man . . . with so much . . . operating beyond reach. No checks, no balances. It would be so simple for good to become evil, evil good. Malcolm said your . . . term isn't guided by a calendar."

"It is not. I am elected for life. Only I can terminate my office."

"And pick your successor?"

"I have influence. The council, of course, has the final disposition."

"Then I think you're more dangerous."

"I do not deny it."

30

THE TRIP to Montego was far easier than the circuitous march from the Martha Brae. To begin with, most of the journey was by vehicle.

Malcolm, his robes replaced by Saville Row clothing, led Alexander around the lake to the southeast, where they were met by a runner who took them to the base of a mountain cliff, hidden by jungle. A steel lift, whose thick chains were concealed by mountain rocks, carried them up the enormous precipice to a second runner, who placed them in a small tram, which was transported by cable on a path below the skyline of the forest.

At the end of the cable ride, a third runner took them through a series of deep caves, identified by Malcolm as the Quick Step Grotto. He told Alex that the Quick Step was named for seventeenth-century buccaneers who raced from Bluefield's Bay overland to bury treasure at the bottom of the deep pools within the caves. The other derivation—the one many believed more appropriate—was that if a traveler did not watch his feet, he could easily slip and plummet into a crevice. Injury was certain, death not impossible.

McAuliff stayed close to the runner, his flashlight beamed at the rocky darkness in front of him.

Out of the caves, they proceeded through a short stretch of jungle to the first definable road they had seen. The runner activated a portable radio; ten minutes later a "desert jeep" came out of the pitch-black hollows from the west and the runner bid them good-bye.

The crude-looking vehicle traveled over a criss-cross pattern of back-country roads, the driver keeping his engine as quiet as possible, coasting on descending hills, shutting off his headlights whenever they approached a populated area. The drive lasted a half-hour. They passed through the Maroon village of Accompong and swung south several miles to a flat stretch of grassland.

In the darkness, on the field's edge, a small airplane was rolled out from under a camouflage of fern and acacia. It was a two-seater Comanche; they climbed in, and Malcolm took the controls.

"This is the only difficult leg of the trip," he said as they taxied for takeoff. "We must fly close to the ground to avoid interior radar. Unfortunately, so do the ganga aircraft, the drug smugglers. But we will worry less about the authorities than we will about collision."

Without incident, but not without signaling several ganga planes, they landed on the grounds of an outlying farm, southwest of Unity Hall. From there it was a fifteen-minute ride into Montego Bay.

"It would arouse suspicions for us to stay in the exclusively black section of the town. You, for your skin, me, for my speech and my clothes. And tomorrow we must have mobility in the white areas."

They drove to the Cornwall Beach Hotel and registered ten minutes apart. Reservations had been made for adjoining but not connecting rooms.

It was two o'clock in the morning, and McAuliff fell into bed exhausted. He had not slept in nearly forty-eight hours. And yet, for a very long time, sleep did not come.

He thought about so many things. The brilliant, lonely, awkward James Ferguson and his sudden departure to the Craft Foundation. Defection, really. Without explanation. Alex hoped Craft was Jimbo-mon's solution. For he would never be trusted again.

And of the sweetly charming Jensens . . . up to their so-respectable chins in the manipulations of Dunstone, Limited.

Of the "charismatic leader" Charles Whitehall, waiting to ride "nigger-Pompei's horse" through Victoria Park. Whitehall was no match for the Halidon. The Tribe of Acquaba would not tolerate him.

Nor did the lessons of Acquaba include the violence of Lawrence, the boy-man giant . . . successor to Barak Moore. Lawrence's "revolution" would not come to pass. Not the way he conceived it.

Alex wondered about Sam Tucker. Tuck, the gnarled rocklike force of stability. Would Sam find what he was looking for in Jamaica? For surely he was looking.

But most of all McAuliff thought about Alison. Of her lovely half laugh and her clear blue eyes and the calm acceptance that was her understanding. How very much he loved her.

He wondered, as his consciousness drifted into the gray,

blank void that was sleep, if they would have a life together.

After the madness.

If he was alive.

If they were alive.

He had left a wake-up call for 6:45. Quarter to twelve, London time.

Noon. For the Halidon.

The coffee arrived in seven minutes. Eight minutes to twelve.

The telephone rang three minutes later. Five minutes to noon, London time. It was Malcolm, and he was not in his hotel room. He was at the Associated Press Bureau, Montego Bay office on St. James Street. He wanted to make sure that Alex was up and had his radio on. Perhaps his television set as well.

McAuliff had both instruments on.

Malcolm the Halidonite would call him later.

At three minutes to seven—twelve, London time—there was a rapid knocking on the hotel door. Alexander was startled. Malcolm had said nothing about visitors; no one knew he was in Montego Bay. He approached the door.

"Yes?"

The words from the other side of the wood were spoken hesitantly, in a deep, familiar voice.

"Is that you . . . McAuliff?"

And instantly Alexander understood. The symmetry, the timing was extraordinary; only extraordinary minds could conceive and execute such a symbolic coup.

He opened the door.

R. C. Holcroft, British Intelligence, stood in the corridor, his slender frame rigid, his face an expression of suppressed shock.

"Good God. It is you . . . I didn't believe them. Your signals from the river . . . There is nothing irregular, nothing at all!"

"That," said Alex, "is about as disastrous a judgment as I've ever heard."

"They dragged me out of my rooms in Kingston . . . before daylight. Drove me up into the hills—"

"And flew you to Montego," completed McAuliff, looking at his watch. "Come in, Holcroft. We've got a minute and fifteen seconds to go."

"For what?"

"We'll both find out."

The lilting, high-pitched Caribbean voice on the radio proclaimed over the music the hour of seven in the "sunlight paradise of Montego Bay." The picture on the television set was a sudden fade-in shot of a long expanse of white beach . . . a photograph. The announcer, in overly Anglicized tones, was extolling the virtues of "our island life" and welcoming "alla visitors from the cold climates," pointing out immediately that there was a blizzard in New York.

Twelve o'clock London time.

Nothing unusual.

Nothing.

Holcroft stood by the window, looking out at the blue-green waters of the bay. He was silent; his anger was the fury of a man who had lost control because he did not know the moves his opponents were making. And, more important, why they were making them.

The manipulator manipulated.

McAuliff sat on the bed, his eyes on the television set, now a travelog fraught with lies about the "beautiful city of Kingston." Simultaneously, the radio on the bedside table blared its combination of cacophonic music and frantic commercials for everything from Coppertone to Hertz. Intermittently, there was the syrupy female Voice-of-the-Ministry-of-Health, telling the women of the island that "you do not have to get pregnant," followed by the repetition of the weather . . . the forecasts never "partly cloudy," always "partly sunny."

Nothing unusual.

Nothing.

It was eleven minutes past twelve London time.

Still nothing.

And then it happened.

"We interrupt this broadcast . . ."

And, like an insignificant wave born of the ocean depths—unnoticed at first, but gradually swelling, suddenly bursting out of the waters and cresting in controlled fury—the pattern of terror was clear.

The first announcement was merely the prelude—a single flute outlining the significant notes of a theme shortly to be developed.

Explosion and death in Port Antonio.

The east wing of the estate of Arthur Craft had been blown up by explosives, the resulting conflagration gutting most of the house. Among the dead was feared to be the patriarch of the Foundation.

There were rumors of rifle fire preceding the series of explosions. Port Antonio was in panic.

Rifle fire. Explosives.

Rare, yes. But not unheard of on this island of scattered violence. Of contained anger.

The next "interruption" followed in less than ten minutes. It was—appropriately, thought McAuliff—a news report out of London. This intrusion warranted a line of moving print across the television screen: "Killings in London Full Report on News Hour." The radio allowed a long musical commercial to run its abrasive course before the voice returned, now authoritatively bewildered.

The details were still sketchy, but not the conclusions. Four high-ranking figures in government and industry had been slain. A director of Lloyds, an accounts official of Inland Revenue, and two members of the House of Commons, both chairing trade committees of consequence.

The methods: two now familiar, two new—dramatically oriented.

A high-powered rifle fired from a window into a canopied entrance in Belgravia Square. A dynamited automobile, blown up in the Westminster parking area. Then the new: poison—temporarily identified as strychnine—administered in a Beefeater martini, causing death in ten minutes; a horrible, contorted, violent death . . . the blade of a knife thrust into moving flesh on a crowded corner of The Strand.

Killings accomplished; no killers apprehended.

R. C. Holcroft stood by the hotel window listening to the excited tones of the Jamaican announcer. When Holcroft spoke, his shock was clear.

"My *God* . . . Every one of those men at one time or another was under the glass—"

"The what?"

"Suspected of high crimes. Malfeasance, extortion, fraud . . . Nothing was ever proved out."

"Something's been proved out now."

Paris was next. Reuters sent out the first dispatches, picked up by all the wire services within minutes. Again the number was . . . four. Four Frenchmen—actually, three French men and one woman. But still four.

Again, they were prominent figures in industry and government. And the M.O.s were identical: rifle, explosives, strychnine, knife.

The French woman was a proprietor of a Paris fashion house. A ruthless, hated, sadistic lesbian long considered an associate of the Corsicans. She was shot from a distance as she emerged from a doorway on the St. Germain des Pres. Of the three men, one was a member of the president's all-important Elysée Financial; his Citroën exploded when he turned his ignition on in the Rue de Bac. The two other Frenchmen were powerful executives in shipping companies—Marseilles-based, under Paraguyan flag . . . owned by the Marquis de Chatellerault. The first spastically lurched and died over a café table in the Montmarte—strychnine in his late-morning espresso. The second had his chest torn open by a butcher's knife on the crowded sidewalk outside the Georges Cinque Hotel.

Minutes after Paris came Berlin. The Berlin of the Bonn government. There were only rumors out of the East—sirens were heard beyond the bridges, the Wall; police radios were intercepted—but nothing was clear.

In Bonn it was clear.

On the Kurfurstendam Strasse, the *Unter Schriftfuhrer* of the Bundestag's *AuBenpolitik* was shot from the roof of a nearby building as he was on his way to a luncheon appointment. A *Direktor* of Mercedes Benz stopped for a traffic light on the Autobahn, where two grenades were thrown into the front seat of his car, demolishing automobile and driver in seconds. A known narcotics dealer was given poison in his glass of heavy lager at the Grand Hotel, and an appointee of the *Einkunfte Finanzamt* was stabbed expertly—death instantaneous—through the heart in the crowded lobby of the government building.

Rome followed. A financial strategist for the Vatican, a despised cardinal devoted to the church militants' continuous extortion of the uninformed poor, was dropped by an assassin firing a rifle from behind a Bernini in St. Peter's Square. A *funzionario* of Milan's Mondadori drove into a cul-de-sac on the Via Condotte, where his automobile exploded. A lethal dose of strychnine was administered with cappuccino to a *direttore* of customs at Rome's Fiumicino Airport. A knife was plunged into the ribs of a powerful broker of the *Borsa Valori* as he walked down the Spanish Steps into the Via Due Macelli.

London, Paris, Berlin, Rome.

And always the figure was four . . . and the methods identical: rifle, explosives, strychnine, knife. Four diverse, ingenious modi operandi. Each strikingly news-conscious, oriented for shock. All killings the work of expert professionals; no killers caught at the scenes of violence.

The radio and the television stations no longer made attempts to continue regular programming. As the names came, so too did progressively illuminating biographies. And another pattern emerged, lending credence to Holcroft's summary of the four slain Englishmen: The victims were not ordinary men of stature in industry and government. There was a common stain running through the many that aroused suspicions about the rest. They were individuals not alien to official scrutinies. As the first hints began to surface, curious newsmen dug swiftly and furiously, dredging up scores of rumors, and more than rumor—facts: indictments (generally reduced to the inconsequential), accusations from injured competitors, superiors, and subordinates (removed, recanted . . . unsubstantiated), litigations (settled out of court or dropped for lack of evidence).

It was an elegant cross section of the suspected. Tarnished, soiled, an aura of corruption.

All this before the hands on McAuliff's watch read nine o'clock. Two hours past twelve, London time. Two o'clock in the afternoon in Mayfair.

Commuter-time in Washington and New York.

There was no disguising the apprehension felt as the sun made its way from the east over the Atlantic. Speculation was rampant, growing in hysteria; a conspiracy of international proportions was suggested, a cabal of self-righteous fanatics violently implementing its vengeances throughout the civilized world.

Would it touch the shores of the United States?

But, of course, it had.

Two hours ago.

The awkward giant was just beginning to stir, to recognize the signs of the spreading plague.

The first news reached Jamaica out of Miami. Radio Montego picked up the overlapping broadcasts, sifting, sorting . . . finally relaying by tape the words of the various newcasters as they rushed to verbalize the events spewing out of the wire service teletypes.

Washington. Early morning. The undersecretary of the budget—a patently political appointment resulting from openly questioned campaign contributions—was shot while jogging on a back-country road near his residence in Arlington; the weapon was a high-powered rifle, probably with a telescopic sight, fired from a hill above the road. The body was discovered by a motorist at 8:20; the time of death estimated to be within the past two hours.

Noon. London time.

New York. At approximately seven o'clock in the morning, when one Angelo Dellacroce—reputed Mafia figure—stepped into his Lincoln Continental in the attached garage of his Scarsdale home, there was an explosion that ripped the entire enclosure out of its foundation, instantly killing Dellacroce and causing considerable damage to the rest of the house. Dellacroce was rumored to be . . .

Noon. London time.

Phoenix, Arizona. At approximately 5:15 in the morning, one Harrison Renfield, international financier and real-estate magnate with extensive Caribbean holdings, collapsed in his private quarters at the Thunderbird Club after a late party with associates. He had ordered a predawn breakfast; poison was suspected, as a Thunderbird waiter was found unconscious down the hall from Renfield's suite. An autopsy was ordered . . . Five o'clock, Mountain time.

Twelve, noon. London.

Los Angeles, California. At precisely 4:00 A.M. the junior Senator from Nevada—recently implicated (but not indicted) in a Las Vegas tax fraud—stepped off a launch onto a pier in Marina del Ray. The launch was filled with guests returning from the yacht of a motion-picture producer. Somewhere between the launch and the base of the pier, the junior Senator from Nevada had his stomach ripped open with a blade so long and a cut so deep that the cartilage of his backbone protruded through spinal lacerations. He fell among the revelers, carried along by the boisterous crowd until the eruptions of the warm fluid that covered so many was recognized for the blood that it was. Panic resulted, the terror alcoholic but profound. Four in the morning. Pacific time.

Twelve noon. London.

McAuliff looked over at the silent, stunned Holcroft.

"The last death reported was four in the morning . . . twelve o'clock in London. In each country four died, with four corresponding—identical—methods of killing . . . The Arawak units of four—the death odyssey . . . that's what they call it."

"What are you talking about?"

"Deal with the Halidon, Holcroft. You have no choice; this is their proof . . . They said it was only the tip."

"The tip?"

"The tip of the Dunstone iceberg."

"Im*poss*ible demands!" roared R. C. Holcroft, the capillaries in his face swollen, forming splotches of red anger over his skin. "We will *not* be dictated to by goddamn *niggers!*"

"Then you won't get the list."

"We'll *force* it out of them. This is no time for treaties with *savages!*"

Alexander thought of Daniel, of Malcolm, of the incredible lakeside community, of the grave of Acquaba . . . the vaults of Acquaba. Things he could not, would not, talk about. He did not have to, he considered. "You think what's happened is the work of savages? Not the killings, I won't defend that. But the methods, the victims . . . Don't kid yourself."

"I don't give a *damn* for your opinions . . ." Holcroft walked rapidly to the telephone on the bedside table. Alex remained in a chair by the television set. It was the sixth time Holcroft had tried to place his call. The Britisher had only one telephone number he could use in Kingston; embassy telephones were off-limits for clandestine operations. Each time he had managed to get a line through to Kingston—not the easiest feat in Montego—the number was busy.

"Damn! Goddamn it!" exploded the agent.

"Call the embassy before you have a coronary," said McAuliff. "Deal with them."

"Don't be an ass," replied Holcroft. "They don't know who I am. We don't use embassy personnel."

"Talk to the ambassador."

"What in God's name for? What am I supposed to say? 'Pardon me, Mr. Ambassador, but my name's so-and-so. I happen to be . . .' The bloody explanation—if he'd listen to it without cutting me off—would take the better part of an hour. And then the damn fool would start sending cables to Downing Street!" Holcroft marched back to the window.

"What are you going to do?"

"They've isolated me, you understand that, don't you?" Holcroft remained at the window, his back to McAuliff.

"I think so."

"The purpose is to cut me off, force me to absorb the full impact of the . . . past three hours . . ." The Britisher's voice trailed off in thought.

McAuliff wondered. "That presupposes they know the Kingston telephone; that they shorted it out somehow."

"I don't think so," said Holcroft, his eyes still focused on the waters of the bay. "By now Kingston knows I've been taken. Our men are no doubt activating every contact on the island, trying to get a bearing on my whereabouts. The telephone would be in constant use."

"You're not a prisoner; the door's not locked." Alex suddenly wondered if he was correct. He got out of the chair, crossed to the door and opened it.

Down the corridor were two Jamaicans by the bank of elevators. They looked at McAuliff, and although he did not know them, he recognized the piercing, controlled calm of their expressions. He had seen such eyes, such expressions high in the Flagstaff mountains. They were members of the Halidon.

Alex closed the door and turned to Holcroft, but before he could say anything, the Britisher spoke, his back still to Alex.

"Does that answer you?" he asked quietly.

"There are two men in the corridor," said McAuliff, pointlessly. "You knew that."

"I didn't know it, I merely presumed it. There are fundamental rules."

"And you still think they're savages?"

"Everything is relative." Holcroft turned from the window and faced Alex. "You're the conduit now. I'm sure they've told you that."

"If 'conduit' means I take back your answer, then yes."

"Merely the answer? They've asked for no substantive guarantees?" The Englishmen seemed bewildered.

"I think that comes in Phase Two. This is a step contract, I gather. I don't think they'll take the word of Her Majesty's obedient servant. He uses the term 'nigger' too easily."

"You're an ass," said Holcroft.

"You're an autocratic cipher," replied McAuliff, with equal disdain. "They've got you, agent-mon. They've also got the Dunstone list. You play in *their* sandbox . . . with their 'fundamental rules.' "

Holcroft hesitated, repressing his irritation. "Perhaps not. There's an avenue we haven't explored. They'll take you back . . . I should like to be taken with you."

"They won't accept that."

"They may not have a choice—"

"Get one thing straight," interrupted Alex. "There's a survey team in the Cock Pit—white *and* black—and *no one's* going to jeopardize a single life."

"You forget," said Holcroft softly—aloofly. "We know the location within a thousand yards."

"You're no match for those guarding it. Don't think you are . . . One misstep, one deviation, and there are mass executions."

"Yes," said the Britisher. "I believe just such a massacre took place previously. The executioners being those whose methods and selections you admire so."

"The circumstances were different. You don't know the truth . . ."

"Oh, come off it, McAuliff! I shall do my best to protect the lives of your team, but I'm forced to be honest with you. They are no more the first priority for me than they are for the Halidon! There are more important considerations." The Englishman stopped briefly, for emphasis. "And I can assure you, our resources are considerably more than those of a sect of fanatic . . . coloreds. I'd advise you not to change your allegiances at this late hour."

The announcer on the television screen had been droning, reading from pages of script handed to him by others in the studio. Alex couldn't be sure—he had not been listening—but he thought he had heard the name, spoken differently . . . as if associated with new or different information. He looked down at the set, holding up his hand for Holcroft to be quiet.

He *had* heard the name.

And as the first announcement three hours ago had been the prelude—a single instrument marking a thematic commencement—McAuliff recognized this as the coda. The terror had been orchestrated to a conclusion.

The announcer looked earnestly into the camera, then back to the papers in his hand.

"To repeat the bulletin. Savanna-la-Mar. Shooting broke out at the private Negril airfield. A band of unidentified men ambushed a party of Europeans as they were boarding a small plane for Weston Favel. The French industrialist Henri Salanne, the Marquis de Chatellerault, was killed along with three men said to be in his employ . . . No motive is known. The marquis was the houseguest of the Wakefield family. The pilot, a Wakefield employee, reported that his final instructions from the marquis were to fly south of Weston Favel at low altitude toward the interior grasslands. The parish police are questioning . . ."

Alex walked over to the set and switched it off. He turned to Holcroft; there was very little to say, and he wondered if the Intelligence man would understand.

"That was a priority you forgot about, wasn't it, Holcroft? Alison Booth. Your filthy link to Chatellerault . . . The expendable Mrs. Booth, the bait from Interpol . . . Well, you're *here*, agent-mon, and Chatellerault is dead. You're in a hotel room in Montego Bay. Not in the Cock Pit. Don't talk to me about resources, you son of a bitch. You've only got one. And it's me."

The telephone rang. McAuliff reached it first.

"Yes?"

"Don't interrupt me; there is no time" came the agitated words from Malcolm. "Do as I say. I have been spotted. M.I.5 . . . native. One I knew in London. We realized they would fan out; we did not think they would reach Montego so quickly—"

"Stop running," broke in Alex, looking at Holcroft, "M.I.5 will cooperate. They have no choice—"

"You damn fool, I said *listen!* . . . There are two men in the corridor. Go out and tell them I called. Say the word 'Ashanti.' Have you got that, mon? *'Ashantee.'* "

Alex had not heard the Anglicized Malcolm use "mon" before. Malcolm was in a state of panic. "I've got it."

"Tell them I said to get out! *Now!* The hotels will be watched. You will all have to move fast—"

"Goddamn it!" interrupted Alex again. "Now you listen to me. Holcroft's right here and—"

"McAuliff." The sound of Malcolm's voice was low, cutting, demanding attention. "British Intelligence, Caribbean Operations, has a total of fifteen West Indian specialists. That is the budget. Of those fifteen, seven have been bought by Dunstone, Limited."

The silence was immediate, the implication clear. "Where are you?"

"In a pay phone outside McNabs. It is a crowded street; I will do my best to melt."

"Be careful in crowded streets. I've been listening to the news."

"Listen well, my friend. That is what this is all about."

"You said they spotted you. Are they there now?"

"It is difficult to tell. We are dealing with Dunstone now. Even we do not know everyone on its payroll . . . But they will not want to kill me. Any more than I want to be taken alive . . . Good luck, McAuliff . . . We are doing the right thing."

With these words, Malcolm hung up the telephone. Alexander instantly recalled a dark field at night on the outskirts of London, near the banks of the river Thames. And the sight of two dead West Indians in a government automobile.

Any more than I want to be taken alive . . .

Cyanide.

We are doing the right thing . . .

Death.

Unbelievable. Yet very, very real.

McAuliff gently replaced the telephone in its cradle. As he did, he had the fleeting thought that his gesture was funereal.

This was no time to think of funerals.

"Who was that?" asked Holcroft.

"A fanatic nigger who, in my opinion—which I realize doesn't interest you—is worth a dozen men like you. You see, he doesn't lie."

"I've had enough of your sanctimonious claptrap, McAuliff!" The Englishman spat out his words in indignation. "Your fanatic doesn't pay one million dollars, either. Nor, I suspect, does he jeopardize his own interests for your well-being, as *we* have done constantly. Furthermore—"

"He just did," interrupted Alex as he crossed the room. "And if I'm a target, so are you."

McAuliff reached the door, opened it swiftly, and ran out into the corridor toward the bank of elevators. He stopped.

There was no one there.

31

IT WAS a race in blinding sunlight, somehow macabre because of the eye-jolting reflections from the glass and chrome and brightly colored metals on the Montego streets. And the profusion of people. Crowded, jostling, black and white; thin men and fat women—the former with their goddamned cameras, the latter in foolish-looking rhinestone sunglasses. Why did he notice these things? Why did they irritate him? There were fat men, too. Always with angry faces; silently, stoically reacting to the vacuous-looking, thin women at their sides.

And the hostile black eyes staring out from wave after wave of black skin. Thin, black faces—somehow always thin—on top of bony, black bodies—angular, beaten, slow.

These then were the blurred, repeating images imprinted on the racing pages of his mind.

Everything . . . everyone was instantly categorized in the frantic, immediate search for an enemy.

The enemy was surely there.

It had been there . . . minutes ago.

McAuliff had rushed back into the room. There was no time to explain to the furious Holcroft; it was only necessary to make the angry Britisher obey. Alex did so by asking him if he had a gun, then pulling out his own, furnished him by Malcolm on the night before.

The sight of McAuliff's weapon caused the agent to accept the moment. He removed a small, inconspicuous Rycee automatic from a belt holster under his jacket.

Alexander had grabbed the seersucker coat—this too furnished by Malcolm on the previous night—and thrown it over his arm, concealing his revolver.

Together the two men had slipped out of the room and run down the corridor to the staircase beyond the bank of elevators. On the concrete landing they found the first of the Halidonites.

He was dead. A thin line of blood formed a perfect circle around his neck below the swollen skin of his face and the extended tongue and blank, dead, bulging eyes. He had been garrotted swiftly, professionally.

Holcroft had bent down; Alexander was too repelled by the sight to get closer. The Englishman had summarized.

Professionally.

"They know we're on this floor. They don't know which rooms. The other poor bastard's probably with them."

"That's impossible. There wasn't time. *Nobody* knew where we were."

Holcroft had stared at the lifeless black, and when he spoke, McAuliff recognized the profound shock of the Intelligence man's anger.

"Oh, *God,* I've been *blind!*"

In that instant, Alexander, too, understood.

British Intelligence, Caribbean Operations, has a total of fifteen West Indian specialists. That's the budget. Of those fifteen, seven have been bought by Dunstone, Limited . . .

The words of Malcolm the Halidonite.

And Holcroft the manipulator had just figured it out.

The two men had raced down the staircase. When they reached the lobby floor, Holcroft stopped and did a strange thing. He removed his belt, slipping the holster off and placing it in his pocket. He then wound the belt in a tight circle, bent down, and placed it in a corner. He stood up, looked around, and crossed to a cigarette-butt receptacle and moved it in front of the belt.

"It's a signaling device, isn't it?" McAuliff had said.

"Yes. Long-range. External scanner reception; works on verticle arcs. No damn good inside a structure. Too much interference . . . thank heaven."

"You wanted to be taken."

"No, not actually. It was always a possibility, I knew that . . . Any ideas, chap? At the moment, it's your show."

"One. I don't know how good it is. An airfield; it's a farm, I guess. West, on the highway. Near a place called Unity Hall . . . Let's go." Alex reached for the knob on the door to the lobby.

"Not that way," said Holcroft. "They'll be watching the lobby. The street, too, I expect. Downstairs. Delivery entrance . . . maintenance, that sort of thing. There's bound to be one in the cellars."

"*Wait* a minute," McAuliff had grabbed the Englishman's arm, physically forcing him to respond. "Let's you and I get something clear. Right now . . . You've been *had. Taken.* Your own people sold you out. So there won't be any stopping for phone calls, for signaling anyone on the street. We run but we don't stop. For anything. You do and you're on your own. I disappear. I don't think you can handle that."

"Who in hell do you think I'm going to get in touch with? The Prime Minister?"

"I don't know. I just know that I don't trust you. I don't trust liars. Or manipulators. And you're both, Holcroft."

"We all do what we can," replied the agent coldly, his eyes unwavering. "You've learned quickly, Alexander. You're an apt pupil."

"Reluctantly. I don't think much of the school."

And the race in the blinding sunlight had begun.

They ran up the curving driveway of the basement garage, directly into a tan Mercedes sedan that was not parked at that particular entrance by coincidence. Holcroft and Alexander saw the startled look on the face of the white driver; then the man reached over across the seat for a miniature transistorized radio.

In the next few seconds Alex witnessed an act of violence he would never forget as long as he lived. An act performed with cold precision.

R. C. Holcroft reached into both his pockets and took out the Rycee automatic in his right hand, a steel cylinder in his left. He slapped the cylinder onto the barrel of the weapon, snapped in a clip, and walked directly to the door of the tan Mercedes Benz. He opened it, held his hand low, and fired two shots into the driver, killing him instantly.

The shots were spits. The driver fell onto the dashboard; Holcroft reached down and picked up the radio with his left hand.

The sun was bright; the strolling crowds kept moving. If any knew an execution had taken place, none showed it.

The British agent closed the door almost casually.

"*My God . . .*" It was as far as Alex got.

"It was the last thing he expected," said Holcroft rapidly. "Let's find a taxi."

The statement was easier made than carried out. Cabs did not cruise in Montego Bay. The drivers homed like giant pigeons back to appointed street corners, where they lined up in European fashion, as much to discuss the progress of the day with their peers as to find additional fares. It was a maddening practice; during these moments it was a frightening one for the two fugitives. Neither knew where the cab locations were, except the obvious—the hotel entrance—and that was out.

They rounded the corner of the building, emerging on a free-port strip. The sidewalks were steaming hot; the crowds of gaudy, perspiring shoppers were pushing, hauling, tugging, pressing faces against the window fronts, foreheads and fingers smudging the glass, envying the unenviable . . . the shiny. Cars were immobilized in the narrow street, the honking of horns interspersed with oaths and threats as Jamaican tried to out-chauffeur Jamaican for the extra tip . . . and his manhood.

Alexander saw him first, under a green and white sign that read "MIRANDA HILL" with an arrow pointing south. He was a heavyset, dark-haired white man in a brown gabardine suit, the jacket buttoned, the cloth stretched across muscular shoulders. The man's eyes were scanning the streams of human traffic, his head darting about like that of a huge pink ferret. And clasped in his left hand, buried in the flesh of his immense left hand, was a transistorized walkie-talkie identical to the one Holcroft had taken out of the Mercedes.

Alex knew it would be only seconds before the man spotted them. He grabbed Holcroft's arm and wished to God both of them were shorter than they were.

"At the corner! Under the sign . . . Miranda Hill. The brown suit."

"Yes. I see." They were by a low-hanging awning of a free-port liquor store. Holcroft swung into the entrance, begging his pardon through the swarm of tourists, their Barbados shirts and Virgin Island palm hats proof of yet another cruise ship. McAuliff followed involuntarily; the Britisher had locked Alex's arm in a viselike grip, propelling the American in a semicircle, forcing him into the crowded doorway.

The agent positioned the two of them inside the store, at the far corner of the display window. The line of sight was direct; the man under the green and white sign could be seen clearly, his eyes still searching the crowds. "It's the same radio," said Alex.

"If we're lucky, he'll use it. I'm sure they've set up relays . . . I know him. He's Unio Corso."

"That's like a Mafia, isn't it?"

"Not unlike. And far more efficient. He's a Corsican gun. Very high-priced. Warfield would pay it." Holcroft clipped his phrases in a quiet monotone; he was considering strategies. "He may be our way out."

"You'll have to be clearer than that," said Alex.

"Yes, of course." The Englishman was imperiously polite. And maddening. "By now they've circled the area, I should think. Covering all streets. Within minutes they'll know we've left the hotel. The signal won't fool them for long." Holcroft lifted the radio as unobtrusively as possible to the side of his head and snapped the circular switch. There was a brief burst of static; the agent reduced the volume. Several nearby tourists looked curiously; Alexander smiled foolishly at them. Outside on the corner, underneath the sign, the Corsican suddenly brought his radio to his ear. Holcroft looked at McAuliff. "They've just reached your room."

"How do you know?"

"They report a cigarette still burning in the ashtray. Nasty habit. Radio on . . . I should have thought of that." The Englishman pursed his lips abruptly; his eyes indicated recognition. "An outside vehicle is circling. The . . . W.I.S. claims the signal is still inside."

"W.I.S.?"

Holcroft replied painfully. "West Indian Specialist. One of my men."

"Past tense," corrected Alex.

"They can't raise the Mercedes," said Holcroft quickly. "That's it." He swiftly shut off the radio, jammed it into his pocket, and looked outside. The Corsican could be seen listening intently to his instrument. Holcroft spoke again. "We'll have to be very quick. Listen and commit . . . When our Italian finishes his report, he'll put the radio to his side. At that instant we'll break through at him. Get your hands on that radio. Hold it no matter *what*."

"Just like that?" asked McAuliff apprehensively. "Suppose he pulls a gun?"

"I'll be beside you. He won't have time."

And the Corsican did not.

As Holcroft predicted, the man under the sign spoke into the radio. The agent and Alex were beneath the low awning on the street, concealed by the crowds. The second the Corsican's arm began to descend from the side of his head, Holcroft jabbed McAuliff's ribs. The two men broke through the flow of people toward the professional killer.

Alexander reached him first; the man started. His right hand went for his belt, his left automatically raised the radio. McAuliff grabbed the Corsican's wrist and threw his shoulder into the man's chest, slamming him against the pole supporting the sign.

Then the Corsican's whole face contorted spastically; a barking, horrible sound emerged from his twisted mouth. And McAuliff felt a burst of warm blood exploding below.

He looked down. Holcroft's hand held a long switch-blade. The agent had ripped the Corsican's stomach open from pelvis to rib cage, severing the belt, cutting the cloth of the brown gabardine suit.

"Get the radio!" commanded the agent. "Run south on the east side of the street. I'll meet you at the next corner. *Quickly* now!"

Alex's shock was so profound that he obeyed without thought. He grabbed the radio from the dead hand and plunged into the crowds crossing the intersection. Only when he was halfway across did he realize what Holcroft was doing: He was holding up the dead Corsican against the pole. He was giving *him* time to get away!

Suddenly he heard the first screams behind him. Then a mounting crescendo of screams and shrieks and bellowing roars of horror. And within the pandemonium, there was the piercing shrill of a whistle . . . then more whistles, then the thunder of bodies running in the steaming-hot street.

McAuliff raced . . . *was* he running south? *was* he on the east side? . . . he could not think. He could only feel the panic. And the blood.

The blood! The goddamn blood was all over him! People had to see that!

He passed an outdoor restaurant, a sidewalk café. The diners were all rising from their seats, looking north toward the panicked crowds and the screams and the whistles . . . and now the sirens. There was an empty table by a row of planter boxes. On the table was the traditional red-checked tablecloth beneath a sugar bowl and shakers of salt and pepper.

He reached over the flowers and yanked the cloth, sending the condiments crashing to the cement deck, one or all smashing to pieces; he did not, could not, tell. His only thought was to cover the goddamn blood, now saturated through his shirt and trousers.

The corner was thirty feet away. What the hell was he supposed to do? Suppose Holcroft had not gotten away? Was he supposed to stand there with the goddamn tablecloth over his front looking like an imbecile while the streets were in chaos?

"Quickly now!" came the words.

McAuliff turned, grateful beyond his imagination. Holcroft was directly behind him, and Alex could not help but notice his hands. They were deep red and shining; the explosion of Corsican blood had left its mark.

The intersecting street was wider; the sign read "QUEEN'S DRIVE." It curved upward toward the west, and Alex thought he recognized the section. On the diagonal corner an automobile pulled to a stop; the driver peered out the window, looking north at the racing people and sounds of riot.

Alex had to raise his voice to be heard. "Over there!" he said to Holcroft. "That car!"

The Englishman nodded in agreement.

They dashed across the street. McAuliff by now had his wallet out of his pocket, removing bills. He approached the driver—a middle-aged black Jamaican—and spoke rapidly.

"We need a ride. I'll pay you whatever you want!"

But the Jamaican just stared at Alexander, his eyes betraying his sudden fear. And then McAuliff saw: The tablecloth was under his arm—how did it get under his arm?—and the huge stain of dark red blood was everywhere.

The driver reached for the gearshift. Alex thrust his right hand through the window and grabbed the man's shoulder, pulling his arm away from the dashboard. He threw his wallet to Holcroft, unlatched the door, and yanked the man out of the seat. The Jamaican yelled and screamed for help. McAuliff took the bills in his hand and dropped them on the curb as he pummeled the black across the sidewalk.

A dozen pedestrians looked on, and most ran, preferring noninvolvement; others watched, fascinated by what they saw. Two white teenagers ran toward the money and bent down to pick it up.

McAuliff did not know why, but that bothered him. He took the necessary three steps and lashed his foot out, smashing one of the young men in the side of the head.

"Get the hell out of here!" he roared as the teenager fell back, blood matted instantly along his blond hairline.

"McAuliff!" yelled Holcroft, racing around the car toward the opposite front door. "Get in and drive, for God's sake!"

As Alex climbed into the seat, he saw what he knew instantly was the worst sight he could see at that moment. A block away, from out of the milling crowds on the street, a tan Mercedes Benz had suddenly accelerated, its powerful, deep-throated engine signifying its anticipated burst of speed.

McAuliff pulled the gearshift into drive and pressed the pedal to the floor. The car responded, and Alex was grateful for the surge of the racing wheels. He steered into the middle of Queen's Drive, on what had to be Miranda Hill, and immediately passed two cars . . . dangerously close, nearly colliding.

"The Mercedes was coming down the street," he said to Holcroft. "I don't know if they spotted us."

The Britisher whipped around in the seat, simultaneously withdrawing the Rycee automatic and the transistorized radio from both pockets. He snapped on the radio; the static was interspersed with agitated voices issuing commands and answering excitedly phrased questions.

The language, however, was not English.

Holcroft supplied the reason. "Dunstone has half the Unio Corso in Jamaica."

"Can you understand?"

"Sufficiently . . . They're at the corner of Queen's Drive and Essex. In the Miranda Hill district. They've ascertained that the secondary commotion was us."

"Translated: They've spotted us."

"Can this car get a full throttle?"

"It's not bad; no match for a Mercedes, though."

Holcroft kept the radio at full volume, his eyes still on the rear window. There was a burst of chatter from the tiny speaker, and at the same instant McAuliff saw a speeding black Pontiac come over the incline in front of him, on the right, its brakes screeching, the driver spinning the wheel. "Jesus!" he yelled.

"It's theirs!" cried Holcroft. "Their west patrol just reported seeing us. Turn! The first chance you get."

Alex sped to the top of the hill. "What's he doing?" He yelled again, his concentration on the road in front, on whatever automobiles might lie over the crest.

"He's turning . . . side-slipped halfway down. He's righting it now."

At the top of the incline, McAuliff spun the wheel to the right, pressed the accelerator to the floor, and raced past three automobiles on the steep descent, forcing a single approaching car to crowd the curb. "There's some kind of park about a half a mile down." He couldn't be sure of the distance; the blinding sun was careening off a thousand metal objects . . . or so it seemed. But he couldn't think of that; he could only squint. His mind was furiously abstracting flashes of recent memory. Flashes of another park . . . in Kingston: St. George's. And another driver . . . a versatile Jamaican named Rodney.

"So?" Holcroft was bracing himself now, his right hand, pistol firmly gripped, against the dashboard, the radio, at full volume, against the seat.

"There's not much traffic. Not too many people either . . ." Alex swerved the car once again to pass another automobile. He looked in the rear-view mirror. The black Pontiac was at the top of the hill behind them; there were now four cars between them.

"The Mercedes is heading west on Gloucester," said Holcroft, breaking in on Alex's thoughts. "They said Gloucester . . . Another car is to proceed along . . . Sewell . . ." Holcroft translated as rapidly as the voices spoke, overlapping each other.

"Sewell's on the other side of the district," said McAuliff, as much to himself as to the agent. "Gloucester's the shore road."

"They've alerted two vehicles. One at North and Fort streets, the other at Union."

"That's Montego proper. The business area. They're trying to cut us off at all points . . . For Christ's sake, there *is* nothing else left!"

"What are you talking about?" Holcroft had to shout; the screaming tires, the wind, the roaring engine did not permit less.

Explanations took time, if only seconds—there were no seconds left. There would be no explanations, only commands . . . as there had been commands years ago. Issued in the frozen hills with no more confidence than McAuliff felt now.

"Get in the back seat," he ordered, firmly but not tensely. "Smash the rear window; get yourself a clear area . . . When I swing into the park, he'll follow. As soon as I'm inside, I'm going to swerve right and stop. *Hard!* Start firing the second you see the Pontiac behind us. Do you have extra clips?"

"Yes."

"Put in a full one. You've used two shells. Forget that goddamn silencer, it'll throw you off. Try to get clean shots. Through the front and side windows. Stay away from the gas tank and the tires."

The stone gates to the park were less than a hundred yards away, seconds away. Holcroft stared at Alex—for but an instant—and began climbing over the seat to the rear of the automobile.

"You think we can switch cars—"

Perhaps it was a question; McAuliff did not care. He interrupted. "I don't know. I just know we can't use this one any longer and we have to get to the other side of Montego."

"They'll surely spot their own vehicle . . ."

"They won't be looking for it. Not for the next ten minutes . . . if you can aim straight."

The gates were on the left now. Alex whipped the steering wheel around; the car skidded violently as Holcroft began smashing the glass in the rear window. The automobile behind swerved to the right to avoid a collision, its horn blaring, the driver screaming. McAuliff sped through the gate, now holding down the bar of his own horn as a warning.

Inside the gates he slammed on the brakes, spun the wheel to the right, pressed the accelerator, and jumped the curb of the drive over onto the grass. He crashed his foot once again onto the brake pedal; the car jolted to a stop on the soft turf. In the distance strollers in the park turned; a couple picnicking stood up.

Alex was not concerned. In seconds the firing would start; the pedestrians would run for cover, out of the danger zone. Away from the fire base.

Danger zone. Fire base. Cover. Terms from centuries ago.

So then it followed that the strollers in the park were not pedestrians. Not pedestrians at all.

They were *civilians*.

It *was* war.

Whether the civilians knew it or not.

There was the sudden, ear-shattering screech of tires.

Holcroft fired through the smashed rear window. The Pontiac swerved off the drive, hurtled over the opposite curb, careened off a cluster of tropic shrubbery, and slammed into a mound of loose earth, dug for one of a thousand unending park projects. The engine continued at high speed, but the gears had locked, the wheels still, the horn blasting in counterpoint to the whining roar of the motor.

Screams could be heard in the distance.

From the civilians.

McAuliff and Holcroft jumped out of the car and raced over grass and concrete onto grass again. Both had their weapons drawn; it was not necessary. R. C. Holcroft had performed immaculately. He had fired with devastating control through the open side window of the Pontiac. The automobile was untouched but the driver was dead, sprawled over the wheel. Dead weight against the horn.

The two fugitives divided at the car, each to a door of the front seat, Alexander on the driver's side. Together they pulled the lifeless body away from the wheel; the blaring horn ceased, the engine continued to roar. McAuliff reached in and turned the ignition key.

The silence was incredible.

Yet, still, there were the screams from the distance, from the grass.

The civilians.

They yanked at the dead man and threw the body over the plastic seat onto the floor behind. Holcroft picked up the transistor radio. It was in "on" position. He turned it off. Alexander got behind the wheel and feverishly tugged at the gearshift.

It did not move, and the muscles in McAuliff's stomach tensed; he felt his hands trembling.

From out of a boyhood past, long, long forgotten, came the recall. There was an old car in an old garage; the gears were always sticking.

Start the motor for only an instant.

Off—on. Off—on.

Until the gear teeth unlocked.

He did so. How many times, he would never remember. He would only remember the cold, calm eyes of R. C. Holcroft watching him.

The Pontiac lurched. First into the mound of earth; then, as Alex jammed the stick into *R*, backward—wheels spinning furiously—over the grass.

They were mobile.

McAuliff whipped the steering wheel into a full circle, pointing the car toward the cement drive. He pressed the accelerator, and the Pontiac gathered speed on the soft grass in preparation for its jarring leap over the curb.

Four seconds later they sped through the stone gates.

And Alexander turned right. East. Back toward Miranda Hill.

He knew Holcroft was stunned; that did not matter. There was still no time for explanations, and the Englishman seemed to understand. He said nothing.

Several minutes later, at the first intersecting road, McAuliff jumped the light and swung left. North. The sign read "CORNICHE ANNEX."

Holcroft spoke.

"You're heading toward the shore road?"

"Yes. It's called Gloucester. It goes through Montego and becomes Route One."

"So you're behind the Dunstone car . . . the Mercedes."

"Yes."

"And may I presume that since the last word"—here Holcroft held up the transistorized walkie-talkie—"any

of them received was from that park, there's a more direct
way back to it? A faster way?"

"Yes. Two. Queen's Drive and Corniche Road. They
branch off from Gloucester."

"Which, of course, would be the routes they would
take."

"They'd better."

"And naturally, they would search the park."

"I hope so."

R. C. Holcroft pressed his back into the seat. It was a
gesture of temporary relaxation. Not without a certain
trace of admiration.

"You are a *very* apt student, Mr. McAuliff."

"To repeat myself, it's a rotten school," said Alexander.

They waited in the darkness, in the overgrowth at the
edge of the field. The crickets hammered out the passing
seconds. They had left the Pontiac miles away on a deserted back road in Catherine Mount and walked to the
farm on the outskirts of Unity Hall. They had waited
until nightfall before making the last few miles of the
trip. Cautiously, shelter to shelter; when on the road, as
far out of sight as possible. Finally using the tracks of
the Jamaica Railway as their guideline.

There had been a road map in the glove compartment
of the automobile, and they studied it. It was maddening.
Most of the streets west of Montego proper were unmarked, lines without names, and always there were the
alleys without lines. They passed through a number of
ghetto settlements, aware that the inhabitants had to be
sizing them up—two white men without conceivable business in the area. There was profit in an assault on such
men.

Holcroft had insisted that they both carry their jackets,
their weapons very much in evidence in their belts.

Subalterns crossing through hostile colonial territory,
letting the nigger natives know they carried the magic
firesticks that spat death.

Ludicrous.

But there was no assault.

They crossed the Montego River at Westgate; a half-
mile away were the railroad tracks. They ran into an
itinerant tramp enclave—a hobo camp, Jamaica-style—

and Holcroft did the talking.

They were insurance inspectors for the company; they had no objections to the filthy campsite so long as there was no interference with the line. But should there be interference, the penalties would be stiff indeed.

Ludicrous.

Yet no one bothered them, although the surrounding black eyes were filled with hatred.

There was a freight pickup at Unity Hall. A single platform with two wire-encased light bulbs illuminating the barren site. Inside the weather-beaten rain shelter was an old man drunk on cheap rum. Painstakingly they elicited enough information from him for McAuliff to get his bearings. Vague, to be sure, but enough to determine the related distances from the highway, which veered inland at Parish Wharf, to the farm district in the southwest section.

By 9:30 they had reached the field.

Now, Alex looked at his watch. It was 10:30.

He was not sure he had made the right decision. He was only sure that he could not think of any other. He had recalled the lone farmhouse on the property, remembered seeing a light on inside. There was no light now. It was deserted.

There was nothing else to do but wait.

An hour passed, and the only sounds were those of the Jamaican night: the predators foraging, victims taken, unending struggles—immaterial to all but the combatants.

It was nearly the end of the second hour when they heard it.

Another sound.

An automobile. Driving slowly, its low-geared, muted engine signalling its apprehension. An intruder very much aware of its transgression.

Minutes later, in the dim light of a moon sheeted with clouds, they watched a lone figure run across the field, first to the north end, where a single torch was ignited, then to the south—perhaps four hundred yards—where the action was repeated. Then the figure dashed once more to the opposite end.

Another sound. Another intruder. Also muted—this from the darkness of the sky.

An airplane, its engine idling, was descending rapidly.

It touched ground, and simultaneously the torch at the north end was extinguished. Seconds later the aircraft came to a stop by the flame at the south end. A man jumped out of the small cabin; the fire was put out instantly.

"Let's go!" said McAuliff to the British agent. Together the two men started across the field.

They were no more than fifty yards into the grass when it happened.

The impact was so startling, the shock so complete, that Alex screamed involuntarily and threw himself to the ground, his pistol raised, prepared to fire.

Holcroft remained standing.

For two immensely powerful searchlights had caught them in the blinding convergence of the cross-beams.

"Put down your weapon, McAuliff," came the words from beyond the blinding glare.

And Daniel, Minister of Council for the Tribe of Acquaba, walked through the light.

32

"WHEN YOU came into the area you tripped the photo-electric alarms. Nothing mysterious."

They were in the automobile, Daniel in front with the driver, Holcroft and Alexander in the back seat. They had driven away from the field, out of Unity Hall, along the coast into Lucea Harbor. They parked on a deserted section of a dirt road overlooking the water. The road was one of those native offshoots on the coastal highway unspoiled by trespassing tourists. The moon was brighter by the ocean's edge, reflecting off the rippling surface, washing soft yellow light over their faces.

As they were driving, McAuliff had a chance to study the car they were in. From the outside it looked like an ordinary, not-very-distinguished automobile of indeterminate make and vintage—like hundreds of island vehicles, made from the parts of other cars. Yet inside the fundamental difference was obvious: It was a precision-tooled mobile fortress . . . and communications center. The windows were of thick, bullet-proof glass; rubber slots were evident in the rear and side sections—slots that were for the high-blasting, short-barreled shotguns clamped below the back of the front seat. Under the dashboard was a long panel with dials and switches; a telephone was locked into a recess between two microphones. The engine, from the sound of it, was one of the most powerful Alex had ever heard.

The Halidon went first class in the outside world.

Daniel was in the process of dismissing McAuliff's astonishment at the events of the past two hours. It seemed important to the minister that he convey the reality of the situation. The crisis was sufficiently desperate for Daniel to leave the community; to risk his life to be in command.

It was as though he wanted very much for R. C. Holcroft to realize he was about to deal with an extremely sensible and hard-nosed adversary.

"We had to make sure you were alone . . . the two of you, of course. That you were not somehow followed. There were tense moments this afternoon. You handled yourselves expertly, apparently. We could not help you. Congratulations."

"What happened to Malcolm?" asked Alex.

Daniel paused, then spoke quietly, sadly. "We do not know yet. We are looking . . . He is safe—or dead. There is no middle ground." Daniel looked at Holcroft. "Malcolm is the man you know as Joseph Myers, Commander Holcroft."

McAuliff shifted his gaze to the agent. So Holcroft the manipulator was a Commander. Commander Holcroft, liar, manipulator . . . and risker-of-life to save another's.

Holcroft reacted to Daniel's words by closing his eyes for precisely two seconds. The information was a professional burden he did not care for; the manipulator was outflanked again.

"Do I have a single black man working for me? For the Service?"

The minister smiled gently. "By our count, seven. Three, however, are quite ineffectual."

"Thank you for enlightening me. I'm sure you can furnish me with identities . . . They all look so much alike, you see."

Daniel accepted the clichéd insult calmly, his smile disappearing, his eyes cold in the yellow moonlight. "Yes. I understand the problem. There appears to be so little to distinguish us . . . from such a viewpoint. Fortunately, there are other standards. You will not be needing the identities."

Holcroft returned Daniel's look without intimidation. "McAuliff conveyed your demands. I say to you what I said to him. They're impossible, of course—"

"Please, Commander Holcroft," said Daniel rapidly, interrupting, "there are so many complications, let us not compound them with lies. From the beginning your instructions were clear. Would you prefer we deal with the Americans? Or the French? The Germans, perhaps?"

The silence was abrupt. There was a cruelty to it, a blunt execution of pain. Alexander watched as the two enemies exchanged stares. He saw the gradual, painful cognizance in Holcroft's eyes.

"Then you know," said the Englishman softly.

"We know," replied Daniel simply.

Holcroft remained silent and looked out the window.

The Minister of the Halidon turned to McAuliff. "The global mendacity, Doctor. Commander Holcroft is the finest Intelligence officer in the British service. The unit he directs is a coordinated effort between the aforementioned governments. It is, however, coordinated in name only. For M.I.5—as the prime investigatory agency—does not apprise its fellow signatories of its progress."

"There are good and sufficient reasons for our actions," said Holcroft, still looking out the window.

"Reduced to one, is that not right, Commander? . . . Security. You cannot trust your allies."

"Our counterparts are leak-prone. Experience has confirmed this." The agent did not take his eyes off the water.

"So you mislead them," said Daniel. "You give false information, tell them you are concentrating in the Mediterranean, then South America—Argentina, Nicaragua. Even nearby Haiti . . . But never Jamaica." The minister paused for emphasis. "No, never Jamaica."

"Standard procedure," answered Holcroft, allowing Daniel a brief, wary look.

"Then it will not surprise you to learn that this mistrust is shared by your foreign confederates. They have sent out teams, *their* best men. They are presently tracing down every scrap of information M.I.5 has made available. They are working furiously."

Holcroft snapped his head back to Daniel. "That is contrary to our agreement," he said in an angry monotone.

The minister did not smile. "I do not think you are in a position to be sanctimonious, Commander." Daniel shifted his eyes again to Alexander. "You see, McAuliff, since Dunstone, Limited, was a London-based conglomerate, it was agreed to give the first-level assignment to British Intelligence. It was understandable; M.I.5 is the best in the free world; the Commander its best. On the theory that the fewer clandestine services operating, the less likely were breaches of security, the British agreed to function alone and keep everyone current. Instead, they continuously furnished erroneous data." Daniel now permitted himself a minor smile. "In a sense, they were justified. The Americans, the French, and the Germans were *all* breaking the agreement, none had any intention of keeping it. Each was going after Dunstone, while claiming to leave the field to the English . . . Dunstone *has* to be dismantled. Taken apart economic brick by economic brick. The world markets can accept no less. But there are so many bricks . . . Each government believes that if only it can get there first—get the Dunstone list before the others . . . well, arrangements can be made."

Holcroft could not remain silent. "I submit—whoever you are—that we are the logical . . . executors."

"The term 'logic' being interchangeable with 'deserving.' I will say this for your cause. God, Queen, and Empire have paid heavily in recent decades. Somewhat out of proportion to their relative sins . . . But that is not our concern, Commander. As I said, your instructions were clear at the outset: Get the Dunstone list at all costs. The cost is now clear. We will give you the list. You will get out of Jamaica. That is the price."

Again, the silence; once more, the exchange of analyzing stares. A cloud passed over the Montego moon, causing a dark shadow to fall over the faces. Holcroft spoke.

"How can we be sure of its authenticity?"

"Can you doubt us after the events of the day? Remember, it is in our mutual interest that Dunstone be eliminated."

"What guarantees do you expect from us?"

Daniel laughed. A laugh formed in humor. "We do not need *guarantees,* Commander. We will *know.* Can you not understand that? Our island is not a continent; we know every liaison, conduit, and contact with whom you function." The smile from the laugh formed in humor disappeared. "These operations will stop. Make whatever settlements you must, but then no more . . . Give—really give—Jamaica to its rightful owners. Struggles, chaos, and all."

"And"—the Englishman spoke softly—"if these decisions are outside of my control—"

"Make no mistake, Commander Holcroft!" Daniel's voice rose, cutting off the agent. "The executions that took place today began at noon. London time. And each day, the chimes in Parliament's clock tower ring out another noon. When you hear them, remember. What we were capable of today, we are capable of tomorrow. And we will add the truth of our motives. England will be a pariah in the community of nations. You cannot afford that."

"Your threat is ludicrous!" countered Holcroft, with

equal fever. "As you said, this island is not a continent. We'd go in and destroy you."

Daniel nodded and replied quietly. "Quite possibly. And you should know that we are prepared for that eventuality. We *have* been for over two hundred years. Remarkable, isn't it? . . . By all you believe holy, pay the price, Holcroft; take the list and salvage what you can from Dunstone. You *do* deserve that. Not that you'll salvage much; the vultures will fly in from their various geographies and dive for the carrion. We offer you time, perhaps only a few days. Make the best of it!"

A red light on the panel beneath the dashboard lit up, throwing a glow over the front seat. There were the sharp, staccato repeats of a high-pitched buzzer. The driver reached for the telephone and pulled it to his ear, held it there for several seconds, and then handed the instrument to Daniel.

The Minister of the Halidon listened. Alexander saw his face in the rear-view mirror. Daniel could not conceal his alarm.

And then his anger.

"Do what you can but risk *no lives.* Our men are to pull out. *No one* is to leave the community. That is final. *Irreversible!*" He replaced the telephone in its upright recess firmly and turned in the seat. He looked first at Alexander and then at Holcroft, keeping his eyes on the Englishman as he spoke sarcastically. "British *expertise,* Commander. John Bull *know-how* . . . The West Indian Specialists, M.I.5, Caribbean, have just received their orders from Dunstone. They are to go into the Cock Pit and intercept the survey. They are to make sure it does not come out."

"Oh, my God!" McAuliff pitched forward on the seat. "Can they reach them?"

"Ask the eminent authority," said Daniel bitingly, his eyes wide on Holcroft. "They are his men."

The agent was rigid, as though he had stopped breathing. Yet it was obvious his mind was operating swiftly, silently. "They are in contact with the radio receivers . . . the signals transmitted from the campsite. The location can be pinpointed—"

"Within a thousand yards," cut in Alex, completing Holcroft's statement.

"Yes."

"You've got to stop them!"

"I'm not sure there's a way—"

"Find one. For Christ's sake, Holcroft, they're going to be killed!" McAuliff grabbed Holcroft by the lapels of his jacket, yanking him forward viciously. "You *move,* mister. Or I'll kill you!"

"Take your hands—"

Before the agent could finish the obvious, Alexander whipped his right hand across Holcroft's face, breaking the skin on the Englishman's lips. "There isn't anything more, *Commander!* I want those guarantees! *Now!"*

The agent spoke through rivulets of blood. "I'll do my best. All I've ever given you was . . . our best efforts."

"You son of a bitch!" McAuliff brought his hand back once again. The driver and Daniel grabbed his arm.

"McAuliff! You'll accomplish *nothing!"* roared the minister.

"You tell *him* to start accomplishing!" Then Alexander stopped and turned to Daniel, releasing the Englishman. "You've got people there." And then McAuliff remembered the terrible words Daniel had spoken into the telephone: *Risk no lives. Our men . . . pull back. No one is to leave the community.* "You've got to get on that phone. Take back what you said. *Protect them!"*

The minister spoke quietly. "You must try to understand. There are traditions, revelations . . . a way of life extending over two hundred years. We cannot jeopardize these things."

Alexander stared at the black man. "You'd watch them *die? . . .* My *God,* you *can't!"*

"I am afraid we could. And would. And we should then be faced with the taking of your life . . . It would be taken as swiftly . . ." Daniel turned up the collar of his shirt, revealing a tiny bulge in the cloth. *Tablets, sewn into the fabric.* ". . . as I would bite into these, should I ever find myself in a position where it was necessary. I would not think twice about it."

"For God's sake, that's *you!* They're not you; they're no part of you. They don't *know* you. Why should they pay with their lives?"

Holcroft's voice was startling in its quiet incisiveness. "Priorities, McAuliff. I told you. For them . . . for us."

"The accidents of war, Doctor. Combat's slaughter of

innocents, perhaps." Daniel spoke simply, denying the implication of his words. "Things written and unwritten—"

"*Bullshit!*" screamed McAuliff. The driver removed a pistol from his belt; his action was obvious. Alexander looked rapidly back and forth between the Minister of the Halidon and the British Intelligence officer. "Listen to me. You said on that phone for them to do what they can. You. Holcroft. You offered your . . . goddamned 'best efforts.' All right. Give *me* a chance!"

"How?" asked Daniel. "There can be no Jamaican police, no Kingston troops."

The words came back to Alexander. Words spoken by Sam Tucker in the glow of the campsite fire. A quiet statement made as Sam watched the figure of Charles Whitehall and the black giant, Lawrence, talking in the compound. *They're our protection. They may hate each other . . .*

They're our protection.

McAuliff whirled on Holcroft. "How many defectors have you got here?"

"I brought six specialists from London—"

"All but one has sold out to Dunstone," interrupted Daniel.

"That's five. How many others could they pick up?" McAuliff addressed the Halidonite.

"On such short notice, perhaps three or four; probably mercenaries. That is only a guess . . . They would be more concerned with speed than numbers. One automatic rifle in the hands of a single soldier—"

"When did they get the Dunstone orders?" asked Alex swiftly, breaking off Daniel's unnecessary observations.

"Within the hour is our estimate. Certainly no more than an hour."

"Could they get a plane?"

"Yes. Ganga aircraft are always for hire. It would take a little time; ganga pilots are a suspicious breed, but it could be done."

Alex turned to Holcroft. The agent was wiping his lips with his fingers . . . his goddamn fingers, as if dusting the pastry crumbs off his mouth during tea at the Savoy! "Can you raise the people monitoring the signals from the campsite? With that radio?" McAuliff pointed to the panel under the dashboard.

"I have the frequency—"

"Does that mean *yes?*"

"Yes."

"What is the point," asked Daniel.

"To see if his goddamn specialists have reached them. To get the position—"

"You want our plane?" interrupted the Minister of the Halidon, knowing the answer to his question.

"*Yes!*"

Daniel signaled the driver to start the car. "You don't need the position. There is only one place to land: the grassland two miles southwest of the campsite. We have the coordinates."

The automobile lurched out of the parking area, careened off the primitive border, and sped into the darkness toward the highway.

Holcroft gave the frequency-band decimals to Daniel; the minister transmitted them, handing a microphone to the British agent.

There was no pickup.

No answer over the airwaves.

"It will take time to get a plane . . ." Daniel spoke quietly as the car roared over the wide roadway.

Alex suddenly put his hand on the minister's shoulder. "Your runner, the one who used the name of 'Marcus.' Tell him to get word to Sam Tucker."

"I have instructed our men to pull out," answered Daniel icily. "Please remember what I told you."

"For Christ's sake, send him back. Give them a chance!"

"Don't you mean . . . give *her* a chance?"

McAuliff wanted—as he had never wanted anything before—to kill the man. "You had to say it, didn't you?"

"Yes," replied Daniel, turning in his seat to look Alexander in the eye. "Because it is related to the condition on which you have use of the plane . . . If you fail, if the woman is killed, your life is taken also. You will be executed. Quite simply, with her death you could never be trusted."

Alexander acknowledged the penetrating stare of Daniel the Halidonite. "Quite simply," he said, "my answer is easy. I'll give the firing order myself."

R. C. Holcroft leaned forward. His speech was measured, precise as ever. "I am going in with you, McAuliff."

Both Daniel and Alex looked at the Englishman. Holcroft, in a few words, had quietly moved into a strangely defenseless position. It astonished both men.

"Thank you." It was all McAuliff could say, but he meant in profoundly.

"I'm afraid that is not possible, Commander," said Daniel. "You and I . . . we have matters between us. If McAuliff goes, he goes alone."

"You're a barbarian." Holcroft spoke sharply.

"I am the Halidon. And we *do* have priorities. Both of us."

33

MCAULIFF nosed the small plane above cloud cover. He loosened the field jacket provided him by the driver of the car. It was warm in the tiny cabin. The Halidon aircraft was different from the plane he and Malcolm had flown from the field west of Accompong. It was similar to the two-seater Comanche in size and appearance, but its weight and maneuverability were heavier and greater.

McAuliff was not a good pilot. Flying was a skill he had half mastered through necessity, not from any devotion. Ten years ago, when he had made the decision to go field-commercial, he had felt the ability to fly would come in handy, and so he had taken the prescribed lessons that eventually led to a very limited license.

It had proved worthwhile. On dozens of trips over most continents. In small, limited aircraft.

He hoped to Christ it would prove worthwhile now. If it did not, nothing mattered anymore.

On the seat beside him was a small blackboard, a slate common to grammar school, bordered by wood. On it was chalked his primitive flight plan in white lettering that stood out in the dim light of the instrument panel.

Desired air speed, compass points, altitude requirements, and sightings that, with luck and decent moonlight, he could distinguish.

From the strip outside Unity Hall he was to reach a height of one thousand feet, circling the field until he had done so. Leaving the strip perimeter, he was to head southeast at 115 degrees, air speed 90. In a few minutes he would be over Mount Carey—two brush fires would be burning in a field; he would spot them.

He did.

From Mount Carey, maintaining air speed and dropping to 700 feet, he was to swing east-northeast at 84 degrees and proceed to Kempshot Hill. An automobile with a spotlight would be on a road below; the spotlight would flicker its beam into the sky.

He saw it and followed the next line on the chalkboard. His course change was minor—8 degrees to 92 on the compass, maintaining air speed and altitude. Three minutes and thirty seconds later, he was over Amity Hall. Again brush fires, again a fresh instruction; this, too, was minimal.

East-northeast at 87 degrees into Weston Favel.

Drop altitude to 500 feet, maintain airspeed, look for two automobiles facing each other with blinking headlights at the south section of the town. Correct course to exactly 90 degrees and reduce air speed to 75.

The instant he reached the Martha Brae River, he was to alter course 35 degrees southeast, to precisely 122 on the compass.

At this point he was on his own. There would be no more signals from the ground, and, of course, no radio contact whatsoever.

The coordination of air speed, direction, and timing was all he had . . . everything he had. Altitude was by pilotage—as low as possible, cognizant of the gradual ascent of the jungle hills. He might spot campfires, but he was not to assume any to be necessarily those of the survey. There were roving hill people, often on all-night hunts. He was to proceed on course for exactly four minutes and fifteen seconds.

If he had followed everything precisely and if there were no variants of magnitude such as sudden wind currents or rainfall, he would be in the vicinity of the grasslands. Again, if the night was clear and if the light of the moon was sufficient, he would see them.

And—most important—if he spotted other aircraft, he was to dip his right wing twice. This would indicate to any other plane that he was a ganga runner. It was the current courtesy-of-recognition between such gentlemen of the air.

The hills rose suddenly, far more rapidly than McAuliff had expected. He pulled back the half wheel and felt the updrafts carry him into a one-o'clock soar. He reduced the throttle and countered the high bank with pressure on the left pedal; the turbulence continued, the winds grew.

Then he realized the cause of the sudden shifts and cross currents. He had entered a corridor of harsh jungle showers. Rain splattered against the glass and pelted the fuselage; wipers were inadequate. In front of him was a mass of streaked, opaque gray. He slammed down the left window panel, pulled out the throttle, went into a swift ten-o'clock bank, and peered down. His altimeter inched toward 650; the ground below was dense black . . . nothing but jungle forest, no breaks in the darkness. He retraced the leg from the Martha Brae in his mind. Furiously, insecurely. His speed had been maintained, so too his compass. But there had been slippage; not much but recognizable. He was not that good a pilot—only twice before had he flown at night; his lapsed license forbade it—and slippage, or drift, was an instrument or pilotage problem corrected by dials, sightings, or radio.

But the slight drift had been there. And it had come from aft starboard. Jesus, he was better in a sailboat! He leveled the aircraft and gently banked to the right, back into the path of the rain squall. The windshield was useless now; he reached across the seat and pulled down the right window panel. The burst of noise from the crossdrafted openings crashed abruptly through the small cabin. The wind roared at high velocity; the rain swept in streaking sheets, covering the seats and the floor and the instrument panel. The blackboard was soaked, its surface glistening, the chalk marks seemingly magnified by the rushing water sloshing within the borders.

And then he saw it . . . them. The plateau of grassland. Through the starboard—goddman it, *right* window. A stretch of less-black in the middle of the total blackness. A dull gray relief in the center of the dark wood.

He had overshot the fields to the left, no more than a mile, perhaps two.

But he had reached them. Nothing else mattered at the moment. He descended rapidly, entering a left bank above the trees—the top of a figure eight for landing. He made a 280-degree approach and pushed the half wheel forward for touch down.

He was at the fifty-foot reading when behind him, in the west, was a flash of heat lightning. He was grateful for it; it was an additional, brief illumination in the night darkness. He trusted the instruments and could distinguish the approaching grass in the beam of the forelamps, but the dull, quick fullness of dim light gave him extra confidence.

And it gave him the visibility to detect the outlines of

another plane. It was on the ground, stationary, parked on the north border of the field.

In the area of the slope that led to the campsite two miles away.

Oh, God! He had not made it at all. He was too late!

He touched earth, revved the engine, and taxied toward the immobile aircraft, removing his pistol from his belt as he manipulated the controls.

A man waved in the beam of the front lights. No weapon was drawn; there was no attempt to run or seek concealment. Alex was bewildered. It did not make sense; the Dunstone men were killers, he knew that. The man in the beam of light, however, gave no indication of hostility. Instead, he did a peculiar thing. He stretched out his arms at his sides, lowering the right and raising the left simultaneously. He repeated the gesture several times as McAuliff's craft approached.

Alex remembered the instructions at the field in Unity Hall. If you sight other planes, dip your right wing. *Lower* your right wing . . . arm.

The man in the beam of light was a ganga pilot!

McAuliff pulled to a stop and switched off the ignition, his hand gripped firmly around the handle of his weapon, his finger poised in the trigger frame.

The man came up behind the wing and shouted through the rain to Alex in the open window. He was a white man, his face framed in the canvas of a poncho hood. His speech was American . . . Deep South, Delta origins.

"Gawd*damn!* This is one busy fuckin' place! Good to see your white skin, man! I'll fly 'em and' I'll fuck 'em, but I don' *lak* 'em!" The pilot's voice was high-pitched and strident, easily carried over the sound of the rain. He was medium height, and, if his face was any indication, he was slender but flabby; a thin man unable to cope with the middle years. He was past forty.

"When did you get in?" asked Alex loudly, trying not to show his anxiety.

"Flew in these six niggers 'bout ten minutes ago. Mebbe a little more, not much. You with 'em, I sup'oze? You runnin' things?"

"Yes."

"They don' get so *uppity* when there's trouble, huh? Nothin' but trouble in these mountain fields. They sure need whitey, then, you betcha balls!"

McAuliff put his pistol back in his belt beneath the panel. He had to move fast now. He had to get past the ganga pilot. "They said there was trouble?" Alex asked the question casually as he opened the cabin door, stepped on the wing into the rain, and jumped to the wet ground.

"Gawd*damn!* The way they tell it, they got stole blind by a bunch of fuckin' bucks out here. Resold a bundle after takin' their cash. Let me tell you, those niggers are loaded with hardware!"

"That's a mistake," said McAuliff with conviction. "Jesus . . . goddamned *idiots!*"

"They're lookin' for black blood, man! Those niggers gonna' lay out a lotta brothers! *Eeeaww!*"

"They do and New Orleans will go up in smoke! . . . Christ!" Alexander knew the Louisiana city was the major port of entry for narcotics throughout the Southern and Southwestern states. This particular ganga pilot would know that. "Did they head down the slope?" McAuliff purposely gestured a hundred yards to the right, away from the vicinity of the path he remembered.

"Damned if they was too fuckin' sure, man! They got one a them Geigers like an air-radar hone, but not so good. They took off more like down there." The pilot pointed to the left of the hidden jungle path.

Alex calculated rapidly. The scanner used by the Dunstone men was definitive only in terms of a thousand-yard radius. The signals would register, but there were no hot or cold levels that would be more specific. It was the weakness of miniaturized long-distance radio arcs, operating on vertical principles.

One thousand yards was three thousand feet—over a half a mile within the dense, almost impenetrable jungle of the Cock Pit. If the Dunstone team had a ten-minute advantage, it was not necessarily fatal. They did not know the path—he didn't *know* it either, but he had traveled it. Twice. Their advantage had to be reduced. And if their angle of entry was indirect—according to the ganga pilot, it was—and presuming they kept to a relatively straight line, anticipating a sweep . . . the advantage conceivably might be removed.

If . . . if he could find the path and keep to it.

He pulled up the lapels of his field jacket to ward off the rain and turned toward the cabin door above the wing of the plane. He opened it, raised himself with one knee to the right of the strut, and reached into the small luggage compartment behind the seat. He pulled out a short-barreled, high-powered automatic rifle—one of the two that had been strapped below the front seat of the Halidon car. The clip was inserted, the safety on. In his pockets were four additional clips; each clip held twenty cartridges.

One hundred shells.

His arsenal.

"I've got to reach them," he yelled through the downpour at the ganga pilot. "I sure as hell don't want to answer to New Orleans!"

"Them New Orleens boys is a tense bunch. I don't fly for 'em if I got other work. They don' lak nobody!"

Without replying, McAuliff raced toward the edge of the grassland slope. The path was to the right of a huge cluster of nettled fern—he remembered that; his face had been scratched because his hand had not been quick enough when he had entered the area with the Halidon runner.

Goddamn it! Where *was* it?

He began feeling the soaked foliage, gripping every leaf, every branch, hoping to find his hand scratched, scraped by nettles. He *had* to find it; he had to start his entry at precisely the right point. The wrong spot would be fatal. Dunstone's advantage would be too great; he could not overcome it.

"What are you lookin' for?"

"What?" Alex whipped around into the harsh glare of light. His concentration was such that he found himself unlatching the safety on the rifle. He had been about to fire in shock.

The ganga pilot had walked over. "Gawddamn. Ain't you got a flashlight, man? You expect to find your way in that mess without no flashlight?"

Jesus! He had left the flashlight in the Halidon plane. Daniel had said something about being careful . . . with the flashlight. So he had left it behind! "I forgot. There's one in the plane."

"I hope to fuck there is," said the pilot.

"You take mine. Let me use yours, okay?"

"You promise to shoot me a couple o' niggers, you got it, man." The pilot handed him the light. "This rain's too fuckin' wet, I'm going back inside. Good huntin', hear!"

McAuliff watched the pilot run toward his aircraft and then quickly turned back to the jungle's edge. He was no more than five feet from the cluster of fern; he could see the matted grass at the entry point of the concealed path.

He plunged in.

He ran as fast as he could, his feet ensnared by the underbrush, his face and body whipped by the unseen tentacles of overgrowth. The path twisted—right, left, right, right, *right, Jesus! circles*—and then became straight again for a short stretch at the bottom of the slope.

But it was still true. He was still on it. That was all that mattered.

Then he veered off. The path wasn't there. It was gone!

There was an ear-shattering screech in the darkness, magnified by the jungle downpour. In the beam of his flashlight, deep within a palm-covered hole below him, was a wild pig suckling its blind young. The hairy, monstrous face snarled and screeched once more and started to rise, shaking its squealing offspring from its teats. McAuliff ran to his left, into the wall of jungle. He stumbled on a rock. Two, three rocks. He fell to the wet earth, the flashlight rolling on the ground. The ground was flat, unobstructed.

He had found the path again!

He got to his feet, grabbed the light, shifted the rifle under his arm, and raced down the relatively clear jungle corridor.

Clear for no more than a hundred yards, where it was intersected by a stream, bordered by soft, foot-sucking mud. He remembered the stream. The runner who had used the name of "Marcus" had turned left. Was it left? Or was that from the opposite direction? . . . No, it *was* left. There had been palm trunks and rocks showing through the surface of the water, crossing the narrow stream. He ran to the left, his flashlight aimed at the midpoint of the water.

There were the logs! The rocks. A hastily constructed bridge to avoid the ankle-swallowing mud.

And on the right palm trunk were two snakes in lateral

slow motion, curving their way toward him. Even the Jamaican mongoose did not have the stomach for Jamaica's Cock Pit.

Alexander knew these snakes. He had seen them in Brazil. Anaconda strain. Blind, swift-striking, vicious. Not fatal, but capable of causing paralysis—for days. If flesh came within several feet of the flat heads, the strikes were inevitable.

He turned back to the overgrowth, the beam of light crisscrossing the immediate area. There was a dangling branch of a ceiba tree about six feet long. He ran to it, bending it back and forth until it broke off. He returned to the logs. The snakes had stopped, alarmed. Their oily, ugly bodies were entwined, the flat heads poised near each other, the blind, pinlike eyes staring fanatically in the direction of the scent. At him.

Alex shoved the ceiba limb out on the log with his left hand, the rifle and flashlight gripped awkwardly in his right.

Both snakes lunged simultaneously, leaping off the surface of the log, whipping their bodies violently around the branch, their heads zeroing toward McAuliff's hand, soaring through the soft leaves.

Alex threw—dropped? he would never know—the limb into the water. The snakes thrashed; the branch reeled in furious circles and sank beneath the surface.

McAuliff ran across the logs and picked up the path.

He had gone perhaps three-quarters of a mile, certainly no more than that. The time elapsed was twelve minutes by his watch. As he remembered it, the path veered sharply to the right through a particularly dense section of fern and maidenhead to where there was a small clearing recently used by a band of hill-country hunters. Marcus—the man who used the name of "Marcus"—had remarked on it.

From the clearing it was less than a mile to the banks of the Martha Brae and the campsite. The Dunstone advantage had to be diminishing.

It *had* to be.

He reached the nearly impossible stretch of overgrowth, his flashlight close to the earth, inspecting the ground for signs of passage. If he stepped away from the path now—if he moved into underbrush that had not seen human movement—it would take him hours to find it again. Probably not until daylight—or when the rains stopped.

It was painfully slow, agonizingly concentrated. Bent weeds, small broken branches, swollen borders of wet ground where once there had been the weight of recent human feet; these were his signs, his codes. He could not allow the tolerance of a single error.

"Hey, mon!" came the muted words.

McAuliff threw himself to the ground and held his breath. Behind him, to his left, he could see the beam of another flashlight. Instantly he snapped off his own.

"Hey, mon, where are you? Contact, please. You went off your pattern. Or I did."

Contact, please . . . Off your pattern. The terms of an agent, not the language of a carrier. The man was M.I.5.

Past tense. *Was.*

Now Dunstone, Limited.

The Dunstone team had separated, each man assigned an area . . . a pattern. That could only mean they were in radio contact.

Six men in radio contact.

Oh, *Jesus!*

The beam of light came nearer, dancing, flickering through the impossible foliage.

"Here, *mon!*" whispered Alex gutturally, hoping against reasonable hope that the rain and the whisper would not raise an alarm in the Dunstone ear.

"Put on your light, please, mon."

"Trying to, mon." No more, thought McAuliff. Nothing.

The dancing beam reflected off a thousand shining, tiny mirrors in the darkness, splintering the light into hypnotically flickering shafts.

Closer.

Alex rolled silently off the path into the mass of wet earth and soft growth, the rifle under him cutting into his thighs.

The beam of light was nearly above him, its shaft almost clear of interference. In the spill he could see the upper body of the man. Across his chest were two wide straps: One was connected to an encased radio, the other to the stock of a rifle, its thick barrel silhouetted over his shoulder. The flashlight was in the left hand; in the right was a large, ominous-looking pistol.

The M.I.5 defector was a cautious agent. His instincts had been aroused.

McAuliff knew he had to get the pistol; he could not allow the man to fire. He did not know how near the others were, how close the other patterns.

Now!

He lashed his right hand up, directly onto the barrel of the pistol, jamming his thumb into the curvature of the trigger housing, smashing his shoulder into the man's head, crashing his left knee up under the man's legs into his testicles. With the impact, the man buckled and expunged a tortured gasp; his hand went momentarily limp, and Alex ripped the pistol from it, propelling the weapon into the darkness.

From his crouched agony the Jamaican looked up, his left hand still holding the flashlight, its beam directed nowhere at the earth, his face contorted . . . about to take the necessary breath to scream.

McAuliff found himself thrusting his fingers into the man's mouth, tearing downward with all his strength. The man lurched forward, bringing the hard metal of the flashlight crashing into Alex's head, breaking the skin. Still McAuliff ripped at the black's mouth, feeling the teeth puncturing his flesh, sensing the screams.

They fell, twisting in midair, into the overgrowth. The Jamaican kept smashing the flashlight into McAuliff's temple; Alex kept tearing grotesquely, viciously, at the mouth that could sound the alarm he could not allow.

They rolled over into a patch of sheer jungle mud. McAuliff felt a rock, he tore his left hand loose, ripped the rock up from the ground, and brought it crashing into the black mouth, over his own fingers. The man's teeth shattered; he choked on his own saliva. Alex whipped out his bleeding hand and instantly grabbed the matted hair, twisting the entire head into the soft slime of the mud. There were the muffled sounds of expulsion beneath the surface. A series of miniature filmy domes burst silently out of the soggy earth in the spill of the fallen flashlight.

And then there was nothing.

The man was dead.

And no alarms had been sent.

Alexander reached over, picked up the light, and

looked at the finger of his right hand. The skin was slashed, there were teeth marks, but the cuts were not deep; he could move his hand freely, and that was all he cared about.

His left temple was bleeding, and the pain terrible, but not immobilizing. Both would stop . . . sufficiently.

He looked over at the dead Jamaican and he felt like being sick. There was no time. He crawled back to the path and started once again the painstaking task of following it. And he tried to focus his eyes into the jungle. Twice, in the not-too-distant denseness, he saw sharp beams of flashlights.

The Dunstone team was continuing its sweep. It was zeroing in.

There was not an instant to waste in thought.

Eight minutes later he reached the clearing. He felt the accelerated pounding in his chest; there was less than a mile to go. The easiest leg of the terrible journey.

He looked at his watch. It was exactly four minutes after twelve midnight.

Twelve was also the hour of noon.

Four was the ritual Arawak unit.

The odyssey of death.

No time for thought.

He found the path at the opposite side of the small clearing and began to run, gathering speed as he raced toward the banks of the Martha Brae. There was no air left in his lungs now, not breath as he knew it; only the steady explosions of exhaustion from his throat, blood and perspiration falling from his head, rivering down his neck onto his shoulders and chest.

There was the river. He had reached the river!

It was only then that he realized the pounding rain had stopped; the jungle storm was over. He swung the flashlight to his left; there were the rocks of the path bordering the final few hundred yards into the campsite.

He had heard no rifle fire. There had been no shots. There were five experienced killers in the darkness behind him, and the terrible night was not over . . . but he had a chance.

That's all he had asked for, all that was between him and his command to a firing squad ending his life.

Willingly, if he failed. Willingly to end it without Alison.

He ran the last fifty yards as fast as his exhausted muscles could tolerate. He held the flashlight directly in front of him; the first object caught by its beam was the lean-to at the mouth of the campsite area. He raced into the clearing.

There were no fires, no signs of life. Only the dripping of a thousand reminders of the jungle storm, the tents silent monuments of recent living.

He stopped breathing. Cold terror gripped him. The silence was an overpowering portent of horror.

"Alison. *Alison!*" he screamed, and raced blindly toward the tent. *"Sam! Sam!"*

When the words came out of the darkness, he knew what it was to be taken from death and be given life again.

"Alexander . . . You damn near got killed, boy," said Sam Tucker from the black recesses of the jungle's edge.

34

SAM TUCKER and the runner called "Marcus" walked out of the bush. McAuliff stared at the Halidonite, bewildered. The runner saw his expression and spoke.

"There is no time for lengthy explanations. I have exercised an option, that is all." The runner pointed to the lapel of his jacket. Alex needed no clarification. Sewn into the cloth were the tablets he had seen in the wash of yellow moonlight on the back road above Lucea Harbor.

I would not think twice about it, Daniel had said.

"Where is Alison?"

"With Lawrence and Whitehall. They're farther down the river," answered Sam.

"What about the Jensens?"

Tucker paused. "I don't know, Alexander."

"What?"

"They disappeared. That's all I can tell you . . . Yesterday Peter was lost; his carrier returned to camp, he couldn't find him. Ruth bore up well, poor girl . . . a lot of guts in her. We sent out a search. Nothing . . . And then this morning, I can't tell you why—I don't know—I went to the Jensen tent. Ruth was gone. She hasn't been seen since."

McAuliff wondered. Had Peter Jensen seen something? Sensed something? And fled with his wife? Escaped past the Tribe of Acquaba?

Questions for another time.

"The carriers?" asked Alex warily, afraid to hear the answer.

"Check with our friend here," replied Tucker, nodding to the Halidonite.

"They have been sent north, escorted north on the river," said the man with the usurped name of "Marcus." "Jamaicans will not die tonight unless they know why they are dying. Not in this fight."

"And you? Why you? Is this your fight?"

"I know the men who come for you. I have the option to fight."

"The limited freedoms of Acquaba?" asked Alex softly.

Marcus shrugged; his eyes betrayed nothing. "An individual's freedom of choice, Doctor."

There was a barely perceptible cry of a bird, or the muted screech of a bat, from the dense, tropic jungle. Then there followed another. And another. McAuliff would not have noticed . . . there were so many sounds, so continuously. A never-ending nocturnal symphony; pleasant to hear, not pleasant to think about.

But he was compelled to notice now.

Marcus snapped his head up, reacting to the sound. He swiftly reached over and grabbed Alexander's flashlight and ripped it out of his hand while shouldering Tucker away.

"Get down!" he cried, as he pushed McAuliff violently, reeling him backward, away from the spot where he was standing.

Seven rifle shots came out of the darkness, some thumping into trees, others cracking into the jungle distance, two exploding into the dirt of the clearing.

Alex rolled on the ground, pulling his rifle into position and aimed in the direction of the firing. He kept his finger on the trigger; a shattering fusillade of twenty bullets sprayed the area. It was over in seconds. The stillness returned.

He felt a hand grabbing his leg. It was Marcus.

"Pull back. Down to the river, mon," he whispered harshly.

McAuliff scrambled backward in the darkness. More shots were fired from the bush; the bullets screamed above him to the right.

Suddenly there was a burst of rifle fire from only feet away. Marcus had leaped up to the left and delivered a cross-section barrage that drew the opposing fire away. Alex knew Marcus's action was his cover. He lurched to the right, to the edge of the clearings. He heard Sam Tucker's voice.

"McAuliff! Over here!"

As he raced into the brush, he saw Sam's outline on the ground. Tucker was crouched on one knee, his rifle raised. *"Where?* For Christ's sake, where's Alison? The others?"

"Go down to the river, boy! South, about three hundred yards. Tell the blacks. We'll hold here."

"No, Sam! Come with me . . . *Show* me."

"I'll be there, son . . ." Another volley of shots spat

out of the jungle. Marcus answered from the opposite side of the clearing. Tucker continued speaking as he grabbed the cloth in Alex's field jacket and propelled him beyond. "That black son of a bitch is willing to get his tar ass shot off for us! Maybe he's given me a little time I don't deserve. He's my countryman, boy. My new *landsmann*. *Jesus!* I knew I liked this fucking island. Now get the hell down there and watch out for the girl. We'll join you, don't you worry about that. The *girl*, Alexander!"

"There are five men out there, Sam. I killed one of them a mile back. They must have seen my flashlight when I was running. I'm sorry . . ." With these words McAuliff plunged into the soaking-wet forest and slashed his way to the river bank. He tumbled down the short slope, the rifle clattering against the metal buttons of his jacket, and fell into the water.

South. *Left*.

Three hundred yards. Nine hundred feet . . . a continent.

He stayed close to the river bank, where he could make the best time. As he slopped through the mud and the growth and over fallen trunks, he realized his magazine clip was empty. Without stopping he reached into his pocket and pulled out a fresh clip, snapping the old one out of its slot and slamming the new one in. He cracked back the insertion bar; the cartridge entered the chamber.

Gunfire broke his non-thoughts. Behind him men were trying to kill other men.

There was a bend in the narrow river. He had traveled over a hundred yards; nearer two, he thought.

. . . *my new landsmann* . . . Christ! Sam Tucker, itinerant wanderer of the globe, schooler of primitives, lover of all lands—in search of one to call his own, at this late stage of his life. And he had found it in a violent moment of time in the cruelest wilds of Jamaica's Cock Pit. In a moment of sacrifice.

Suddenly, in an instant of terror, from out of the darkness above, a huge black form descended. A giant arm fell viselike around his neck; clawing fingers tore at his face; his kidneys were being hammered by a vicious, powerful fist. He slammed the rifle butt into the body behind him, sank his teeth into the flesh below his mouth, and lunged forward into the water.

"Mon! Jesus, mon!"

The voice of Lawrence cried as he pummeled McAuliff's shoulder. Stunned, each man released the other; each held up his hands, Alex's awkwardly thrusting out the rifle, Lawrence's holding a long knife.

"My God!" said McAuliff. "I could have *shot* you!"

There was another fusillade of gunfire to the north.

"I might have put the blade in . . . not the handle," said the black giant, waist-deep in water. "We wanted a hostage."

Both men recognized there was no time for explanations. "Where *are* you? Where's Alison and Whitehall?"

"Downstream, mon. Not far."

"Is she all right?"

"She is frightened . . . But she is a brave woman. For a white English lady. You see, mon?"

"I saw, mon," replied Alexander. "Let's go."

Lawrence preceded him, jumping out of the water about thirty yards beyond the point of the near-fatal encounter. McAuliff saw that the revolutionary had tied a cloth around his forearm; Alex spat the blood out of his mouth as he noticed it, and rubbed the area of his kidneys in abstract justification.

The black pointed up the slope with his left hand and put his right hand to his mouth at the same time. A whistled treble emerged from his lips. A bird, a bat, an owl . . . it made no difference. There was a corresponding sound from the top of the river bank, beyond in the jungle.

"Go up, mon. I will wait here," said Lawrence.

McAuliff would never know whether it was the panic of the moment or whether his words spoke the truth as he saw it, but he grabbed the black revolutionary by the shoulder and pushed him forward. "There won't be any more orders given. You don't know what's back there. I do! Get your ass up there!"

An extended barrage of rifle fire came from the river.

Lawrence blinked. He blinked in the new moonlight that flooded the river bank of this offshoot of the Martha Brae.

"Okay, mon! Don't *push!*"

They crawled to the top of the slope and started into the overgrowth.

The figure came rushing out of the tangled darkness, a darker, racing object out of a void of black. It was Alison.

Lawrence reached back to McAuliff and took the flash-light out of Alex's hand. A gesture of infinite understanding.

She ran into his arms. The world . . . the universe stopped its insanity for an instant, and there was stillness. And peace. And comfort. But for only an instant.

There was no time for thought. Or reflection.

Or words.

Neither spoke.

They held each other, and then looked at each other in the dim spill of the new moonlight in the isolated space that was their own on the banks of the Martha Brae.

In a terrible, violent moment of time.

And sacrifice.

Charles Whitehall intruded, as Charley-mon was wont to do. He approached, his safari outfit still creased, his face an immobile mask, his eyes penetrating.

"Lawrence and I agreed he would stay down at the river. Why have you changed that?"

"You blow my mind, Charley . . ."

"You *bore* me, McAuliff!" replied Whitehall. "There was gunfire up there!"

"I was in the middle of it, you black son of a bitch!" *Jesus, why did he have to say that?* "And you're going to learn what the problem is. Do you understand that?"

Whitehall smiled. "Do tell . . . *whitey.*"

Alison slapped her hands off McAuliff and looked at both men. *"Stop it!"*

"I'm sorry," said Alex quickly.

"I'm *not,*" replied Whitehall. "This is his moment of *truth.* Can't you see that, *Miss* Alison?"

Lawrence's great hands interfered. They touched both men, and his voice was that of a thundering child-man. "Neither, no more, mon! McAuliff, mon, you say what you know! *Now!*"

Alexander did. He spoke of the grasslands, the plane—a plane, not the Halidon's—the redneck ganga pilot who had brought six men into the Cock Pit to massacre the survey, the race to the campsite, the violent encounter in the jungle that ended in death in a small patch of jungle mud. Finally, those minutes ago when the runner called "Marcus" saved their lives by hearing a cry in the tropic bush.

"Five men, mon," said Lawrence, interrupted by a new

burst of gunfire, closer now but still in the near-distance to the north. He turned to Charles Whitehall. "How many do you want, *fascisti?*"

"Give me a figure, *agricula.*"

"Goddamn it!" yelled McAuliff. "Cut it out. Your games don't count any more."

"You do not understand," said Whitehall. "It is the only thing that does count. We are prepared. We are the *viable* contestants. Is this not what the fictions create? One on one, the victor sets the course?"

. . . The charismatic leaders are not the foot soldiers . . . They change or are replaced . . . The words of Daniel, Minister of the Tribe of Acquaba.

"You're both insane," said Alex, more rationally than he thought was conceivable. "You make me sick, and goddamn you—"

"Alexander! *Alexander!*" The cry came from the river bank less than twenty yards away. Sam Tucker was yelling.

McAuliff began running to the edge of the jungle. Lawrence raced ahead, his huge body crashing through the foliage, his hands pulverizing into sudden diagonals everything in their path.

The black giant jumped to the water's edge; Alex started down the short slope and stopped.

Sam Tucker was cradling the body of Marcus the runner in his arms. The head protruding out of the water was a mass of blood, sections of the skull were shot off.

Still, Sam Tucker would not let go.

"One of them circled and caught us at the bank. Caught *me* at the bank . . . Marcus jumped out between us and took the fire. He killed the son of a bitch; he kept walking right up to him. Into the gun."

Tucker lowered the body into the mud of the river bank.

McAuliff thought. Four men remained, four killers left of the Dunstone team.

They were five. But Alison Booth could not be counted now.

They were four, too.

Killers.

Four. The Arawak four.

The death odyssey.

Alex felt the girl's hands on his shoulders, her face

pressed against his back in the moonlight.

The grasslands.

Escape was in the grasslands and the two aircraft that could fly them out of the Cock Pit.

Yet Marcus had implied there was no other discernible route but the narrow, twisting jungle path—a danger in itself.

The path was picked up east of the river at the far right end of the campsite clearing. It would be watched; the M.I.5 defectors were experienced agents. *Egress* was a priority; the single avenue of escape would have automatic rifles trained on it.

Further, the Dunstone killers knew their prey was downstream. They would probe, perhaps, but they would not leave the hidden path unguarded.

But they had to separate. They could not gamble on the unknown, on the possibility that the survey team might slip through, try to penetrate the net.

It was this assumption that led McAuliff and Sam Tucker to accept the strategy. A variation on the deadly game proposed by Lawrence and Charles Whitehall. Alexander would stay with Alison. The others would go out. Separately. And find the enemy.

Quite simply, kill or be killed.

Lawrence lowered his immense body into the black waters. He hugged the bank and pulled his way slowly upstream, his pistol just above the surface, his long knife out of its leather scabbard, in his belt—easily, quickly retrievable.

The moon was brighter now. The rain clouds were gone; the towering jungle overgrowth obstructed but did not blot out the moonlight. The river currents were steady; incessant, tiny whirlpools spun around scores of fallen branches and protruding rocks, the latter's tips glistening with buffeted moss and matted green algae.

Lawrence stopped; he dropped farther into the water, holding his breath, his eyes just above the surface. Diagonally across the narrow river offshoot a man was doing exactly what he was doing, but without the awareness Lawrence now possessed.

Waist-deep in water, the man held a lethal-looking rifle in front of and above him. He took long strides, keeping his balance by grabbing the overhanging foliage on the river bank, his eyes straight ahead.

In seconds, the man would be directly opposite him.

Lawrence placed his pistol on a bed of fern spray. He reached below and pulled the long knife from his belt.

He sank beneath the surface and began swimming underwater.

Sam Tucker crawled over the ridge above the river bank and rolled toward the base of the ceiba trunk. The weight of his body pulled down a loose vine; it fell like a coiled snake across his chest, startling him.

He was north of the campsite now, having made a wide half circle west, on the left side of the river. His reasoning was simple, he hoped not too simple. The Dunstone patrol would be concentrating downstream; the path was east of the clearing. They would guard it, expecting any who searched for it to approach from below, not above the known point of entry.

Tucker shouldered his way up the ceiba trunk into a sitting position. He loosened the strap of his rifle, lifted the weapon, and lowered it over his head diagonally across his back. He pulled the strap taut. Rifle fire was out of the question, to be used only in the last extremity, for its use meant—more than likely—one's own execution.

That was not out of the question, thought Sam, but it surely would take considerable persuasion.

He rolled back to a prone position and continued his reptilelike journey through the tangled labyrinth of jungle underbrush.

He heard the man before he saw him. The sound was peculiarly human, a casual sound that told Sam Tucker his enemy was casual, not primed for alarm. A man who somehow felt his post was removed from immediate assault, the patrol farthest away from the area of contention.

The man had sniffed twice. A clogged nostril, or nostrils, caused a temporary blockage and a passage for air was casually demanded. Casually obtained.

It was enough.

Sam focused in the direction of the sound. His eyes of fifty-odd years were strained, tired from lack of sleep and from peering for nights on end into the tropic darkness. But they would serve him, he knew that.

The man was crouched by a giant fern, his rifle between his legs, stock butted against the ground. Beyond, Tucker could see in the moonlight the outlines of the lean-to at the far left of the clearing. Anyone crossing the campsite was in the man's direct line of fire.

The fern ruled out a knife. A blade that did not enter precisely at the required location could cause a victim to lunge, to shout. The fern concealed the man's back too well. It was possible, but awkward.

There was a better way. Sam recalled the vine that had dropped from the trunk of the ceiba tree.

He reached into his pocket and withdrew a coil of ordinary azimuth line. Thin steel wire encased in nylon, so handy for so many things . . .

He crept silently toward the giant spray of tiny leaves.

His enemy sniffed again.

Sam rose, half inch by half inch, behind the fern. In front of him now, unobstructed, was the silhouette of the man's neck and head.

Sam Tucker slowly separated his gnarled, powerful hands. They were connected by the thin steel wire encased in nylon.

Charles Whitehall was furious. He had wanted to use the river; it was the swiftest route, far more direct than the torturously slow untangling that was demanded in the bush. But it was agreed that since Lawrence had been on guard at the river, he knew it better. So the river was his.

Whitehall looked at the radium dial of his watch; there were still twelve minutes to go before the first signal. If there was one.

Simple signals.

Silence meant precisely that. Nothing.

The short, simulated, guttural cry of a wild pig meant success. One kill.

If two, two kills.

Simple.

If he had been given the river, Charles was convinced, he would have delivered the first cry. At least one.

Instead, his was the southwest sweep, the least likely of the three routings to make contact. It was a terrible waste. An old man, authoritative, inventive, but terribly tired, and a plodding, unskilled hill boy, not without potential, perhaps, but still a misguided, awkward giant.

A terrible waste! Infuriating.

Yet now as infuriating as the sharp, hard steel that suddenly made contact with the base of his skull. And the words that followed, whispered in a harsh command:

"Open your mouth and I blow your head off, mon!"

He had been taken! His anger had caused his concentration to wander.

Stupid.

But his captor had not fired. His taker did not want the alarm of a rifle shot any more than he did. The man kept thrusting the barrel painfully into Charles's head, veering him to the right, away from the supposed line of Whitehall's march. The man obviously wanted to interrogate, discover the whereabouts of the others.

Stupid.

The *release-seizure* was a simple maneuver requiring only a hard surface to the rear of the victim for execution.

And it was, indeed, execution.

It was necessary for the victim to rebound following impact, not be absorbed in space or elastically swallowed by walled softness. The impact was most important; otherwise, the trigger of the rifle might be pulled. There was an instant of calculated risk—nothing was perfect—but the reverse jamming of the weapon into the victim allowed for that split second of diagonal slash that invariably ripped the weapon out of the hands of the hunter.

Optimally, the slash coincided with the impact.

It was all set forth clearly in the Oriental training manuals.

In front of them, to the left, Whitehall could distinguish the sudden rise of a hill in the jungle darkness. One of those abrupt protrusions out of the earth that was so common to the Cock Pit. At the base of the hill was a large boulder reflecting the wash of moonlight strained through the trees.

It would be sufficient . . . actually, more than sufficient; very practical, indeed.

He stumbled, just slightly, as if his foot had been ensnared by an open root. He felt the prod of the rifle barrel. It was the moment.

He slammed his head back into the steel and whipped to his right, clasping the barrel with his hands and jamming it forward. As the victim crashed into the boulder, he swung the weapon violently away, ripping it out of the man's grasp.

As the man blinked in the moonlight, Charles Whitehall rigidly extended three fingers on each hand and completed the assault with enormous speed and control. The hands were trajectories—one toward the right eye, the other into the soft flesh below the throat.

McAuliff had given Alison his pistol. He had been startled to see her check the clip with such expertise, releasing it from its chamber, pressing the spring, and reinserting it with a heel-of-the-palm impact that would have done justice to Bonnie of Clyde notoriety. She had smiled at him and mentioned the fact that the weapon had been in the water.

There were eight minutes to go. Two units of four; the thought was not comforting.

He wondered if there would be any short cries in the night. Or whether a measured silence would signify an extension of the nightmare.

Was any of them good enough? Quick enough? Sufficiently alert?

"Alex!" Alison grabbed his arm, whispering softly but with sharp intensity. She pulled him down and pointed into the forest, to the west.

A beam of light flicked on and off.

Twice.

Someone had been startled in the overgrowth; some *thing* perhaps. There was a slapping flutter and short, repeated screeches that stopped as rapidly as they had started.

The light went on once again, for no more than a second, and then there was darkness.

The invader was perhaps thirty yards away. It was difficult to estimate in the dense surroundings. But it was an opportunity. And if Alexander Tarquin McAuliff had learned anything during the past weeks of agonizing insanity, it was to accept opportunities with the minimum of analysis.

He pulled Alison to him and whispered instructions into her ear. He released her and felt about the ground for what he knew was there. Fifteen seconds later he silently clawed his way up the trunk of a ceiba tree, rifle across his back, his hands noiselessly testing the low branches, discomforted by the additional weight of the object held in place inside his field jacket by the belt.

In position, he scratched twice on the bark of the tree.

Beneath him Alison whistled—a very human whistle, the abrupt notes of a signaling warble. She then snapped on her flashlight for precisely one second, shut it off, and dashed away from her position.

In less than a minute the figure was below him—crouched, rifle extended, prepared to kill.

McAuliff dropped from the limb of the ceiba tree, the sharp point of the heavy rock on a true, swift course toward the top of the invader's skull.

The minute hand on his watch reached twelve; the second hand was on one. It was time.

The first cry came from the river. An expert cry, the sound of a wild pig.

The second came from the southwest, quite far in the distance but equally expert, echoing through the jungle.

The third came from the north, a bit too guttural, not expert at all, but sufficient unto the instant. The message was clear.

McAuliff looked at Alison, her bright, stunningly blue eyes bluer still in the Caribbean moonlight.

He lifted his rifle in the air and shattered the stillness of the night with a burst of gunfire. Perhaps the ganga pilot in the grasslands would laugh softly in satisfaction. Perhaps, with luck, one of the stray bullets might find its way to his head.

It did not matter.

It mattered only that they had made it. They were good enough, after all.

He held Alison in his arms and screamed joyfully into the darkness above. It did not sound much like a wild pig, but that did not matter, either.

35

THEY SAT at the table on the huge free-form pool deck overlooking the beds of coral and the blue waters beyond. The conflict between wave and rock resulted in cascading arcs of white spray surging upward and forward, blanketing the jagged crevices.

They had flown from the grasslands directly to Port Antonio. They had done so because Sam Tucker had raised Robert Hanley on the airplane's radio, and Hanley had delivered his instructions in commands that denied argument. They had landed at the small Sam Jones Airfield at 2:35 in the morning. A limousine sent from the Trident Villas awaited them.

So, too, did Robert Hanley. And the moment Sam Tucker alighted from the plane, Hanley shook his hand and proceeded to crash his fist into Tucker's face. He followed this action by reaching down and picking Sam up off the ground, greeting him a bit more cordially but explaining in measured anger that the past several weeks had caused him unnecessary anxiety, obviously Sam Tucker's responsibility.

The two very young old reprobates then drank the night through at the bar of Trident Villas. The young manager, Timothy Durell, surrendered at 5:10 in the morning, dismissed the bartender, and turned the keys over to Hanley and Sam. Durell was not aware that in a very real sense, the last strategies of Dunstone, Limited, had been created at Trident that week when strangers had converged from all over the world. Strangers, and not strangers at all . . . only disturbing memories now.

Charles Whitehall left with Lawrence, the revolutionary. Both black men said their good-byes at the airfield; each had places to go to, things to do, men to see. There would be no questions, for there would be no answers. That was understood.

They would separate quickly.

But they had communicated; perhaps that was all that could be expected.

Alison and McAuliff had been taken to the farthest villa on the shoreline. She had bandaged his hand and washed the cuts on his face and made him soak for nearly an hour in a good British tub of hot water.

They were in Villa Twenty.

They had slept in each other's arms until noon.

It was now a little past one o'clock. They were alone at the table, a note having been left for Alexander from Sam Tucker. Sam and Robert Hanley were flying to Montego Bay to see an attorney. They were going into partnership.

God help the island, thought McAuliff.

At 2:30 Alison touched his arm and nodded toward the alabaster portico across the lawn. Down the marble steps came two men, one black, one white, dressed in proper business suits.

R. C. Holcroft and Daniel, Minister of Council for the Tribe of Acquaba, high in the Flagstaff Range.

"We'll be quick," said Holcroft, taking the chair indicated by Alexander. "Mrs. Booth, I am Commander Holcroft."

"I was sure you were," said Alison, her voice warm, her smile cold.

"May I present . . . an associate? Mr. Daniel. Jamaican Affairs. I believe you two have met, McAuliff."

"Yes."

Daniel nodded pleasantly and sat down. He looked at Alex and spoke sincerely. "There is much to be thankful for. I am very relieved."

"What about Malcolm?"

The sadness flickered briefly across Daniel's eyes. "I am sorry."

"So am I," said McAuliff. "He saved our lives."

"That was his job," replied the Minister of the Halidon.

"May I assume," interrupted Holcroft gently, "that Mrs. Booth has been apprised . . . up to a point?"

"You certainly may assume that, Commander Holcroft." Alison gave the answer herself.

"Very well." The British agent reached into his pocket, withdrew the yellow paper of a cablegram, and handed it to Alexander. It was a deposit confirmation from Barclay's Bank, London. The sum of $660,000 had been deposited to the account of A. T. McAuliff, Chase Manhattan, New York. Further, a letter of credit had been forwarded to said A. T. McAuliff that could be drawn against for all taxes upon receipt of the proper filing papers approved by the United States Treasury Department,

Bureau of Internal Revenue.

Alex read the cable twice and wondered at his own indifference. He gave it to Alison. She started to read it but
did not finish; instead, she lifted McAuliff's cup and saucer and placed it underneath.

She said nothing.

"Our account is settled, McAuliff."

"Not quite, Holcroft . . . In simple words, I never
want to hear from you again. *We* never want to hear
from you. Because if we do, the longest deposition on record will be made public—"

"My *dear* man," broke in the Englishman wearily, "let
me save you the time. Gratitude and marked respect
would obligate me socially any time you're in London.
And, I should add, I think you're basically a quite decent
chap. But I can assure you that *professionally* we shall remain at the farthest distance. Her Majesty's Service has
no desire to involve itself with international irregularities.
I might as well be damned blunt about it."

"And Mrs. Booth?"

"The same, obviously." Here Holcroft looked directly,
even painfully, at Alison. "Added to which it is our belief
she has gone through a great deal. Most splendidly and
with our deepest appreciation. The terrible past is behind
you, my dear. Public commendation is uncalled for, we
realize. But the highest citation will be entered into your
file. Which shall be closed. Permanently."

"I want to believe that," said Alison.

"You may, Mrs. Booth."

"What about Dunstone?" asked McAuliff. "What's going
to happen? When?"

"It has already begun," replied Holcroft. "The list was
cabled in the early hours of the morning."

"Several hours ago," said Daniel quietly. "Around
noon, London time."

"In all the financial centers, the work is proceeding,"
continued Holcroft. "All the governments are cooperating
. . . it is to everyone's benefit."

McAuliff looked up at Daniel. "What does that do for
global mendacity?"

Daniel smiled. "Perhaps a minor lesson has been
learned. We shall know in a few years, will we not?"

"And Piersall? Who killed him?"

Holcroft replied. "Real-estate interests along the North

Coast who stood to gain by the Dunstone purchase. His work was important, not those who caused his death. They were tragically insignificant."

"And so it is over," said Daniel, pushing back his chair. "The Westmore Tallons will go back to selling fish, the disciples of Barak Moore will take up the struggle against Charles Whitehall, and the disorderly process of advancement continues. Shall we go, Commander Holcroft?"

"By all means, Mr. Daniel," Holcroft rose from the chair, as did the Minister of Council for the Tribe of Acquaba.

"What happened to the Jensens?" Alexander looked at Daniel, for it was the Halidonite who could answer him.

"We allowed him to escape. To leave the Cock Pit. We knew Julian Warfield was on the island, but we did not know where. We only knew that Peter Jensen would lead us to him. He did so. In Oracabessa . . . Julian Warfield's life was ended on the balcony of a villa named Peale Court."

"What will happen to them? The Jensens." McAuliff shifted his eyes to Holcroft.

The commander glanced briefly at Daniel. "There is an understanding. A man and a woman answering the description of the Jensens boarded a Mediterranean flight this morning at Palisados. We think he is retired. We shall leave him alone. You see, he shot Julian Warfield . . . because Warfield had ordered him to kill someone else. And he could not do that."

"It is time, Commander," said Daniel.

"Yes, of course. There's a fine woman in London I've rather neglected. She liked you very much that night in Soho, McAuliff. She said you were attentive."

"Give her my best."

"I shall." The Englishman looked up at the clear sky and the hot sun. "Retirement in the Mediterranean. Interesting." R. C. Holcroft allowed himself a brief smile, and replaced the chair quite properly under the table.

They walked on the green lawn in front of the cottage that was called a villa and looked out at the sea. A white sheet of ocean spray burst up from the coral rock and appeared suspended, the pitch-blue waters of the Caribbean serving as a backdrop, not a source. The spray cascaded forward and downward and then receded back over the crevices that formed the coral overlay. It became ocean again, at one with its source; another form of beauty.

Alison took McAuliff's hand.

They were free.

THE SEVENTEENTH STAIR

Barbara Paul

The velvet silence of the tower hung like a pall around
her . . . she lay, drenched in a chill sweat of terror,
straining to hear the sound that had woken her . . . then
it came again . . . a low sobbing cry echoing through
the lonely chateau.

Rosella Eastwood was summoned to Paris by her
guardian, but when she arrived she found no one to
greet her, only a will bequeathing her the Chateau de
Louismont in the Loire Valley: a place of hated
childhood memories, where she had to face the hatred
of the Louismont family, the agony of loving a man who
could never be free, and the evil secret of the west
tower.

—

POLMARRAN TOWER

Charlotte Massey

Polmarran Tower stood high above the Cornish cliffs,
a landmark for wreckers and smugglers, frowning over
the sea.

Katherine Ainsley came to Polmarran as a governess to
Adelaide Northwood, but found herself drawn into a
vortex of terror. For over the house brooded the spirit of
a woman who had once lived there, a woman whose
very name drew a chilling silence from the Northwoods
of Polmarran, and over Katherine's charge hung the
shadow of a mystery that threatened the lives of both
pupil and governess.

THE SWEENEY

Ian Kennedy Martin

Jack Regan is one of the Heavy Mob.
He's also a loner, intolerant of red tape and
insubordinate to his superiors.
And he just happens to be the best detective in
Scotland Yard's crack Flying Squad.

When Regan receives orders to co-operate with
Lieutenant Ewing, over from America to trace a cop
killer, Regan is pursuing his own case and ignores
them. But he soon discovers that Ewing is as tough as
he is – and a dangerous clash of personalities
develops. As the two cases begin to merge into a
sinister and violent network of IRA provos and
murderers, the two men close in for the kill . . .

Ian Kennedy Martin is the creator of Thames
Television's enormously popular TV series, starring
John Thaw.